THE GATES OF HELL

The Gates of Hell

Geraint V. Jones

ISBN: 0-86381-852-8

Cover design: Dylan Williams

Published with the financial support of the
Welsh Book Council.

First published in 2003 by
Gwasg Carreg Gwalch, 12 Iard yr Orsaf, Llanrwst,
Wales LL26 0EH
☎ 01492 642031   📠 01492 641502
✉ books@carreg-gwalch.co.uk   website: www.carreg-gwalch.co.uk

Acknowledgements

I wish to thank the following:

- Bill Napier, author and Research Astronomer at Armagh Observatory and Philip Woodworth of the Proudman Oceanographic Laboratory, Birkenhead, for kindly providing me with some of the details for my story. (Any embarrassing gaffes will be purely of my own making!);
- my publishers, Gwasg Carreg Gwalch for showing faith;
- the Welsh Book Council for its support;
- my wife Gwenda for her forbearance and support and my son Elfyn for his ceaseless encouragement.

I am particularly indebted to Gwynn C. Griffith and Gwyn M. Lloyd for taking the trouble to read the manuscript and giving me their valued suggestions and advice.

In memory of
my godson
Anthony (Anth)
1975-2002,
tragically killed
in a road accident
'Smiling always with a never fading serenity of
countenance and flourishing in an immortal youth.'

PART 1

The Sword of Damocles

Chapter 1

The eye glinted steely grey in the late afternoon sun, its stare fixed on some distant thought. In profile, the nose was not as aquiline as it once had been. The lips were unusually tense above a chin that had its firmness concealed in the cup of a large hand supported by a tanned forearm, the elbow of which rested on an upturned knee. Elbow to shoulder revealed naked biceps of impressive size, the taut skin adorned with a dragon-slaying-St-George tattoo. The neck was bullish, the torso athletic even in its sitting posture. Wiry dark hair, cropped short and now damp with sweat, matted the head. In silhouette. he mirrored Rodin's 'Thinker'.

His fixed eye, his frozen posture betrayed nothing of his mood, whether pensive or vacant, and the raven's croak, as it crossed his line of vision, failed to draw him out of his reverie. Perhaps he was aware of the sound, perhaps not, as it faded harshly in flight towards a distant cliff towering over a scree-strewn slope. Nor did the constant chatter of skylarks or the distant bleating of worried ewes disturb his concentration.

Perched on a boulder, that was itself sitting precariously on the very edge of a rocky precipice, he continued to stare over the miles of falling undulations towards a crescent-shaped bay in the distance. Eventually, the intensity of his gaze gave way to recognition and through the glare of the late afternoon sun he slowly began to detect little clusters of farm buildings on hillsides here and there, whilst around the edge of the far-off bay larger settlements came into focus. He could name those towns, now; could even tell what their names meant! The thought brought on the briefest of smiles, as he grudgingly paid tribute to the teaching of Ffion Morgan, Rees' daughter.

To the south west, sixteen miles distant, was Caer Môr – *Sea Fort* – so named because of its majestic Edward 1 castle overlooking a wide sandy beach. Ten miles due west and directly in front of him, Portharian – *Silverport* – with its little fishing harbour and marina straddling and strangling the estuary of Afon Arian. Portharian, he reminded himself, was where Simon Carvel now resided, presumably more content than when he'd first arrived in the area eighteen months ago. Furthest and largest of the three towns was Aberheli, clinging to its shingle beach way out on the promontory that formed the northern extremity of the Bay of Branwen. *Salty Estuary*, he had to admit, didn't sound half as lyrical as *Aberheli*! A little to his right, between him and the sea, the scene was dominated by a beautiful U-shaped valley, the sides of which were clothed with indigenous oak forests, and its farmed floor a cluster of green parcels loosely tied together by the meandering string of Afon Arian.

The view was familiar enough to him. From a more northerly angle and a slightly lower trajectory, it was what greeted him every morning when he opened the front door of his cottage, or glanced out through one of its two tiny windows. During the past eighteen months, he'd become more attached to this little bit of earth than he'd ever thought possible in such a short time. He'd begun to throw roots here. 'But how long will it last?' he muttered. 'How will all this change in three months time?' It was a thought that he didn't want to dwell on.

The boulder on which he was sitting was known locally as *Carreg y Cawr* – Titan's Rock. From a distance, it resembled the head of a diminutive preacher straining to peer over the edge of his towering pulpit! *Carreg y Cawr* was one of Mother Nature's little eccentricities. He'd noticed it before, from a distance, but today, for the very first time and to satisfy his own ill-defined curiosity, he'd ventured to climb up here.

Instinctively he turned to gaze at the evidence that he knew to be there, behind him, of the boulder's true source. *'Roche moutonne'.* He uttered the words out loud. The path of a once stone-shod glacier was clearly defined by the striation scars on the slope of polished rock that gently climbed towards him. He tried to imagine the slow but relentless upward path of the ice as it scraped the rock clean of its vegetation before starting on its remorseless downward plucking to chew out a precipice where there had previously been but a sharp descent. And the deposited boulder on which he was now sitting had been that glacier's final word, its farewell punctuation mark, its crowning glory, it's excrement. For a second or two the geographical term eluded him. *'Erratic!'* he finally muttered. 'That's the word for it!' And then, in the didactic manner of his old geography teacher he added aloud, 'The boulder on which I now sit is known as an *erratic!*'

To left and right, distant hills patched with rocky outcrops and heather in early bloom, and dotted white here and there with newly-sheared sheep, rose against the blue of the northern and southern skies. And in the hollow below him, to his immediate right, man had wreaked his own form of destruction, in his search for roofing slate. The quarry, redundant these past thirty-odd years, now revealed the gaping holes of three of its worked-out caverns, as if some giant moles had come up for

8

air, whilst nearby, the pyramidal tip of bluish-grey waste was reluctantly being reclaimed by Mother Nature. From his precarious height, the hollow resembled an open mouth sucking at the mountain air, the caverns now resembling the cavities of extracted molars. Other caverns, he suspected, lay hidden beneath the surface, half drowned by seeping rainwater, their blue-grey wealth forever pilfered from them. This had been but one of the area's smaller workings.

Gingerly, Craig O'Darcy got to his feet and savoured the cool breeze as it filled his lungs. Vaguely, he brushed imaginary lichen off the seat of his mud-flecked shorts. His light-blue running-vest was stained with darker shades of sweat, witnesses to the strenuous ten kilometres that he'd already run. Twelve more lay before him, but he took comfort from the fact that most of those would be downhill and on metal-surfaced roads.

Wistfully, he again pondered about the cataclysm that was waiting in the wings, only this time he did allow his mind to dwell on the thought. Another three months, he reminded himself, and all before him now would suffer a dramatic change, as would every other corner of the globe. On that, at least, the experts were agreed. Unless NASA could work some last-minute magic to divert the danger, then there *would* be asteroidal impact on the twenty sixth of August, three months from now! 'No question about it', they'd said. 'Eros Two will plummet into Antarctica and there *will* be pandemic repercussions.' What those so-called experts hadn't yet been able to agree on was the extent of global devastation, and that was the one strand of hope that people all over the world had been clinging to, these past two years, ever since the news had broken. If there was doubt about the magnitude of the destruction, if the boffins were at odds about the true nature of the threat, as had been demonstrated in endless televised discussions over the past worrying months, then there had to be uncertainty about the impact itself. At least, that was how the sceptics and the optimists had argued all along, a stance also taken by some government spin doctors who were anxious to keep panic and lawlessness off the streets. In the meantime, however, poor Joe Public had been left stranded and confused, not knowing who or what to believe.

Alistair Dalton, Craig's estranged half-brother, and Brussels spokesperson for next Friday night's *'Doomsday Discussion'* panel on the European Skywatch channel, would undoubtedly toe that official line, doing his bit *for the general good*. 'I'll be watching you, big brother!' Craig now muttered. 'Big half-brother!' he added, somewhat resentfully.

9

He tried to recall when he'd last seen Alistair, to actually talk to him. He didn't have to think hard or long, because the occasion had been poignantly engraved on his then young mind – March 18, 2012 – their mother's forty sixth birthday, the day of her third marriage and the eve of her emigrating to California. He hadn't seen either of them, mother or half-brother, since that day. He'd been fourteen at the time – half his present age – and eleven years junior to Alistair, who was then just beginning to find his feet on Whitehall's corridors of power. Many had suspected, Alistair had known, even in those early days, that Big Brother was destined for higher things than Junior Computer Records Clerk.

Ruefully, Craig now recalled that his mother had invited him more than once to visit her at her Palo Alto home; had even sent him an airline ticket once. But, with time, she'd been forced to accept that her youngest son had no intention of forgiving her for leaving him forsaken in the adoptive care of an ailing uncle and a morbid aunt. Alistair, on the other hand, had made no effort whatsoever to keep in touch with his younger brother.

'Anyway, I'll watch Friday's programme, just to hear what Big Brother has to say.'

And with that silent promise, he sprang down from his perch, turned his back on the precipice and on the distant sea and began to pick his way down the striated rock form, pausing but for a moment to survey the undulating moorland now stretching out before him. In the distance and slightly to his left, a black expanse of land showed where the heather had been stripped away and its underlying peat dug up for fuel. Due east and directly ahead, less than a mile away, a sliver of water was catching the late afternoon sun. Its presence surprised him. He'd have to enquire as to its name. *Llyn* something-or-other, no doubt. He knew about Llyn Foel, pronounced Voyle, and Llyn Du – Black Lake – and a few others, because his cross-country fitness runs had brought them to his notice before now. But the one in the distance was new to him. Hardly surprising, he thought, considering its remoteness. Anyway, none of his past runs had given him this altitude or this vista.

To the south-east, the skyline was serrated, like the blade of a fine saw, by the tops of a distant pine forest and he could make out the glinting meanders of a tarmac road winding its way towards it. By now, the forest was but a fraction of its original size. When he'd first arrived in the area, eighteen months ago, it had commanded over twenty square miles of these uplands, but then had come predictions of a big freeze in the wake of the asteroid's impact and people had begun to panic in their desperate bid to stock up on fuel. Governments, under threat of insurrection, had been forced to act. By decree, pine forests had been systematically cut down and sawn into logs to be rationed off to the public. Craig had claimed his allocation, just like everyone else because, for all he knew, he might still be here, in the Pencraig area, when the worst came to the worst. But then again he might not, in which case, he argued, he'd just have to find a way of taking his stock of food and fuel with him, when the time came.

What remained of the forests was now being patrolled day and night by army personnel, guarding against the so-called 'log-thieves' who were forever seeking to satisfy a thriving black market in fuel supplies. And there were similar patrols guarding lowland and upland pastures as well, to thwart the efforts of sheep and cattle rustlers.

A distant glint on the road told him that a car had just emerged from beneath the canopy of pines. How often during those early months, and in all sorts of weather, had he travelled that road, towards Offa's Dyke and the English border, the Norton Jaguar 1500cc superbike purring contentedly beneath him as it ate up the bends and the miles? He smiled now as he recalled those early journeys to Nottingham, to see Sally. Weekdays had dragged, weekends had flown. God! How he and Simon Carvel had hated their posting to this remote, God-forsaken backwater, as it had seemed to both of them at the time. As if Sellafield B itself hadn't been bad enough!

But that was eighteen months ago and much had happened since then, for him at least. For a start, he'd met Rees Morgan, successful businessman and benefactor. And through Rees had come the inevitable contact with the local rugby club and his appointment as player-coach. And as the weeks had passed, and as Sally had distanced herself from him, Craig O'Darcy's life had taken on a new course and a new meaning.

As he reached the tarmac of the open road and, as his strides again began eating up the miles, he felt his feet squelching on the padded soles of his running shoes. Despite a full fortnight of warm sun, the moorland still retained a lot of its moisture, and there had been soggy moss and bog for him to contend with. They were behind him now, though, and the little quarrying town of Pencraig was gradually coming into view as the road curled towards it across the slope. Seven kilometres still to go, he thought, eyeing the distant windows glinting in the late sun. And then that extra kilometre and a half up to Havod. 'Hafod with an f,' he muttered smilingly, as he recalled those disastrous language lessons when he'd first arrived.

'The Welsh *f* is always pronounced as a *v*'. Ffion Morgan, teacher.

'So you don't have an *f* sound in Welsh, then?'

Simon Carvel's smirk had once again been too obvious and Ffion's eyes had narrowed, but she'd retained her cool. 'Your *f* sound in English is denoted in Welsh with a double *ff*, the single *f* in Welsh is the equivalent of your English *v*. Welsh is a phonetic language, Mr Carvel, and pronunciation should pose no problems, not even for you!'

The warning had been there, in the rasp of her voice and the drop of her eyebrows, but Simon hadn't had the sense to heed the signs or to let things be, and with a series of guttural noises in his throat he'd pretended to spit all manner of sounds at his feet. Ffion had looked at him with disdain, like a disapproving pedestrian who had just witnessed a stray dog fouling the pavement. 'Mr Carvel! This is but your second lesson and already you've made your contempt towards my language and my people blatantly clear. Experience tells me that such arrogance stems either from base racial prejudice or from a sense of intellectual inadequacy. In your case, I suspect both.' And with that, she'd curtly dismissed the class, leaving a livid Simon Carvel to seethe under the disapproving gaze of the other fifteen students. Soon after, Simon had left his hotel in Pencraig and moved to the more anglicised coastal town of Portharian, ten miles away.

A tractor and trailer roared around the bend to meet him, bringing in tow a string of impatient lorries and cars that had been held back too long by the winding road. The first of the trucks was now pulling out to overtake the tractor and Craig barely had time to leap the low stone wall to safety, and to glimpse a smirking truck driver raising a stiff finger of defiance at him. For a second, he weighed up the options. Could he run fast enough to catch the bastard before he moved up through his gears? It would be satisfying indeed to drag him out of his cab and to rub some sheep shit over his arrogant face. The option, however, wasn't practicable and he allowed his blood to cool before taking to the road again.

A tractor, four lorries – eight wheelers, all of them – and two cars! Quite an unexpected collection, in days of fuel rationing. The trucks, in convoy, he could explain. They were carrying slate waste, to be dumped along the Kent coast, where a fifty-metre-high embankment, it was said, would withstand the monster tsunamis when they struck in late August! The two cars, on the other hand, had probably been requisitioned by army personnel.

As his pace warmed to its earlier rhythm, his brain struggled to find its previous train of thought. What had he been thinking about? Of course! Simon Carvel! Yes, the man could be arrogant and unbearable at times, and Ffion Morgan certainly wasn't one to suffer fools gladly.

He and Carvel had been at Sellafield B together, employed by INCSU, the International Nuclear Contamination Supervision Unit. They'd hardly known one another in those days, coming as they did from such totally different backgrounds, Simon from a well-heeled Essex family and PSFE schooling, himself from the sort of home life that travelling circus artistes or itinerant preachers might have endured in days gone by. His mother – so she once told him – had been tricked into her second marriage. Patrick O'Darcy, American-Irish and silver-tongued rogue, had duped her into believing that he was Director of CASOC, the Combined American States Opera Company that was touring Europe at the time. In fact, he'd been nothing more than a poorly paid booking clerk. There had followed twelve years of vagrant poverty and constant bickering, before Patrick, on a cold and wet Christmas Eve in 2009, opted out of his marital and parental commitments by simply disappearing. Craig, the only child of the marriage, had been eleven at the time. All efforts to track down the errant husband had failed and two and a half years later, the revised statute on Wedlock, Divorce and Bigamy had allowed his mother to tie the knot with a third husband and to move to the west coast of America to live.

Their gypsy-like existence with Patrick O'Darcy had left young Craig with virtually no hope of qualifying for a Private Sector Funded Education like the one that Simon Carvel had enjoyed. But he'd got by somehow, and years later had done rather well to leave Carlisle University with an A2 Registration in Nuclear Waste Physics.

The summons to the Chief Administrator's Office at Sellafield B, eighteen months ago, had been unexpected to say the least. Even more of a shock had been the CA's blunt message. 'Mr Carvel, Mr O'Darcy! As from next Monday, you're both being posted to Storage Site 5 in North Wales. You'll remain there for the next eighteen months, during which time you will oversee the final stages of the work on the two new storage galleries being built there. The Regional Government takes very seriously the threat of post-collision earthquakes, and if we, in Europe, are fortunate enough, two years from now, to escape relatively unscathed from the predicted AAE, then the last thing that we will then want is to be lethally irradiated from Storage Site 5, or from any other site on these islands.'

'The Antarctic Asteroid Encounter is now one hundred per cent certain, then?'

The CA's pupils had dilated into a cold stare. 'Mr O'Darcy! Make no mistake about it! Unless NASA comes up with an answer pretty quickly then AAE is indeed a hundred per cent certainty. There may be some discrepancy amongst the experts about the scale of global destruction but, as things stand, the impact itself is beyond question. Which is why the construction work on the new underground storage galleries at Site 5 must be carefully monitored at all times, to ensure that the planners' specifications are followed to the very last detail.' With a slight wave of hand, he'd then intimated that the discussion was over. 'I shall expect fortnightly reports, plus any relevant recommendations . . . '

'North Wales! Bloody hell!'

Simon Carvel had made no attempt to hide his displeasure. His tone of voice and his scowl had said it all. Uncharacteristically, however, the CA had chosen to ignore his petulance. 'Storage Site 5 is maintained by a local workforce which will, perhaps, resent your presence . . . '

'Resent?'

'Yes, Mr O'Darcy. They might feel that they have the know-how to oversee the work themselves . . . '

'Ha!'

Again, the CA chose to disregard Carvel's sneering interjection, but not for long 'They might well have a valid argument, of course. Tell me, Mr Carvel! What length of service do you have with INCSU?'

'Nine years. Why?'

At that point, the CA had spent a second or two inspecting his cuticles before looking up and holding Simon Carvel in a fixed meaningful stare. 'In which case, gentlemen, you'll be well-advised to bear in mind that Senior Management at Site 5 – the Site Supervisor and his two Deputies – have a combined service record of ninety seven years between them. All at that one particular site! The three have worked their way up through the ranks to reach their current positions of authority and you should respect them for that. What *they* lack, however, and you don't, are the paper credentials necessary to put a seal on the development, one that Westminster and Brussels will be happy with. The Cardiff Government, for its part, will be sending its own experts, and they'll have a somewhat different mandate to yours. No doubt they will be working more closely than yourselves with the local management team. But that's beside the point, at this moment in time! Suffice it for me to say that *your* fortnightly reports must be compiled independently, and must be based on your own personal observations and professional judgement. They will be presented directly to me, and it will be from those reports that a team of government advisors will compile a comprehensive final report that will receive Whitehall's and Brussels' ultimate seals of approval.'

'Why . . . ?'

'Why the two of you, Mr Carvel? Is that your question?' The Chief Administrator had obviously been prepared for some form of remonstrance. 'Well, why not? Somebody has to go, and the both of you are as qualified as anyone to do the work.' At that point he had swivelled his chair to indicate that the matter was closed and that he would contemplate no further objection. Then, just as they were leaving the room, he'd said, 'By the way, gentlemen! You'll be spending your time in what the Welsh Ministry for Culture call a DLPA, i.e. a Designated Language Preservation Area. It seems that over fifty per cent of the local populace, where you'll be based, still use Welsh as their first tongue and that the area was adopted a few years ago for some kind of linguistic experiment . . . to safeguard the language and the culture, I think . . . Something like that, anyway.'

'And that's got somethin' to do with us?' Carvel's tone was still heavily tinged with the scorn that he attached to the orders he'd just been given.

'To some degree, yes. Mind you, in the face of what's going to happen in eighteen months' time, the experiment will prove pointless anyway – in fact, the Welsh Senate has already acknowledged as much – but feelings and aspirations still run high in some quarters, apparently, so as a show of good will, and to forestall any animosity, I would strongly suggest that you attend a few language classes whilst you're there.' He'd stopped, there, to smile somewhat sympathetically before adding a mischievous parting shot. 'I don't expect you to become fluent, of course . . . '

'I don't believe it!' The door had closed behind them. 'I don't fuck'n believe it!' Carvel had vented his frustration and anger on a litter bin which his left foot sent clattering from wall to wall down the corridor ahead of them. 'Not only is he sendin' me to fuck'n Siberia but he wants me to learn some fuck'n dodo language as well.'

He, Craig, although every bit as resentful as Carvel, had bit a stoic tongue.

'Well say somethin' O'Darcy, for fuck's sake.'

'I don't like it any more than you do.'

But his response had been seen as timid by the fuming Essex man. However, when the time came, both of them had dutifully signed up for a course of evening classes with the redoubtable Ffion Morgan, and in somewhat record time Simon Carvel had had his due comeuppance.

15

The recollection brought on another wistful smile. He had now reached Pencraig High Street.

'Hi, Rocky!'

He raised a cursory hand to acknowledge the greeting from across the road.

To most of his friends and acquaintances in the town, he was known as either *Rocky* or *Coach*. Rees and Sinéad Morgan were about the only ones to call him by his proper name. *Coach* was to be expected. It was what he was, at the club. *Rocky*, on the other hand, had originated in one of Ffion Morgan's evening classes. 'Do you realise, Mr O'Darcy, that your name probably derives from the same word as the one found in the name of this town – Pencraig? Only that they're pronounced rather differently.' She'd left it at that, though, and he'd later asked Rees, her father, to explain. The old man had obliged. '*Your* pronunciation is Irish . . . or Gaelic. In Welsh, it's *Craig* . . . ' He pronounced the vowels phonetically, the *a* as in m*a*n and the *i* as in *i*nn – 'Either way, it means '*rock*'.'

The mistake had been to ask Rees whilst they were both standing at the packed clubhouse bar after a Sunday afternoon match. His question and the old man's explanation had been overheard and some had been calling him *Rocky* ever since.

As he ran, he passed a few solemn-faced pedestrians. Some nodded to him, one or two smiled briefly, and he nodded and smiled in return. Not that he knew them, nor they him, but it was all part of the friendliness of the place, even in these trying times. He liked that. It made him feel at home. For the first time in his life, he felt that he belonged. 'But only until August twenty six!' he thought ruefully. 'Then what?'

There was no hiding the tension and the fearful anticipation behind every friendly nod, etched into every facial wrinkle. There was no escaping, either, the unnerving mood of resignation. For most people, preparation had reached its climax months ago in a surge of panic-buying in readiness for the long 'Arctic winter' that was, quite literally, being predicted in the stars. In Pencraig, as elsewhere throughout the country, throughout the world, shops and supermarkets had seen their stocks disappear virtually overnight and fuel suppliers had been inundated with demands. In towns and cities, store managers and staff had been physically threatened by frenzied shoppers, and private houses had been burgled for their supplies. While stocks lasted, looting had escalated and then, when the shelves eventually ran dry, looters had become highwaymen, hijacking food trucks for their meagre contents and their part-full tanks of fuel. And when undermanned police forces had become powerless and resigned to their own failure, the army had been deployed to keep order as best they could, but even the soldiers were known to be pilfering and secretly feathering their own nests. Then had come reports of attacks and murders in various parts of the country – burglars murdering householders for their stocks; householders, armed with whatever weapons they could muster, and intent on safeguarding their properties at all costs, resolutely lying in wait for the thieves and becoming prisoners and would-be killers in their own homes. And throughout it all, the poor and the ill-prepared had known famine and death.

Reports of similar scenarios had come from all the developed countries whilst in the third world, millions had accepted their fate, as they always had done, in silent and noble resignation.

Fortunately, Pencraig had escaped much of the disorder, thanks mainly to Rees Morgan's foresight and selfless preparation.

'Hi, Coach! See you later?'

'Yea, Les! I'll be there.'

His pace didn't falter and the second row forward who had hailed him from across the street now smiled at such dedication to fitness.

With the sword of Damocles hanging by an ever-stretching thread, talk of rugby practice seemed ridiculous but life had to go on . . . at least for another three months!

On a sudden whim, he left the high street and bore right, up a steep hill that bisected three terraces, one above the other on the slope. Two housewives paused in their solemn jangling to gaze in amazement at him, then shook their heads in disbelief. He glimpsed the question in their minds and in their eyes. Who, on a scorching afternoon in May and with possible extinction just around the corner, could be daft enough to think of personal fitness? *Barmy! . . . Bonkers! . . . Nuts!* Their opinion was plain to see.

He smiled as the slope began to take its toll on his leg muscles. *'Only mad dogs and Englishmen!'* he muttered.

The hill ended in a steep *cul de sac.* At its top end, however, a sturdy style gave access to a footpath that led through rough mountain pasture above the town. He paused to catch his breath and to swat at the cloud of gnats that were getting into his eyes and mouth and ears.

In the distance, still a good kilometre away, with just the ridge of its roof visible against dark rock, nestled Hafod, his home these past fifteen months. About two hundred metres to its right, a huge slate tip poured down the slope to fill what had once been a small ravine. Catching the late sunlight, as it now did, it gave Craig O'Darcy the stunning impression of a frozen cataract.

A cluster of sheep scattered in panic as he drew nearer, drawing, no doubt, the binocular attention of a soldier on some distant hill. At the start of last year's lambing and calving season, the European Agricultural Ministry had imposed a ban on indiscriminate slaughter of livestock because some breeds were in danger of becoming extinct. It hadn't deterred the poachers and the rustlers though, which was why the army had been posted to keep an eye on things.

From here on, his jog was reduced to a crawl, which became a climb on all fours as he zigzagged the final ascent to reach the rough track that cut horizontally across the slope in front of Hafod. The track, now pitted and uneven, had once been the bed for a narrow gauge tramway running from Cefn Quarry to the rubble tip, and the cottage, standing between them, had seen generations of laden and empty wagons come and go. And although the rails of that track had long since disappeared, either corroded into the wet ground or carried off as scrap, the remains of the odd railway sleeper were still to be seen embedded here and there, stubbornly withstanding the tide of decay.

Hafod was a long low building of roughly hewn granite blocks, with its two small windows blinded by slate-grey shutters. It was set against a thirty-foot-high escarpment formed by a geological fault, and its stone structure blended well with the cliff behind. Built originally as a shepherd's summer dwelling, the cottage was exposed to the prevailing westerly winds.

To his left, some fifty metres away in the rock face, yawned the black cavern of a failed mine, whilst further left the skyline was scarred by the tall tips of slate waste marking the location of *Chwarel Cefn*. This had been Pencraig's largest quarry with its row upon row of black underground caverns – a hundred and sixty eight in all – carved out of the bowels of the earth. In its heyday, over eight hundred men had worked here, but then had come the decline and, in 2008, final closure. After that, it soon degenerated into a huge security risk, with subsidence creating treacherous potholes that swallowed many a venturesome sheep. Then, in the summer of 2014, two young lads on an orienteering course accidentally tumbled into such a pothole and plunged fifty feet to their underground deaths. That had led to calls for the whole mine to be fenced off and sealed, leaving the errant owners, faced with impending compensation claims by the families of the deceased, with no option but to go into voluntary liquidation. Less than two years later, Rees Morgan had arrived on the scene, fresh from all sorts of business successes abroad, and had bought Cefn Quarry. After forty five years of exile, he was back on his home patch, intent on repaying his 'great debt', as he called it, to the community that had nurtured him. His entrepreneurial skills had soon silenced the cynics as well as surprising even the most optimistic of his supporters. He'd begun by utilising not the underground workings of the quarry but the apparently worthless slate tips. Others before him, at the turn of the century, had successfully experimented with slate dust, using it in the manufacture of roofing felt and building blocks. Rees Morgan, however, had taken the initiative a significant step further. He'd built a state-of-the-art laboratory on site and employed two of Europe's foremost industrial scientists to come up with a compound that would match the quality of slate in every department. Local cynics had been vociferous in their scepticism at the time, but Rees, by producing the goods, had silenced them all. In a matter of eight months, his lab had produced a resin that could be fused with a molten compound of plastic and rubber to produce a material that was both lighter than and reputedly as durable as the best quality slate. The next stage had been to replicate the permanent colour of slate. That had been accomplished by erecting giant crushers, again on site, into which waste from the century-old tips had been fed. The powdered slate thus produced had then gone into the mix, which was then squeezed under pressure onto fine steel wire mesh in lengthy five-millimetre-deep tray moulds, and allowed to solidify. From there, it could then either be guillotined into conventional slate sizes or marked off in full roofing sheets. Either way, once in place, the material resembled the real thing, showing the grain of the top class 'old vein' slate for which the Pencraig quarries had once been world-renowned. Using brick dust to produce a red tile effect had been a subsequent development. And within four years, the Pencraig Roofing Company, as it came to be called, was able to supply not only slate and tile material but also wood effect for roofing log cabins. By halving both the weight and the cost of roofing material, Rees Morgan had collared the world market almost overnight and had overturned the ill fortune that had dogged this part of North Wales for so long. In two years, the size of his workforce grew to three hundred and fifty; in four years it was over twelve hundred, and still they hadn't been able to keep up with the orders that were coming in. Even so, Rees' entrepreneurial hunger had not been sated. He'd then turned his attention to memorial headstones and here again his slate, granite and Carrara marble effects had become instant successes.

Craig had met Rees Morgan within the first fortnight of his arriving from Sellafield B. The reputation and unique properties of the Pencraig roofing product had been brought to his notice and it hadn't taken him long to realise that the material, because of its high tensile attributes and fine steel reinforcement would make ideal interior wall cladding for the underground galleries being constructed at Storage Site 5. That it was produced locally and to whatever sheet size and thickness required, made its application even more ideal. He hadn't shared his thoughts with Simon Carvel though, but had made his recommendation in his very first fortnightly report to the CA. The idea had found immediate favour in Sellafield, London and Brussels, much to Simon's chagrin, and Pencraig Roofing had received the lucrative European contract at a time when demand for roofing material had fallen off completely in the wake of Doomsday predictions. This had led to a healthy mutual respect developing between Rees and himself, a respect that had soon grown into close friendship, despite the difference in age. And then, one day, had come the proposition:

'I've heard that you play stand-off for Lancashire Hornets? That you were in the side that won the European League Trophy two years ago. Is that right?'

A modest smile had been Craig's only reply.

'Do you still turn out for them?'

'Not often. Work commitments make it difficult, these days.'

'Then how would you like to become player coach of Pencraig?'

He'd laughed rather nervously before starting to make his excuses: 'Thanks for the offer, Mr Morgan, but I'll have to turn it down. For one thing, I'm no coach. Never have been! And anyway, I . . . '

But the ageing Welshman wasn't used to refusals. 'Hold on! Listen to the proposition first. For a start, you won't be paid a penny for your services. Pencraig is an amateur set-up, pure and simple, and will remain so.'

He'd smiled on hearing that. Not exactly the sort of opening gambit to bring pressure to bear! But Rees, with characteristic self-assurance, had continued regardless. 'You'll remember what happened to professional sport in Europe twenty years ago?' He'd paused briefly there. 'Come to think of it, maybe you don't. Too young! Anyway, all that greed – personal and corporate – almost killed off some sports, football and rugby in particular. The fans got fed up and they began shunning the turnstiles. Which wasn't a bad thing, as it turned out, because it gave new life to amateur sport.' His glint of pleasant recollection was short-lived, though, and he made a clucking sound with his tongue. 'But by today, as you know only too well, the old corrupt professionalism has crept back in. Lancashire Hornets probably pay you well for your services, don't they . . . ?'

The old man had immediately regretted the question. ' . . . But that's none of my business, is it? All I will say is that no brown envelopes change hands at Pencraig . . . '

It was an impassioned argument from him.

'It's not that, Mr Morgan! It's just that I'm too involved with my work at the moment. I wouldn't have the time. Anyway, if what they say's going to happen . . . this asteroid . . . '

'Let's not dwell on that! It might never happen. Just listen to the offer, that's all! You love it here. Right? You love the rural life.'

Craig had nodded. No point in denying that he felt more contentment now than he'd ever felt before, despite the predictions of doom.

'Then how would you like your own cottage in the wilds?' Rees had smiled before continuing. 'Not too far from where I live, actually! It's called Hafod. Used to be a shepherd's summer residence in the old days. Lay in ruins for years, until I had it done up recently . . . re-roofed, refurbished to its former glory. And I want it lived in! Stone floor throughout, open fireplace, bare walls, no bathroom, no running water – water supply comes from a spring at the back of the house. No water closet either!'

'Closet?'

'Toilet.'

Craig had laughed out loud then. 'And those are your incentives? No brown envelopes and no creature comforts!'

But Rees had pretended not to hear. 'I know you'll love it, because you love your solitude. And as an added incentive, I'll arrange flying lessons for you, and you can then borrow my helicopter at weekends. You'll get to see your girlfriend in Nottingham in a quarter of the time that it now takes you on that superbike of yours.'

Craig O'Darcy smiled now as he recalled the conversation of so many months ago. Rees was a wily old character who had sussed his man out well. He'd known that the cottage offer would have its appeal. And he'd known that the helicopter offer would carry the day.

'Two practice sessions a week, and the odd game on Sunday should you be available . . . And the name's Rees, not Mr Morgan!'

It was as if the old man had known even then that the love affair with Sally wouldn't last, and before long, Craig O'Darcy, ex part-time professional stand-off for Lancashire Hornets, was turning out as unpaid player coach of Pencraig RC, at a time when league fixtures all over the country were being cancelled because of growing transport difficulties. Very soon, he was wondering why Rees Morgan had bothered to recruit him at all. He wasn't to know, at the time, that the old man was working to a very different agenda to his own.

Behind him the meanders of Afon Arian were beginning to bleed under a reddening sky and a path of colour was starting to show on the waters of the far-off bay. Early street lights helped delineate the seaside settlements of Caer Môr, Portharian and Aberheli. The only blot on an otherwise perfect scene was the thirty acre caravan site on the southern outskirts of Pencraig, with its uniform rows of tightly packed static vans; a recent development to accommodate some of those residents of Caer Môr and Aberarian who had already vacated their seaside homes to escape the predicted coastal flooding in three months time. Whereas the area's weathered tips of slate blended naturally with the surrounding landscape, this regiment of pastel coloured vans looked distinctly ugly and out-of-place, a forewarning that the pattern of life here was about to change forever.

Despite the lengthening shadows, the low sun still gave off unnatural warmth for the time of year. He wiped his brow with the back of his hand and turned to walk the twenty metres or so to the front door of his cottage home. Near the door, on a slate slab that still retained the sun's warmth, his pet sheepdog lay curled and still, until the sound of his footsteps roused it from its slumber. It now jumped to its feet and ran panting and yelping down the path to meet him, until its five-metre-long tether gave out and the animal was yanked back. In the ten months that he'd owned it, he'd never given it a name. *Dog* had seemed adequate enough, somehow.

'Well, Dog, have you missed me?' He playfully tousled the black head and a limp ear. Living as he was in such an isolated spot, Dog was not just company but also a guard against unwelcome visitors.

The coolness of the clean slate floor and the bare granite walls of Hafod welcomed him in a pleasant embrace. Having thrown open the shutters to allow what little evening light could enter through the pair of tiny windows, he then fetched a jug, took it outside to fill at the spring and drank profusely from it. The ice-cold water felt like new life flowing down his gullet. He also topped up Dog's stainless steel bowl and listened to the parched tongue lapping it all up.

It was so hard to accept that all this was coming to an end.

Chapter 2

'Life's been good to me, Craig. I'm seventy two . . . pushing seventy three . . . and God has been kind.'

They were sitting in the lounge bar, Rees nursing a glass of brandy, Craig cupping his pint glass of orange and lime in both hands. The room was about a quarter full; groups of young women mainly – wives and girlfriends of the rugby squad.

For months, Pencraig Recreation Club had been rationing its drinks to three units per member per week, a cup of tea or coffee being the equivalent of a single measure of spirit or a half pint of beer. Consequently, most members were now limiting their social activities to one evening a week – preferably Saturday or Sunday – and were reserving their three unit ration for that one session. No one complained. In fact they felt privileged, because every other club and tavern in Pencraig had had to close its doors months ago, with virtually no hope of getting any fresh supplies.

Rugby practice had finished almost an hour ago but most of the squad were still either enjoying the pool and sauna or using the facilities of the snooker hall or the squash and badminton courts. The Club committee had wanted to close the heated pool and the sauna booths in order to save valuable energy but Rees Morgan had strongly and successfully argued that maintaining the facilities helped to keep up morale of members, most of them Pencraig Roofing employees.

But even when alcohol was in plentiful supply, Rees had been able to discourage heavy drinking amongst the players, and there had grown within the Pencraig rugby squad a keen but healthy rivalry towards achieving the highest possible levels of fitness, so that by now many of them regarded beer and spirits as a negative to their efforts.

'Listen, lads . . . !' It was late June 2024, with only a fortnight having elapsed since the world being told of the incoming asteroid and Rees had taken it upon himself to call a squad meeting. ' . . . No one knows for certain what things will really be like when the worst comes to the worst, but one thing's for sure, rugby won't be a priority by then . . . !'

That had brought a nervous laugh from some, a throaty grumble from others.

' . . . In a little over two years from now, when this thing drops on us . . . *if* it drops on us . . . Well! You hardly need me to tell you that this world of ours is going to change dramatically.'

Rees' quiet self-assurance had commanded a polite hearing, even from the least intelligent members of the squad.

'They tell us that conditions will, at best, resemble those of a Siberian winter, and that they'll last for months . . . years even . . . depending on which expert opinion you're prepared to listen to. Anyway, we're all going to be needing adequate supplies of food and warm clothing for ourselves and our families and the sooner we start preparing, the better. But that's something to discuss later. For now, I want to stress the importance of physical fitness once those conditions hit us. You all watch the TV! You've heard the predictions! Extreme weather . . . crime and lawlessness . . . anarchy . . . survival of the fittest . . . dog eat dog . . . That sort of alarmist talk. But we'd be fools not to take some of it seriously. In many respects, it *is* going to be every man for himself, which is why I'm telling you now that your personal fitness will be crucial to every one of you when the hard times come and you have families to fend for.'

He'd then gone on to labour the point and as he did so, all plans for success on the rugby field had paled into insignificance.

'But I'm hoping that we can work for one another, as well as for those sections of the community that won't be able to cope with the conditions.'

That was when they began to appreciate Rees Morgan's agenda. During the next few weeks, the extent of that agenda became clear to them. To begin with, a part-time professional with Lancashire Hornets, called Craig O'Darcy, was brought in as team coach. Then, Rees had moved quickly and had offered the entire rugby squad, all twenty five of them, a new role to play during their working hours, a role that they'd taken to with varying degrees of enthusiasm and success. Under the auspices of Pencraig Roofing, they'd been supplied with a fleet of lorries and vans, a fifty million euro fund and a mandate to travel far and wide for food and fuel, warm clothing and bedding supplies. And when prices had become inflated in the wake of panic buying, Rees had doubled the size of the fund. 'What the hell!' he'd said, in his astute matter-of-fact way. 'Once this thing falls on us, my money's going to count for nothing anyway.'

The Provenders, as the squad soon came to be affectionately known, were first of all charged with procuring the goods which were then to be rationed to Pencraig Roofing employees and to the pensioners and the disabled in the community. The squad was split up into teams of two, three or four in number, with each group being given a *carte blanch* to operate on its own initiative, and with the added incentive of a small percentage of whatever provisions they could acquire. During that first month, the levels of initiative had varied greatly. Whereas one team of four had struggled within a fifty mile radius to obtain meagre provisions, others had ventured much further afield and their efforts had been generously rewarded. Team S (*S* for Steve) – four in number – had taken two cattle trucks, with long trailers attached, up to the Scottish Highlands where they'd successfully bid for a large herd of the highland breed. On their return, a highly delighted Rees Morgan had bought the local abattoir and the services of its butchers and had installed huge refrigerated storage units on site at Cefn Quarry. In Mid Wales, Team P (*P* for Phil) had paid well over the odds for a full flock of mountain sheep – 1,460 in number – and had returned to a hero's welcome from the others. Team K (*K* for Keith) enjoyed similar success in Dumfries-shire, where they were able to stock a huge refrigerated lorry with fresh Solway-farmed salmon. Soon after that, however, Whitehall and Brussels put a lid on the brokering of such deals, but the move only served to establish a flourishing black market in refrigerated meats.

Two of the teams were given a different directive. They were charged with acquiring as much warm clothing as possible and their initiative had taken them past the middle men and directly to two large Manchester factories where they used hundreds of fleeces as bargaining power for a fifty-fifty share of the finished sheepskin coats.

In the meantime, another squad, six in number – Team O (*O* for Owain), together with wives and girlfriends – were entrusted with setting up a huge store in the centre of town from which other local people, non-employees of Pencraig Roofing, could buy their provisions at cost price. Rees had sensibly argued that the only way to avoid lawlessness and insurrection – locally, at least – was to ensure that everybody had access to food, fuel and warm clothing. Not all, though, had taken advantage of the offer. Some had been too slow to make the most of it, whilst others had just laughed at the predictions of doom. When told, Rees had merely shrugged a disappointed shoulder and said, 'Well, you know what they say about taking a horse to water.'

Craig's face now creased in a little smile of respect as he regarded the old man taking a sip of his brandy. 'Yes, you've done well for yourself, Rees, but I suspect that Fate had nothing to do with it. Anyone who's as shrewd as you are and who works as hard as you do, is bound to succeed . . . deserves to succeed. Luck has nothing to do with it, I reckon.'

'Don't misquote me, my friend! I said *God*, not *Fate* . . . not *Luck*.'

At that, the little Welshman looked away as some raised voices came through from the other bar. It gave Craig a few seconds to contemplate the rugged features and the slight torso. He looks more like fifty two than seventy two, he thought. The body was sinewy with hardly any excess weight, the weather-beaten features resembling supple leather, the hands that gripped the edge of the table large and rough from early years of manual toil. His clothes – dark grey corduroy trousers and light grey crew-neck cotton sweater – were unassuming, the one being well-tailored and of the finest quality, whilst the other, with its black and gold motif, was just an ordinary run-of-the-mill Pencraig RC casual-wear sweatshirt. Despite his mere five feet seven inches, Rees Morgan could pose a commanding presence in any company, with his rugged looks and full head of wiry grey hair, brushed back above the ears. A beard would look well on him, Craig thought, but personal vanity's not in the man's nature. Yes, life had been good to him; had given him features that were striking if not overly handsome; had given him a strong but warm personality; had given him an ease and a self-assurance to blend into any company, and an ability to converse engagingly at any level. And he had Sinéad for wife! Sinéad! The undoubted jewel in Rees' crown and a striking personality in her own right. During those times of recession, when he'd had to struggle to succeed, Rees had relied heavily on his wife's support. Whether playing host to potential customers or contending with serious business competitors, her redoubtable persuasiveness had invariably won through, helped not a little by the brightness and depth of green flirtatious eyes, flashing white teeth, eye-catching cleavage, flame-red hair, soft brogue and contagious Irish laughter. Rees, more than anybody, realised the asset that she was, and had been, to him. Even now, at fifty four, she retained a beauty and a poise that could turn the heads of younger men, Craig himself amongst them.

'By the way, lad, . . .' The old man's attention had returned. 'I'll need to inspect those underground galleries of yours next week, just to satisfy myself, as well as your bosses, that the joints in the cladding have been well and truly sealed. How much work is there left?'

'Three weeks at the most.' Craig had been the first to be told of Whitehall's concerns; concerns emanating from an ill-founded report submitted by Simon Carvel. 'But you needn't worry.'

'I won't!' Rees' self-assurance said it all. 'And then?'

'What do you mean?'

'When those three weeks are up, what happens to *you*? Do you stay here? Or do you go back to Sellafield?'

'Who knows? One of us – Carvel or myself – will have to oversee the storing of the plutonium waste in Gallery 2.' He smiled a rueful smile. 'The local management is quite capable of shouldering that responsibility, but they're only answerable to the Welsh senate, as you know. Whitehall will need its own assurance. So Carvel or myself will have to stay on until Gallery 2 is finally sealed. Then, in all likelihood, I'll be recalled to Sellafield.'

'And then what?'

Craig's quizzical look begged further explanation and Rees continued, 'I mean, where will you be when it happens?'

'The impact, you mean? Somewhere high up in Cumberland, I expect. And well out of reach of those bloody huge waves that they're promising us.' His laugh carried very little humour.

'Don't you think it stupid that you should be moving at all? It won't leave you much time to prepare for what's ahead . . . to stock up on supplies and things.'

Craig shrugged. 'Not much choice really, if I'm ordered back. Either that or forfeit my last two months' rations from Central Depot. Anyway I've been doing a bit of hoarding already, Rees . . . as you'd expect. I've got a good supply of logs and peat stashed away in that cavern next to Hafod . . . and if I'm still here when the time comes, then I presume that I'll still have the generator, if I need it?'

When Rees Morgan had renovated and refurbished the cottage, he'd installed a sizeable wood burner in the old ingle-nook chimney and had housed a mobile generator at the rear of the building so that Craig would have an adequate supply of electricity.

'Petrol and diesel?'

'Yes. I've got a bit put by.' He had, in fact, five ten-gallon drums of each, filled to the brim, all well-hidden behind the log pile in the old workings.

'How about food? Clothing?'

Craig smiled. 'Hafod isn't all that big . . . ,' implying that his storage space was limited. He took comfort from the fact that in addition to the supplies that Rees had already provided him with, he had also, over the past months, been rationing his Posting Allocation. And as far as clothing was concerned, he had his warm skiing gear stashed away, plus the Himalayan-style sleeping bag and the cold-weather outfit that the Lancashire Hornets had supplied him with for the squad's Pre-season Toughening Adventure in Lapland, a few years ago. And the wet-suit that he'd often used on holiday – snorkelling on the Great Barrier Reef and off the Greek isles, or diving in the cold Norwegian fjords – might also prove invaluable under extreme conditions.

'Where would you rather be, though?' There was a persistence in

Rees' tone. 'With your family . . . ? Where are *they* based?'

Craig's smile turned rueful. For months, he'd successfully avoided this subject. 'Not much of a family, I'm afraid. My mother's living in California with her third husband. My father's missing, presumed dead . . .'

The Welshman's face clouded with sudden compassion. 'I'm sorry. Which war?'

Craig laughed. 'My old man went missing by design. I just prefer to think of him as dead! It's easier that way.'

'Ah!' No more questions were needed. Rees Morgan had grasped the situation. 'He was Irish.'

'Why? Is deceit a trait of the Irish?' It was meant as a weak joke to hide his discomfort but he bit his lip as he realised his gaffe. Sinéad was Irish! 'I mean . . . ,' he mumbled. 'How did you know?'

'That he was Irish?' Rees smiled rather sympathetically, unaware of Craig's embarrassment, and then, with a half laugh, 'O'Darcy! Hardly English, is it?'

Craig also laughed, with some discernible relief. 'American Irish in fact.'

'No other relatives?'

'None to hold on to, I'm afraid. I do have a brother, a half brother, from my mother's first marriage but . . . Which reminds me of a favour I wanted to ask of you, Rees.' And without waiting for his friend to respond, he continued, 'I've heard that Alistair – that's my brother's name – is to be Brussels' official spin doctor on Friday night's *'Doomsday Discussion'* programme on Skywatch and I was wondering . . .'

'Hei!' Rees' face took on a mixture of surprise and pleasure. 'You never let on that you had friends in high places!'

Craig smiled sadly. 'Brother, yes; friend, no. We haven't seen each other for the best part of fifteen years, and I won't be particularly worried if I don't see him for another fifteen, if ever.'

Rees eyed him keenly for a second or two. 'So what's the favour?'

'As you know, I never bothered with a TV wallscreen for the cottage . . . never felt the need for it, . . . until now.'

'No problem! You can have one of mine.'

Craig felt suddenly embarrassed. 'No need for that,' he muttered. 'It's just that . . . well, maybe I don't want to *see* Alistair ever again, but I wouldn't mind *hearing* his pearls of wisdom on Friday evening, and I was thinking that if you and Sinéad intend watching it, well . . . I had thought of watching it here, at the Club, but . . .'

Rees sensed his discomfort and finished his sentence for him. ' . . . but

28

they're more likely to be watching that holiday quiz show in here!'

Because public alarm had given way to melancholy and then to a mood of sombre indifference, few people now watched the *Doomsday Discussions*, no longer wanted to be reminded of their fate. They preferred to think of everything as normal, and that summer holidays were still an option. Who could blame them? A little self-delusion wouldn't harm anybody. And yet, sooner rather than later, the realisation was going to return, and then there *would* be panic on the streets!

'That's not the reason, actually. It's just that this place will be shut by then. The fact is, Rees, the programme doesn't start until half past eleven, and that's rather late!'

'No problem. We'll be watching anyway. You'll be more than welcome, son. Tell you what! Come early, and you can have that promised tour of the old underground workings.'

It had been something they'd often talked about, ever since Craig had shown an interest in the bygone process of slate mining but, for one reason or another, they'd never got round to the final arrangements.

One of the perks of the job at Storage Site 5 was being his own boss and being able to please himself as to the hours that he worked. As long as his fortnightly report landed punctually on the CA's desk in Sellafield, then no questions were ever asked.

'Yes, I'd like that.' He'd heard so much about the scale of the workings at Cefn Quarry, reputedly the largest underground mine in the world at one time. 'How long will we need, do you reckon?'

'An hour or so, just to give you an idea of the way things used to be done around here. Tell you what! Call at the Plas round about four o'clock, then we'll go up to the quarry, have our quick tour and then you can join us for supper. You can then stay to watch your programme. How does that sound?'

'That's very decent of you, Rees. Thank you.'

'But I should warn you that Ffion will also be there.'

Craig watched the smile crease the corners of the old man's eyes. It was a shared knowledge between them that he and Ffion weren't on the most friendly of terms. Although sixteen months had since elapsed, Craig knew that Rees' daughter still bore a grudge against him for the incident involving Simon Carvel. She'd been mistakenly convinced at the time that he'd played a part with Simon in disrupting her lessons. True, by persevering with the evening classes after Simon had left, he had made an effort to redeem himself and to make amends for his colleague's vulgarity but she'd been reluctant to ease the tension between them and that, in turn, had stifled his own inclination towards compromise, which was why he hadn't signed on for a second term. The course hadn't lasted long after that, anyway. People had more serious things to worry about.

'What say you? Will you run the gauntlet?'

They laughed and Craig nodded.

He left the club earlier than usual that night, before his friends could join him from their 'S & S' – their swim and sauna. Out on the car park, he mounted the Norton Jaguar 1500, but before pulling on his helmet he gazed long and hard at the clear night sky, as if expecting the rogue asteroid to reveal itself. 'What if I was up there, in Rees' helicopter, when the impact comes? Would I avoid the worst of it?' The naivety of the thought brought on an involuntary smile.

He had but a fleecy-lined track-suit to keep out the night air, but it was adequate, because for late May the climate was inordinately warm. The bike purred loudly as it took the steep hill in its stride, a hill that would, if he wished, take him over the Dunant Pass and on towards the north Wales coast. To left and right, moonlight glinted with an ethereal quality on the slate of the waste tips, causing him now to recollect the bout of melancholy and dejection that those very same tips had brought on when he'd first arrived in the area, eighteen months ago. Then, they'd been swathed in mist and cold drizzle, and the total greyness of sky and surroundings had been oppressive, to say the least. 'How miserable can this fuck'n place get?' had been one of Simon's more memorable quotes at the time.

Half way up the hill, he indicated a right turn off the main road and into a wide entrance. The security recognition system acknowledged the badge that he now held aloft and the heavy gates slid open and just as silently closed behind him. The Norton's headlights swept over an expanse of shining tarmac and picked a large house out of the shadows of tall conifers up on his left. Plas Cefn, home of Rees and Sinéad Morgan, was an impressive three-floored edifice of trimmed granite blocks with three large ground-floor bow windows looking out on a veranda which, in turn, overlooked well-kept gardens. Beds of waving tulips reflected the bike's halogen headlights, the whites and the yellows like a welcoming committee of little bright faces, the reds and the purples more reserved and blushing. There was but one incongruity – steel bars straddled all the windows. Rees had had them put up some months ago, *'in readiness,'* as he put it, *'for the difficult times to come.'* They made the place look like a prison. Up to the left of the house and well away from the conifers, the silent rotors of the six-passenger Humming Bird shimmered in the moonlight that bathed the helipad.

Once past the house, the square of tarmac led onto a road that gently climbed across the slope towards the huge industrial complex that had once been Cefn Quarry and which was now the home of Pencraig Roofing. Here, a dozen large buildings, lit up as if by daylight, were sited along a three hundred yard long platform of rock that had been carved out of the hillside, at the far end of which yellow diggers and earth-movers restlessly reflected the night lights and indicated the further development that was in progress. Their intermittent revving was all part of the constant rumble of machinery that echoed within the amphitheatre of quarried crags. The house and the site were roughly half a mile apart.

Taking a left, Craig aimed the Norton Jaguar onto a narrow off-shoot track that curled around the base of an undisturbed slate tip. From there on, the track wound its way up between other tall tips until it reached the level of the old track-way that eventually led to Hafod. All in all, it was a bumpy ride, but three minutes later he was parking the bike under one of the cottage windows and tousling Dog's ears in acknowledgement of the welcome that he was getting. The dial of his watch showed twenty past ten. Below him, the street lights of Pencraig gave up a soft orange glow, mantle-shaped over the town, whilst in the distance, the twinklings of the coastal towns – Caer Môr, Portharian, Aberheli – were a poor imitation of the star-studded sky.

*　　*　　*

Sinéad Morgan had recognized the bike and its rider as it passed her on the hill. She now guided the dark green Mercedes into the nearest available parking space to the clubhouse. She was here to pick up her husband, to be his *chauffeur* home. Rees would never risk driving with alcohol on his breath, however little he'd consumed. The law was prohibitive and Rees respected the fact. It was a restraint that irked his wife, though. Did he have to be so bloody fastidious, so habitual, in everything that he did?

Without bothering to lock the car, she strode towards the main door, her knee length dress swaying to and fro with the movement of her shapely hips. The moonlight played along the restless tresses of her hair.

'Ah, Sinéad my love!' Rees rose to greet her. 'Thank you for coming. No inconvenience, I hope?' The gratitude was sincere. 'If you'd been a couple of minutes earlier you'd have seen Craig O 'Darcy.'

'Yes. To be sure, he passed me on the hill. Did I not recognise the

31

bike?' Her Bantry accent was as strong as ever and it still pleased him to listen to it.

'He'll be joining us for dinner tomorrow night. Hope you don't mind?'

A stern look moved like a cloud over her attractive face. 'But surely, husband, you remember that Ffion will be with us?'

Rees half laughed. 'Yes, I did remember, and I *have* warned Craig. He didn't seem to mind.'

The cloud now became a scowl. '*He* didn't mind? What if *Ffion* minds?'

'Nonsense! Why should she? Craig is a presentable enough young man, and can be good company. Anyway, it's about time the two of them sorted out their little differences and misunderstandings, and tomorrow night will be as good a time as any.'

Sinéad licked her upper lip as she contemplated a reply, but then thought better of it and walked away to a nearby table where five young women were engaged in lively conversation punctuated by raucous laughter. As they all turned their heads to greet her, their welcome was obviously genuine. Two of them pointed to an empty chair in an instinctive invitation for her to join them, but she politely declined and indicated that she couldn't stay because her husband was waiting to leave. In the meantime, Rees himself, having watched her briefly, now moved towards the door.

Sinéad didn't hurry. She visited every occupied table, either to greet or to hold brief conversations with everyone in the room. Rees smiled as he watched her. Her ease and her composure pleased him.

Eventually she said her goodbyes and they both left for the car. The ride back home was quieter, more strained, than of late.

Chapter 3

He was preparing to leave the site early for his appointment with Rees when he caught sight of Simon Carvel striding down the two-hundred-metre-long corridor into Gallery 2. He'd shunned the trolley transport, preferring to walk the underground distance, and Craig couldn't help but wonder why. As usual, Carvel – or Rottweiller as he was often referred to amongst the workforce – was dressed in a dark suit, on the lapel of which his silver name-tag now glinted spasmodically as he moved under the corridor's triple row of fluorescent lights. Those same lights also drew notice to the thinness of his fair hair which now seemed to grow like a halo around his head. *Hardly a saint though!* Craig O'Darcy thought, with a wry smile, as he stood waiting for the Essex man to reach him.

Gallery 2, although nearing completion, was already a good two months behind schedule, a fact that was, in itself, causing considerable concern in Cardiff, Whitehall and Brussels. All it needed now, though, was another fifty metres or so of cladding on one of its walls before the remainder of the flasks of plutonium rods from various parts of the country, as well as from north-east France and the Low Countries, could be trundled in for safe storage. But, with just three months left to complete the work, people in high places were becoming increasingly agitated. And although a fortnight had passed since the completion of storage work in Gallery 1, the decision to permanently seal it off had had to be delayed because of Simon Carvel's report on the 'suspect cladding joints'.

Work on the two galleries, begun almost four years ago, had been providential to say the least, considering the threat that was now being posed by the incoming asteroid. They were vast underground affairs, each a quarter of a mile square, each expanse of roof supported by twelve-by-twelve rows of reinforced concrete pillars. Three silver-bright tracks of standard gauge tramway rutted the wide corridor floor that Carvel was now treading, each one leading from railway sidings on the surface to a complicated sets of points that sent capillary tracks down every one of the twelve storage rows. Outside, in the covered sidings, convoys of lead-coated flasks, delivered along the main line direct from France and the Low Countries, not to mention Sizewell, Hinckley Point and Dungeness, waited to be trundled underground for permanent storage.

The twelve billion euro scheme, and another like it in the highlands of Scotland, had been prioritised by EMNWD, the European Ministry for

Nuclear Waste Disposal, back in 2022 and work had begun without even the Welsh and Scottish Senates, let alone regional councils and the local populace, being consulted. Predictably, opposition to the project and particularly to the Ministry's high-handedness, had been hostile, with pressure groups staging sit-ins and organising rallies to create as much disruption as possible. But the confrontation had been anticipated and the disruption had been short-lived. EMNWD had come prepared to North Wales with two armed companies of the European Land Force equipped with full powers to suppress any civil disobedience and insurrection, and that had given the Tory press a field day of *'Don't say we didn't warn you, years ago, about German and French pretensions in Europe!'*

Carvel eventually arrived and stood glaring defiantly. 'Wha' the hell's goin' on, O'Darcy?' Although faced with a man five inches taller, and broader by far than himself, he was making no attempt to curb his belligerence. ' . . . Was it you who rubbished my concerns about these fuck'n joints in the claddin'?'

His bark sounded more like a terrier's than a Rottweiller's.

Craig ran his forefinger along the broken bridge of his nose and cast a quick look over his shoulder to see if there was anyone else within earshot. 'You filed your report, I filed mine. If mine contradicted yours then that's too bad, mate.'

'Too bad? Is that all you can fuck'n say? We're dealin' 'ere with national security and all you can fuck'n say is *Too bad?*'

A number of workmen in the gallery now turned towards the source of the tirade, a fact that either escaped Carvel's notice or else his concern.

Although eight years senior to him, Simon Carvel no longer commanded the respect of his younger colleague. 'National security? Don't be so bloody dramatic, for God's sake! There's bugger all wrong with the seals on these plate connections . . . ' With a sweep of the hand he indicated the gallery walls behind him. ' . . . and well you know it! So don't play stupid games. Both of us know why you cried wolf, Simon . . . '

The Rottweiller glared. 'If you're suggestin' that just because this fuck'n panel claddin' was your idea in the first place that I'm in some way biased against it . . . '

O'Darcy didn't wait for him to finish. 'Can you give a better reason? Anyway, you can make your complaint direct to the manufacturer next week, when Rees Morgan visits the site.' And with that he turned and summoned a trolley-cart to take him back up to the surface, knowing that he'd just added fuel to Carvel's vindictiveness; knowing also that Rees

Morgan would be more than capable of holding his own in any argument.

*   *   *

'Would you be believing that Rees is delayed at the office? But he'll be wanting me to phone him now, that you've arrived?'

Sinéad turned and walked ahead of him into the spacious foyer of Plas Cefn. Did he detect a tenseness in her tone?

'Thank you, Mrs Morgan. Are you sure that it's not an inconvenience for me to be joining you later . . . to watch the programme?'

At that, she seemed to think better of her attitude and turned to smile at him. 'And to have supper with us, Craig. No, no inconvenience whatsoever. And surely, have I not told you before to forget this *Mrs Morgan* formality. Sinéad be the name I was born with!'

She dialled on her C-phone and gazed at her husband's face as it appeared on the little screen in her hand. 'Dear husband!' she greeted him playfully in her Irish lilt. 'Your guest awaits you.'

Craig, not entirely at ease, once more sensed that he was imposing but his edginess was again dispelled as she turned to face him with her smile, inviting him to follow her into the front lounge. Her dark emerald dress was as becoming as anything he'd ever seen her wear. It emphasised the flame in her hair and the deep colour of her eyes and as she played her tongue over her capped white teeth, Craig felt a sudden urge to approach her, just to see how she would respond to him. She was, without doubt, the most sensuous female that he'd ever been in company with and as she looked at him with her laughing eyes, she seemed to sense his need.

'Sit down, Craig! My husband surely won't be long. You'll excuse me. There'll be work for me in the kitchen.'

The moment was gone and he felt a mixture of relief and frustration as his eyes followed her well shaped calves out of the room. He sensed that she'd been playing with him.

He walked over to the bay window and gazed awhile over the garden and down in the direction of the town which was hidden from him by a huge slate tip that clung to the hillside about half a mile away. Apart from the garden and its flowers, not much else of interest was to be seen. Plas Cefn, built just over a hundred years ago, had originally been intended as a summer residence for the Derbyshire family who owned the quarry at the time, but it hadn't been a particularly good choice of site, with mountains closing in on all sides. And as the quarry had

35

flourished, the surrounding slopes had become clothed with slate waste in semi-pyramidal piles whilst way to the left, the quarry workings had denuded the area down to the bare rock. Whoever had planted the sweep of tall pines between house and quarry, had done so to obliterate the scars from view.

He turned his back on the window. The room was impressively decorated. To his right, a grandfather clock claimed the space between the frame of the door and the corner. Until now, he'd been deaf to its loud ticking and its rough mechanical movements. The space between the door and the other corner was taken up by another piece of antique furniture, one that he couldn't give a name to or speculate as to its original function. In some respects it resembled a double-decker tallboy, fashioned from dark oak and with amateurish carvings all around its edges. It had to be very old! And probably priceless! Directly opposite him, on the far wall, stood a large Welsh dresser displaying willow-patterned plates and tureens of various sizes. Original brass handles glowed on the drawers and cupboards of its lower half. The wall to his left had two large watercolour originals in heavy gilded frames, one hanging directly above the tiled fireplace with its black slate mantle-piece, the other an overly ornate backdrop to the baby grand piano that glistened ebony black. The leather three piece that commanded the centre of the room, although blending well with everything else around it, was, in fact, a more recent acquisition, but manufactured to appear old and worn. Under it, on the lustrous block floor, lay a large square of thick carpet, of either Indian or Persian origin.

Craig found himself wondering whose taste was reflected here. Husband's? Or wife's? He decided that it could be that of either or both of them. The watercolours, he felt sure, were of local scenes but as he made to cross the floor towards them, a movement in the room's gable-end window drew his attention. A grey wheel-convertible Leech Land Rover was pulling up outside and he saw Rees nimbly climbing out of it.

'Sorry to have kept you waiting, my friend. Decisions had to be made. You know how it is. Shall we go?'

Typically brief and to the point, he'd come no further than the front door. Craig followed him out and into the extra-long-base Leech.

'Sinéad knows when to expect us back,' he explained, sensing Craig's wavering.

They drove the half mile up to the quarry site, passing the huge bilingual Pencraig Roofing sign on the way. Craig had had his tour of the site's surface complex many months ago, prior to suggesting the cladding for the new galleries at Storage 5. He'd already seen, and studied at first hand, Rees' replicating process for slate and tile, and had visited the huge crushing plant.

They needed to stop just long enough at the stores to pick up their white nylon oversuits, hard hats with head beams and batteries attached, and a pair of wellington boots each, before proceeding to the first mine entrance, two hundred yards further on. The adit, roughly six feet high by six wide, was barricaded with thick steel bars resembling those of a prison cell.

'That was the very first thing I had to do after buying the quarry,' Rees explained. 'Health and Safety Authorities wouldn't have it otherwise. Nor me for that matter,' he added. 'Every entrance had to be sealed off. Couldn't risk Jo Public wandering inside at will and in all likelihood getting killed.'

Craig tried peering into the darkness beyond the bars but could see no further than a few yards. 'We'd get our feet wet going in there,' he said, noticing the water that had collected in the entrance. 'That's why we've got the wellingtons, I presume. How many were there?'

'Mine entrances? Four in all. We'll be entering at a lower level than this, where it's a little drier under foot. '

Craig held his breath when they began the precarious downward journey along one of the quarry's original inclines, one that had carried a dual tramway. Although he knew that Rees had released the extra wheels to convert the vehicle into a six wheeler, he still half expected the 6 X 6 to start sliding on the steep descent. His sigh of relief was audible when they reached the bottom, where they turned left onto a rough track that horizontally traversed the waste tip. This, he realised, was the tip that he'd looked at earlier, the one that hid Pencraig from view from the house.

'We're not going down those, I hope?' Here and there on the slope below him, he could see at least three other inclines leading to lower levels, and narrow paths zigzagging their way up and across the plethora of slate waste. As he looked, he was vaguely reminded of a Snakes & Ladders board. Apart from a patch of greenery, resembling a small park, way down to his left and near the main road into the town, and the odd bush of wild rhododendron that had somehow taken root and even flourished in amongst the slate waste, all else was grey and cold and unyielding. And yet there was a character to the place, just like its people.

Rees laughed. 'No, not the way you think, but we could make the journey underground, if you like.'

Craig looked at him dubiously and the Welshman smiled. 'You'll see what I mean in a minute or two,' he added. 'Here we are.'

They'd left the slate waste behind them and the Leech LR was pulling-up outside an adit that was slightly larger than the previous one. This was sealed not with steel bars but with solid aluminium double doors bolted into the rock.

'You certainly took no chances with this one.' There was a hint of wonderment in Craig O'Darcy's voice. 'Anybody would think that you had the Crown Jewels in there.'

Rees again smiled, donned his hard hat with head beam and battery attached and pulled on his rubber boots. He watched Craig do the same. Then he approached the metal doors, key in hand.

'These shafts were the work of the miners . . . '

They were out of the sunlight now and peering into a long straight tunnel, Rees erect, Craig stooping because of the low headroom. Craig felt the chill of the rock and of the wintry draught. He could smell the dust and the stagnation and the decay.

' . . . In these quarries, the term *miners* was used specifically to refer to the men who dug out these tunnels . . . '

'Granite?' He directed his beam at the shaft wall.

'Yes. Quarry engineers-cum-geologists would decide where the slate beds lay and where best on the hillside to start digging for them. A quarry's profitability depended greatly on how near the surface those beds were, because in those days, blasting out these shafts could be a long and expensive business. This one, for instance . . . ' Rees rolled his head so that his beam played restlessly on the distant darkness, giving his younger companion the impression of peering into the murky depths of a bottomless pool. ' . . . took sixty metres to find the slate. Others are longer, some much shorter. Some turned out to be total failures, which meant that the miners would have had to work for weeks for next to no pay. It was payment by results in those days.' And then, sensing Craig's question, he added, 'Quarry owners were a greedy and heartless breed!'

Their echoing footsteps filled the eerie tunnel. There was no sign of the tramway that had once carried the wagons of rubble and slate slabs out into the open; in fact, it seemed to Craig that the shaft floor had been flattened and improved and that it had been in recent use.

'This is where they hit the slate. This is the first chamber on this level.'

Rees had turned his head to reveal a yawning cavern on their left, causing Craig to catch his breath at the unexpected sight. It's entrance, he reckoned, was about twenty five feet wide but it opened out, at right angles to the tunnel itself, to a height and a depth that suggested a vastness that he couldn't properly fathom. Using his own light as best he could, he stepped forward, grateful to be out of his stoop, and began to explore what seemed to be an impenetrable darkness.

'Can you see where the bore holes were?' Rees' voice had an uncanny, even icy, quality to it. The beam of his head-light was directed at the looming chamber wall.

Craig looked at the many drilling scars on the rock face.

'That's the work of the rockmen. In the old days, all that boring had to be done by hand; powered drills didn't come until much later. They would carefully decide where best to bore each hole, then they'd pack it with black powder and blast out the slate which was then sent up to the mills in huge lumps, to be sawn and split and trimmed by the quarrymen. Two rockmen down here would supply their two partners up in the mill and the size of their wage packets at the end of the month depended on the number of finished slates that they were able to produce between them in that time.'

'Piecework.'

'That's right.'

'How did they get up there?' Craig was studying some bore holes high up on the almost vertical chamber wall. 'The rockmen I mean.' He spoke in a semi-whisper, without really knowing why.

'Chains! Heavy chains were hung from up there . . . ' Rees' beam traversed the cavern wall near the roof until it picked out a large and rusty metal ring. ' . . . and then the rockman would hang on to that whilst drilling.'

'You're joking!'

'No. He'd hang upright, suspended on one leg which was coiled by the chain. That meant that he had both hands free to drill, whilst his other leg kept him at a workable distance away from the rock face.'

The younger man felt genuinely interested and tried to imagine the difficulty of such a manoeuvre. 'There must have been accidents.'

'Fatalities, yes. Especially in the early days when they had to work by candlelight; not to mention those early deaths from silicosis, when lungs became rock hard from breathing in too much dust.'

Craig could dimly make out the roof of the chamber climbing at an angle away from him to a maximum height of some sixty feet. The aura of the place made him feel as though he'd entered an unlit cathedral and he half expected to hear a choir's chant reverberating in the darkness.

Rees seemed to sense his thought. Without warning he broke out in song with the opening notes of the Welsh air 'All Through the Night', his bass voice resonating in the chilly blackness –

'Holl amrantau'r sêr ddywedant,
Ar hyd y nos . . . '

– his breath creating a little puff of vapour with each exhalation.

'How's that for acoustic?' Without waiting for a reply, he turned and led the way back into the tunnel, speaking over his shoulder as he did so. 'Safety rules dictated that a pillar of rock, twenty yards wide, had to be left between each chamber, to ensure against roof falls.'

They didn't linger long at the second chamber, less still at the third and not at all at the next three.

'How many are there?'

'On this level, nine.'

They'd reached the top of an incline which dropped at a sharp angle into an impenetrable darkness.

'And how many levels?'

'Two above this one – you saw the adit to one of them – and . . . ' He fell into a silent count. ' . . . fifteen below.'

'Fifteen?' The astonishment was genuine. 'With nine chambers on every level?'

'More on some, fewer on others. There are a hundred and sixty eight of these chambers in all, the lowest of them well below sea level.'

'Which means that this mountain that we're in is more empty than solid ?' He didn't know how else to express his wonder.

'Not quite true, actually. You've got to remember that the lower levels, from the G down, are now completely flooded. In the old days, pumps were in permanent use to keep the workings dry . . . '

'G? What does that mean?'

'Each level was designated with a letter, beginning with A at the very top.'

'So, if there were two above this one and fifteen below, then the lowest was . . . ?'

'The R.'

'And today they're all obsolete.' It wasn't a question, merely a statement.

'Not quite. Let's go down.'

The steep incline could have been a tricky descent indeed if it hadn't been for the roughly hewn stone steps down one side. Rees led the way and they both fell silent as they gingerly picked their way down, one behind the other, with Craig imagining all sorts of worrying scenarios if they were to lose their way in the darkness. What if they took a wrong turning? What if their batteries ran out? What if one of them was to fall and break a leg? Or worse! What if the old man had a heart attack? What if he died?

He didn't want to dwell on the thought. 'It's chilly down here.'

'The temperature's more or less constant all year round. The miners and the rockmen would feel the chill in summer and a relative warmth in winter . . . Right! Now we've reached the D floor, but I want to take you down another two levels.'

'O!' He wanted to ask *'But what's the point? I've already got the gist of it.'* but he chose to keep quiet rather than question the old man's decision.

They followed the D for some fifty yards or so – back, Craig thought, in the direction from which they'd come along the upper floor – until they arrived at the head of another incline. Down they went, seemingly into the bowels of the earth. As he picked his way from step to step, forever stooping lest he bang his head on the low roof, he recalled a visit that he'd made to a copper mine in the Lake District some years previously but the scale of that, he realised now, was nowhere near as impressive or as frighteningly claustrophobic as this.

Rees lingered only long enough on the E to point with his head beam to what remained of a rusty wagon half blocking the passage in the distance. Then they were descending again, down another seemingly endless incline, their restless headbeams dancing on the tunnel wall as this one disappeared in a constant curve, below them. Not for the first time, Craig felt a chill other than that of the cold draught that was coming up to meet them.

At first he thought that the dark grey of the tunnel wall had taken on a lighter hue but then he caught his breath. 'There's someone down there, Rees! There's a light!'

The little Welshman neither answered him nor slowed his step.

When they came to the end of their descent, Craig O'Darcy saw that their way was blocked by steel bars similar to what he'd seen previously. Beyond the bars, traces of tramway curled right, to join a well lit passageway.

'What *is* this place, Rees?' Even as he spoke, he felt ashamed of his whispers. 'What the hell's going on here? What's that hum?'

'You'll see.' The little man had been busy rummaging in a bunch of keys, then part of the steel bars swung open on well-oiled hinges and they both passed through, Rees pausing to lock the gate behind them.

'How squeamish are you, son?'

'Squeamish? What do you mean?' He felt ill-at-ease. 'What *is* this place?'

The dim lights along the roof of the tunnel ran in both directions, spaced every ten yards or so, but there was no other sign of life nor any sound except that of their own breathing and the distant humming noise that Craig had already enquired about. The tunnel was wider, higher than anything that he'd seen so far. Beneath his feet was smooth black tarmac.

'We're on the F now. Every level below this is flooded.'

'Every chamber?'

'Every single one is full of water.'

Craig did a rough calculation. 'Twelve levels. That's a lot of water.' He'd done some risky deep sea diving in his time but the thought of venturing into those dark depths and getting lost really made his skin crawl. 'Why do you ask if I'm squeamish?'

'Does the sight of a coffin upset you?'

'Not usually. Down here it might!' And he tried to laugh off his unease.

'It's just that I wanted you to see another use that I've made of these old workings.'

There was room for them now to walk side by side and Craig had no need to stoop. A chamber soon yawned to their right and two sets of head beams were directed into its blackness. Then, as Rees threw a switch on the chamber entrance wall, the interior became bathed in a soft bluish floodlight to reveal a cavern similar to what Craig had already seen, only this one was decked on two sides – to the left and straight ahead – and to roof height, with partitioned shelving. Some partitions were larger than others, bringing to mind the staggered shelves that he'd seen in some libraries. These partitions, however, would have held giant books. His first thought was that it was all part of Rees' preparations for what was now termed 'the post impact period'. This, he imagined, was to be a huge food or fuel storage unit. He certainly wasn't prepared for the true explanation when it came.

'Here! Wear this!'

From a cabinet on the chamber wall, the little man produced a nose and mouth mask before continuing towards the next cavern. Craig complied.

'Seven years ago, the town's governing council were faced with a bit of a predicament. The local cemetery was filling up and suitable alternative land wasn't available. The land around here, as you well realise, if very rocky and to dig a grave in it can cost the earth.' He laughed drily. 'And that's not meant as a pun! Anyway, cremation wasn't an alternative as far as a lot of families were concerned . . . '

'And you thought . . . ' The sentence went unfinished but he'd said enough to imply a level of comprehension.

'Why not?'

They reached the next chamber, the entrance to which was blocked off, from the passage they were in, with large metal-framed glass doors.

Another switch was thrown and the tinted glass that was one minute reflecting his head beam back at him suddenly became a window for him to look through. The sight that greeted him, although half expected, was probably the most eerie that Craig had ever witnessed and he was grateful for the mask to stifle his surprise. He was gazing at similar shelving to that of the previous cavern, only here there were coffins present; a variety of coffins in white, black or woodgrain, the white ones reflecting the floodlighting with a bluish incandescence, like white-shirted dancers caught in a discotheque's flashing strobes. A quick count revealed that there were about forty coffins in all, perched here and there along the topmost shelves. A parked forklift, shining and silvery, indicated how they'd been placed there.

'Come on. The next one will give you a better idea.' A flick of the switch cast everything into darkness again and they moved on. 'You'd be surprised how popular this idea proved to be.' Rees was smiling. 'I've had literally thousands of applications from people who want to book their own family vault. And many of them from people who aren't that old! Enquiries came from far afield.' He chuckled. 'You'd be surprised how far some people are prepared to travel to be buried.'

'I can understand why.' He was getting over his astonishment.

Rees stopped to look up at him. 'Can you?'

'Yes. Cremation isn't an option for me either . . . '

'You've thought about that? At your age?' The old man seemed amused.

'Of course! As have those applicants you've just mentioned! On the other hand, the thought of being screwed into a box and buried under six feet of earth isn't particularly appealing either, I can tell you, . . . especially if you're as claustrophobic as I am. But this . . . ' He pointed to the chamber which they were now approaching. ' . . . this is an option that I would definitely consider . . . as long as the lid was left off the coffin, and the lights were left permanently on. How do I apply, Rees?'

The older man laughed. 'Strictly reserved for local ratepayers, my friend, but if you're still around in about fifty years time, then come and see me again and I'll see what I can do for you.'

They'd reached the glass doors of the next chamber and the lights, here again, were duly switched on.

'This was the first chamber to be used. As you see . . . ' He waved a hand to indicate the size of the passageway behind them. ' . . . we had to expand to allow for our special hearse to be driven in here. The scaffolding that you see is made of reinforced plastic . . . '

'And the different-sized partitions?'

'To suit family demands! Some compartments can take up to four coffins, others just one or two. We made an exception with one family who wanted room for six . . . ' He pointed towards the topmost layer. ' . . . Parents and four children. The kids are up there, poor souls, burnt to death in a house fire. The parents are still alive; still live in Pencraig. Tragic! Anyway, every partition in this chamber is now occupied, or part-occupied I should say. All the empty spaces that you see are reserved for remaining family members.'

'Charming!' Craig noted that the spaces outnumbered the coffins.

'Bear in mind that it's only seven years since we've been using this place.'

'And the humming noise, of course, . . . ' He'd just become aware of it again. ' . . . is the air conditioning.' Otherwise, he thought, this place would be reeking putrefaction.

He'd noticed that the lights in the tunnel roof only ran for another fifty metres or so. There, a pair of huge aluminium double doors barred the way. Rees duly produced a key and Craig sighed aloud when the tarmac beneath his feet led him out into unexpected fresh air and warm sun, and directly into the neat little park with its flower beds and weeping willows that he'd spotted earlier, from above. Never had sky seemed bluer nor grass greener and never had air been fresher! He looked at his watch. They'd been an hour and forty minutes underground and in that time he'd seen but a fraction of the mine. He was now standing at the foot of the slope, near the exit – or entrance! – to Level F. And below his feet . . . ? To comprehend the scale of the workings down there was beyond him.

'This is as far as the mourners are allowed to come.' The old man, white hardhat in hand, turned, having shut and locked the doors behind him. He was referring to the oasis of warm green in a world of cold grey.

He pointed. 'Over there you'll see an open air chapel where services can be held if requested.'

Craig tried to imagine the feelings of relatives as they watched a hearse, bearing the coffin of a loved one, disappear into a black hole in a mountainside that was clothed with slate rubble. *Not everyone's idea of heaven*, he thought. *More like the other place!*

Rees seemed to read his mind. 'We use special lighting and sound effects for the last journey and there's a screen on which mourners can watch the coffin being taken to its last resting place. They can even order a video recording of the event. All done in a very dignified and discreet manner, I can assure you.'

'I'm impressed, Rees.' And he was.

'Thank you. But now you've got a stiff climb ahead of you.'

Somewhere up there, on a ledge on the slate-strewn slope, the Leech LR awaited them. Craig reckoned that they'd descended nearly two hundred feet but the stiff climb that Rees had just mentioned was infinitely more preferable to a return journey along those underground passages. He shuddered, despite himself. 'Bloody hell!' he thought, as he contemplated all that he'd just seen and heard. 'What a burial mound!'

Then, squinting in the late sun, he began following in Rees Morgan's footsteps, as the older man gingerly picked his way up through the slate rubble. 'Look out, in case I dislodge some of this stuff!' he shouted over his shoulder and Craig heeded the warning.

They had the equivalent of three levels to climb, to reach the LLR.

*　　*　　*

Simon Carvel, with a book of crosswords tucked under his arm, chose the empty bar rather than his hotel room. It was a quarter past six and he'd had a vile day. Not only had O'Darcy ridiculed him but a group of the *fuck'n locals* had then had the nerve to challenge his authority by rejecting his instruction to re-align one of the cladding panels. That had led to an unseemly confrontation, one that had resulted in threats of industrial action. The occasional insult in Welsh hadn't helped either. He knew enough of the fuck'n language to know what 'Bastard Sais!' meant.

The empty optics and the covers over the pumps were a depressing sight, while the fact that no delivery was expected from the brewery in the foreseeable future added to his melancholy. The crowd that he usually drank and played cards with here – the REs, or Reluctant Ex-pats, as they liked to refer to themselves – now no longer met; no longer had incentive to meet. After all, an evening of poker or solo was no fun unless accompanied by a few pints. And once the others came to know that his monthly posting allocation included a bottle of Islay whisky, then things had turned really sour. Their hints that he could organise gambling sessions in his hotel room and acknowledge their friendship with 'a tot or two', took things too far, in his opinion. 'Fuck'n scroungers, the lot of them!'

One of the few perks that came with the job at Storage Site 5 was the 'posting allocation' that had begun to arrive soon after the period of panic buying had stripped every store in the country of its food and alcohol supplies. Every month, for the past year and a half, he and O'Darcy, like all other government employees in key jobs, had been receiving a large box of provisions direct from Central Government Depot. And as added incentive to keep them at their job, they'd also been given an any-two-from-three option – beer (two dozen cans), whisky (litre bottle) or cannabis (two hundred grammes). 'It's no more than we deserve,' he often whined, 'for being exiled to this fuck'n back-of-beyond. I wouldn't have stuck it here otherwise. No doubt, O'Darcy would have – he seems to like the place, and the fuck'n people – but not me. Not Simon Carvel!'

The sense of monotony now returned, and with it the reproach. 'If I hadn't raised the business of those fuck'n panel joints, I could have been out of 'ere by now.' He knew what he'd done, and why he'd done it, and now he had to live with the consequences of his own vindictiveness. He'd cut his own nose . . . !

The rest of the workforce at Site 5 also received special supplies, known in their case as 'Site Rations'. The condition laid on them was that each month's schedule had to be completed on or before time. A delay in the work meant a delay of delivery. Site rations were meagre, however, if compared with the posting allocation that Carvel and O'Darcy received, but the men weren't to know that. To them and their families, those rations were critical at a time when salaries, as such, meant very little. While shelves in food stores remained bare, then money counted for nothing, especially since even the black market was unable to meet demands.

'Coffee . . . ! And put it on my room bill.'

Dave, the Haven Hotel's long-serving barman and now general dogsbody, had seen him arrive and had followed him into the lounge bar. Although not too fond of the Haven's solitary resident, he now paused long enough to question his black looks before retreating dutifully to the kitchen. When he returned, cup in hand, he saw that the disgruntled Essex man had made his way to a corner table and that his head was now buried in one of the crosswords.

'What do you make of these fuck'n Welsh, Dave?'

The barman, after an instinctive glance around the room to make sure that no locals had slipped in unnoticed, screwed his small face and shrugged his narrow shoulders, as if unsure how else to respond. He'd heard the question from Carvel so many times before. At first, he'd tried to humour the hotel's long-term guest by adding his own little bit to discredit the natives, but things had got out of hand since then. Carvel, he realised, had become paranoid.

'Had a bad day, then?'

*   *   *

'Help yourself to a bath or a shower . . . '

The offer had come as soon as the two of them arrived back at Plas Cefn. Rees was aware of the lack of such facilities at Hafod.

' . . . Dinner won't be ready for . . . '

He'd then looked long at his watch, as if unsure when they'd be sitting at table.

' . . . at least another hour.'

Craig, hands black from groping in semi-darkness along the underground tunnel walls and face streaked with dirty perspiration, had gratefully accepted the offer.

'Believe me, a hot bath will be a welcome luxury,' he'd said. 'But first of all I'll have to pop up to Hafod for a change of clothing.'

Rees had smiled. 'You've had to sweat more than usual this evening, haven't you, pal? Fine, then! But take the Leech. It'll be better than the bike.'

It had been his first time at the wheel of the LLR and he'd been impressed, to say the least, with the vehicle's performance, powered by its hydrogen cell.

Now, as he skipped down the stairs of Plas Cefn, in collarless white shirt and clean light-blue cotton trousers, feeling refreshed and scented, he wondered what sort of evening awaited him. Judging from the smell of cooking coming from the kitchen, he was in for a sumptuous meal. A bottle of wine even? Rees, after all, was used to his luxuries, and his larder was undoubtedly well-stocked in readiness for the hard times ahead. But what the atmosphere at table would be like, with Ffion present, was another question entirely. Her stubborn resentment towards him would undoubtedly take the shine off his evening.

'Feeling better?' Rees had emerged scowling from the room to the left at the bottom of the stairs.

'Much.'

'Then join me for a drink.'

Although the scowl had now disappeared, the reason for it soon became evident to Craig as he followed the older man into the room and saw him point briefly towards a wallscreen TV.

'If we're not careful we'll soon have total anarchy.' While making his way towards the corner cocktail bar he used the volume control to underline what he meant.

'... the forty fifth to be murdered in Liverpool alone during these past six months. Anthony Blaydon, the city's outspoken parliamentary representative, has again voiced the concerns of his electorate, castigating the local constabulary's ineptitude and the Westminster coalition government's apparent indifference to the increasing state of lawlessness on Merseyside and in other towns and cities throughout England ...'

'You could say that we've been lucky around here to have escaped that sort of thing.' Rees now darkened the wall screen, thus silencing the newscaster, 'Although God only knows how long before it starts catching up with us as well.'

'What happened this time?'

'A man in his mid-fifties in Toxteth, shot dead while trying to safeguard his rations. Apparently, his killers – eight of them in all – could have been no older than twelve or thirteen!' The old man snapped open a can of beer and held it out for his guest.

'Thanks, Rees ... Junkies?'

'Seems so.'

Recently there had been a spate of crimes all over England and Wales, with a worrying increase in the number of drug-crazed gangs that were terrorising ordinary homes at all times of day or night. With food stores and fuel depots either empty or heavily guarded, the target of those gangs had now become the meagre food and fuel rations of the most vulnerable within their communities, supplies that were then passed on to the black market in exchange for heroin or cocaine or whatever hallucinatory substance offered escape from reality. A few weeks ago, one such gang had brazenly barged their way into an old people's country home near Southport and had stripped the place not only of food but also of all bedding and heaters, before callously breaking all the windows to leave the elderly inmates open to the elements. On leaving, the leader of the gang had been heard to shout, *'We cain't affurd to support fewkin parasites!'*

'This sort of thing is bound to reach us, sooner or later, Craig.' Rees sounded genuinely worried. His voice had a flint edge to it. 'If we're not careful, we're going to find ourselves ambushed by that kind of trash . . . ' A wave of the hand towards the dark screen indicated to whom he was referring. 'They've started already in many rural areas; gangs, local and otherwise, making lightning raids. We've had our problems here, as you know, but they're nothing compared to that.' He again indicated the screen. 'We're just lucky, so far, that things haven't got out of hand here.'

'You're probably right . . . I suppose.' He didn't know how else to respond.

'Worrying little incidents, yes, but relatively insignificant up till now. No organised crime as such. But we ought to prepare ourselves.'

'Prepare? How?'

'Pencraig will need to be protected. The few policemen that we have here won't be able to offer enough security, and if the worst comes to the worst then there's no telling where their allegiance will lie.'

Craig allowed himself time to consider what had been said. 'What do you suggest, though?'

It was obvious that Rees had already mulled long and hard over the problem.

'Security squads. We'll have to form security squads.'

Craig O'Darcy laughed nervously at the thought. Although not large, Pencraig did, after all, have a population of over nine thousand, and a small army would be required to protect the whole town.

Rees sensed his doubt.

'Listen to me, Craig. As you've just heard, things have got bad enough as it is in some places, but can you imagine what it's going to be like in three months time, if the predictions we've been hearing become fact? When that time comes, what do you think is going to happen to the policemen and the soldiers who are currently keeping things fairly under control around here? Money – their salaries, if at all paid! – will count for nothing. Loyalty will count for nothing.'

The old man's brow was creased with genuine concern.

' . . . Their priorities will become selfish ones, just like those of the rest of us.'

'And they'll have their guns!' Craig's comment, although alive with sudden perception, was also tinged with resignation.

'Exactly! Unless, of course, somebody in authority recognises the danger in time and strips them of their armoury.'

'But you don't honestly think that the police and the army will . . . '

'It's possible. Good God, of course it is! Okay! As things are at the moment, there's not too much to worry about. Every policeman and soldier receives his posting allocation, his monthly food and fuel ration from Central Depot, just like you do. But that's the only incentive left, isn't it, to keep you all at your jobs? What happens when that arrangement comes to an end in a few weeks' time? When that bloody great rock falls on us, there's no telling what things are going to be like . . . '

Sinéad had appeared in the doorway to signal that the meal was ready. Her gleaming hair was pulled tight over the ears and tied at the back of her head. She had on an olive green trouser suit partly hidden by a smock apron, purple in colour.

' . . . We'll be there in a minute, love. Just give us time to finish our beer.'

She pretended a doleful smile of resignation and returned to her kitchen.

'What if things get so bad that the monthly food supplies don't get delivered? Have you thought about that, Craig? How long do you think the constabulary and the military will stay at their posts to protect us?'

The implication didn't bear thinking about. 'We'll just have to hope for the best, Rees. What else can we do?'

'I've already taken my fears to the highest possible level. Whether they'll be listened to is another matter entirely. But we should take some precautions for ourselves.'

'Such as?'

'I've already said. Security squads! Someone who'll be prepared to patrol the streets of this town and to suppress insurrection before it can take hold.'

Craig's eyes widened with incredulity. 'Who would do that? If the police won't . . . '

'The rugby squad! The Provenders! They're fit! They're strong! They're more than capable!' Rees was now sitting on the edge of his chair, the beer in his glass barely touched. 'As you well know, lad, I've still got a sizeable store of food and fuel under lock and key. Come the time, what if I was to offer a token ration to the squad teams – to the Provenders? Do you think they'd accept?'

Although he seemed anxious for Craig's opinion, Rees had already done his thinking and was obviously confident in his own assessment of the situation. What he wanted was not so much the younger man's approval as his willingness to help set things up.

'It worked before, Rees . . . to bring in food. Worked very well, I'd say. And it'll work again. But *you're* the one to ask them. They're not likely to refuse *you*.'

'And you?'

The question surprised Craig. 'What do you mean?'

'I mean, will you help with the recruiting? In other words, will you stay?' The riveting gaze was both challenging and beseeching. Then the smile creased the older man's temples. 'Of course you will! Come on! Let's go and have supper.'

*   *   *

'I'm sorry, Mr Carvel, but I have some bad news, I'm afraid.' Owen Thomas, owner of the Haven, had been waiting for him to finish his evening meal before approaching his table. He now stood, apparently more nervous than apologetic, looking down on his solitary guest. 'Truth is, I no longer have any option but to close the hotel down.'

There followed a few seconds silence; enough time for Carvel to digest the *bad news*.

' . . . You've been expecting as much, I know. You've noticed how meagre the meals have become . . . ' The little bald hotelier almost added *'You've complained often enough,'* but thought better of it. 'You'll appreciate, I'm sure, that it's become practically impossible to run a hotel these days, what with the food and fuel rations and everything.'

For a month or more, the Rottweiller had seen this coming; there had been hints from more than one quarter of the intent to shut up shop and he'd more or less resigned himself to the fact that he'd have to find other lodgings. That didn't mean, though, he now told himself, that he had to hide his annoyance.

'No doubt you've put enough by for your own use.' The half smile half smirk was the closest that he could muster to disguise his displeasure and it pleased him to see the frown that now furrowed the little man's brow and the flush of his puffed cheeks.

'No more than you yourself, Mr Carvel. I have a family to care for.'

The comment sounded more of an accusation than anything else. Like a lot of other people, the hotelier knew about the PA – the Posting Allocation – that Simon Carvel, and others like him, received from Central Depot every month. The fact that so-called government workers

51

received such preferential consideration was a source of indignation to many. What the hotelier didn't know though, as far as his solitary remaining guest was concerned, was where all those rations then went. Of one thing he was certain though, they were being stored locally. But where?

Owen Thomas didn't like Simon Carvel. No point denying the fact. Come to that, neither did a lot of other people. The man was too sarcastic, too selfish, too full of himself. He might boast a string of local acquaintances but there were no real friends amongst them. The Haven, the proprietor now told himself, would be a healthier place with him gone. Fifteen months ago, when hotel owners had the incentive of extra food rations for providing board and lodging for key government workers, Carvel had been made more than welcome here. But those incentives had been withdrawn weeks ago, ironically around the time when Simon Carvel had expected to be leaving the area for good.

Despite Owen Thomas' blunt announcement, Carvel, for his own part, had reason to feel satisfied with the way things had gone for him. Soon after moving from Pencraig to Portharian, he'd begun stocking-up on food and fuel. At the time, he'd been fortunate to rent, from an ageing widow, a lock-up garage in the fairly well-lit back-lane, directly opposite the Haven Hotel's car park and in sight of his own bedroom window, from where he could keep an eye on the property. He'd been very careful not to mention the renting arrangements to anyone else, and he'd visit the garage only once a month to deposit his latest *box of goodies* as he liked to refer to his allocation from Central Depot. On those occasions, he took extreme care not to be seen entering the garage. He'd park his car – a Ford Ra (2 litre), with the box of rations safely locked in its boot – in the most concealed corner of the hotel car park, opposite the lock-up; then he'd wait in his room until dark and until the coast was clear before using the fire escape to slip out of the hotel unnoticed, collect the box from the car and then furtively secrete it with the rest of his food and fuel cache. Apart from the main up-and-over metal door, the garage also had a single side door that opened onto a narrow and little-used footpath that formed a capillary connection between two back lanes. The path was shadowed on one side by a six foot high garden wall and a thick overhang of un-pruned trees and bushes. On this door, Carvel had fitted his own extra Chubb locks, ensuring that the only way to gain entry, other than with keys, was to take an axe or a sledgehammer to it. He'd also taken the precaution of jamming the up-and-over from the inside. It had been to his advantage that the old woman who owned the lock-up had had no close family and that she'd conveniently passed away during that very first winter after giving him the garage key. Not only did he have the ideal hiding place, but it was also rent free!

The contents of the boxes were intact except for perishables like butter, yogurt, bacon packs, fresh fruit et cetera. He'd also helped himself to the odd bottle of whisky and wallet of cannabis because, as he kept telling himself, he deserved at least some solace for staying-on in this god-awful backwater. In addition, he prided himself on some successful under-the-counter bargaining that he'd done over the past few months with the local hyperstore manager. In return for fuel coupons, which he had no problem in claiming from Central Depot to cover ghost visits to Storage Site 5, he'd been getting stocks of tinned food and items of warm clothing.

He now allowed himself a sarcastic smile. The decision to close the hotel held no fears for him.

'So you're kicking me out?' The scorn filled the eyes and the voice.

'I've no option, sir. After all, I did warn you some weeks ago that things were getting worse. And now that the government has done away with all hotel quotas . . . '

'When?'

'Pardon?'

'When do you want me out of here?'

The little man did his best to ignore the harsh tone with its total lack of civility. 'I thought a week's notice would be fair. Next Friday? Should give you time to make other arrangements.'

For answer, the Rotweiller churlishly got to his feet, in so doing pushing at the chair with the back of his legs to send it toppling. 'Friday then!' And without a further word, he stamped out of the dining room, leaving the middle-aged hotelier to do the clearing-up.

*　*　*

It was after eight by the time they sat to eat. If Craig had anticipated an exotic dinner, then he was disappointed. But if he'd hoped for a meal that was more sumptuous than gastronomic, then he couldn't have been dismayed. The leg of Welsh lamb, dressed with fresh young mint, had been cooked to near perfection and although the portion on his plate – on all plates – was somewhat frugal, the same could not be said of the tureens of vegetables, particularly the one that contained the tasty fried mushrooms and onions. Craig doubted if he'd ever enjoyed home

53

cooking of this quality. Not that he'd tasted much home cooking anyway! His mother, he now recalled ruefully, had never been particularly fond of pots and pans and hot stoves.

Conversation during the meal was spasmodic but polite. Everyone seemed intent on making the most of the food whilst it was still hot. Sinéad was the most talkative, Ffion the least. She'd helped her mother to carry things to table and had then sat down with a brief smile to her father and a cursory nod to their guest. If her attitude towards Craig was a source of embarrassment to her father, it didn't show.

'That was an excellent meal, Mrs Morgan. It's been a long time since . . . '

'Mary mother of God! Surely, have I not told you that the name is Sinéad!' The rebuke was coupled with a faint smile. 'Anyway, it'll be Ffion who did most of the cooking.'

Her daughter, however, was already on her way to the kitchen with her hands full of dirty crockery. She neither turned nor paused in her stride to acknowledge her mother's tacit compliment. As Sinéad turned to follow her out of the room, Craig could not help but notice the difference between them – Sinéad elegant in her tailored trouser suit, erect and graceful despite three inches of stiletto heels; Ffion, shapeless in an ill-fitting pair of fawn slacks and an oversized brown top that could well have been intended for maternity wear, or even as a man's shirt. The worn trainers, the dishevelled short hair, the lack of make-up, further underlined the gulf between mother and daughter. Sinéad had charm, Ffion didn't. Sinéad took pride in the way she looked, her daughter didn't. The one had eye-catching beauty, the other a more austere, intimidating manner. And yet, the younger woman had an attractiveness and an appeal that Craig couldn't easily define. And he knew, from seeing her at the club swimming pool, that beneath her unstylish dress she had a shapely, muscular body that never failed to draw lascivious looks from all the men present, he himself included.

'Oh! I knew there was something I wanted to ask you, Rees . . . I was up on Titan's Rock . . . um! Carreg y Cawr . . . the other day . . . '

'Cawr!' Ffion's voice was raised from the kitchen. She was correcting his pronunciation. 'Cawr not Core! –aw- as in Aw! when somebody kicks you.'

Rees laughed, not seeming to realise his daughter's bad manners or his guest's discomfort. 'Once a teacher, always a teacher!'

'Cawr!' Craig involuntarily corrected himself. 'Anyway, I'd interrupted my run to go up there, just for the view . . . '

'Worth it?'

'Definitely! But I noticed a lake that I hadn't seen before . . . Out on the open moor.'

Rees' face suggested that he needed more information.

'North east. Perhaps three quarters of a mile away.'

The Welshman smiled with recognition. 'Llyn Rhos. Private fishing for Pencraig Roofing employees. I bought the rights five years ago. Had it stocked with brown trout.' He laughed. 'Too remote though. Apart from poachers, very few are prepared to make the walk.'

'Poachers?' Craig was bemused. 'How do they get the fish out? Nets?'

'Otter boards.'

'Oh!' His face suggested that he was none the wiser.

'An otter board has a length of nylon fishing line tied to it. There could be up to twenty five or thirty flies dangling from that line, so that when the otter board is fully out on the lake, and the line is extended, then the flies will bob on the surface and the fish will rise to them. It's just an illegal way of fly fishing, that's all. A traditional form of poaching in these parts.'

'So how do they get the line out? Do they need a boat?' He felt genuinely interested.

'The board is shaped in such a fashion that it will swim out as you apply tension to the line from the shore. Same sort of principle as flying a kite, I suppose. Then, when his line is fully extended, the poacher will walk along the bank and watch the fish taking the flies.'

'And that's an effective way of catching trout?'

'As effective as any. Whereas an ordinary fly fisherman would consider four or five fish a good catch, a poacher with an otter board might expect perhaps ten times that many.'

'You seem to know a lot about it, Rees.'

The older man detected the mischievous note of suspicion and laughed. 'Yes. I might tell you about it sometime.'

Sinéad and Ffion had appeared with the dessert. Again, nothing particularly exciting, just a large bowl of apple stew accompanied by an even larger bowl of steaming rice pudding. Craig felt somewhat disappointed, a fact that Ffion immediately picked up on.

'We've got a saying in Welsh, Mr O'Darcy: *Yng ngena'r sach y mae dechra cynilo.* In other words, you've got to be sparing whilst times are good; the time to start saving is when your larder is full.'

He blushed; again embarrassed by her. 'It looks lovely,' he mumbled, 'but I just can't eat any more, I'm afraid. I'm full.'

'Please yourself.' She knew it to be a lie. Knew also that she'd embarrassed him.

'And will you be attending morning mass?' Rees was addressing his wife, in an attempt to dispel the tension.

'To be sure.' Sinéad was surprised by his question. 'Do I not always go to mass, husband?'

'What about you, Craig? Do you go to church?'

'No. Never have done, I'm afraid.'

'Not even now, when things are looking so bad for us? To pray, I mean.'

'What? To ask God to deflect the asteroid?'

He hadn't meant to sound cynical and immediately regretted the words.

'Many people do, you know.' Rees smiled. 'Two years ago, the one remaining nonconformist chapel in this town was due to shut down, leaving us with just the Church of Wales and the Roman Catholic church. Not that *their* future was very bright either, judging by the dwindling number of worshippers. Anyway, news of the threat from the asteroid gave them all a new lease of life. Look at them today! Both churches and chapel are full to overflowing for every service. There's even talk of re-opening Bethel chapel at the other end of town. That's the one that was converted into a cinema about twenty five years ago. Ironic, don't you think?'

'Understandable, I suppose. If it gives people hope, if it takes their minds away from what's about to happen . . . '

Rees helped himself to rice pudding. 'But not you, Craig?'

The Welsh pronunciation of his name still fell strange on his ears. 'No, not me.'

'Why is that?'

It was Ffion's question but he directed his answer at Rees. 'To me, God is of Man's making. A figment of his imagination . . . An escape from reality, if you like, because Man just can't accept his own mortality.' He wanted to admit that he'd never been to a church service in his life and wouldn't know how to begin praying. He wanted to tell them that he'd been to St Paul's and York Minster, to Notre Dame and Sacre Coeur, to Milan's Il Duomo and the Vatican's Sistine Chapel, but only to admire the art and the architecture.

'So, come the night of August the twenty fifth, with Armageddon just a few hours away, you won't be getting on your knees?'

There was a persistence in Ffion's tone that Craig wasn't comfortable with.

'What for? I'd only feel as if I was talking to myself.' Knowing that she wouldn't let go, he decided to set his own agenda. Attack, after all, was said to be the best form of defence. 'What has religion ever done for the world, except to split it and to create strife? Look at Ireland years ago!' He realised his gaffe, but it was too late. ' . . . No disrespect intended, Mrs . . . I mean, Sinéad . . . '

She smiled. 'None taken, to be sure. But it'll be those godless Protestants who were to blame there, would you not be thinking?'

He smiled back. She was humouring him. 'Catholic and Protestant, Moslem and Jew, Moslem and Christian, Jew and Christian, Moslem and Hindu, Orthodox and Unorthodox . . . Intolerance wherever you look.'

'Politics more than religion perhaps?'

'Both, Rees! Both!'

'You're being simplistic, Mr O'Darcy.'

He felt the sting of her words.

'Am I, Miss Morgan? In what way?'

'Christianity teaches us to love and to respect one another, even our enemies. It teaches us that selfishness is a sin. Tell me, is there anything in Christian teaching that you disagree with?'

'Well, yes. For one thing, that Christ was the son of God. It's a recognised fact, today, that the concept of Christianity owes more to early Egyptian religion than to anything else, and that the so-called divine birth of Christ replicates the magical birth of Horus in Egyptian mythology.'

'Oh! You *have* been reading, Mr O'Darcy! But tell me, what is God?'

Her undisguised sarcasm was annoying and he let her believe that he'd got his information from books rather than from the TV history channels.

'I've told you . . . '

'That you're a non-believer. So you have. But what is the concept of God that you find so difficult to accept?'

A quick glance told Craig that Rees and Sinéad were enjoying the verbal exchange.

'The concept of God as a benign old man, smiling or scowling as the mood suits Him.'

'And whose concept is that? Yours? It's certainly not mine.'

'That's how He's generally depicted, isn't it?'

'Is it?' She was being sceptical. 'But even if it were, it would still be *your* concept . . . wouldn't it? *Man's* concept. Nothing more, nothing less.'

'I'm not sure that I get the drift of your argument.'

'The *drift* of my argument, as you call it, Mr O'Darcy, is this: Man creates his own concept of God and then decides that he can either (a) use

Him for his own ends – you've already mentioned the conflict between religions – or (b) turn around, as you seem to be doing, and state brazenly that your own concept of the Almighty is ridiculous and incredible. I find that naïve. Don't you?

Rees, decided to intervene, perhaps to take some of the pressure off Craig 'God, surely, is just a word for something that is impossible to define. All we know is that there is some terrific power within this universe, a power that we have to respect and to fear. The fact that we can't even begin to comprehend that power doesn't mean that it doesn't exist. Modern-day scientists find it hard to accept that there are certain things that are way beyond their understanding. Call it pride, call it arrogance, call it what you will. It's their failing, not . . . not . . . '

Craig sensed his hesitancy. 'Not God's!' he prompted, with a wide grin, feeling suddenly more relaxed.

'It doesn't matter what name we use, lad. The point is that the power is still there! Still unexplained!' The old man's eyes were bright as he warmed to the discussion. But now he turned on his daughter. 'Mind you, having said that, I have to agree with Craig as well. Yes, there are others – some would call them simpler folk, more naïve, more superstitious perhaps, and we must count ourselves . . . ' He indicated himself and his family. ' . . . amongst them – who need to have a material image or a tangible form of what they can't understand, of the power that they refer to as *God*. They need idols, icons or whatever.'

'And you honestly believe that Man can tap that power?' Craig was doing his best not to sound too sceptical.

'Yes, I do, but only on the right wavelength.'

This time the younger man couldn't restrain his cynicism. 'Like picking up the C-phone and dialling G.O.D?'

'If you like, yes!' Rees wasn't smiling. 'But you can't do that without total faith, and that's what we're lacking in this day and age. We live in a materialistic world, son. We're self-satisfied and we're selfish. We don't need help do we? Don't need God, if you like! We don't feel the need to tap into that great universal energy . . . at least, not until something happens to bring us to our knees. And whatever you may think, we're being brought to our knees at this very moment in time. That's why the churches and the chapels and the temples and the synagogues all over the world are full to overflowing.' He pointed towards a small screen on the dining room wall. 'You've seen what's happening in other parts of the world. Even the Yanks are feeling vulnerable . . . '

'But the idea of life everlasting! To me, that's . . . that's . . . ' He wanted to say *ridiculous* but settled for ' . . . illogical.'

'Why?' Ffion again. 'Because it's inconceivable?'

'Incomprehensible. Yes. Who'd want to live forever, anyway? Not me.'

'How do you know? How can you say that without knowing what quality of afterlife is on offer to you?'

'Oh, come on, Miss Morgan! *Everlasting*! Can *you* comprehend that?'

'No more than I can comprehend Time itself or the length and breadth of the Universe. Tell me, Mr O'Darcy, how many bed bugs do you have?'

'Pardon?' He was clearly taken aback and he showed it by laughing humourlessly.

'Daughter!'

But Rees raised a hand to silence his wife's interruption. The verbal encounter, as well as the show of formality between the two, amused him.

'From all accounts, you probably have thousands of bugs in your bed. But don't worry! It's not just you. We all have them. Can't be seen, of course, because they're microscopic . . . '

Craig, not knowing where she was leading him, made a show of looking perplexed.

' . . . In the course of its lifetime, each of those tiny creatures will probably see not much more than a square inch of your mattress.' She paused for effect before adding, 'On the other hand, of course, their lives only last a few hours.'

He smiled patronisingly, as much as to suggest that she was struggling to get her argument across but at the same time knowing that she wasn't.

'Through the eyes of each of those little creatures, Mr O'Darcy, how big do you reckon your bed appears to be?'

His smile broadened. 'I've no idea, Miss Morgan. *You* tell *me*.'

'Your small bed is their world. It's immense. Agree?'

'Granted. So?'

'So, how far do you think my mother and father's bed is for them? For *your* bugs, I mean. And my bed, down in town? How far do you reckon that is?'

'They'd know nothing about them, obviously. I'm afraid that I don't see your point.' He did, though, and it gave him the uncomfortable feeling that she was on her way to settling the argument.

'I think you do, Mr O'Darcy. I think you do. As far as your little bugs are concerned, my bed and every other bed in Pencraig, would have to be seen as the outer reaches of their universe. Would you agree?'

'If you say so.' Yes, he could see what was coming.

'Do you think that your little microscopic creatures could comprehend that there are other beds, other galaxies if you like, as far away as Cardiff or London? Not to mention California, Hong Kong, Australia . . . '

'Fair enough. I get the point.'

'But do you, though?'

Her persistence was irksome.

' . . . Your bugs can't even comprehend the vastness of this *Earth*, leave alone that of the Universe.'

'I wish you wouldn't refer to them as *my* bugs.'

Only Sinéad smiled. Rees was absorbed in his daughter's reasoning.

Ffion ignored the interruption. 'Any more than they can comprehend Time. They only live a few hours, but some creatures have shorter lifespans than *your* bugs even! Some midges, for instance, count their lives in minutes. Now then, if they had the brain power . . . which they don't of course . . . do you think they could comprehend the lifespan of a cat, say? For somebody who only lives for a few minutes, a life of ten years must be inconceivable. Don't you think so? And if you could tell them that there are humans who live to be a hundred, or giant tortoises who get to be three hundred years old, then they'd probably think of that as life everlasting and they'd tell you that the concept was ridiculous.'

What could he say? She was effectively throwing his own words back at him. He bowed his head to acknowledge defeat. '*Touché!* What you're saying is that I have the brain power of bed bugs.'

Rees smiled, Sinéad laughed.

'Not you personally, Mr O'Darcy, but mankind in general. We have no real concept of time and space, have we? But we're unwilling to accept the fact.'

'In the name of Mary mother of God, can we not now talk about something else? Something that a simple little Irish colleen can understand?'

This time, Rees accepted his wife's intervention and with natural ease he changed the course of the conversation. 'And how many miles did you run the other day if you got as far as Carreg y Cawr?'

'About fourteen I suppose.' He sighed, feeling the relief of someone who had just escaped from prison.

'You should take Ffion with you next time. She could do with the extra exercise.'

Whether Rees meant it as a joke or not, Craig couldn't tell. Ffion didn't need the exercise, they all knew that. She was herself a fitness fanatic, only that she confined her efforts mostly to circuit training at the club gym where she consistently proved herself equal to some of the men. She also did some light jogging and was a strong swimmer in the pool. Craig had seen her in bathing costume, and he recalled again how the sight of her firm, shapely body always aroused him. He saw her now give her father a withering look but Rees merely smiled back at her like a mischievous schoolboy.

After that, silence reigned until they'd all finished their meal.

'When can we expect Tristan to arrive?' Ffion had reached out for the empty dishes and was forming neat piles of them.

Craig caught a quick sideways glance between Sinéad and Rees but nothing was said. Who was Tristan, he wondered.

'More wine?' Rees tilted the bottle in the direction of his glass.

'No more, thanks.' When he'd first seen the red wine uncorked he'd been pleasantly surprised by his host's extravagance at a time of such need. It was common knowledge, after all, that the shelves of every single wine store in the country had been emptied months ago, with no hope whatsoever of seeing them replenished in the foreseeable future. But then he realised that wine was no longer high on anyone's list of necessities, that there were far more important priorities.

'Unless you'd be thinking of helping Ffion and myself with the dishes, then I'd be suggesting that the two of you make yourselves scarce. Would you not be better drinking brandy in the lounge? Or even risking some exercise in the night air?' She turned on her heel, not waiting for a response.

'She's got a point, Rees.'

'Then let's go for a walk.' He looked at his watch. 'Your programme won't be starting for another forty five minutes.'

The quarry lights and the distant harsh sounds of machinery, in particular the constant grinding of the crushers, spoilt an otherwise perfect late spring evening. The air was warm, the gentle breeze invigorating.

'Look at that sky!'

Craig did, and felt some of the wonderment that he'd detected in Rees' voice. The dark blue that paled dramatically towards the west had a hue and a quality that reminded him of clear Pacific or Caribbean depths waning into the shallows. More often than not, the stars seemed merely pasted onto a cold and uninteresting sky, but tonight they were glittering diamonds in a three-dimensional setting. Way to their left, the moon was nearing the full.

'Orion!' he pointed, as he searched for recognisable constellations. 'The Hunter!'

'You know your stars, then?'

He laughed lightly. 'Not really. Just a few. I wish I knew more. Those three close together are what are known as Orion's Belt.'

Rees' gaze followed the direction of his raised finger.

'Some maintain that the Giza pyramids were set out to replicate them.'

'What for?' There was a cold practicality in the old man's tone.

'I'm not too sure, actually. Just something I once heard, that's all. Some connection with the Egyptian gods. And that bright one . . . ' His raised arm moved slightly down and left. 'That's Sirius, the Dog Star.'

'Oh? And why *Dog* star?'

'Well, every hunter has a dog at his heels, so why not Orion?'

Craig smiled, but Rees remained serious.

'It's what we *can't* see up there that should be worrying us, my friend.'

A silence followed, as they strolled in their shirt sleeves in the direction of the quarry, but with no intention of getting that far. Eventually, the reason for Rees' pensiveness became apparent.

'In a way, you know, that third world famine three to four years ago and all those dreadful epidemics could have been a blessing in disguise . . . I mean, just imagine the predicament the world would be in now if all those extra millions who died then were alive today?'

'Those extra millions, as you refer to them, would at least have had three or four more years of life.'

'Ah! But what quality of life? Wouldn't they have been years of scraping and suffering?'

There was no callousness in the old man's reasoning, just a tone of practicality.

'You see, the difference between then and now is that we now have a world-wide shortage. These days, even America and Federal Europe are badly feeling the pinch. If the populations of middle-eastern and African countries hadn't been so decimated four years ago, imagine the extra strain on world food supplies now. We'd be seeing much more famine and suffering in the western world as well . . . '

Although the argument seemed somewhat perverse to him, Craig could nevertheless recognise, and to some extent sympathise with the reasoning behind it.

' . . . I mean, look at what happened two years ago, when the news about the asteroid was made public. Look how quickly the situation got out of hand then. You know yourself, son, how panicky people got, the whole world over. Within a month at the most, every hyperstore in the country had been stripped clean – if not by paying customers then by night-time looters. It was as if a plague of locusts had descended on a field of grain. And not just in Britain but in every prosperous country throughout the world. Fifteen million plus have since died in the US alone! Fifteen million! And God only knows how many in Federal Europe.'

'Yes, I realise that, Rees. I realise that people are still dying of famine by the thousands every day, even here in Britain. Survival of the fittest, I suppose.'

'Of the more fortunate you mean! Survival of the better off and the better prepared.'

Craig thought he could detect a note of moral guilt in the old man's tone and decided to spare him the agony.

'I really enjoyed that meal tonight, Rees.' Even as he uttered the words, he realised how incongruous they sounded after what had just been discussed, but he continued regardless, 'I just hope that my being there didn't spoil it for you . . . As a family, I mean.'

As Rees paused briefly in his stride to look at Craig, the moonlight froze on his silver hair and in his penetrating eyes. 'What do you mean?'.

'Well . . . um . . . it's just that . . . that your daughter didn't seem too comfortable with . . . well, with my being there.'

The old man laughed out loud. 'Nonsense!'

'She was very quiet, very distant, throughout the meal. And then . . . Well, afterwards she seemed to take pleasure in putting me down.'

'Ha! There's nothing that she likes better than a good lively argument. You've already had a taste of that! But don't take it to heart. She doesn't dislike you personally. I know that for a fact.' Then, as if he'd said more than he intended, he added, 'But the evening is far from over, my friend. You could find that, up to now, she's just been winding herself up!'

'Sounds ominous! Perhaps I'd better leave whilst the going's good.'

Rees continued to smile even though he detected some intent in Craig's tone. 'Don't worry, I'm sure you'll be more than a match for her . . . next time.' But his words lacked real conviction.

'The truth is, she's never really forgiven me for what happened in her evening class, eighteen months ago. Has she told you?'

'About your friend's attitude? Yes, she did refer to it at the time.'

'She's very . . . What's the word? . . . very intense, isn't she.' A statement more than a question.

Rees looked at him. 'Intense?'

Craig nodded. 'On most things, I feel.'

Rees' eyes were still questioning.

'On the language issue, for instance.'

'Ah! But only when she feels threatened.'

'Threatened? How?'

'I doubt whether you'd understand.'

'Try me.'

They'd reached a point of return and they now paused before slowly retracing their steps. Rees mulled a while over his answer.

'In my grandparents' day . . . my adoptive grandparents I should say . . . over half the people of Wales spoke the language. But in Pencraig, the figure was more like ninety eight per cent! Anyway, by the turn of the century, it was down to twenty per cent nationally . . . a little over sixty five here. The national statistic being quoted nowadays, however, is twelve per cent, and you've a fair idea what it's become locally!'

'There's been quite a decline then! What caused it?' He'd have preferred to question the word 'adoptive' but decided otherwise.

Rees suddenly laughed dismissively. 'No. I'll not be drawn! Not tonight of all nights! No longer of any consequence anyway, is it?'

Although the threat of Eros 2 was always there, at the back of their minds, Craig hoped that the conversation wasn't now going to return to the asteroid and Rees seemed to sense as much.

'You see, Craig, Ffion dreamt of . . . ' He hesitated, as if groping for the right words. ' . . . of returning the language to its former glory, I suppose you'd call it.' He grinned with some pride. 'She had a vision, I think, of making Pencraig a shining example to the rest of Wales. That was her dream, and the dream became a kind of crusade, I suppose!' The grin suddenly gave way to a more serious countenance. 'I don't know if you realised it or not, but those language courses of hers were voluntary and unpaid. In fact, she even paid the rent on the classroom out of her own pocket. And that went on for six years or more.'

'I hadn't realised.'

'Few people did. Anyway, what disappointed . . . what frustrated Ffion more than anything else was the Cardiff Senate's negative response when she lobbied them to adopt the scheme in other areas.' He laughed somewhat bitterly. 'They weren't just reluctant but downright opposed to it. Can you believe that? Even tried to legislate against it, here in

Pencraig!'

'But they changed their minds.' Craig could recall what the CA at Sellafield B had told Carvel and himself all those months ago.

'You could say that.' Rees' grin was now broad and mischievous. 'But only after I threatened to re-locate Pencraig Roofing in Cumbria or Scotland.'

'Would you have done that?'

'What do you think . . . ? Anyway, we've had too much serious discussion already for one night, I'd say.'

'Bed bugs and stuff, you mean?'

The old man nodded, before adding mischievously, 'Maybe you'd like to tell Ffion to her face that she's too intense?'

It was Craig's turn to laugh out loud. 'No thanks!'

They'd reached the house.

Chapter 4

'*Bon soir . . . Je m'appelle Anita Beuwerk . . .*'

She was tall, blonde and shapely, wearing a deep-orange coloured dress that revealed long slits on both tanned thighs as she paced elegantly across the studio floor towards the camera. The satiny material, cupped tightly around her firm breasts, shimmered as floor-lights from below and unseen spotlights from above and behind suddenly bathed her in bright yellow, encompassing her whole body in a spectacular halo that gave her a goddess-like presence. Her voice, husky and low, relied much on the pencil microphone that was trained on her lips.

' . . . This is *Doomsday Discussion* on Skywatch Channel, coming to you from yet another of the world's great cities . . . '

As she spoke, there appeared on screen the usual alphabetic instructions for instant translation. 'For Arabic press 1 on your handset; for Chinese press 2; Danish 3; English 4; French 5; German 6; Japanese . . . ' and so on through the whole gamut of mainstream languages to Russian, Spanish and finally Swedish.

The background music, electronically produced, had an eerie quality and as she drew nearer, the soft pulse that pervaded it grew stronger, into a more distinct throb, to suggest a threat inexorably closing in. In the meantime, the embracing yellow gradually gave way to amber that rapidly deepened through hues of vermilion, purple and finally a midnight blue filled with stardust. Her face, now filling the screen, had a cold, almost death-like beauty.

A heavy sigh from Ffion suggested that such dramatic presentation was not to her liking.

' . . . Last month we were in Adelaide, Australia; prior to that in London, Buenos Aires, Jerusalem, Peking, Cape Town, Tokyo, Reykjavik, Delhi, Cairo, . . . ' She had a relaxed, confident air about her. South African by birth but now a naturalised American, Anita Beuwerk was anything but the empty-headed bimbo that some journalists and cartoonists had attempted to portray her as, during the early days of the *Doomsday* series. Nowadays, she enjoyed international renown.

'It's twenty one thirty hours European time . . . ' Her accent reflected neither the harshness of her Afrikaner childhood nor the drawl of her adoptive state of Virginia. 'Here, in the studios of *Televisione Francais* in Paris, I am again joined by a number of leading world authorities . . . '

She paused long enough in mid-sentence to indicate, with a backward gesture of her right hand, the studio behind her. But, apart from a bank of flat screens adorning its rear wall, the studio was empty. However, with the continuing throb of the music, albeit lower now in volume, and the icy blue lighting that still bathed the scene, the bareness had an aura, a hypnotic ambience.

'. . . to discuss what is now being uncompromisingly referred to as the August Armageddon . . . '

The studio lights softened and progressively returned to normal. From studio camera distance, it was difficult to detail what each screen – eight in number – was showing. Regular viewers, however, would know that they were views of the programme's host city; in this case, the French capital – A trafficked Champs de Elysees, darkly illuminated under its ration of neon lights . . . Notre Dame, face in deep shadow, bald dome glistening under a clear night sky . . . the Seine, alternating between sluggish black and mercurial silver . . . a spiritless Arc d'Triomphe belying its name . . . Sacre Coeur a pale spectre through the gloom . . . Versailles minus its palatial glory . . . Airport Charles de Gaul dark and still. And as the radiant Anita Beuwerk stepped aside, the studio camera zoomed patiently in on a spectral Eiffel skeleton that had moonlight dancing on its exposed ribs,

'Tonight's programme will feature Professor Henri Karembeu of the Observatoire de la Côte d'Azur here in France . . . Dr Chuck Larson, Professor of Biology at Ottawa University, . . . Dr Matt Flescher, Director of the NASA-Ames Research Center in Moffett Field, California but tonight speaking to us from the Glenn Research Center in Cleveland, Ohio . . . ' With each name, a face appeared on a wall screen, Karembeu replacing a subdued Avenue des Champs Elysees, Larson instead of Notre Dame . . . Dr Flescher, the NASA-Ames Director, for the sluggish Seine.

The soft, husky voice continued its introduction. ' . . . Professor Marta Thomson of AAO, the Anglo-Australian Observatory, joins us from the Siding Spring Observatory in Australia, geophysicist Sion Tudor is in Oxford, England, oceanographer Reinhard von Papen in Reykjavik, meteorologist Alan Scheiner in Sutherland, South Africa and Jiang Ch'un, world-renowned botanist, in Beijing. And to complete tonight's panel, Alistair Dalton in Brussels. As a leading civil servant, he will respond on behalf of the combined European governments and will hopefully give viewers an update on the efforts of INDE, the International Natural Disasters Evasion Task Force.

Craig pressed forward in his seat to get a clearer view. Alistair had changed! His brother was fuller of face than he remembered him and his hair had thinned appreciably. The eyes seemed colder, more calculating, lying deeper in their sockets, whilst the bags under them were testimony to long hours of worry and sleepless nights.

Rees Morgan had noticed the movement. 'That's your brother?'

'My half-brother . . . Yes.'

The studio camera was retreating slowly to reveal the full bank of screens, each framing its own expert face. Anita Beuwerk now stood slightly to one side of them, ready to launch the discussion.

'Must be highly thought of in Brussels! Quite a responsibility on his shoulders tonight.'

Rees sounded genuinely impressed. Craig, however, chose to remain silent, concerned lest Alistair should somehow make a complete fool of himself. The feeling surprised him. *So what?* he thought hurriedly. Hadn't he disowned his half-brother years ago? And hadn't Alistair disowned him?

'We'll begin this *Domesday Discussion* in the way that we have begun all others, by asking for the very latest update on *Eros 2*, the asteroid that's threatening not only the future of our civilization but possibly, also, the future of life as we know it on earth. As viewers of this programme will know, all the world's leading observatories, by courtesy of NASA and its Hubble B space telescope, and Europe's own GAIA space telescope of course, have been able to track the progress of *Eros 2* over the past two years, ever since the threat became known, and the Observatoire de la Côte d'Azur is no exception. Let us, therefore, turn first of all to Professor Henri Karembeu for an update. *Bonsoir*, Professor, and welcome to the programme.'

'*Merci, madamoiselle Beuwerk . . . et bonsoir á tous.*' Karembeu's thick grey hair was wild and un-combed, as if he'd just appeared out of a wind tunnel, whilst his heavy, dark-rimmed glasses, lying rather lop-sided on the bridge of his nose, gave further credence to that impression.

'In the month that has passed since I last presented this programme – from Adelaide at the time – can you tell us, Professor, whether anything has changed? Are you still convinced – and by *you* I do, of course, mean the astronomical fraternity – that *Eros 2* will collide with Earth during the early hours GMT of August twenty six?'

Rees pressed button 4 for sub-titled translation.

'Nothing has changed, *madamoiselle*. I would very much like to be able to offer your viewers good cheer, but it is not possible, no? *Eros 2* is now within one hundred million miles of Earth and is mid-way through its final orbit. As predicted by NASA months ago, it will strike our planet at exactly 0212 GMT on the morning of August twenty six.'

'Let me remind our viewers worldwide . . . ' On cue, she turned towards another studio camera and Karembeu and the split screen temporarily disappeared. ' . . . that, on the programme, all references to hour of impact will be Greenwich Mean Time. You, the viewers, will know to convert that to local time, according to the time zone that you are in.' The split screen suddenly returned. 'And the point of impact, Professor? Does that remain the same?'

'*Mais oui*! We are agreed, are we not?'

The question, seemingly directed to others on the panel, was Anita Beuwerk's cue.

'Dr Flescher, in Ohio! Good evening! Or should I say good afternoon.'

'Good afternoon, Anita! You look stunning!'

The face that filled the screen – mid-thirties, rugged, handsome – oozed self-assurance. Matt Flescher, Director of the NASA-Ames Research Center, despite being the youngest to have ever filled the post, had a brashness and an arrogance that radiated over-confidence.

The presenter coloured briefly, her hint of a smile suggesting that the unveiled flattery had both surprised and pleased her.

'Thank you, doctor. And to return the compliment may I say that it's both a pleasure and an honour to have you with us on the programme. We've had spokesmen from NASA before now, but to have the Director himself is quite a catch for us . . . '

A snort from Ffion suggested that she was averse to such public fawning.

'Now then, Dr Flescher, can you first of all confirm for our viewers worldwide that the point of impact on the morning of August twenty six will definitely be somewhere on the continent of Antarctica?'

'*Somewhere*, Anita? I can do better than that.'

As he spoke, the lens of the camera filming him at the NASA-Ames Center in Cleveland panned out to reveal that he was half-standing half-sitting on the edge of his desk and that the previously out-of-focus white background was in fact a blown-up map of the continent in question. Longitudinal lines radiated from the Pole, cutting across latitudinal ones, thus giving the impression of a dart board awaiting the arrival of a projectile. With aplomb and with the aid of a long pointer, Matt Flescher now turned to indicate a specific region.

'Eros 2, Anita, will plough into this area known as Queen Maud Land, exactly on point of intercept of thirty degree longitude with seventy degree parallel. Hypervelocity prior to impact will be 18.2 kilometres per second, sixty five thousand five hundred and twenty kph, which converts to forty thousand nine hundred and fifty mph . . . '

He paused briefly for effect, as if waiting in mid sentence for an audience gasp of astonishment.

' . . . Explosive execution will equal ten thousand Mt. That's something that Earth can just about contend with, I think. We can thank our stars – No pun intended! – that Eros 2 is no bigger than it is, that it's velocity is not greater and that it's not in retrograde orbit . . . '

'Pompous ass! Who's he trying to impress?'

There was an exasperation in Ffion's tone that Craig could respond to, because Flescher's arrogant demeanour grated a raw nerve in him also. But since her question wasn't directed at anyone in particular, least of all himself, then he remained tight-lipped.

'For our viewers worldwide Dr Flescher, and for the benefit of our interpreters, can I ask you to explain in layman's terms what that means?'

'Sure thing.' The condescending look on his face suggested that this was what he'd expected anyway. 'Let me put it this way! The explosive potential of any asteroid hitting this planet will depend on three main factors – size of the beast, its velocity and speed of rotation and finally, whether orbit is retrograde or otherwise . . . '

On a cue from the programme producer, Anita Beuwerk interrupted the flow. 'Can we therefore discuss each of those factors as far as Eros 2 is concerned, doctor? Size to begin with. In previous programmes we have been told that Eros 2 is roughly a kilometre in length by a fifth wide. Is . . . '

He again anticipated her question. 'Let's be more specific, shall we? Over-all length of Eros 2 is eleven hundred and twenty seven metres, which is well over the kilometre that has previously been quoted on your programme. Width, however, varies. Shaped somewhat like an egg timer, Eros 2 is two eighty seven and a half metres at its narrowest, three nine nine at its broadest. You have its speed – eighteen point two kilometres per second – and, if viewed from the ground, it tumbles anti-clockwise at a rate of one full rotation per 221 minutes thirty two seconds.'

'Prat!'

The word was mumbled. Ffion was obviously objecting to Flescher's preoccupation with detail and his inflated self-importance. Craig winced in anticipation of what her reaction might be, later in the programme, to his brother's contribution.

'You can be that precise?'

A hint of tedium had become apparent even in Anita Beuwerk's voice but the Director of NASA-Ames Research seemed deaf to it.

70

'Sure thing, Anita! Sure thing! We have the technology! For instance, radar detection can pinpoint an asteroid's geocentric distance to within a few kilometres at any given time and can determine its exact line-of-sight velocity . . . '

'Then why don't you save the world, Mr Cleverclogs?'

Rees laughed briefly. 'Relax, Ffion! Let's hear what else the man has to say.'

'In previous programmes we've heard reference to *density* and *composition*, Dr Flescher. What can you tell us about Eros 2 in that respect? . . . But be as brief as possible, please, so that we can bring in other members of the panel.'

'No problem, Anita! For a start, Eros 2 is carbonaceous. That means that some of it will burn off as it enters Earth atmosphere. But just imagine if it had a metal consistency! Nickel-iron for instance! . . . Gee! That would be some projectile!'

'How certain are you, doctor?'

'That it's carbonaceous? One hundred per cent, Miss Beuwerk! One hundred per cent! You're aware, surely, that we've had a working module sitting on that little rock for the past eight months, feeding us with all sorts of detailed information?'

'Yes, I do realise that, doctor.' There was now a distinct edge to her voice. 'Can we move on? You mentioned angle of entry. Explain to our viewers the relevance of that, please. And also the significance of the term *retrograde*.'

Dr Matt Flescher picked up a hand set, pointed it at the wall map behind him and pressed a button. Antarctica vanished, to be replaced by a large but blank computer screen.

'Let me introduce Eros 2.'

Craig wasn't the only one in the room to catch his breath as the stellar scene materialised. He heard gasps from the other three, not least from Ffion. Against a rather blurred background, the rogue asteroid Eros 2 filled the screen. Its only visible movement was its rate of rotation and even that was but minimal.

'Count the turns and you'd come up with six and a half every twenty four hours.'

The large screen suddenly split into three, with the intimidating asteroid still commanding by far the greater part of it. The remainder, a strip down the right hand side, showed Anita Beuwerk and Dr Matt Flescher, framed one above the other, both looking in the direction of the larger screen section.

'Is that a computer simulation, doctor?'

The American chuckled smugly. 'That, dear lady, is Eros 2 at this exact moment in time – allowing, that is, for speed of light over ninety eight and a half million miles – as seen from Hubble B. You are actually looking at that son of a bitch as it now hurtles towards us.'

'Hurtling, Doctor? There doesn't seem to be any movement, apart from the rotation.'

'That baby's moving all right.' He made a show of looking at his watch. 'It's about fifteen thousand miles closer now, Anita, than it was when you introduced your programme. But because of the vast distance involved, fifteen thousand is barely perceptible. Wait until it's within a million of us, though! Jees! Then you'll get an idea of its hypervelocity.'

'I can't wait!' The hint of sarcasm suggested that she didn't appreciate his insensitivity.

'Now let's take a closer look, shall we?' Flescher must have used the control on the hand set because the camera now zoomed in to detail the surface of Eros 2. 'See the craters? That little lump of rock has been spinning its way through space for tens of millions of years, . . . and now it's finally found a place to roost.' The smile could be heard in his voice. 'Now wait! . . . Any second now! . . . There! Can you see it?' The tip of his pointer came into view to indicate a growing speck of silver that had appeared with the rotation. 'That's Marilyn, our darling little bombshell module. She's there to tell us how our friend is behaving every second of every day.'

'Good for Marilyn!' The intolerance was now unmistakable. 'But the other one is hardly a friend, Doctor! However, you were going to tell us about angle of entry?'

'Earth's gravity will curve it in to a twenty nine degree angle of descent . . . '

'Too steep to be deflected by Earth's atmosphere?'

Again the condescending smile. 'A much smaller, much slower object would either burn up on entry or explode in the atmosphere, like the Tanguska bolide of 1908. But not this baby!'

'The angle . . . Good or bad, doctor? Or should I ask *Bad or worse?*'

'*Worse* would be twenty nine degree retrograde. *Bad* is what we have. *Good* – Don't you think, Miss Beuwerk? – would be no strike at all. The shallower the angle, the more Earth atmosphere that our friend will have to pass through, causing a fraction more burn up and a minimal reduction in speed. Nothing to make any perceptible difference, though.'

'*Ten thousand Mt explosive execution* were your words, Dr Flescher.

What you are saying – Am I correct? – is that the impact will result in an explosion equivalent to ten thousand million tons of TNT?'

'One hundred p.c. correct, young lady.'

She ignored his patronizing tone. 'And *retrograde*, doctor? What could that mean?'

'Let me demonstrate.' Another touch of button and Eros 2 disappeared. In its place, a computer simulation of the universe, showing the nine planets orbiting the Sun. Flescher's face, and that of the presenter, remained, still looking in the direction of the bigger screen. 'This is us.' Pointer tip again appeared, to indicate Earth. 'Third rock from the Sun and all that!' He said the words as if weary of the cliché. 'Now here's the ecliptic.' Earth orbit appeared faintly in yellow, its restiveness indicating the direction of movement. 'We're travelling at over two and a half million kilometres per day through space – velocity varying between twenty nine point three and thirty point three kilometres per second. Bear in mind also that this little planet of ours is spinning on its axis at speeds of up to sixteen hundred kilometres per hour, depending on where on the globe you happen to be. So, if you're sitting slap bang on the equator, then that's a thousand mile an hour spin! Now here's where our baby's coming from.' Another orbit now appeared, this time shown faintly in red. 'At eighteen point two kilometres per second! And with an aphelion of one point zero two five AU that means that it crosses Earth's path twice every year, coming and going as it were. AU, Miss Beuwerk, stands for Astronomical Unit . . . ' He'd anticipated her question. ' . . . i.e. the mean distance between Sun and Earth. Our wayward little friend has been avoiding us for all those millions of years, but on twenty five August at eighteen twelve Cleveland time – zero two twelve August twenty six GMT, as your French professor just mentioned – it's decided to drop in on us.'

Despite the flippancy, there was no hint of a smile on Flescher's face, nor on Anita Beuwerk's.

'You see that the elliptic – and by that I mean the asteroid's orbit – moves in the same general direction as the ecliptic, i.e. Earth orbit, but crossing at these points here.' The restive nature of both yellow and red orbits on screen, with further help from the pointer tip, clarified the detail. 'So, when our little Eros comes in to land it will be travelling in the same general direction as we are. Whereas . . . ' Another touch of button threw the red elliptic into a mirror image of itself, reversing its flow. ' . . . if we had it coming towards us . . . Jees! The gates of hell would really be swinging open for us then.'

He allowed a second or two for the concept to become clearer.

'Equate it to being in an automobile accident. You're travelling on the freeway . . . say in a truck or a Greyhound bus . . . at, say, a mere hundred and fifty kph and a guy in a Cadillac comes up from behind at, say, two hundred and he rams your fender. You'd survive, I'd say. What do you think? Now, at those same speeds, imagine that the Cadillac comes at you from the front, head on. Truck . . . bus . . . whatever you're in . . . I'd say you're done for.'

'So Eros 2 is the Cadillac coming from behind. The one coming from the front would be the retrograde. Right?'

'You're not just a pretty face, Miss Beuwerk.'

'*Digon yw digon!**' Ffion had got to her feet. 'Where did they find this idiot, anyway? I'm going to make coffee.'

'I'll be coming to help you, daughter.' Sinéad also got up. 'This high-falutin mummery is beyond the limits of my little Irish intellect, to be sure.' She tousled Rees' hair as she passed behind his chair and he smiled lovingly over his shoulder at her.

Craig also smiled, envious of the close family unit, but he didn't for one second swallow Sinéad's diffidence. She was astute; she was intelligent.

' . . . hope to come back to you during the programme, Dr Flescher. I'd like now to ask our other guests to respond to what they've just heard, starting, if I may, in Siding Spring on the other side of the world, with Professor Marta Thomson of AAO. Good evening, professor. Early morning at your end of the world. Thank you for joining us.'

'You're welcome.' Marta Thomson was an austere-looking middle-aged lady, with greying hair, prominent eyes, rather wide nostrils and strong white teeth that parted her lips involuntarily. She had a heavy Australian accent and Craig half-expected to hear the word 'sport' added to her response.

'You've heard Dr Flescher's comments. Do you wish to pick up on certain points that he made?'

'I'm afraid that Siding Spring can't compete with NASA technology . . . '

'But it was you, not NASA, who first spotted Eros 2? I *am* right?'

'Of course. Pure luck though. You have to bear in mind that there are literally thousands of earth-crossers up there but that they're as hard to find as a croc in a goldfish bowl.' Her smile was full of teeth. 'They're not like comets. They don't draw attention to themselves . . . '

'Explain the difference to our viewers, professor.'

'Sure thing! Most comets are just huge blocks of ice with nuclei of dust

* '*Enough is enough!*'

or rocks. They're visible because they are continually outgassing. That's what gives them their comae . . . their tails. Asteroids. however, have lost all their volatile gasses. In that sense they are dormant, and that makes them bloody difficult to find, Miss Beuwertk. As your Dr Flescher just said, Eros 2 is carbonaceous, rather than metallic . . . '

'And carbonaceous is preferable.'

Marta Thomson laughed. 'I suppose it is, if you prefer being fatally clubbed with a cricket bat rather than with an iron bar. But carbonaceous is not preferable in terms of finding the damn thing. In fact, it's just about the least detectable, being less bright than the metallic ones. Unless you're lucky enough to have your scope trained on that one tiny section of sky that it crosses at that particular moment in time, then it's gone before you know it's been there. Sometimes, they're only spotted *after* they've passed us by . . . going away from us! In which case, it would be too late anyway, if you get my meaning. For example, when Eros 1 was spotted in 2001, it was already too late because it had crossed Earth orbit three weeks before it was seen! A couple of months before that . . . ' She looked down as if to check her facts. ' . . . asteroid 2000YA, as it was tagged, missed Earth by a mere four hundred and eighty thousand miles. It was fifty yards wide and travelling at twenty miles per second. And then, a few months *after* Eros 1, in January 2002, asteroid 2001YB5 whizzed us by, just three hundred and ninety thousand miles away from us. It was three hundred and thirty yards across and it wasn't spotted until a month before it crossed Earth orbit. Three close shaves in a matter of eighteen months or so. Underlines the NEO problem doesn't it, Miss Beuwerk.'

'NEO?' For a second or two, the programme presenter seemed perplexed. 'Ah! Of course! Near Earth Objects! . . . But three hundred and ninety thousand miles? You'd call that a near-miss, professor?'

'For definition, Miss Beuwerk, some of us prefer *near-hit* to *near-miss*. However, to answer your question! In intergalactic terms, three hundred and ninety thousand was *very* close, believe you me. In fact, had YB5 crossed our path four hours earlier then we'd certainly have known about it.'

'You mean, it would have collided with us.'

The astronomer in Siding Spring nodded her head solemnly.

'Okay, so what you're saying is that Earth struck lucky in years 2001 and 2002, but that that's not going to be the case in 2026. This year, our luck runs out! Is that it? . . . '

Again she paused for the nod of confirmation.

'. . . Now then, Professor Thomson, can you now give us your version of the sighting of Eros 2? I gather that you were present in the observatory at Siding Spring at the time of discovery?'

'That's right. Exiting stuff it was too. Greatest birthday present I've ever had.' Her toothy grin filled the screen.

'You mean you were celebrating your birthday on that day?' The attractive presenter could be seen smiling graciously.

'That's right. My forty eighth! God knows where the last six years have gone.' Despite her austerity, she had a friendly, disarming manner.

Craig O'Darcy caught the fraction of astute excitement in Anita Beuwerk's eye before it was just as quickly disguised with a playful look of womanly mischief. 'Now you've told the whole world your age, professor.'

'So I'm fifty four! No great shakes, young lady!'

'And you were celebrating your fiftieth when Eros 2 spoilt your party.'

'Spoilt? My God! It made my day . . . !' She paused. 'Did I say fiftieth? No, surely!' Her face reflected her uncertainty. 'I meant forty eighth, anyway. Not that it matters. I'll be lucky to see another one, don't you think?' Large eyes, large teeth again filled the Australian screen.

Anita Beuwerk in Paris, showed no amusement. Her face was grave, her look calculating, disguising an inner excitement.

'What you are saying, professor, is that you first spotted Eros 2 six years ago, in 2020. When were you able to determine that it was going to strike Earth?'

'We kept our scope on that radiant . . . '

'*Radiant* being . . . ?'

'The direction of origin. It was coming at us from Centaurus. Not from that constellation, of course,' she laughed, 'but from that part of our sky . . . '

'Yes, I get the drift.'

'And sure enough, twelve months and nineteen days later, there it is again, waving to us as it goes by.'

'Closer?'

'Indeed so. One hundred and twenty two thousand miles closer, in fact. We had recorded its presence, naturally, and had already informed NASA, so that Hubble B could also track it.'

'And the following year?'

'There, again! Closer still! When it showed up for a third consecutive year, that's when our calculations revealed the worst for us.'

'Would that be 2022? Four years ago?' She was struggling for composure.

'2022. Yes, of course.'

'What *is* she getting at, Rees?' Craig got up to accept the mug of coffee that Ffion was offering him. 'Thank you.' He smiled and she nodded slightly in acknowledgement.

'What you are saying, professor, is that the AAO – the Anglo Australian Observatory – and NASA became convinced of the danger . . . one hundred per cent so . . . in 2022?'

Suddenly, a look of consternation swept across the astronomer's face, as if she'd just realised a gaffe that she'd made, whilst at the same time a cloud of displeasure darkened Anita Beuwerk's good looks as she reluctantly listened to her producer's hurried instructions in her ear.

'Thank you, professor!' Her tone, however, implied that she was more peeved than grateful, just as an interrogator might be at being interrupted when on the point of extracting a confession. 'We'll now join geophysicist Sion Tudor in Oxford. Good evening, Professor Tudor. Now then, you've heard what's already been discussed . . . '

Craig could still detect a petulance in her voice, and it intrigued him.

' . . . As a geophysicist, can you give us the likely scenario for the morning of August twenty six?'

'I can indeed. If the facts that have been provided by NASA are one hundred per cent correct, and we must assume that they are, then the planet is in for a torrid time indeed. Dr Flescher has already given us an indication of the magnitude of impact. Ten thousand megaton, I believe he said?'

'That's right, professor. What, in your considered opinion, will be the extent of the damage?'

'Difficult to judge exactly. What I will say with any certainty, though, is this – An explosion of that magnitude will not only change the shape of this planet but also cause either a slight shift of Earth's axis or, alternatively, an unwelcome adjustment of plate tectonics. Such a major change occurred during the K/T incident . . . '

'We have heard K/T mentioned in previous programmes, Professor Tudor, but can you briefly remind our viewers?'

'Certainly. The K/T impact occurred some sixty five million years ago – give or take a million . . . !' His smile was brief and sardonic. 'Hence K for Kreide, which is German for Cretaceous, and T for Tertiary, to refer to what has come to be known as the Cretaceous –Tertiary period. A large lump of rock – quite a bit bigger than the one we're expecting – plummeted into the Youcatan region of Central America. The town of Chicxulub now marks the spot, we're told.'

'And that's the impact that's thought to have wiped out the dinosaurs, I believe.'

'So they say.'

'How could that be, professor? Can you explain how an impact in one part of the world could create such extensive global devastation?'

Creases appeared along the wide Celtic forehead, pushing the heavy eyebrows down to hood the deep sockets beneath. 'Consider, for a start, the explosion itself. God only knows the magnitude of K/T but ours, according to NASA, will be the equivalent of ten thousand million tons of TNT. Quite a bang, I'd say. Nothing within a radius of at least a thousand miles could survive that. But that'll be just the beginning! Such an impact will send ejecta – some of it perhaps as big, if not bigger, than the damn asteroid itself – miles up into the ionosphere and that will then fall back to earth like a meteoroid shower over an ever-expanding radius, some of it hot enough to cause global firestorms that could incinerate much of the Earth's biomass. The jungles and grasslands of Africa, for instance, will become raging infernos, as will the pampas regions of South America and even the equatorial forests of the Amazon basin . . . ' His face showed little emotion. He was pragmatic if nothing else.

Rees Morgan sat motionless, the mug of coffee raised almost to his lips but held there in limbo. Craig and the others – Sinéad back in her chair, Ffion standing behind her father's – felt equally disturbed by what they were hearing.

' . . . We'll have earthquakes and volcanic activity and tsunamis on a scale never before witnessed by man, and the south polar icecap, a million years old in parts according to glaciologists, will vaporise in an instant.'

'And such a scenario is likely, do you think?

'You'd better believe it, Miss Beuwerk! You had better believe it!'

'But to what degree? Earthquakes, for instance?'

'One can only surmise. Mount Erebus, not too distant from the point of impact, is an active volcano. That indicates a plate tectonics weakness beneath Antarctica itself. Who knows what degree of activity can result? But we'll *see* some . . . guaranteed! . . . and on a grand scale, I fear, as new vents are opened up for the mantle plume . . . '

'That being?'

'That being the reservoir of molten lava that's forever seeking a way of breaking through the Earth's upper crust, the lithosphere . . . And just think of the shudder that the impact and the explosion will send up the spine of the South American continent and through into the Rockies.

What'll happen in the San Andreas Fault in California is anybody's guess. And for certain, we're going to see some alarming climatic changes.'

'Thank you, professor. That's my cue for moving on to my next guest, world renowned German oceanographer, now based in Reykjavik . . . Professor Reinhard von Papen. Good evening, professor.'

'Good evening, Miss Beuwerk.'

They both smiled within their respective frames.

* * *

Simon Carvel sat in his room in the Haven, chair pulled up to within two yards of the small screen, so that he could see as much detail of Anita Beuwerk as possible. She was really something, wasn't she? He'd share his bed with her any day . . . or night preferably! The hips on her! And those provocative thighs that appeared all too briefly with each movement of a shapely leg! He shifted uneasily as he felt himself stirring.

His hands cupped a tumbler holding a generous measure of Scotch. He now brought it to his lips with a certain contentment. It had not been an unfruitful day, he reminded himself. At least he'd succeeded in finding alternate lodgings to this dump. Granted, a static van up in Pencraig of all places wasn't his idea of paradise but what the hell . . . ! Another month or so and he'd be gone, anyway. Back to civilization where he belonged! His plans were made, and they didn't include Sellafield B either. 'When tha' fuck'n rock drops out of the sky,' he told himself for the umpteenth time, 'I'll be well away from 'ere.' He'd be safely camped in his mountain retreat in the Chilterns, in Buckinghamshire and his parents would be joining him there. The house was big enough. Hadn't he had the foresight to build on to it, within the last two years, a two-bedroomed extension and a large conservatory? Just the place to ride out the storm, he now reminded himself smugly. As he sipped, he felt the whisky adding to his inner glow.

'Professor von Papen, you've heard what Professor Tudor had to say. Earthquakes, volcanic activity on a wide scale, tsunamis . . . Is that the sort of scenario that you envisage? And if so, what effect will they have on the world's oceans?'

Reinhard von Papen looked distinctly German. Middle aged, pale handsome features, fair hair meticulously combed, gold wire-rimmed glasses, piercing blue eyes and a relaxed confident air. He looked both refined and gracious.

'Given the facts supplied by NASA . . . ' His English was smooth, not in the least bit guttural. ' . . . then I must agree with Professor Tudor. Without question, we are facing destruction of global proportions, not least from our oceans.'

'Can you elaborate, professor?'

'Most surely, *fraulein*. The immediate result of Eros 2 striking our Earth will be the explosion. Doctor Flescher of NASA has explained that, and Professor Tudor of Oxford has elucidated further. What you wish to know is what effect the earthquakes and the volcanic eruptions will have on the world's oceans? Quite simply, *Fraulein* Beuwerk, the sea will create more devastation than all else put together. Bear in mind, first of all, that seventy point eight per cent of our globe is covered with water. Now consider that Antarctica contains ninety per cent of the world's ice, the equivalent of roughly seventy per cent of its fresh water! Now then, your geophysicist in Oxford referred briefly to the immediate meltdown of the polar icecap. As he so rightly said, much of the snow and ice will vaporise immediately, only to fall back very soon as rain, sleet, snow . . . In time, sea levels will rise dramatically. But that time we *will not have!*' He made a point of emphasising the last three words. 'Professor Tudor made reference to tsunamis, did he not?'

'He did indeed. We have been warned of them in previous programmes, as you know, but just in case some of our viewers had not tuned in before tonight, perhaps you would be kind enough to explain what a tsunami really is.'

Simon Carvel sighed out loud, took a gulp from the tumbler and slid lower in his uncomfortable bedroom chair. He knew what was coming. He'd heard it all before.

'Tsunami is a Japanese word meaning *harbour wave*. It is unlike any ordinary wave which just skims over the surface of the ocean, growing only when it reaches the shallows. Such a wave is wind propelled. A tsunami, on the other hand, is a deep water wave. The whole sea moves, vertically as it were, not just its surface, so that when it eventually reaches the shallows it can grow quickly to hundreds of metres high.'

'So the coasts of South America and South Africa could be in real danger?'

'My dear *fraulein*! In the aftermath of the Eros 2 impact and the resulting violent sub-oceanic activity . . . earthquakes, volcanic eruptions *et al* . . . such tsunamis will pound every ocean boundary around the world, for weeks, possibly months, perhaps years. It is new to us only because of its scale. Some of your older viewers in Hawaii might remember, and not without some trepidation I am sure, what happened in the year 1960.'

He paused briefly, enough for Anita Beuwerk to feel the need to intervene. 'Remind us, professor.'

'A violent earthquake in Chile in 1960 created a tsunami that wreaked havoc in *Hawaii, sixteen thousand* kilometres away!' The place and the distance, he stressed. 'Many lost their lives.'

Judging by her slightly surprised look, the Hawaiian event had been unknown to her until now. 'Sixteen thousand kilometres? Could the people of Hawaii not have escaped to the mainland? Surely they had enough warning?'

'Not so, *fraulein*. For one thing, a tsunami is barely perceptible in deep water. It may be only four or five metres high, but when it reaches a continental shelf, when it hits the shallows and its movement is restrained, then it can suddenly build up to a terrifying thirty or forty metres or more, depending of course on the degree of violence of the original cause. Couple that with the fact that it can travel at the speed of a jet aeroplane and you will have some indication of the sort of threat that a tsunami can pose.'

'So what grade tsunamis are we talking about here, professor, if an ordinary earthquake could cause such a disaster back in 1960?'

'Much worse to be sure. It is possible that some coastlines could be hit by waves over a mile high . . . Three miles even!'

'Good grief!' Anita Beuwerk was genuinely shaken. A prediction of that magnitude hadn't been made on any of her previous programmes.

Simon Carvel laughed drily and refilled his glass. 'German git! Whoever 'eard of a mile-'igh fuck'n wave?'

He'd heard enough, flicked through the channels until he found *Channel Sexwatch.*

* * *

'That's really frightening!'

'Possible though. But only in the southern hemisphere I should think. If they get this far north . . . ' Craig paused briefly. ' . . . well, they'll have lost their sting won't they? The tsunamis, I mean.'

Ffion looked unconvinced and he didn't pursue the logic.

Von Papen continued, as if challenging the very point that Craig had made. 'Consider this! In the aftermath of the explosion, the Southern Ocean will become a boiling cauldron and, in no time at all, the shores of

Argentina, South Africa, Australia and New Zealand will be awash, not just pounded but engulfed by scalding waves hundreds, perhaps thousands, of metres high. The tsunamis will naturally go through a process of cooling as they push north, but they'll still be warm enough to cause considerable climatic change even in the northern hemisphere. And even when they reach the north polar icecap which is just a mass of floating pack ice . . . '

'I think I have the gist of what you are saying, professor. With it being spring already, the pack ice is even now breaking up . . . is it not? . . . as the Gulf Stream gets warmer . . . But with the much warmer tsunamis . . . '

'Exactly, *fraulein* Beuwerk! Exactly! Furthermore, you must take into account that there is no land at the North Pole. The ice there is sitting in water . . . water that will become considerably warmer after the impact.'

'Yes, I do get your drift, professor. The North Pole will quickly melt and we can expect sea levels to rise rapidly and dramatically.'

'I fear so, young lady. I fear so. But not so much, of course, from the Arctic icecap itself because that is merely displacing its own mass of water, so the meltdown there shouldn't make all that difference to sea levels. But the grounded ice sheets of Greenland and the Antarctic are a different story. When they melt . . . ! And if conditions cause the glaciers of the Alps and the Andes and the Himalayas also to melt, well . . . '

The presenter waited for him to finish his sentence, but then realised that Von Papen expected the viewers to use their imagination.

'What sort of sea changes can we expect though, professor? Will we see the oceans rise by centimetres . . . metres? . . . What?'

'Satellite altimeters tell us, Miss Beuwerk, that the average thickness of the Antarctic icecap is about one and a half kilometres. That's almost a mile thick! In total, we are talking here in terms of something like thirty million cubic kilometres of ice! Or, if you prefer, seven million cubic miles of it! If all that melts, well . . . Does that explain why Professor Tudor referred to the changing shape of our planet?'

'And to what extent would that be, professor? What levels are we talking about here?'

Reinhard von Papen pulled a face, as if to imply *Anybody's guess!* Then, following four or five seconds' deliberation, he ventured, 'I estimate that sea levels will eventually settle at anything between seventy and eighty metres above what we now have. I should stress, however, that not all oceanographers agree with me. Some confirm whilst others are quite sceptical of my calculations. But whatever the end result, we can be certain that low coastland areas all around the world will disappear; all estuaries and mature valleys will be swamped. Think, for example, of those giant tsunamis attacking the shores of Brazil or western Africa . . . Just imagine what will become of the Amazon basin . . . the Congo . . . ! They will largely disappear under water. Countries will literally shrink overnight. In the United States, for instance, Louisiana . . . Mississippi . . . huge areas of Texas and Alabama . . . will disappear as the floodplain of the Mississippi river becomes permanently flooded. Add to those the Everglades of Florida and the eastern seaboard of Georgia, North and South Carolina, Virginia, Maryland, Delaware, New Jersey . . . '

A voice of protest was heard coming from the direction of one of the other screens and Anita Beuwerk raised a hand as if to quell the remonstrance. 'One minute, please!'

Reinhard von Papen continued. 'I do not wish to cause panic, but the sad plight of Venice during the last decade will be as nothing compared to what will now happen. Great cities like Houston, New Orleans, Memphis, even St Louis could well vanish forever, not to mention Washington, Baltimore, New York . . . '

The same protesting voice was again heard.

'Please, Mr Dalton! Let Professor von Papen finish. You will have your opportunity shortly.'

Rees Morgan chuckled, but without much humour. 'Your brother's getting a bit hot under the collar, Craig!'

'Hm! . . . Half brother!'

'Please continue, professor.'

'The United States is a great country, *fraulein* . . . very large . . . which is why I use it as an example, you understand . . . '

He allowed time for Anita Beuwerk to respond. She did so by nodding sagely.

' . . . Now if the Mississippi basin is flooded from the south, and similar flooding occurs from the north, up the St Lawrence and into the Great Lakes, causing them to overflow their banks, then Detroit and Chicago will also be affected, and the Appalachian Mountains will virtually become an island, cut off from the western states. In other words, the United States could lose in all over a tenth of its land area.'

'The Great Lakes? Surely not, professor? Even if the giant tsunamis get past all the locks on the St Lawrence, what about the Niagara Falls?'

'You think I exaggerate, *fraulein*! But I think not. I am merely considering the possibilities. A large tsunami hitting the Gulf of St Lawrence will, despite the deflection, create a bore of startling proportions that will travel upriver at an alarming rate, literally pushing the waters of the great river before it, just like a huge retreating dam. What I am predicting is that for a short time, the waters of the St Lawrence will actually be moving backwards! But only until the bore loses its initial power, of course. Then the flow will return. But the process will be repeated time and time again as the tsunamis continue, following shocks and aftershocks from the sort of violent disruptions that Professor Tudor referred to! By then the damage will have been done of course. Quebec and Montreal will have been swept away by the very first tsunami, along with all those other towns and cities on the St Lawrence and along the banks of Ontario. Judging by what we've heard from NASA, I would say that such a scenario is beyond question. The level of Lake Ontario will rise dramatically. I even believe it possible for the other Great Lakes, beyond the Niagara, to be affected as their waters are held back.'

'It is a horrifying thought, professor. And presumably we shall see similar results all over the world?'

'Unfortunately, that is so. We shall see much loss of land and life. The Indian sub-continent will be left dangling off Asia like an inverted pear on a tree, with the Punjab as its supporting stem; Malaysia will all but disappear; Australia will shrink dramatically, as will the country you are in at the moment, *fraulein*; great cities will be washed away . . . London, Lisbon, my own Hamburg; I also fear for the great historical regions of the world, in particular the plains of the Tigris and the Euphrates, the so-called Cradle of Civilisation, and of course the treasures of the Nile, not to mention Rome and Istanbul.'

'You paint a very dismal picture, Professor von Papen.'

'Doom and gloom merchant!' The words were Craig's. He'd just seen the genuine concern on Sinéad's face as she'd clutched at her daughter's hand and his instinctive reaction was to say something, anything, however puerile, to dispel those fears.

'I paint the picture that I see, Miss Beuwerk. People need to be warned, don't you think? Certain governments have with-held information; they have talked half-truths.'

'I must protest . . . ' Alistair was champing at the bit.

'You will, indeed, have your opportunity to protest, Mr Dalton. But first I wish to turn to Professor Alan Schreiner, a meteorologist based in Cape Town, who tonight joins us from the Astronomical Observatory in Sutherland. Good evening, professor.'

'Good evening, Anita.'

'Having listened to the opinions of our other guests so far, what scenario do you envisage on and after August twenty six? Are you as pessimistic about the outcome?'

'Very much so, I'm afraid. I too have heard some of NASA's predictions before today. Given that they are anywhere near the mark, then things do not look good for the planet, for sure.'

'As a meteorologist, what do you regard as the greatest threat to mankind, professor?'

Schreiner's features, granite-like beneath a shaven head, were momentarily distorted as he considered his response. 'Your last speaker . . . von Papen was the name? . . . painted a very dismal picture . . . exaggerated, some might claim . . . '

'Is that your view?' She was quick to grasp at the straw. 'That Professor von Papen's deductions are an exaggeration?'

The stern features hardened. 'You did not hear me say that, young lady! But I would question one or two things . . . '

'Such as?'

'The extent of devastation, mainly. The concept of the Appalachian Mountains becoming an island, for one thing. The waters of the St Lawrence, a mighty river, being pushed back is another.' He paused, seeming to reconsider his position. 'But who am I to question Professor von Papen's opinion? He's the oceanographer, after all! He's the expert in the field! And I presume that that's why you invited him to take part in your programme.'

'Quite so, Professor Schreiner! Quite so!' She gave the impression of having been effectively slapped on the hand for appearing to discredit her previous guest by allowing the discussion to take place at all. 'Can we therefore turn to your specialist field of meteorology and ask you whether you foresee any major weather changes in the wake of Eros 2?'

'You asked me earlier what I thought would be the greatest threat to mankind, post impact . . . ' He closed his eyes briefly, in thought. 'None of your other guests have pulled any punches and neither will I. The predictions that concern me most are those that were made by the man in Oxford . . . '

'Professor Sion Tudor?'

'That's the guy! He talked of wide-scale conflagration; he talked of earthquakes on a global scale; he predicted violent volcanic activity . . . We've heard such predictions before, and I've always tried to take them with a good pinch of salt, but your Professor Tudor was bloody convincing, was he not? And after listening to him . . . ' He paused to consider. 'Well, let's just say that I'm willing to re-think my position.'

'You mean it gets worse than you'd originally thought?'

'Indeed it does . . . if Tudor is right, if Dr Flescher is right. Let's deal with the various aspects of what they predicted. The explosion for a start! Tudor talked of huge lumps of ejecta falling back to Earth. What he forgot to mention was the hot ash and submicron dust that will shoot up into the atmosphere and remain in heliocentric orbit for months, maybe years. Neither did he mention the threat from subsequent windstorms. He talked of conflagration . . . the burning of tropical and equatorial forests and grasslands, but he didn't mention the huge pall of smoke that will consequently encircle the equatorial belt, nor the massive amount of carbon dioxide being released. He referred to volcanoes blowing their tops and to new vents in the Earth's crust spewing not just hot lava and miles-high columns of volcanic dust but all sorts of other pyrotoxin gasses and fumes that will poison our environment. An accumulation of sulphur dioxide in the atmosphere, for instance, will be absorbed by moisture in clouds, and sulphuric acid will fall as rain. Imagine the result of such precipitation on plants and crops . . . !'

A camera in the Brussels studio momentarily showed a frustrated Alistair Dalton mouthing some form of silent protest to a switched-off microphone. The producer had obviously decided to cut off all lines of interruption.

' . . . All in all, the atmosphere will suffer wide-scale chemical changes. Gradually, the stratospheric ozone will be eaten away, so that when our skies eventually clear, any survivors will be exposed to solar ultraviolet flux. Before that, though, Earth will have to endure months, probably years, of smoke, cloud and dust cover which will block the Sun's light and warmth and bring on extreme Siberian conditions. Worse still, the hydrological cycle will gradually come to a halt. Without warm sunlight there can be no evaporation, no evaporation means no rain, no rain means drought, drought means famine. But we probably won't be around long enough for that to be a problem.'

When he stopped speaking, it was sudden and unexpected, leaving Anita Beuwerk in stunned silence for a second or two. She soon regained her composure, however.

'Thank you Professor Schreiner. It seems that you offer the world very little hope.' She now turned full face towards the camera. 'We are now half way through our programme and it's time for a commercial break, followed by the news bulletin.'

'Well, well! . . . ' Rees was first to break the silence.

'Unequivocal!' Sinéad was looking to the others. 'Is that the word that

I'd be looking for?'

Craig moved his head in a thoughtful half nod of agreement. Ffion remained silent.

Rees spoke, his forehead creased by a worried frown. 'That's just about the most uncompromising bit of discussion we've heard since the *Doomsday* series began. I honestly don't know what to make of it all. Last month there was a lot of hope on offer; tonight, none.'

'There was something odd about that Australian interview, don't you think?' Craig looked at each of them in turn, anxious to dispel his own disquiet as much as theirs.

Sinéad and Ffion waited for him to continue.

'All that nonsense about that woman's birthday, for one thing. As if anything mattered anymore!' He kept looking around. 'What did you make of it, Rees?'

'She established, for one thing, that they knew for certain about the impact back in 2022, almost two years before they broke the news to the rest of the world.' By 'she' Rees meant Anita Beuwerk; by 'they' he was referring to the chosen few of world governments.

'Maybe so, but what the hell? What difference will it make now, anyway? At least it saved us from an extra two years of worrying, didn't it?'

Ffion, though, was more absorbed with her father's pensiveness than with Craig's questions. Suddenly, her eyes lit up with understanding. 'The famine! That's what caused it!'

Rees Morgan looked his daughter in the eye. Both faces wore the same shocked look. 'Exactly!'

'Christ!'

Sinéad: 'Don't you be blaspheming now, daughter!'

Suddenly, Craig's mind engaged gear as well. 'They died because the West was buying in all the food?' He was referring to the many hundreds of millions who had perished of hunger during the past four years. Parts of South America, North Africa, the Middle East, Russia, Asia, the Indian sub-continent had suffered immense losses, their populations more or less wiped out by the famine and by crippling diseases. Unexplained anthrax had broken out in Russia, typhoid and diphtheria in India, cholera in Brazil and Peru, whilst an unknown bacterium had swept through a belt of African countries with equally devastating effect, leaving doctors and scientists at their wits' end and in a mood of total resignation. In Nigeria, Cameroon, Gabon, Chad, Zaire . . . , only pockets of stubborn survivors now remained. Between them, the famine and the epidemics had almost halved the world's population in a matter of months.

The realisation, now put into words out loud, stunned the four of them.

'That's what that Beuwerk woman was after!'

'Yes.' Rees continued to sound stunned, his eyes unmoving as he acknowledged Ffion's dazed reaction. 'That's what she was after.'

'And they shut her up! Somebody in that studio told her to drop it! Somebody with a lot of political clout phoned in to ask her . . . no, to *order* her . . . to drop her line of questioning, after that Australian astronomer let slip about the date when the asteroid was first spotted.'

Craig took up the reasoning. 'And while all those millions were dying of hunger in the rest of the world, Europe and America and other developed countries were keeping quiet about the asteroid whilst secretly and systematically buying in all the available food. And that's not the only thing to make sense!' His eyes shone with a new realisation. 'The Storage Sites in Scotland and here! Work on *those* started four years ago! I remember the astonishment in Sellafield B at the time, when we heard about the massive programme. It didn't make sense to any of us. No one could explain the need for all that extra storage, nor where the waste was going to come from. Remember the force they used to quell the protests? Now it all makes sense, doesn't it? All those flasks containing plutonium rods, sitting in the sidings in Site 5, waiting to be stored!' His voice had become more agitated. 'I see it all now! They've been de-commissioning every reactor in Europe, so that the plutonium can be put into safe storage. Hm! They've been planning for a hell of a lot longer than they've let on.'

*　*　*

When Simon Carvel eventually switched back from *Sexwatch* to *Doomsday Discussion*, the programme was drawing to its close with the Beijing botanist Professor Jiang Ch'un discussing the disaster that would result from thick smoke and dust encircling the Earth. No sunlight meant no solar warmth and therefore no photosynthesis.

'Fuck'n slit-eyed git!' He felt good; better than he'd done for quite a while. The whisky had something to do with it, he thought, but he owed more to the joint of cannabis that he'd just finished. He smiled, breaking out into song again. '*O, ma love! Ma darlin', I hunger for yer touch, A long lonely time . . .* ' Top of the Hit Parade! He laughed out loud. *Hit Parade?*

Where the hell had that jargon suddenly come from? Anyway, great song! Great recording by The New Age Phantoms! Made him feel nostalgic. *'Time goes by, so sloooowly . . . '* The old songs were always the best. *'An' time can mean so much. Are you still miiiine? I need yer . . . '*

'Shut up, for God's sake!'

It was a woman's voice, an angry voice, from the corridor outside.

Stuff 'er! He'd roll himself another joint and turn the volume up on the small bloody silly telly.

Some balding civil servant was striving to get an important point across and the sexy presenter was having trouble to pin him down with questions.

' . . . it all boils down to NASA, and the viewers should realise that. We've listened to some very alarmist opinions from the rest of tonight's panel . . . ridiculous talk of mile-high waves, of boiling seawater, global conflagration, an Earth without rain, without drinking water . . . We've listened to nonsense about permanent darkness and Siberian winters the world over, hurricane force winds of unimaginable intensity, sulphuric acid falling as rain . . . And how about the one where the Gulf of Mexico becomes one with the Great Lakes? And makes an island of the Appalachian Mountains . . . !'

The tone of his voice was loaded with a sarcasm that struck a chord with the way Simon Carvel suddenly felt. 'You tell 'em, mate! You tell the bitch! And give 'er one while yer at it!'

The small screen was split down the middle, with Alistair Dalton and Anita Beuwerk, face profile, seemingly looking straight at one another.

'Really, Mr Dalton! What we have heard so far, tonight, have been the opinions of professionals, each one an expert in his or her own particular field.'

'But opinions on what, Miss Beuwerk?'

'What do you mean, Mr Dalton?' She seemed perplexed by his question. 'Opinions on the events of August twenty six, of course, and the likely aftermath.'

'Ah! Not so, young lady! That's where I beg to differ. Think back . . . !'

She continued to look half-annoyed, half-confused, waiting for him to explain.

'Every one of your experts . . . and I don't for a second doubt that they do indeed represent the very best in their respective fields, Miss Beuwerk . . . every one of them based his or her judgement on what Dr Flescher, the NASA Director, had to say . . . ' He looked down as if to consult notes that he had made. 'Professor Karembeu of the Observatoire de la Côte d'Azur used the words *As predicted by NASA* . . . ; Professor Marta Thomson in Australia, a lady whom I met when I visited Siding Springs three months ago and whose work I have nothing but the highest regard for, hinted that she'd needed to be convinced by NASA; Sion Tudor of Oxford, whom I know personally by the way, used these words . . . ' Again he lowered his eyes to quote. *'If the facts that have been provided by NASA are one hundred per cent correct* . . . ; Professor Reinhard von Papen said something similar – . . . *given the facts supplied by NASA.* Professor Schreiner was the only one of them not to refer directly to NASA, but he did admit to relying heavily on Professor Tudor's opinion, and Sion Tudor, as we've just heard, relies on NASA.'

'Your point, Mr Dalton?'

'My point, young lady, is that NASA is working to its own agenda. Dr Flescher's account, impressive to say the least and doubtless containing many facts, was nevertheless over-dramatic and scaremongering and, if I may say so, very American. For me, and for many others I'm sure, it smacked of Hollywood.'

'Damn right it did!' Simon Carvel had difficulty getting his thick tongue around the words, so he angrily decided to wet it with yet another gulp of whisky. 'Tell the fuck'r not to talk so much crap.'

'But what has NASA to gain?' Despite herself, Anita Beuwerk felt intrigued, wanting to pursue the point. *'Go for it!'* The producer in her ear was giving her the mandate she wanted.

The civil servant in Brussels needed no urging, however. 'Who knows? Perhaps it suits them to create panic . . . Maybe the CIA is involved!'

It was a clever gambit on Alistair's behalf. Only a few months previously, CEG, the Combined European Governments, had fallen out with the United States Senate at an Emergency General Meeting of the United Nations when CEG had publicly accused America of deploying its military in various parts of the world to commandeer by force all available foodstuffs, and the CIA had been seen as the mainspring behind the campaign. World opinion, what was left of it, was now very much against the States, with the CIA being perceived as a vile Gestapo-like organisation, responsible not only for the third-world famine but also for the mass genocide caused by the earlier epidemics. By openly criticising the U.S., Alistair Dalton was taking the easy route towards discrediting the claims of all the other members of tonight's *Doomsday* panel. But by claiming that they had been cleverly misled by NASA, he was at the same time safeguarding the good name of each and every one of them.

'Are you suggesting, Mr Dalton, that the United States may be working to a hidden agenda?'

'Yea! Of course they are!' Simon Carvel was shouting angrily at the screen, the whisky spilling out of the glass as he tried to hold his balance. 'Bloody Yanks!'

A third section appeared on screen showing Matt Flescher mouthing his protest, but his microphone had been conveniently switched off. The Director of NASA-Ames was obviously irate; tight at the gills and white around the nostrils.

'I'm not in a position to prove anything, Miss Beuwerk . . . ' Alistair was now the picture of modest geniality. ' . . . but they have been known to work to their own private agenda in the past, have they not? However, all I maintain is that Dr Flescher's predictions are over-exaggerated; whether deliberately or in ignorance is not for me to say. You must remember that we, too, have our team of experts from the European Space Agency to advise us, and they assure me that the impact, if it happens – and I say *if!* – will be nothing like the ten thousand megaton which Dr Flescher claims. In fact, it will be more in the region of seven point five megaton . . . '

Matt Flescher was seen open-mouthed, and shaking his head in disbelief.

Alistair continued in a subdued but reassuring voice, 'Now there's no need for me to tell your educated audience, Miss Beuwerk, that there's a very great difference between an explosion the equivalent of ten thousand million tons of TNT, as Dr Flescher claims, and one that can be no bigger than seven point five Mt.'

'But how can two predictions be at such variance?'

Craig's brother simply smiled benignly to suggest that the answer was obvious, whilst the NASA Center Director was seen fuming, either because he was being wrongly accused of incompetence or that he was being shown up as a liar and a scaremonger. Alistair Dalton was crafty enough to know which interpretation the viewers would prefer.

'You said *if*, just now, Mr Dalton. Are you suggesting that there's a possibility that Eros 2 might miss us?'

'It is possible, yes . . . '

This time, Flescher was shown raising both hands above his head in an expression of utter disbelief.

' . . . Some of NASA's revelations are, without doubt, factual . . . '

Revelations was a canny choice of word, Craig thought, implying that there was still a lot being concealed. 'For instance, we neither disagree on the velocity of Eros 2 – eighteen kilometres a second . . . ' His smile broadened mischievously. 'Sorry! Eighteen *point two* kilometres per second . . . sixty five thousand five hundred and twenty kph, which converts, of course, to forty thousand nine hundred and fifty mph . . . nor on the density and composition of the asteroid. Bear in mind that Hubble B isn't the only lookout up there.' An upward gesture with the hand indicated outer space. 'Our GAIA space telescope is just as reliable.'

The glass tumbled out of a listless hand, spilling its contents onto the bedroom carpet but Simon Carvel was too far gone to care. His chin rested heavily on his chest, keeping the mouth tightly closed and muting a drunken snore.

' . . . By the way, Miss Beuwerk, Dr Flescher forgot to point out that his baby, as he likes to refer to it, would be an also-ran in any Asteroid Derby. A real slowcoach, in fact . . . if you'll pardon the mixed metaphors!' Alistair's smile was mischievous. 'Some of the bigger boys can touch forty, fifty . . . even seventy kilometres per second. I could give you that in kph and mph of course, but I don't want to bore your viewers.'

* * *

'That brother of yours is taking the mickey! And that NASA bloke knows it!' Rees had straightened up in his chair.

Craig's only response was an unsmiling nod and a quiet sigh of relief. Alistair was indeed impressive; he, Craig, had feared otherwise. What was not clear to him, though, was why he should care whether his brother made a fool of himself or not. Hadn't they both chosen their separate ways? Hadn't they willingly cut the blood chord that was supposed to bind them together? And neither of them had ever regretted doing so; certainly not Alistair.

'I think he's very clever . . . '

Coming from Ffion, that was indeed a compliment.

' . . . and devious.'

Oh well! he thought.

' . . . nor do we disagree on the size of the asteroid – give or take a centimetre or two!' Alistair Dalton again smiled as he emphasised Flescher's regard to detail. 'Nor do we disagree with the angle of entry – twenty nine degrees – . . . but . . . ' He paused and his face took on a new seriousness. ' . . . I am told that there is a remote chance that Earth's atmosphere might still do enough to deflect it back into deep space . . .

never to bother us again. Well, not for another hundred million years at least!' Once more he permitted himself a knowing grin whilst Flescher, at the NASA Center, was now seen to laugh in scornful disbelief.

'Viewers will indeed welcome that glimmer of hope, Mr Dalton, but can you tell them to what extent INDE, the International Natural Disasters Evasion task force, has been deployed?'

'There is little more that can be done by the Force. As you know, until fairly recently we have been working in conjunction with NASA . . . '

'And what brought the partnership to an end?'

'Many reasons, Miss Beuwerk, but most of them cannot be aired in public. However, I can refer to one basic disagreement very early on. CEG – the Combined European Governments – were advised that the best course of action was to detonate a number of nuclear devices as close as possible to Eros 2 in an effort to deflect it. Blow it off course, as it were, so that it would pass us by. NASA, however, maintained that those same bombs had to be detonated at the tail of the asteroid.'

'Behind it?' She sounded genuinely surprised. 'To what effect?'

'In an attempt to increase its velocity.'

'*Increasing* its speed? I don't understand the strategy, Mr Dalton.'

'Neither did I, quite frankly, my dear. I understood the argument of course – propel the asteroid forward so that it crossed Earth's orbit early and so missed us.'

'But you didn't think that was practical?'

'No.' He was unequivocal. 'Not in the limited time available, it wasn't. And we were proved right, unfortunately. Apollo Nova 2 was launched from Cape Canaveral over two and a half years ago, carrying a specially constructed module with three nuclear bombs on board. It reached its rendezvous with Eros 2 on March the fifteenth of this year . . . the Ides of March!' he added sardonically. ' . . . and the devices were detonated.'

'And the effect?' She made no attempt to disguise her pessimism.

'Imperceptible.'

'I don't think our viewers even knew about that attempt, Mr Dalton. I certainly didn't.'

'Of course not.' A bitterness had crept into Alistair's voice. 'After all, NASA only informs us about its successes, never its failures.'

'Hm! Hopefully we'll have time to let Dr Flescher respond to that comment before the end of the programme, Mr Dalton. In the meantime, let me ask you a question that's been asked before on this programme. Would it not have been better to bombard Eros 2 with nuclear weapons, to blow it to bits as they say?'

Alistair smiled patronisingly. 'Not practicable, I'm afraid! We did give it some thought, of course, and the considered opinion of our space scientists was that a number of large detonations on or near the surface of the asteroid itself might . . . just might . . . have found a weakness that would not only break it up but even deprive it of much of its impetus.'

'So where was the impracticality?'

'Depending on their size, some of the resulting fragments might even burn up in our atmosphere or explode as bolides before they reached earth. A break up would certainly reduce the kinetic energy of the whole.'

'But?'

'The risk was too great. If I can use the analogy, it's far better to have an alp the size of Mont Blanc plummeting into the snowy wastes of Antarctica, than to risk three or four Ben Nevises or Snowdons falling God-only-knows-where around the world.'

Anita Beuwerk nodded sagely. 'Yes, I get the point, as do our viewers I'm sure. But to get back to the original bone of contention between yourselves and NASA. You say that NASA won the argument?'

Alistair Dalton shrugged. 'Couldn't have been otherwise, could it? Apollo Nova was theirs! If it's your ball then everybody has to play your game.'

'But you really think that the European option might have worked? The deflection?' She sounded cynical, her questions rhetorical. 'Same problem, after all! Same number of bombs!' Then, as an afterthought, she added, ' . . . Dr Flescher showed us, earlier, the NASA module that has already been deposited – if that's the relevant verb – on Eros 2. Could not both plans have been attempted? NASA's and yours?'

'They could have, had NASA waited. The truth is that their first launch, with module Marilyn aboard, was due to happen anyway. They'd originally planned to drop their little blonde bombshell as they like to refer to it – named, by the way, after some obscure Hollywood star of the last century – onto another asteroid called JE08 which is due to pass within three million miles of Earth in early October. News of Eros 2 brought on a hurried change of plan . . . '

On a cue from the programme's producer, Dr Matt Flescher in the NASA-Ames Center was again seen in a split screen. He was shown growing in frustration, and shaking his head vehemently to deny Alistair Dalton's account of what had taken place, but there was no operational microphone to pick up his arguments.

'And when was Marilyn launched?'

'On board Apollo Nova 1, a good six months ahead ot Nova 2.'

'Three years ago!' She stressed each word. 'And is it now too late to attempt the European option?'

Alistair nodded smugly. 'I can reveal that our *Icarus* will rendevouz with Eros 2 in thirty eight days time and that the single nuclear bomb on board will be detonated a few hundred kilometres in front of the asteroid, but not directly in its path. That way we hope to render it harmless, at least as far as our little planet is concerned.'

'By deflection?'

Alistair again nodded sagely and smiled.

'Thank you, Mr Dalton. We appreciate your contribution to the debate. You have given our viewers hope. So, on behalf of them all . . . indeed, on behalf of the whole of Mankind . . . I say *God speed, Icarus!*'

The civil servant's smile became a broad grin, suggesting that he, personally, wasn't in the least bit concerned about the future. Then he was gone, and two new faces appeared on screen.

'We had hoped to return to the NASA Center before the end of the programme but time is of the essence, I fear, and we still have two other guests to consult . . . '

A final shot of Dr Flescher showed him irately throwing his pointer like a spear across the room.

' . . . Doctors Chuck Larson and Jiang Ch'un are, respectively, the world's leading biologist and botanist . . . '

Rees Morgan turned down the sound. 'That brother of yours came over very well, Craig. But how much of it was genuine, do you think?'

*   *   *

As the bike's headlight carved its way up through the starlit quarry workings, Craig felt an inner satisfaction following Alistair's performance. Rees had been impressed, as had Sinéad, as probably had Ffion. The credits at the end of the programme had supplied website addresses and he'd made a note of Alistair's on his C-phone memory pad. Before going to bed tonight, he'd send his congratulations, and he'd leave his own name and address and number. Despite everything, it would be nice to hear from his brother again, because apart from an estranged mother seven thousand miles away, who else did he have? At this moment in time, he needed to belong to somebody.

Dog was there to welcome him as usual, excited, yapping, tail flaying, pulling dementedly at its extended chain.

He stopped the bike's purring and yanked the heavy machine onto its stand. A lamb bleated out of the distant darkness, answered repeatedly by a worried ewe, until mother and offspring were eventually reunited.

Sheep stopped bleating, Dog stopped yapping, chain stopped rattling, leaving only the muted hum of the generator to intensify the silence. Moonlight had turned the roofs of Pencraig to silver but beyond the town an eerie whiteness, slowly creeping in from the sea, had already filled the valley of Afon Arian. The mist, he knew, would climb and envelop everything before morning.

A night for poachers, he thought, with their crossbows and silent darts! A night that would keep the Army Rangers busy, protecting the depleted flocks.

As he stepped indoors and threw a switch, Hafod, with its tightly shuttered windows and cold slate floor, offered little comfort. The single light-bulb revealed a table, still displaying the remains of his last meal, set against a bare stone wall, with chair pushed away, just as he'd left it that morning. Next to the table, a double-decked cupboard with a microwave oven perched on top. In the corner, five strong cardboard boxes piled one above the other; what he'd manage to ration of his posting allowance over the past months. Side by side against another wall, a fridge and a second-hand chest freezer, the latter crammed tight with a variety of meats – pork, venison, beef, lamb, rabbit, trout and salmon, plucked pheasant and quail. He owed it all to Rees, he reminded himself. But the thought only made him melancholy as he recalled the comfort and the warm family atmosphere that he'd so recently left behind. The solitary easy chair, the small rug, the wood-burner standing cold and black in the shadow of the open fireplace, all emphasised the room's lack of cheer.

He sat at the table, consulted his C-phone for his brother's e-mail address, then dialled. What message would he leave? Whatever it would be, it would have to be punched in, word for word, since Alistair's voice recognition programme at the other end wouldn't be able to transmit the message on screen, simply because it wasn't familiar with Craig's inflection and intonation. Slowly he punched in the words 'Saw you on *Doomsday Discussion*. Much impressed. Warm congratulations. Get in touch. C-phone number . . . ' His finger hovered over the SEND button. No! Too ingratiating, he thought, especially if Alistair didn't care a damn anyway. So he deleted and tried again – 'Saw you on *Doomsday Discussion*. Congratulations. You look well, brother. Regards, Craig.' He read the words out loud, added his own C-phone number and pressed SEND.

Chapter 5

The morning was misty and wet. *Glaw mynydd* they called it here – mountain rain; a steady, seemingly unending drizzle wrapped in a greyness that enveloped everything, from distant hills to garden gates. From his front door, Craig could see no further than Dog's extended leash. On the bike, he was reduced to a respectable crawl. All sounds, even the harsher ones from the nearby quarry site, were muted and alien, belonging as if to another world. After a fortnight of clear skies and warm sun, the rain wasn't unwelcome; the mist was.

It was Saturday morning but he'd still have to go to work, if only for a couple of hours. Progress at Storage 5 had reached a critical stage. By the end of tomorrow night's shift, all the cladding panels would be in place, and Gallery 2 would at last be ready. It was imperative, therefore, that the next few hours be carefully recorded in his penultimate report before he and Simon Carvel sanctioned the transfer of the remaining flasks of uranium to their final resting place.

Looming out of the mist, the huge concrete edifice of Nuclear Site 5 looked like a towering mausoleum. NS5 had been obsolete these past ten years, its suspect reactors long cooled. But the wide road of fresh tarmac that skirted the building, running parallel to an equally-new railtrack, indicated a more recent development. Knowing that he now had a straight mile stretch from here to Gallery 2, Craig opened the Norton's throttle to feel the power of the engine beneath him and to see the mist whip by him in waves.

He sensed that something was wrong as soon as he leapt off the trolley cart. The men were idle, grouped in agitated conversation, and Craig noticed that Alun Evans, the shift charge, was in amongst them, as involved as any of the others in what was being discussed.

There were only seven of them. At one stage there would have been forty workers per shift down here in the gallery, but the work was now nearing completion and only one team was required to fix the few remaining panels.

His arrival was hardly noticed, nor did they pay any attention to his echoing footsteps as he approached. Their talk was in Welsh.

'Problems, Alun?' His question was mere curiosity and not in any way suggesting criticism of their idleness. He had no direct authority over the workforce. His role, and Simon's, had been merely consultative all along.

The shift charge extricated himself from the group, his face a picture of concern. 'Good morning, Craig.'

They walked towards one another.

'Anything wrong?'

'Not on site, no. You haven't heard the news, then?'

'News? No. I've come straight to work. I've heard nothing . . . You know where I live!' he added with a brief smile to suggest Hafod's remoteness.

The rest of the men also drew nearer, to be involved in the revelation of disturbing news.

'Two killed in Pencraig last night. One of them a policeman.'

'Good God!' He looked from one serious face to another. 'Accident?'

'Worse, I'm afraid. It seems that a gang raided a number of houses in town. After food they were . . . and cash of course. Cash for drugs.'

'Good grief! Who else, apart from the policeman, was killed?'

'An old bloke. Seventyish. He and his wife moved here when he retired about eight years ago. Came from Durham way, we think. God only knows what will become of her, now.'

'How were they killed, though?'

'Shot! The bastards had a gun! I heard the shots!' This information was volunteered by another of the group, whom Craig knew by name.

'Where did it happen, Brian? Where do you live?'

'You know the Quarryman's?'

Craig nodded. He'd been to the pub a couple of times.

'The old guy and his wife live in that end house opposite . . . At least he did until last night,' Brian added bitterly. 'The two of them used to pass our house every morning. Daily walk, sort of thing.'

'So why was he shot?'

'He probably wouldn't give them what they wanted.' It was Alun Evans again. 'Or couldn't, more likely! From what we've heard . . . ' His brief gesture towards the others suggested that he was about to impart a consensus of information. ' . . . the gang had already raided three or four houses in the street. Somebody must have called the police.'

'And they sent a car with two cops! Can you believe it?' Craig, this time, knew the face but not the name. 'Two cops to tackle a gang with guns! Bloody pathetic, I say!'

A chorus of mumbled expletives endorsed the comment.

'They shot the cop as he was getting out of the car. The other one, the driver, managed to get away. They then shot the cop again, and laughed. At least that's what I heard.'

'Did anybody recognise them? Were they local?'

'Most likely. Local accents were heard, anyway. There were five of them, according to some accounts, three according to others! Bill, here, was told that they all wore balaclavas.' Then, realising that all his information was hearsay, he added, 'Anyway, that's what we heard on our way in, this morning.'

Craig's C-phone rang and he reached for it from the leather case dangling at his waist. As he moved away from the group, he pressed the REVEAL button and Rees Morgan appeared on screen. He was sitting at his desk in his office at Pencraig Roofing and looking directly into the lens of the phone camera on the wall opposite.

'Rees.'

'Craig! You've heard?' The brow was furrowed.

'About the murders? Yes. Just now.'

'Where are you?'

'At work. I'm in Gallery 2 at the moment.'

'We have to talk. When can we meet? This afternoon? . . . No! Better still, *I'll* come over to see *you*, if that's okay? I need to check those cladding joints, don't I?'

'Two birds with one stone!'

The old man smiled ruefully. 'Something like that! I'll be with you in . . . an hour? I take it that that mate of yours is going to be there as well? The one who complained about the joints?'

'Colleague perhaps, Rees, but hardly a mate. Meet us in Gallery 1. He should be there by now.'

'Okay! See you then.'

At the touch of a button, the old man faded from the screen. Craig now dialled Carvel's number. Seven . . . eight . . . He counted the buzzes. Thirteen . . . fourteen . . . twenty . . . twenty one . . .

He should have answered by now! Why the hell wasn't he carrying his phone with him?

'Yea?' The voice was gruff and muffled, the tone angry. 'Wha' the hell do you want?'

Craig scowled. He could read the signs. Simon was still in bed, suffering a bad hangover most likely, his face probably half buried in the pillow. On a whim, he threw a handkerchief over the mouthpiece and disguised his voice as best he could. 'Carvel? Where the hell were you? Your phone's been buzzing for ages.'

'Who . . . ?'

'What's the matter with you, man? This is the CA here.'

Simon Carvel was suddenly wide awake. 'Sellafield? The CA? Yea, of course! Sorry! Took me some time to register who it was.'

'Where are you now? I mean this instant?'

'Uh! . . . 'alf way between Galleries 1 and 2.'

Craig smiled. Carvel was a compulsive liar. 'Good! Now return to Gallery 1. The suppliers of those cladding panels are sending a rep over to see you. He'll be there within the hour. You need to explain to him the problem with those joints and get him to sort it out soon, or else you're going to be stuck there for the duration. You get my drift, Carvel?'

'Of course . . . Uh! Actually, I think I've already settled the problem of the joints.'

'Let's hope so. You can explain how in your next report. Oh! and Carvel . . . '

'Yea?

'Get O'Darcy to join you there.'

Craig smiled. Simon's brain must be really woozy to have been fooled by that! He could imagine him rushing around like a headless chicken now, to get dressed and to be up here in time.

He turned. Alun Evans was within a couple of yards of him, smiling broadly. He'd obviously heard the conversation and twigged what was going on. Craig smiled back at him – a roguish smile – and winked. 'Not a word, Alun! Not a bloody word! Right?' The shift charge raised a playfully accusing finger. *'Diawl drwg wyt ti, O'Darcy!*'* he said, knowing that Craig knew enough basic Welsh to understand.

* * *

One arrived early, the other late, giving Rees and Craig the chance for the talk that the old man had wanted.

'You know what I want to discuss, Craig. Those killings last night! Remember the idea I mentioned to you yesterday?'

'The vigilantes?'

'Yes.' Rees looked as worried as Craig had ever seen him. 'After what happened last night, something will have to be done. Things can only get worse. Whoever did that, whoever killed the old man and that policeman, if they get away with it, are going to try again. No doubt about that. Somehow or other, they'll have to be sorted out before things get too bad. You agree, I take it?'

Craig nodded somewhat reluctantly. He could foresee all sorts of pitfalls in Rees' plan.

'If I get four or five of the lads together tomorrow afternoon, before

* *You're a bloody rogue, you are!*

100

training, can I rely on you for support?'

'Just four or five?'

'To start off with, yes. A few of the squad captains; only those who showed initiative and leadership qualities during the food campaign.'

'Who did you have in mind?'

Rees produced a little notebook from which he now quoted. 'Keith, for one. His squad did very well to bring in that stock of salmon. Glyn Hughes is another . . . Sparks, I think, they call him. He and his partner came up trumps with all that warm clothing from Manchester. Steve, of, course. He ran a good team . . . '

'The highland cattle.'

Rees nodded. 'And Phil.'

'He got the sheep!'

'That's four. I was thinking of adding Owain to the list. He did well with running the shop in Pencraig. Showed a lot of integrity and good sense, I thought. Do you agree?'

'Yes. And I could name a few more. Squad members rather than team leaders, I mean.'

'I *hope* you can! For this plan to work, I reckon we're going to need at least twenty that we can depend on. Five teams of four, minimum, I thought. But I'd rather get these . . . ' He pointed to his notebook. ' . . . the ones that I've just named, to suggest their own additions to the list. They'll know who they can work with. They'll know who they can depend on.'

'And they've got to be rugby squad members?'

'Preferably. Because they're already a close-knit group; they know one another; they've worked closely together before. But more importantly, they're strong and they're fit and they're disciplined.'

'I suppose so, but I have my reservations, Rees.'

As the old man's gaze hardened to a stare, Craig hastened to explain. 'Not with the personalities, I mean, but with the danger involved.'

'Ah, yes! The risks! Don't think that I haven't weighed those up. Don't think that I haven't done a lot of soul-searching before now. The killings last night . . . knowing that these thugs now have guns . . . hasn't helped, believe you me. But what option do we have? Unless we do something, and quickly, then we'll soon be over-run, just as they have been in the big towns. For all we know, it might have been a gang from Wrexham or Liverpool that was responsible for last night's attack.'

'No, I don't think so. It seems that most of those, last night, had Welsh accents. The gang was local, I think.'

'Let's hope so. We might then be able to deal more effectively with the problem.'

The C-phone rang and Craig plucked it out of the leather case on his waist. 'Yes?'

'O'Darcy? Carvel here! I've just 'ad a message from Sellafield a few minutes ago. The CA wants you in Gallery 1. Now! That Rees Morgan bloke, of Pencraig Roofin', is sendin' somebody over to discuss the claddin' joints. I'm waitin' for you.'

'Waiting? Where?'

'Wha' do you mean, *Where?*'

'Where are you waiting for me?'

'Gallery 1. Where the hell do you think I am?'

Craig adopted his most innocent tone of voice. 'That's funny, Simon! I'm in Gallery 1 now, and I can't see you anywhere.'

The silence on the line meant that Carvel was temporarily lost for words. Then, 'What the hell are you doin' in Gallery 1, anyway?'

With a wink to the Welshman, Craig continued, 'Talking to Mr Rees Morgan . . . personally! The CA phoned me almost an hour ago to meet the two of you here. He told me that you were already here, waiting for the both of us. He was obviously mistaken, though.' Then, on the spur of the moment, he decided to twist the blade a little further. 'Actually, he phoned back a few minutes ago, just to check that Mr Morgan had arrived.'

'Shit!'

The word was whispered and not meant to be overheard. Craig, however, picked up on it.

'Don't worry, my friend! I covered for you. Told him that you were still in discussion with the workforce and that you were on the brink of settling the problem of the joints.' He waited a few seconds before adding, 'Hope I did right? That was the only excuse I could think of at the time.'

A grunt for an answer was followed by an unwilling 'Yea'.

'After all, Simon, the sooner we get to settle the problem, the sooner our work gets finished and the sooner we can get out of here.'

'Hm! I'll be there now.'

When he realised that Carvel had switched his phone off, Craig's smile broadened.

'What are you up to, I wonder?' Rees was also smiling.

'Here he comes now!' Craig's ear had recognised the power of the Ford Ra two litre even before it emerged out of the mist. Rees took his cue and made a meal of looking critically at his wristwatch.

'Um! Sorry I'm late!' But there was more petulance than apology in his tone.

'Let's get on with it, Carvel. I'm a very busy man.' With a peeved look, Rees Morgan strode towards the trolley car that would take them down the long ramp into Gallery 1. Craig, smiling, kept up with him, leaving Simon to hurry after them in undistinguished fashion.

'This gallery is now fully loaded, I believe?' Rees sat next to a still-smiling Craig O'Darcy who was driving the trolley car, with Simon taking a back seat.

'Yeah! Has been for some time.'

'And you're unable to seal it off, because of a problem with the joints?'

'Well, yeaaah!' A hint of uncertainty had replaced the usual aggression in Carvel's voice. 'But I think we've overcome the problem now . . . Actually, you needn't have come. Um! . . . I'd meant to contact you later today, to tell you.'

'Not good enough Mr Carvel!' Rees had taken to the part and Craig loved him for it. 'That's my product that's lining these galleries and I take a very serious view when doubt is cast on its quality.'

They'd reached the bottom of the two hundred metre long ramp and were now facing row upon row of brand new lead-lined flasks, each containing two hundred and twenty rods of active plutonium. Every so-called *flask*, ten metres in length and heavier than two full-grown elephants, was mounted on wheels that had allowed it to be transported along the main line railway network from various parts of Britain and the Continent. They were bigger than the standard flasks that had, for years, been used to transfer plutonium rods from the various nuclear stations to be reprocessed at Sellafield. Whereas those had been designed to be used and re-used, these, however, had been specially constructed as permanent coffins for the highly radioactive rods. The effort and the cost had been enormous but it had been deemed the quickest and the most effective way of dealing with the problem.

Rees continued. 'The sooner you get this place sealed off, the better. I'm personally not happy to spend too much time down here. For all I know, there could be contamination here.'

'No need to worry on that count.' Simon laughed briefly, glad to be assertive. 'Any contamination, and these sensors . . . ' He pointed to the nearest one. ' . . . would send every light in the place flashin' and every alarm screamin'.'

The old man's 'Hm!' suggested that he needed more convincing.

'Anyway, let's get on with it. Show me where the faults are.'

'Were. As I said, we've now sorted 'em out.'

'But the problem? What was it?' Craig had the impression that Rees was going for the jugular. 'I want you to be particularly specific.'

'Weeell . . . Minor, really! But we had to be one 'undred p.c. certain, you understand?'

'Show me then.'

Simon Carvel led the way uncertainly between some of the flasks, choosing a section of wall at random. 'It's just that a few of these didn't bind tightly enough.'

Rees peered closely at the seam that he was pointing at. The tongue and groove joint between the two panels not only fitted perfectly but had been secured tight with a quick-drying sealant . 'Looks alright to me.'

'Yeah. This one is well sealed, but one or two of the others, on that far wall, wouldn't bind quite so well.' He didn't even sound convincing. 'There's no point in walkin' that far. Anyway, you needn't worry. Everythin's okay now. We sorted the problem.'

'Oh? And how did you do that?'

'Uh? . . . Oh! . . . Um! Just by realignin' them.'

Irritably, Rees turned on his heel. 'That's nonsense, my friend! Unless you can show me a specific fault then I'd say that you've brought me out here on a wild goose chase. Wouldn't you?'

Carvel mumbled indignantly under his breath.

The old man again turned, to face him. 'Just make sure that your next report approves the cladding and the joints . . . What's the phrase? . . . *one hundred p.c.* You can be sure that I'll be checking with your Chief Administrator in Sellafield, just to make sure that he, too, is *one hundred p.c.* satisfied. Good day gentlemen.'

He jumped into the trolley car's driving seat and left them there, to make their own way to the surface. Craig O'Darcy smiled secretly, not only impressed with the way that Rees had dealt with Simon but also thankful that the old man had been discerning enough not to show any great familiarity towards he himself.

Chapter 6

The following day, Sunday, seven men turned up for the meeting at the Club, prior to rugby training – the five listed in Rees' notebook plus Craig O'Darcy as *Coach*, and Rees Morgan himself. Directly after leaving Storage Site 5 the previous day, the first thing that the old man had done was to contact each of the five personally and, without disclosing the purpose of the meeting, had stressed the need for secrecy. Each one had agreed to attend and had solemnly promised to do so without telling even their very closest family.

'Thank you for coming.'

He looked at each in turn. They'd now taken their seats at the heavy oak table in the Club Committee Room on the first floor of the building, their curiosity heightened by the way they'd been spirited up here via the back stairs and by the fact that Rees Morgan had then proceeded to lock them all in, lest they be interrupted.

'I'll make this brief and to the point, but before I go any further, you've got to give me your word that you'll not mention, outside this room, anything of what we're about to discuss. . . . especially if you decide to refuse what I'm going to ask of you.'

His penetrating blue-grey eyes paused long enough on each of them to coerce a brief nod of agreement.

'Thank you! Right then! Let me first of all explain that I've called this meeting as a direct result of what happened in this town on Friday evening. Not that I hadn't thought about it before that, mind you. Long and hard, in fact. So let me get straight to the point . . . '

He now stood up and began pacing the room, leaving five pairs of enquiring eyes to follow him back and forth, whilst Craig watched the faces for their initial reaction to what was being said.

'During the next three months, expect things to get worse. That's the reality of the situation. If Friday's killings shocked you, then expect to be shocked again, soon, because this is but the start, I fear. You've been hearing for months what's been happening in the big cities, how criminals are running riot. It's the same all over the world. But now the cancer is reaching the more rural areas as well. It's on our own doorsteps, and its no exaggeration to say that nobody will be able to feel safe again in his own home. You've seen how little regard these louts have for law and order. You've seen how ineffective the police can be, simply because they lack the numbers to deal with these animals. Imagine sitting at home with the rest of your family and a gang bursts in and demands all the food and clothing that you've been so carefully stocking up over these past two years. They'll have guns, maybe, so what do you do? What *can* you do? Just one man against a gang of . . . ' Pausing briefly for effect, he left his sentence unfinished. 'What I want your opinion on is this – Do you think the rugby squad has a contribution to make towards dealing with the problem?'

Again he paused, and Craig realised that, rather than offering a plan himself, he wanted the suggestion to come from them.

'What? Just the six of us?' Steve was looking around at the others, Craig included.

'No. We'd need more. We've called you five here simply to discuss the idea.' By using the plural pronoun, Rees wanted to make it quite clear that Craig was already in the fold; already convinced and involved. 'We chose you because the two of us have such a high regard for the way that you tackled that other challenge. You all showed exceptional qualities of leadership then, and you got the job done. And because of that, because of you, there are a lot of people in this town today, and in Pencraig Roofing in particular, who literally owe you their lives. It's because of the initiative which you showed then that we've asked you here today.'

The sincerity with which he spoke made all five of them feel a warm satisfaction. Rees now looked inquiringly towards Craig, inviting a contribution from him.

'What we want from this meeting today, lads, is a consensus on what can be done in the face of the growing violence . . . if anything! . . . If you feel that we can do nothing, then so be it! At least we'll have given the problem our consideration. What Mr Morgan and I were wondering was whether we had enough squad members that we could rely on. After all, this is a little different to what you did before.' Now, Craig thought, was the time to add an incentive. 'As you know, every member of the squad, apart from Tony the Neck, is employed by Pencraig Roofing. Your boss has decided that whoever volunteers for this duty won't be expected to do any other work. Not only that, but he will also receive a box of groceries every week; not much, obviously, in these difficult times, but enough to supplement the family rations.'

'Whatever it is you expect of us, how will we explain why we're not at work?'

'You needn't worry about that, Owain. I'm sure your boss will come up with something.'

'Let's get this straight, Coach!' Glyn Hughes, otherwise known as Sparks because he was employed as electrician by Pencraig Roofing, had got to his feet. 'What you and Mr Morgan are suggesting . . . what you want from us . . . is for us to form gangs of vigilantes to patrol the streets of this town?'

'*Gangs* is not the word I'd use, Sparks. I prefer *teams*. But otherwise, I think you've got the gist of it. As Mr Morgan said earlier, the sole purpose of this meeting is to discuss the idea, that's all. If you think it's at all practical, then let's air it further. If not, then we'll drop it, but at least we'll have given it our consideration. What we want to ask of you is this – If need be, would each of you be able to raise a team of four – yourself and three others? Lads whom you could completely rely upon, bearing in mind, of course, the need for utter and complete secrecy.'

It was Rees' turn to watch the hesitant faces as they wrestled with various suspicions and uncertainties. 'Secrecy is all important,' he repeated, 'because if the Vigilantes are formed . . . '

The name had a romantic ring to it as it rolled off his tongue.

' . . . then their identities will have to be well protected, to avoid revenge attacks.'

'Does that mean wearing masks?' The question held a hint of scepticism.

'It probably does, Steve. I anticipate the teams having to wear dark clothing at night, and ski-mask-type headgear. But that'll also be open to discussion. Every member will be supplied with short-wave radios so that they can keep in constant touch with one another and call for immediate help should that be necessary.'

'Would we be armed?'

'Guns, no! . . . Truncheons? I would say yes.'

'Sounds like something straight out of Hollywood!' Keith's laugh hid a degree of apprehension.

Rees, however, remained poker-faced. 'Yes, you're probably right. But as far as I can see, there's little option.'

'This is one hell of an important decision.' Owain spoke without looking up, his forefinger tracing a line of woodgrain in the table. 'Where would we stand with the police? What if one of us was to get caught? What if one of us was to get shot?'

'There'll be risks. No one's denying that. But are they risks worth taking?' There was a sadness in the old man's voice now. 'The police will be told of your involvement, I promise you that. They'll receive an anonymous message pledging practical help from well-meaning ratepayers who prefer to remain faceless.'

'And they'll accept that?'

'In normal circumstances they wouldn't, but we're not dealing with normal circumstances anymore, are we? In view of the current escalation in crime, I should think that they'll welcome your involvement with open arms.'

'But how would it work though? What would we have to do?'

Craig looked at Phil, who was the youngest there. 'Two teams on duty every night. Working in pairs. Keeping to the shadows, listening for any noise of disturbance. If anything happens then Rule 1 will be to inform the others over the radio and then wait until all four of you meet near the scene of the crime. Then you decide how best to tackle the situation. And if the worst comes to the worst, then I presume that the other teams, those off-duty, will be willing to respond to an emergency call.'

'The baddies could be long gone by then.'

Craig disregarded the touch of flippancy. 'Maybe. Maybe not. We're not going to catch them all, that's for sure. But we want to make our presence felt.'

'And if we catch somebody, what then?'

'We make an example of him, Sparks.'

'And how would we do that?'

'Again that's something to be discussed between you.'

'I propose that whoever we catch should be stripped of their clothes, gagged, then tied to lamp posts in very public places and left there until daylight. Make a spectacle of them. Humiliate them. Then the police can deal with them.'

One or two grunts suggested sympathy with Steve's suggestion and Craig saw his chance. 'So you reckon that the plan is feasible? You think you could each raise a team? Each of you would need to find three others to join you. Remember, though, that whoever you choose will have to be completely dependable and will be expected to agree to some form of secrecy code.' He smiled. 'I know that that sounds bloody dramatic, but you'll agree that safeguarding your identities must be given A1 priority.'

A good fifteen seconds elapsed before any sign of a decision. Eventually it was Sparks who broke the silence. 'Actually, I don't see that we have any choice, do we? If any of those buggers broke into my house and threatened my wife and kids, then I'd like to think there was somebody I could turn to; who'd be willing to help me deal with the problem . . . Okay! Count me in!'

One by one the others, too, agreed, albeit rather reluctantly.

'I'm glad.' And the old man obviously was, judging by the satisfied look on his face. 'What I'd like you to do now is to discuss amongst yourselves who best to have in your teams and to pass your lists on to me. But, again for the sake of confidentiality, I urge you not to approach any of them yourselves, even if they're your best mates. Let me do that. Once we have a full list, I personally intend to assess every individual, to make sure that he's reliable and fully committed to what we're doing. I'm going to leave you to it.' At the door, he turned and afforded himself a grateful smile. 'Well done, boys! That was a brave decision.'

* * *

On his way home, Craig was surprised to see droves of people coming towards him along the high street. He reckoned that there were at least two hundred of them, filling both pavements to overflowing. And not all were glum, either! There were many who smiled and chatted as if they'd just left their worries and their cares behind them. In the distance, he could see a similarly large crowd dispersing in the opposite direction.

Suddenly, it dawned on him. He checked his watch. Quarter to seven! They were coming from evening service!

He slowed the bike down to a crawl, lest someone should inadvertently step out in front of him. Few paid him any attention.

'Hi!'

It was the wave more than the greeting that drew his attention. Lowri Daniels, flanked by two friends, had perched herself on the edge of the curb. She'd seen him coming, had recognised the Norton, and now seemed anxious for him to stop and talk. He obliged, pulling up the visor on his helmet as he did so.

They'd had a brief affair some months ago. He'd dated other girls since, but nothing serious.

'Long time no see!' Her broad smile revealed sparkling white teeth, whilst the twinkle in her eyes told him how glad she really was to see him again. Her friends, sensing as much, walked on, giggling.

'How are you Lowri?'

'Fine. It's nice to see you, Craig. Where've you been hiding?'

He smiled, debating whether he wanted to date her again. It was a fortnight or more since he'd been out with someone; since he'd last had sex.

'How about a lift home?'

He recoiled slightly. The come-on was a bit strong, he felt.

'No helmet!'

'Who cares?' She had an infectious laugh.

'Hop on then!'

The long slits of her skirt were accommodating as she threw a leg over the pillion and Craig couldn't help wondering how incongruous the sight must seem to the other worshippers as they walked by. Lowri wasn't one to care, though, as she threw her arms around his waist and held on tighter than was necessary.

'Was it worth it?' The closed visor muffled his voice but she heard him just the same.

'What do you mean?' She stretched to rest her chin on his shoulder and so get her lips as close to his helmeted ear as possible. 'Was what worth what?'

'Chapel!'

'Oh, that!' There was now a hint of embarrassment in her laugh. 'First time, actually! Gwenith and Caroline were keen to go, so I went with them. Never again, though!'

'Why's that?'

'Did nothing but bloody pray for almost an hour. Enough to give anyone a stiff neck. That wimp of a minister started things off. Said something about how important it is for everyone to have hope . . . to believe and to trust in God.' She giggled out the words. 'How important it is for us all to pray.'

'Pray for what?'

'I don't know, do I? Forgiveness, I suppose. He kept going on about God punishing us for our sins.'

'And what did you pray for? What sins did you want forgiveness for, I wonder?''

She couldn't see his smile as he egged her on.

'I prayed for that bloody great lump of rock up there to give us a miss . . . Fat chance of that though, is there? Anyway, the minister then said that whoever else wanted to pray could get up and do so. Bloody hell! About five hundred of them got up one after the other!'

He laughed at her exaggeration. 'Five hundred?'

'Well, you know what I mean! Anyway, about five or six stood up, one after the other, and they all went on and on about the same bloody thing. I tell you, I almost got up and walked out. Caroline felt the same, actually.'

Because of the helmet he wore, she had to shout to make herself understood, giving others within earshot reason to scowl at her as they walked past. There was one smiling face amongst them, though. It took a second or two for the face behind the smile – a mocking smile, he thought! – to define itself. Rees' daughter!

Ffion Morgan was dressed in a one-piece black suit, tighter fitting than her usual wear. Her hair, boyishly cut, was also better groomed than he'd seen it. In the Club gym, where he usually came across her, she'd invariably be dressed in loose-fitting tracksuits or joggers, her face and hair damp with perspiration. Even on Friday evening, for that meal at her parents' house, she hadn't made this sort of effort.

She paused long enough in her stride for him to see the disdain in her eyes as she took in the scene, and Lowri in particular. Under her gaze, he suddenly became aware of the amount of bare thigh that his pillion rider was showing and, for some reason that he couldn't explain, he felt momentarily embarrassed. He revved the Norton, threw a brief nod in her direction, and took off at a greater speed than he would have liked. His mirror told him that she didn't even bother to watch him go, but her display of contempt had etched itself on his mind.

'Where are you taking me, then?' With the wind whipping the words off her lips, she now had to shout louder than ever.

Back to Hafod! That had been his original intention. But Ffion's quiet derision had brought on a change of mind. He knew where Lowri lived and he now aimed the bike towards that part of town.

'You said you wanted a lift home.'

'It doesn't have to be straight away, though!'

'Sorry, Lowri! I've got a lot to do.'

Her disappointment could be detected in her silence; a mood that, by the time they'd reached her front door, had developed into an outright sulk.

'Thanks . . . ' But her mumbled ' . . . for nothing!' went unheard.

By the time she'd closed her front door behind her, the Norton was a good two hundred metres away.

Chapter 7

The rest of the week was uneventful. Whilst Simon Carvel supervised the final stages of sealing Gallery 1, Craig O'Darcy saw to the transfer of flasks from the railway sidings to Gallery 2. He also informed the CA at Sellafield that the work had begun and that the site was now ready to receive the rest of its quota, which was awaiting dispatch from nuclear centres all over Britain and Federal Europe. Craig knew that for the next few weeks, Storage Site 5 would once more be a hive of activity, with trains arriving daily with their long convoys of uranium-laden flasks.

The extra responsibility now on his shoulders helped to dampen the disappointment that he'd felt as the last few days had slipped by. He had expected Alistair to acknowledge his message but nothing came. 'Not surprising, I suppose,' he told himself. 'If I hadn't watched that programme, then *I* wouldn't have bothered with *him*, either. We never were close, anyway. To hell with him!' But the disappointment still lingered.

*   *   *

In the meantime, Simon Carvel moved from The Haven Hotel in Portharian to his new lodgings in Pencraig. The static van, that had been allocated to him through Central Office influence, was impressive to say the least, giving him so much more room, so much more privacy than he'd had up to now. It had four bedrooms – two double, two single – a small bathroom and a well-equipped kitchen-cum-lounge. 'When will your family be joining you?' The question had come from a prying neighbour and his lie of 'Next week, sometime' had been made to cover for the preferential treatment that he'd received. Not that his conscience bothered him that he'd been allocated accommodation adequate for a family of six. He merely regarded his good fortune as 'One of the perks of the job'.

What few possessions he owned had been brought up by car. The lock-up garage and its contents had been left untouched. He'd deliberated long and hard about that, before ultimately coming to the conclusion that his stockpile of food and drink was safer left where it was, under good lock and key, rather than in a flimsy-framed caravan that even a child could break into. There'd be no problem in popping down every few days – every day even, if necessary – just to make sure that everything was intact. It was barely ten miles away, after all! Then, in readiness for the day when he'd be leaving the area for good, he would swap his Ford Ra for a sturdy van or truck. He had everything figured out.

Simon Carvel knew that he had more reason than most to feel satisfied.

* * *

By the following Saturday, Rees Morgan had received the names of another nineteen potential vigilantes, four more than he'd expected. The initial five – the Team Leaders as they were once again referred to – had come up with the suggestion of working a substitute rota. That was fine, as far as Rees was concerned, as long as every one on the list was reliable. He then proceeded to interview each of them, individually. It proved a lengthy process, having first of all to explain the covert nature of the work without actually telling them what it was all about; then, after ensuring each one's interest and pledge of confidentiality, revealing details of the proposed plan. Only two had refused outright but even they, after they'd had time to re-consider, had had a change of mind and had decided to throw in their lot.

Rees had reason to feel content with his total success rate. The next step would be to acquire enough short wave radios and powerful halogen torches for everybody and to draw out a timetable for each group. Then they would have to discuss nightly patrol routes so as to cover as many of the town's back lanes as possible. Keeping to the shadows, remaining unseen, would be imperative, he told them, whilst at the same time being within earshot of any likely disturbance.

As usual, those who turned up for rugby practice on Sunday evening, were split into two teams – Reds and Greens – for a game of thirty minutes each half. This had become the adopted pattern, ever since league fixtures had had to be cancelled due to fuel shortage and on-going travel restrictions. The squad knew that O'Darcy, as Coach, expected all-out commitment from each and every one of them, just the same, so as to maintain the highest possible levels of fitness and ruthlessness, but this week he issued a stern warning against reckless and dangerous tackling. Most but not all of the squad understood why.

* * *

'Do you reckon that all this is necessary, then?'

The two were huddled in a shop doorway, out of the drizzle.

Phil, after glancing briefly at his partner's dripping headgear, now noticed the disenchanted look on his face and smiled ruefully. 'Time'll tell. Let's hope there's no trouble on our first bloody shift though.'

They'd both temporarily curled their ski-masks up above their ears, because of how unpleasantly warm and damp they'd become, to leave their faces open to the cold night air.

'Whose idea was it? Originally I mean. Was it the old man's?' Tony the Neck, Pencraig RC's sixteen stone hooker, was as squat and as strong as a young ox. For him, circuit training and strenuous workouts in the gym weren't a drudge, as for most of the other squad members, but pure enjoyment, and there was nothing that he liked better than three rounds of serious sparring in the ring. He'd earned his nickname! *The Neck* referred to the fact that there wasn't a shirt with a big enough collar-size to fit him. A plumber by trade, but also an all-round handyman, he'd now moved on to owning and running a thriving builders' merchant business.

'Yea, I think so. But Coach probably had something to do with it as well, I'd say.'

They'd completed one careful stage of their allocated route without seeing or hearing anything untoward. At the other end of town, Sparks and partner were also nearing the end of their first patrol. For both teams, what had started out as a bit of an adventure had now become tedious and disagreeable, due mainly to the incessant drizzle.

'What time is it, anyway?'

Phil peered at his watch but couldn't make out the position of the fingers on it. 'Don't know.' He couldn't be bothered reaching through the wet for the halogen torch in an inside coat pocket. 'Half two to three, I reckon.'

'Another two hours! Bloody 'ell!'

It had been decided that every shift should only cover the hours of darkness. They'd been patrolling since half past ten and would continue to do so until half past four, when the first light of dawn would begin to show.

The inaction didn't suit The Neck. Despite the weather, he'd much prefer being stripped to his running shorts and doing press-ups, out in the open road if need be.

During their patrol, there was little chance of them being spotted by anyone, unless by would-be criminals. The streets of Pencraig, like those of every other town and city throughout the country, became deserted once the sun went down. People feared for their lives, for their families, for their belongings.

'Bed will be nice after this.'

The Neck grunted. 'Do you think the others have seen anything?'

'Hardly. They'd have called us. It's agreed.'

Whatever the nature of any disturbance, it had been decided that both teams on duty should become involved. 'No undue risks! Is that clear?' Rees Morgan had been adamant on that point, as on most others.

'Who has Sparks got as partner tonight, then?'

'Gareth, I think.'

'What's that?'

Suddenly, both of them became aware of faint shouting in the distance.

'Where's it coming from?' Phil had already pulled his mask down again, to cover his face. 'Can you tell?'

The mist and the rain were dampening the sounds, making it difficult to decide where exactly the voices were coming from.

'Cae Top, I reckon. What do you think?'

By now the two of them were out of the doorway and running. Cae Top was one of the newer housing estates in Pencraig, situated on a gentle slope overlooking the northern end of town, about five hundred metres from where they now stood. It was an area with which they were both well acquainted.

Phil quickly gained a couple of metres on his heavier partner whose pounding feet were sending shudders from one pavement slab to another.

'Call the others, Phil!' The Neck's heavy breathing was due more to his size than to any lack of fitness. 'I think they're getting closer. They're coming this way.'

'P calling G! P calling G! Are you there? Answer!' Without breaking stride, he'd got the radio to his ear.

'What's happening?' Sparks – G for Glyn – could hear the exited breathing and the noise of running. 'Where the hell are you?'

'Commotion near Cae Top. Coming our way. We're running up College Road right now and making for Meirion Crescent.'

'Wait for us! Be with you in minutes. Wait for us!'

Phil stopped and brought The Neck also to a halt. He knew that the other team was at least half a mile away and that it could well be too late by the time they got there. The shouting was getting closer and they could now make out a man's voice, almost breathless.

'What do we do? Do we wait for the others?'

But Pencraig RC's number one hooker wasn't one to stand on ceremony or on agreed procedure. 'To hell with it! Let's get him!'

Suddenly the shouting changed, when another screaming voice was raised, intermingling with the angry shouting that they'd already become familiar with.

'Around the corner!' Phil was informing his partner of how close they now were.

He hardly glimpsed the dark shape as it brushed right past him and straight into the human wall behind, bringing out a wail of surprise and fear. When Phil turned, all he could see was a bundle of flailing arms and legs being lifted off the ground.

'S'only a boy!' The Neck sounded disappointed.

Meanwhile, the shouting around the corner continued unabated, punctuated by barely intelligible utterances like ' . . . little bastard! . . . fucking thief! . . . teach . . . bloody lesson!' and screams of pain. Someone, it seemed, was being murdered, and frightened lights were appearing one by one in many upstairs windows.

As he turned the corner, Phil could make out, in the beam of his torch, a grown man viciously kicking at a writhing form on the ground and then bending to strike out with his clenched fist. His face, pallid and wet, was contorted with rage.

'Hi! That's enough!'

Instinctively, the man straightened in a stance to guard himself against attack, his eyes narrowing as they peered suspiciously into the beam of light. He was about as tall as Phil himself, although less broad of shoulder. The bundle on the ground continued to writhe and to moan.

'What's going on?' Phil tried to put as much authority as possible into his voice.

'What's it to you?' The stranger was sensing that the challenge wasn't as threatening as he'd first feared. As far as he could tell, only one dark figure stood behind the torch and whoever was there was neither policeman nor armed militia.

Phil's beam was now directed towards the ground where a young lad of about twelve or thirteen was trying to hide his guilty face behind a raised hand that also served to stifle his sobs.

'We make it our business, mate!'

The man's belligerence, tinged with suspicion, suddenly gave way to fear as another dark shape – shorter, broader – appeared beside the first, with a flailing body tucked under one of its arms. A sudden light from an upstairs window further heightened his anxiety by revealing to him that both faces were masked. His tone became instantly apologetic.

'Look, here!' He prodded at the prostrate form with his foot. 'I caught this little bastard and his mate breaking into my house. What was I supposed to do? It's the third time in the past fortnight.'

'Not us!' The voice of protest came from the lad trapped under Tony the Neck's arm.

'Don't listen to him! I caught the little buggers red-handed.' The concern could still be heard in the man's voice. He still didn't know what he was up against.

'Just tonight, that's all! Never before! Honest!' The Neck had now propped the protesting lad up on his feet but still had him by the collar.

'What were you after?' It was Phil's question.

'Food, that's all.'

'That's *all*? . . . That's *all*?' The man's voice was again raised, his tone implying that his food supply was the most valuable commodity that he possessed.

'Alright! Go on home! We'll deal with it now.'

'*You'll* deal with it? Who the hell *are* you, anyway?' He was regaining some of his composure but then Sparks and partner came running around the corner, torch beams cutting like lasers through the shimmering drizzle. 'Who . . . ?'

'The Vigilantes, that's who! Now go back home to your family in case there are other thieves around. We'll deal with these, and with any others that we catch.'

The man, after a moment's thought, turned away, muttering under his breath.

'Now then, Vigilantes! What shall we do with these little no-gooders?' The Neck's voice was deep and threatening, and purposely dramatic. 'Do you reckon we should string 'em up? That's what we do with good-for-nothing thieves isn't it? String 'em up!' His hold on the boy tightened, bringing out a squeal of fear more than pain.

'I'm for cutting their selfish little fingers off.' Like The Neck, Sparks too had realised the need to put the fear of God into the two youngsters.

'So, you're food thieves, are you?' Phil had got hold of the one on the ground and was now dragging him, groaning, to his feet, his pimply face mirroring the pain from the beating he'd just had.

'Never . . . done it . . . before.' The words were uttered between sniffles.

'Huh! And we're supposed to believe that?'

''s the trewth, like.' This one had a faint Scouse accent; the other was unmistakably Welsh.

'Yes. We never done this sort of thing before. Honest!'

'Honest? Ah! So you're honest are you? Well tell us then, what happened to your honesty tonight?'

Both fell silent.

'Answer me! Why tonight?'

Still no reply.

Sparks stepped closer to the one that The Neck had by the scruff. 'We're wasting time. Let's deal with them here and now. Where's your blade, Joe?'

Although no one knew the Joe he was referring to, the threat proved effective.

'His dad told us to.'

'Oh? And who's his dad?' He turned on the one whom Phil was holding. 'And who is your dad then, you little terror? Where do you live?'

'Not tellin yuh!'

'Fair enough! No skin off my nose, boyo. I'll just make sure that you won't lay your dirty little fingers on anybody else's property ever again. Hold his hand out!' Sparks directed the light of his torch at the blade of the Stanley knife, now gleaming wet, in his other hand. 'I'll give you one more chance, lad. Your dad's name?'

Although badly bruised and now quaking with the additional threat, the boy was still reluctant. 'Yur goin to 'urt 'im, like?'

It was Phil who answered, and in a tone less threatening than Sparks'. 'Maybe not this time. Just a warning for him . . . for now. You have the word of the Vigilantes on that. But . . . '

The promise, and the implied threat from the unfinished sentence proved enough.

''is name's Frank Taylor, like.'

'What did you say? Speak louder, boy!'

'Frank Taylor.'

'Taylor, did you say? Frank Taylor?' Sparks was shouting, as if he wanted every bedroom window to hear. 'And what's *your* name?'

'Nick.'

'Huh!' from The Neck. 'Baptised to be a thief were you?'

'And where do you live?'

'Quarry Bank.'

'*Where* in Quarry Bank? And I want the truth . . . because we're going there, now!'

'Number seven.'

'And you?' Phil had now turned to the other. 'What's your name?

'Alwyn Edwards.'

'And where do *you* live?'

'Eleven Quarry Bank.'

'And who's *your* father?'

'He doesn't know anything about this. Honest!'

'Let us be the judge of how honest you are, laddie! His name?'

'Colin.'

'Right then! I think we'll be having friendly little words with both your dads. Let's go!'

As they set off, a woman's voice was heard to call 'Bless you!' from a nearby open window.

The two boys were frog-marched home without any effort being made to keep to the shadows or to keep voices down, the logic being that people, now in their beds, needed to know that their streets were being patrolled at night.

When they reached the Quarry Bank estate, The Neck half dragged his charge up to the front door of number eleven and Sparks held his finger on the bell. A light appeared in an upper window and an angry voice was soon heard making its way down the stairs.

'Who the hell . . . !' The door was flung open, revealing an overweight man dressed only in pyjama trousers. His hair was tousled and his eyes still full of sleep.

'Colin Edwards?' The Neck pushed the lad forward arm's length but still kept a firm grip on his collar. 'Your son?'

'Who . . . ?' Fear sprang to his eyes as his dim passage light picked out two of the sinister visitors. 'Who the hell are you?' He barely glanced at his son.

'Is this your lad?' Sparks stressed each word and the boy started sobbing again.

'Yea. What's he done? Who are . . . ?' He paused because he'd now seen movement from other black shapes beyond the arc of his passage light.

'A warning, Mr Edwards! Your son's a thief. Next time, he won't get off lightly. Nor will you. So watch your step.'

With that, The Neck hurled the lad forward, straight into his father's paunch, a collision that caused them both to yelp and splutter.

119

'Deal with him, or expect another call from us!' And with Sparks' stern warning, the four of them turned and led their second captive towards the fourth house down.

The performance was repeated at No. 4 Quarry Bank, but Frank Taylor, lean and ferret-like and not yet forty, dressed in filthy T-shirt and boxer shorts, proved to be a more stubborn customer, because once he'd got over his initial shock at seeing the masked strangers and once he'd realised that they were nothing more than self-styled law-enforcers, he then became abusive and intimidating, threatening to call the police. In reply, Tony the Neck merely laughed and, stepping over the threshold, grabbed him by his over-long hair and yanked him out into the night air, evoking a shout of protest tinged with pain and fear. A shove now drove the barefooted Taylor straight into the arms of the other two – Phil and Gareth – who were blocking the garden path, his rancid breath and foul-smelling wear causing them to recoil as if he'd aimed a punch at them.

As the father involuntarily vacated the doorway, an ashen-faced family group, that had gathered behind him at the bottom of the stairs, now moved forward in mumbling protest, led by the eldest son, a cocky youth of fifteen, perhaps sixteen. None of them, however, ventured any further than the doorstep.

'You miserable punk!' The Neck was making no effort to keep his voice down, hoping to wake more neighbours so that they too could witness the lesson that was about to be taught. 'You sorry son-of-a-bitch!'

'Mr Taylor!' Sparks also spoke loudly, and with sham civility. 'Your boy was caught tonight trying to steal food from law-abiding taxpayers . . . '

More lights were beginning to appear, more windows being opened.

' . . . Nowadays, as far as we're concerned, stealing food is just about the worst crime imaginable. Anybody who does what your lad did tonight deserves to have his fingers chopped off.' He began to prod the boy's father so fiercely in the chest that he toppled back into Phil's arms, knocking against his own son in doing so. 'But sending your own lad, a boy of thirteen, out to do your dirty work for you is even more disgusting . . . '

'Who says tha I did tha, like?'

'Ah! So your son's a *liar* too, is he? Maybe we should cut off his tongue as well as his fingers.'

'Yuh did, Da! Yuh did tell me to steal food, like.'

'Shutch yuh mouth, yuh little bastard!'

The vigilantes now sensed a difficulty. They'd purposely drawn attention to themselves because it was policy, under the circumstances, to

120

make their presence as widely known and as widely felt as possible, in order to deter future offenders. But they also knew that once the eyes of the public were on them, as they were now, then they'd have to show that they could deal effectively with any problem that arose, otherwise their position could be weakened rather than strengthened. Frank Taylor's insolence and shamelessness threatened to undermine their authority and Sparks, recognising the fact, turned to address the others. 'I find both guilty. How about you?'

'Guilty!'

'Guilty!'

'Guilty!'

The enactment sounded so dramatic that all four were glad of the headgear to mask their mood.

'So what's the sentence?' Sparks was calling for a kangaroo court.

Gareth: 'String them up by their feet from the nearest tree, I say.'

Tony the Neck: 'I say cut off one of the boy's fingers but take two off the man.'

'First offence!' Phil's voice suggested tolerance. He was still in bodily contact with both father and son and he could feel the tenseness mounting in them. 'I say throw them in the river for now, just as a warning.'

'So it's my casting vote, then?' Sparks turned to the father, again with mock civility. 'Tell me, Mr Taylor. Which sentence do you think I should pass? Do we string you up? . . . Do we collect fingers as souvenirs? . . . Or do we just throw you into Bridge Pool?'

There was no ready response but the man was obviously shaken.

Sparks turned to the others. 'Okay, I've decided! We take two fingers off him . . . ' He pointed to the man. ' . . . and we throw the other one off the bridge.'

'Tell 'em the trewth, Dad! Tell 'em the blewdy trewth.'

His son's sobbing coupled with the sight of the blade appearing out of the Stanley knife proved to be enough for Frank Taylor. He suddenly slipped out of Phil's grip and onto his knees on the path. He'd begun to tremble uncontrollably.

'Okay! Okay! So I told 'im to find us soom fewkin fewd. So wha? We wus starvin, wasn't we? An' there's no blewdy fewd in the shops is there, like?'

He was scared but not repentant. Obviously, to him, stealing was his moral right. This angered The Neck, who now got hold of him again by his mangy hair.

'Listen, you worthless piece of shite! If I had my way I'd drown you in the town's sewerage beds, and no one would be any bloody wiser. And if we catch you or any of your grotty family with your dirty little paws on somebody else's property again, then that's exactly what I'll be doing.' He shook him by his hair, provoking squeals of pain, then he let him go. 'And I mean it!'

They left the pimply lad standing over his cowering father, with the rest of the family looking on. No voice of gratitude was heard this time from any of the neighbours but the four of them knew that some would now be feeling safer in their beds whilst others would be thinking twice about venturing out with any criminal intent of their own.

'That was good!' The Neck was peering at his watch, having rolled up his soaking wet ski-mask. They were now well away from Quarry Bank Estate and keeping to the shadows once more. 'That hour went quickly!'

'Yea! Never thought we'd have anything to do tonight . . . very first shift an' all.' The voice was Gareth's. 'Quite a coincidence, don't you think?'

'I'm not too sure!' It was Phil's response. 'There's more going on than we ever imagined.' 'You didn't hear that other chap, did you? – the one who caught the Taylor boy – saying that he'd had break-ins twice, before tonight. All within the last fortnight! And that's just *one* house! God knows how much more of this sort of thing has been going on! Okay, granted we've been hearing about some of it – after all, that's why we agreed to this work – but I'm thinking now that we may have underestimated the scale of what's happening.'

'Yea! I reckon that we've got our work cut out for us.' Judging by his animated tone and the spring in his heels, Tony the Neck was relishing the thought.

Chapter 8

Over the next five weeks, The Neck's prediction proved to be correct. During that time, the Vigilantes had to cope with a number of incidents, from petty theft and intimidating behaviour to more serious offences like aggravated assault and an attempted killing. Every team experienced at least one case to deal with, some as many as seven or eight, and by and large they succeeded in meting out punishment befitting the crimes. They'd come to realise, though, that they were only touching the tip of a criminal iceberg.

Rees Morgan had reason to feel gratified with the results. As the days and the weeks passed, not only had he been receiving first-hand reports from Craig O'Darcy about the Vigilantes' activities, but he'd also been keeping his ear close to the ground, for up-to-date public and police response. He heard that there had been a dramatic reduction in petty crime, a fact welcomed by everyone except the criminals themselves, whilst an official police report, although not openly endorsing the work of the Vigilantes, used clauses like *'the welcome constraint shown by the faceless law-enforcers'* and the *'not unacceptable levels of correction used'*. The jargon made him smile. The double negative, he thought, was always a handy tool.

It was July, and the total workforce at Storage Site 5 had been whittled down to a mere twenty five men. Gallery 1 had finally been sealed and its entrance blocked off with thousands of tonnes of concrete delivered by a ceaseless convoy of huge eight-wheeler ready-mix cement lorries, and now a similar process was nearing completion in Gallery 2. Other than the depleted workforce, only senior management and a skeleton clerical staff remained. Any day, Craig O'Darcy and Simon Carvel expected recall to Sellafield B, but whilst the one had long-since decided not to comply, the other was busily involved with preparations to move his personal possessions, lock, stock and barrel, to his safe retreat in the Chiltern Hills in Buckinghamshire. With just forty two days to go to countdown, he had finally negotiated a deal to exchange his Ford Ra for a five year old Mercedes covered-truck. Not that he needed anything as big but he'd had to accept that beggars couldn't be choosers. Any form of large transport had become almost impossible to get hold of, especially along lowland coastal areas, where the whole population was on the move. He'd had to search long and hard on the internet before being finally successful and even then he'd had to make a three-hundred-and-eighty-mile round trip to finalise the deal and to collect the vehicle.

Craig O'Darcy had just begun typing his final report to the CA in Sellafield when the C-phone on the desk beside him started ringing. He cursed out loud, thinking that any call at this time of day could only mean extra work. Petulantly, he jabbed at the REVEAL button but continued to type. 'Yea?'

'Craig? Is that you?'

The voice seemed vaguely familiar but he had a sentence to finish typing.

'Yea! Craig O'Darcy here. Who's speaking?'

'Can't you see me? Don't you have a C-phone? Alistair here!'

The report was instantly forgotten as he saw his brother's face, in close-up, filling the small screen. He pushed away his keyboard and excitedly perched the phone in its stead.

'Alistair! Yes, Craig here. How are you?' It surprised him how relieved and how enthused he felt at receiving the call.

'Apologies, little brother! I should have contacted you before now, but I've hardly had a second to myself. You know how it is.'

'Yes, I can imagine.' But he couldn't, not really. 'How are you then, Alistair? It's been a long while. I'm glad to hear your voice.' And he truly was.

'And me yours. You don't have a camera? I'd like to see you.'

'Afraid not. Anyway, *I* can see *you*, and you're looking well.' Which wasn't true! Alistair had bags like bellows under his eyes and, judging by its pallor, his skin hadn't felt warmth of sun for months if not years.

'I was glad to get your message. I had no idea where you were or how to contact you.'

Craig was surprised by the sincerity that he could both hear and see, and for the first time that he could remember, he felt a genuine affection towards his older brother.

' . . . Where are you now?'

'North Wales, finalising some plutonium storage work for INCSU. And you?'

'Whitehall at this moment in time. I'll be going back to Brussels later in the week.'

'And mother? Have you any idea how she is?' The question slipped out even before he realised that he was going to ask it.

'Spoke to her . . . ' Alistair's brow furrowed in thought. ' . . . week before last, must have been. She's looking well. But older, as you'd expect.'

'Where is she? Still in California?'

'Yes. Only, she and Max moved out of Palo Alto some months ago . . . '
He hesitated, choosing his words. 'I'd say he's been good for her, Craig.
Max, I mean. It's ironic perhaps, considering how uncertain the future
now is, but I'd say that she's happier now than she's ever been. Good
luck to her, I say. Didn't have much of a life until she met Max, did she? I
don't know whether you ever realised the fact? My old man was as much
of a bastard as yours, I think. Anyway, she seems much more content
since marrying Max. They're now settled somewhere high up in the
Sierra Nevada, in the Yosemite National Park.'

'The Sierra Nevada! She's going to be safe, then.' Then as he saw his
brother grimace, he added, 'Not safe?'

'Depends.'

'On what?'

'Extent of stress in the San Andreas Fault. But they *should* be alright
up there, though, provided there are no major landslips in their area, or
virgin volcanic activity.'

'You didn't sound too worried about that sort of thing on *Doomsday
Discussion*. In fact, I thought that you came over very well on it. You've
certainly eased a lot of worries for some people, me included.'

Alistair smiled a rueful smile. 'In five weeks time, Craig, where are
you likely to be?'

'Here. Why do you ask?'

'You're welcome to join Sue and myself in the south of France . . . the
foothills of the Maritime Alps. I've got a big enough villa there . . . '

Craig presumed that Sue was either wife or partner.

' . . . And I've got enough food stacked away to last us for years.'

'Years? Wow! I'm impressed. Friends in high places, must have!
Anyway, thanks just the same, Alistair, but I've already made my
arrangements at this end of the world.'

'How high above sea level are you?'

'Just over five hundred metres. Why do you ask?'

He saw his brother's eyes move up in their sockets, implying that he
was making a quick calculation.

'Yes . . . ' The tone was guarded. ' . . . that should be enough. And
what about food and drink?'

'Enough for about six or seven months, I'd say.'

Alistair's brow furrowed. 'You'll need more.'

Craig laughed. 'Easier said than done, big brother!'

'Then I'll send you some. Expect a truckload within four or five days'
time. I'll need your address.'

All of a sudden, Craig O'Darcy felt ill at ease. Alistair's intensity had begun to worry him. He knew that his brother had been playing down Matt Flescher's predictions on *Doomsday Discussion,* but to what degree? 'What about the attempt to deflect the asteroid?'

The silence at the other end was ominous. Then, in subdued tones, 'Lost in space, I'm afraid . . . Computer failure.'

Craig winced. The person at the other end of the line neither looked nor sounded anything like the one who had oozed such confidence on *'Doomsday Discussion'*

'How far off the mark was that NASA fellow, would you say, Alistair?'

'Honest answer?'

'Honest answer.'

'Well, quite frankly, little brother, he wasn't far off at all.'

'But you said . . . '

Alistair smiled wanly at him out of the small screen. 'Lesser of two evils, I'm afraid, old boy. In such situations, national security has to take precedence . . . '

Craig couldn't help but smile, himself. *'Such situations,* as you call them, are hardly common occurrences!'

Alistair disregarded the flippancy. 'Can't risk public disorder, panic on the streets . . . that sort of thing.'

'So Flescher was telling the truth and you weren't?'

Again the condescending smile. 'That about sums it up, I'm afraid.'

It took Craig a few moments to gather his thoughts. 'And that oceanographer? What was his name?'

'Von Papen.'

'Was he exaggerating?'

'Probably.'

'But not much?'

'Hard to tell.'

'And the South African? The meteorologist? What about him?'

'Schreiner? No, he wasn't too far off either, I'm afraid.'

Craig sat in stunned silence for four or five seconds. Alistair's optimistic assessment on *Doomsday Discussion* had given him false hope and that hope had now been shattered.

'Craig? Are you still there?'

'I'm still here.'

'You believed me, then? On the programme, I mean. I couldn't have been *that* convincing, could I?'

'Afraid so. But that was the whole point, wasn't it? National security and all that.'

Alistair, detecting a hint of sarcasm, uttered a deep sigh of resignation. 'Anyway, listen! I'm more than willing to give you the very latest expert prognosis, if you like? Provided, of course, that you don't do anything silly, like quoting me to the media or going public on the internet.'

Craig remained quiet and his brother interpreted the silence as concurrence.

'The coast of Britain, particularly the south-west, won't escape those tsunamis that von Papen talked about. Okay, so the professor painted the extreme possibilities but that doesn't change the fact that our more exposed coastline will feel the brunt of some bloody giant waves. Not to his degree of prediction, granted, but certainly close to about three hundred metres high. And that's not just high! That's mountainous! They'll pound our shores for days on end . . . months, years even, depending on the extent of the tremors and undersea activity in the wake of the impact. Following that, sea levels are bound to rise dramatically by several metres with the melting of the polar icecaps.'

'And Schreiner? What about his predictions?'

'As he said, Craig . . . If Sion Tudor's assessment is anything to go by, then we can expect those huge tremors and violent volcanic eruptions not only in the South Atlantic and South Pacific but possibly much wider afield. He mentioned the San Andreas fault in California as one area of instability. The Phillipines is another. The Mediterranean even, where I'm going! Plate tectonics being what they are, then there's no telling where weaknesses in the Earth crust will be revealed.'

Craig O'Darcy again fell silent. His brother waited for his response.

'Give me the practical scenario, Alistair. Impact . . . ten thousand megaton explosion . . . tsunamis, in the northern hemisphere, up to two or three hundred metres high . . . higher even . . . disappearance of polar icecaps . . . All those are assured?'

'Afraid so.'

'Subsequent earthquakes and volcanic activity . . . you can't be sure about.'

'That's right. But highly likely!'

'Global conflagration? Sort of thing that Tudor and Schreiner mentioned?'

'Possible but unlikely, at least to the degree that they were on about. Nothing combustible in Antarctica, after all. Is there?' He smiled wearily.

'But they both mentioned burning ejecta falling back to earth hundreds of miles away from the blast area, causing . . . *global firestorms*, I believe they called them . . . *that will incinerate much of the Earth's biomass.* That's what they predicted, wasn't it?.'

Alistair pulled a face to suggest more than one degree of uncertainty. 'There have been a hell of a lot of predictions during these past two years, Craig, all coming from so-called experts. *Of course* there'll be some amount of conflagration, but hardly on a *global* scale. *Of course* there'll be earthquakes and volcanic activity in the wake of the impact but hardly equal to what Sion Tudor or von Papen talked about.'

'But *you* must be worried? *You're* moving house! To the Maritime Alps!'

'No choice, have I? Sue and I will have to move somewhere. London's not an option anymore. London will go! Nothing surer! Brussels will go!'

'Go?'

''With the tsunamis! With the rising sea level!'

'You mean . . . ?'

'The whole world's going to change, Craig, just as von Papen and the others predicted. Not to the same extent, hopefully, but you can be damn sure that life on Earth won't ever be the same again. There'll be massive loss of life, for one thing. Possibly on the scale of those epidemics, three or four years ago.'

'What caused those, Alistair? The epidemics, I mean. Did we . . . Whitehall, MI6 . . . have anything to do with them?'

'Good heavens, no!' His face and his voice displayed genuine shock at the question.

'CIA then?'

This time, he pulled a face as if to grant the possibility.

Craig's fingers drummed the desk top in front of him but he decided not to pursue the point further. 'Hopefully, most people will have moved in time to higher ground.'

Alistair now came out in mirthless cackle. 'The world over? Don't bet on it, little brother. Don't bet on it. There are tribes of the Amazon, for instance, who don't even know of the *existence* of Eros 2, leave alone anything else. And that goes for many other remote parts of the world – in Africa, Asia . . . communities in Siberia, Mongolia, Tibet.'

'What remains of them!'

'Their populations you mean?' Alistair, sensed the lingering criticism in his brother's voice but felt no obligation to deny again any Whitehall involvement in the epidemics being referred to. 'Yes, you're right. What remains of them.'

'Tibet, Siberia, Mongolia . . . the places you just mentioned . . . They'll be well out of danger, though.'

'From the sea, yes, but not from the extremes of cold weather that we'll all have to contend with.'

It was Craig's turn to laugh, albeit tinged with cynicism. 'If anybody can survive the cold, it'll be the Tibetans and the Siberians!'

'Ah! Don't bet on that either! Not if they're unprepared, they won't! If submicron dust from wide-scale eruptions, and smoke from burning biomass, . . . if they blanket the Earth and cut off the sun's warmth, then God help us all! If toxic gasses don't kill us off then we'll all probably freeze to death, whatever part of the globe we live in.'

'But *you're* thinking of survival! *You* obviously reckon that you've got a chance. Are the foothills of the Maritime Alps going to be any different? What made you choose the south of France anyway?'

'Two reasons in particular. For a start, the tsunamis won't affect the Mediterranean to any great extent. The narrow Straits of Gibraltar will throttle them; take the sting out of them; tame their power, if you like. Just like a huge wave-breaker. Mind you, the continent of Africa will have done that anyway which means that only the western fringes of Europe, along the Atlantic coast, will be exposed to them. But that'll include Wales, where you are! You do realize that?' He paused briefly, to underline the full significance of what he was saying. 'Anyway, the second reason for moving to France is that in the foothills of the Maritime Alps we'll be well above the new sea level when that finally settles, whilst at the same time being far enough away from the threat of avalanches or moving glaciers.' When no response came from his brother, Alistair continued. 'The offer still stands, Craig. You're welcome to join us. There'll be enough food, and perhaps more importantly, guaranteed warmth . . . Plenty of heating fuel, warm clothing and so on. Sue and I could do with your help, I'm sure.'

'I appreciate the offer, believe me.' And he did. 'But I've made my bed here in Wales and I think I'll just have to lie in it now.'

'Fair enough. If you've built your nest, then so be it. But you'll have to feather it a damn sight better than you have up to now. Anyway, I wish you the very best of luck, little brother, only remember that you're going to need more than luck to stay alive. You'll need more food, more clothing, more fuel. As I said, I can help you a little, there. Just give me your address.'

Craig did so. He didn't doubt Alistair's word for a second but he felt sceptical about the supplies getting through. No food-carrying vehicle could expect a trouble-free journey through any part of the country, these days; not without an armed escort, at least.

'You do realise, of course, that you'll virtually be living on an island?'

Craig again laughed, this time with nervous uncertainty. 'What do you mean? Don't I already?'

'Well, you heard Reinhard von Papen going on and on about the flooding of the Mississippi basin and the rising levels of the Great Lakes?'

'And the Appalachians becoming an island! You rubbished that idea, if I remember correctly?'

'So I did. But Wales is a smaller kettle of fish altogether. You've heard of the Severn bore?'

'Yes, of course.'

'Four, maybe five metres high at times, as it rolls upstream at something like twenty kilometres an hour. Something to do with the funnel shape of the Bristol Channel, apparently, and the tide being squeezed in as it hits the Severn estuary. But that's just from ordinary tides! Can you imagine what these huge tsunamis are going to do when they hit that funnel at ten . . . twelve . . . perhaps fifteen times the speed? And that's despite the shelter of the Cornish peninsula! Take it from me, Craig . . . ' He could be seen thinking geographically. ' . . . Worcestershire, Warwickshire will literally be swept away. Sea water could be running through the streets of Birmingham. And that's no exaggeration! Something similar will happen with the Dee and the Mersey to the north. Smaller waves, perhaps, but rising levels will see the Cheshire Plain inundated, possibly as far south as the Severn at Shrewsbury. You get the picture?' He paused to let his brother visualise the scene. 'The waters of what is now Liverpool Bay will become one with those of the Bristol Channel. I'm telling you, Craig! Once those sea levels start to rise, the Cambrian massif of Wales will become an island. As will the uplands of Devon and Cornwall. And God only knows how much of England will be left. There'll be no East Anglia, that's for sure. Much of Lincolnshire will go . . . Dorset, Hampshire . . . Look at the lowland areas on your map. That should give you some idea.'

'But the tsunamis aren't going to last forever! The waters will subside.'

'Of course! But only for a time, and even then not to their original levels. A lot of coastal land is going to disappear forever. But before that, those tsunamis are going to cause massive devastation that the world will take hundreds, perhaps thousands of years to recover from.'

Again, Craig laughed uneasily, whilst at the same time playing a nervous finger over the broken bridge of his nose. 'That's pretty dramatic! You're getting to sound more like von Papen every minute.'

No hint of a smile creased Alistair's pallid features, however. 'Take it from me, Craig! Those waves will be taking everything with them. Not just cars and houses and stuff like that, but trees and vegetation. Everything in their path is going to be swept away. But worst of all is that the topsoil will also go. The land will be left bare. In Britain alone, it's estimated that literally hundreds of thousands of acres of arable land are going to be stripped clean of their fertile soil, and anything that's left will be rendered sterile by all that sea water. That'll reverse the natural process of thousands of years, so I'm told. It may sound dramatic to you, little brother, but I see it only as a frightening probability.'

Craig had learnt enough about Nature's slow processes of erosion and deposition to appreciate the extent of what Alistair was saying. The silt and the sediment, that gave valley floors and alluvial plains their fertility, were the deposits of tens of thousands of years. If that loam was removed then it would take Mother Nature just as long again to replace it.

'In fact, that's one reason why many of us are moving to southern France . . . '

Did he detect a hint of guilt in his brother's voice? The *others* referred to were presumably people just as privileged as Alistair himself. They'd had access not only to expert advice and help but also to the resources needed for survival.

'You see, Craig . . . the Rhone valley, just like the rest of the Mediterranean coast, will be protected from the brunt of the tsunamis, and will be left more or less intact. Okay, so the level will eventually rise maybe two hundred feet or more . . . von Papen's prediction wasn't too far off on that either . . . and places like the Camargue will vanish, but when the time comes, when things start to get better, weather-wise I mean, then the Rhone valley is going to be just about the best place in Europe to settle and to farm.'

'In the meantime, though, you're going for the higher ground?'

'Playing safe, yes, because you never know what volcanic activity there'll be in the Mediterranean itself. You know what it's like there . . . Vesuvius, Etna, Stromboli . . . '

'Santorini!' Craig offered.

'Exactly! We can't be too careful. So that's why we've opted for the Maritime Alps to begin with, but close enough to the Rhone Valley to move down there at some later stage. And as I've already said, you're welcome to join us. Your chances of survival will at least double. Think about it.' Suddenly his tone changed. 'Will *you* do *me* a favour now, little brother?' His face had softened and his eyes had moistened and become somewhat beseeching.

'If I can.' Craig failed to see what Alistair could possibly require of him in return for the food and clothing that he'd just promised to send.

'You can! You definitely can!' There was an earnestness about him now. 'I'd like you to give mother a ring. Take it from me, there's nothing that she'd like more. Will you do that for me?'

Craig didn't pause long. 'Yes, okay! No problem. I'll do it now.'

'Better still, try and find a camera so that she can see you as well as listen to you.'

'Yes. I'll do that.' Rees Morgan would allow him the use of his office C-phone and camera. 'I'll do it this afternoon.'

'Good. She'll really appreciate that. And while you're at it, why not call me back, so that I, too, can see what you look like after all these years. Here's her number . . . '

Once Alistair had gone, a wave of forlornness swept over Craig O'Darcy as he suddenly realised how lonely he really was. The dozens of friends here in Pencraig were no substitute for family, were they? When Eros 2 finally came to roost in a few weeks time, families would rally together, giving each other moral as well as practical support. And friendships would count for less. 'When that time comes, what will *you* have, Craig O'Darcy?' The question disturbed him, but not half as much as the answer. 'Freezing months, years maybe, of living alone up in Hafod with just Dog for company. Perhaps to die there! No one to know, far less to care.' It didn't bear thinking about. He fought an impulse to ring Alistair straight back, to accept his offer. But Alistair and Sue were nothing more than strangers to him either! Blood being thicker than water didn't ring true, somehow, in this context.

Without warning, he found himself thinking about Sally in Nottingham. What had been between them had been good, he thought. At least until she stopped loving him. Five and a half years they'd been together, having met at university.

Remembering brought on a nostalgic smile, as he recalled how they'd first met. He'd found her Physics work file, left forgotten on a park bench. 'Sally Lloyd', the cover said! Nothing else. No address. No phone number. It took him days to find her. Enquiries about her whereabouts, her lodgings, proved fruitless, so eventually, one afternoon, he found himself in the Physics block, waiting for lectures to finish. Twenty minutes he'd waited! 'Sally Lloyd? No, sorry.' . . . 'Lloyd you say? Sally Lloyd? No Lloyd in the second year, I'm afraid.' The third student he'd approached had been more helpful. 'Researching, I think. One of the labs would be your best bet. Or the department library, perhaps.' And the library was where he'd eventually found her, hunched over a pile of papers, engrossed in some elaborate series of equations. 'Yours, I believe?' Her relief at seeing the file appearing, as if by magic, on the table in front of her had been a joy to witness. So pleased, she'd been! So thankful! Craig now recalled the gratitude of her upturned face; recalled the twinkling eyes, the parted lips, the tip of a playful tongue between rows of white teeth. 'I can't thank you enough!' That's what she'd said, and everything and everybody in that library, other than her, had suddenly melted away, diffused into a hazy dimness.

Craig now smiled a sadder smile. Yes, the chemistry between Sally and himself had been strong from the word *go*. So what had changed it all? What had upset the formula? His move to North Wales for one thing! Not that estrangement was new to them, what with Craig's week-end commitment to the Lancashire Hornets and all, but they'd been able to spend a few hours together most weekends, thanks to Craig's willingness to travel. And Pencraig had been no further from Nottingham than Sellafield! But Sally had expressed an early annoyance with his move, an inexplicable dissatisfaction with the remoteness of the place. Not that it had meant any great hardship for her. Apart from the one visit that she'd made to North Wales, – in mist and rain, granted – it was Craig who had done all the travelling. Long hours on the bike, in all sorts of week-end weather! And then, just as he was looking forward to getting his helicopter pilot's licence and surprising her with a visit in Rees' Humming Bird, things had come to a head. On one particular visit, her eyes had said it all; they lacked sparkle, lacked interest. 'Who is he, Sal?' 'What do you mean?' 'You know what I mean. You've met somebody else. Who is he?' She'd denied, of course, but her denial had lacked conviction. He'd clung to that denial, though, like a man in quicksand clutching at withered reeds, until he could deceive himself no longer. 'Look here, Sally! You don't have to pretend any more.' Sleepless nights had become intolerable and he'd reached a point of self-respect where he had to know. 'You've lost interest. It's obvious! If I phone you during the week, you actually sound disappointed that it's me. If I mention coming over for the week-end, you're indifferent . . . apathetic even. Why deny it, when I'm giving you the chance to back out? If you no longer feel anything . . . If there is someone else, then for God's sake come out with it. I've been making a fool of myself for long enough and I think I deserve better. I deserve honesty, at least.' But he'd had to leave Nottingham that day without an admission from her and without any firm understanding either way. Inevitably, from then on, the rift had widened until all contact between them had ceased, leaving him numb and confused. Their relationship – *affair* sounded too seedy, somehow! – had ended in the way that *she* had intended and he now respected her less for it. For all he knew, Sally Lloyd could today be married and living in Japan or Timbuktu. But he still felt enough to care! What saddened him now was knowing that she didn't give a damn about him or his whereabouts.

The melancholy of loneliness stayed with him for the rest of the morning. Finishing his report did little to dispel the mood.

* * *

'Well? What's up with you, sourpuss?' Simon Carvel was bubbling. 'Who pissed in *your* fuck'n beer, then?'

Craig felt Simon's hand slap hard on his shoulder as he walked behind him towards his desk but he had neither the desire nor the mental energy to acknowledge the coarse greeting.

'Ah! Who's bin a good boy, then?' Simon had noticed the small pile of pages still lying in the printer's out-tray and had taken a step or two back to pry. 'I see you've finished your report? E-mailed it, have you? Conscientious little bastard aren't you, O'Darcy?'

Ignoring him was probably the best option, Craig thought. *If I let him get to me now, I'll most likely do something I'll regret.* Carvel was just being his usual annoying self.

Whether Simon sensed the aggravation or not was hard to tell. He certainly wasn't taken aback by Craig's reticence. 'Five more days and I reckon that's it. I'll be off like a fuck'n dose o' salts.'

'Five days?' Filling the entrance to Gallery 2 with concrete would take longer than that. At least another fortnight, Craig reckoned.

'I'm just waiting for tha' final posting allocation and then I'm off.' He laughed. 'Reckon you can manage the final lap without me, O'Darcy?'

'Been recalled?' It would be surprising if he had; more so if he'd been the only one to be told about it.

'Recalled? Sellafield B you mean?' The tone was scornful. 'Not a fuck'n chance, mate! Got things to do, places to see!' His good humour was back.

'Oh!' Craig wanted to add, 'I couldn't care a shit anyway, mate!' but decided against it. Out of the corner of his eye, he was aware of Carvel taking his seat at his desk and switching on the laptop.

'I'll just drum out a few words to keep the old man 'appy. Nothin' as fuck'n elaborate as yours, O'Darcy. What the hell! He don' read them anyway.'

Craig knew better. The CA always went through each report with a fine tooth-comb. But that had to be Simon's lookout.

'Where's *your* little 'ideout goin' to be then?'

'Hideout?'

'When this bloody rock falls on Antarctica. Where have you got your stuff stashed away?'

'My stuff?'

'Food, clothes, fuel . . . ? Tha' sort of thing.'

'Oh! Safely locked away . . . as much as I do have.' He didn't trust Carvel enough to confide in him. 'And you?'

'No problem! No problem at all!' The man had the swagger and the conceit of an adolescent. 'Truck ready for packin'. Safe house waitin'.'

'And where's that?'

'Far enough from this fuck'n place, I'll tell you that! *And* that hen coop of a caravan that I'm living in!' He was on a high and getting carried away. 'Buckin'amshire actually! High in the Chilterns. Great place!'

'Oh!' Same disinterested tone as before.

'And I've got food and fuel to last me five months at least. Tha' should carry me over the worst of it.'

Craig smiled humourlessly. 'You reckon?'

'Don't *you*?'

'Depends. Some say it could be years. Others think that we'll never see it through.'

'That's a load of shite, O'Darcy, and you know it. Anyway, once that final food allocation arrives five days from now, then I'm off. Nothin' fuck'n surer! Nothin' to keep me 'ere after tha'. I reckon I'll need a whole day just to load my stuff into the truck, wha' with the fuel and all.'

'You've got it safely stashed away then?'

'Ha! And wouldn't you like to know where.' He was tapping the tip of his nose with his forefinger, as much as to suggest that Craig O'Darcy had been caught prying.

The younger man, irked, got up abruptly, 'Nothing to me what you do with it, mate!', picked his copy of the report out of the computer's out-tray and locked it away in his filing cabinet. He then raised his hand in a curt goodbye and walked out of the room.

Chapter 9

Rees' office at Cefn Quarry was empty when Craig got there. He looked at his watch. Twenty to four. He'd thought for sure that one, at least, of the clerical staff would be around, but there was no sign of anyone. He went to stand in the outer doorway, hoping to catch a glimpse of Rees somewhere on site.

Here and there, men were standing idle, chatting in groups, morosely waiting for the hooter that would bring their shift to an end. Machines stood silent, as they had done for days now. The activity that Craig had come to associate with Pencraig Roofing was no longer evident; hadn't been, he now realised, ever since the work at Storage Site 5 had been completed. Once the final cladding panels had been supplied to complete the government contract, then the site had ground to a painful halt. No orders to meet, no fresh supply of materials to work with.

Craig knew that Rees, would never consider making his workforce redundant, not at this moment in time. Reporting for work, remaining on site to potter around, helped lessen the tedium and the brooding. Not that everybody took advantage of the opportunity, though. In fact, Pencraig Roofing was seeing more truancy now than it had ever done, with Rees turning an uncharacteristic blind eye to it daily.

Two of the uniformed clerical staff were chatting to a group of men about fifty yards away. They had their backs to him and although he would much rather have their permission to use the office phone, he didn't relish shouting to them or interrupting in any way. He therefore walked back into the office and sat in Rees' chair, directly in front of the wall camera. He placed the bit of paper, with his mother's number on it, on the desk beside him and dialled.

He counted the bleeps at the other end. Eight, nine . . . fourteen, fifteen . . . And then, just as he was beginning to think that his mother wasn't home, a man's face appeared. The desk phone had a larger handset and a larger screen than normal but Rees also had the facility to throw the call-recipient's image onto a larger wallscreen. Craig, at the touch of a button, activated the bigger screen and an enlarged face materialised.

Max had aged. From what Craig remembered of him, fourteen years ago, his hair had now thinned to oblivion, apart from the bleach-white tufts brushed neatly back above the ears. He'd grown a moustache, too, also glistening white, whilst his face and shining baldness radiated a healthy-looking tan. All in all, Max had the distinguished appearance of a senior board director, an elder statesman or a venerable Hollywood actor.

'Max Guilder here. Who's calling please?' He was peering at his own screen, in California, trying to recognise his caller.

Even his name was theatrical, Craig thought. 'Hello Max! Craig here! Is mother there?'

For a second, a cloud appeared on his mother's husband's face and Craig suspected that the call wasn't welcome. Then he realised that Max had merely been wrestling with recognition; recognition of name, recognition of features. 'Craig? Is that really you?' And he suddenly filled more of Craig's wallscreen, as if getting closer to his own camera gave him a better view of the caller. 'God! I just can't tell you how happy your mother's going to be. Hold on!'

Max moved out of picture, leaving Craig staring at an empty chair with a couple of full bookshelves behind it. He could hear Max calling 'Lizzie!', his mother's name, and then, further off, 'You're not going to believe who's on the phone!'

She arrived exited and flustered. 'Craig? Is that really you?' She was peering at her own screen even before properly taking her seat.

'How are you, mother? You're looking well.' And she was. She had the same healthy tan as Max and her greying hair had been recently styled. He couldn't help noticing, though, the wrinkles on her upper lip and the slack skin on her throat.

'I can't tell you how relieved I am to hear from you . . . how happy.' Despite the claim, there was a sadness and a nostalgia in her voice and a moistening in her eyes. 'How are you, my boy? How have you been keeping? Are you married? Children?' She didn't pause for answers. 'Am I a grandmother yet? God! How I wish this damn screen was bigger so that I could see you better.' She was staring at her desk handset.

'I'm keeping well, mother.' He immediately regretted the formality of his answer, and allowed himself to smile at her. 'And how are you? You're looking really well. Both of you, actually; Max and yourself. No, I'm not married. No one will have me, I'm afraid.' But what had been meant as a weak joke backfired on him. It seemed to imply that he was destitute and that he was still reproaching her for forsaking him all those years ago. He therefore laughed out loud to dispel the impression. 'To be honest, mother, I'm in a serious relationship.' To claim honesty, whilst lying, didn't bother him. White lies could often be kinder than the truth. 'Have been for four or five years. No children though. We both have our careers.'

He saw her think and then smile. 'Probably better that way, considering what's about to happen.' She paused. 'It won't be a world for children . . . or grandchildren! . . . then, will it?' Tears had formed in the corners of her eyes and she rose a handkerchiefed finger to absorb them before they could wet her cheeks. 'And your partner's name?'

'Um! Ffion! Ffion Morgan!' He gripped the edge of the desk in frustration at his own answer. What had made him name her, of all people? Why hadn't he named Sally?

'Nice name! And what's your career, Craig? Where are you now? Where will you be when . . . ?' She obviously felt no need to finish the last question.

'I'm employed by INCSU, the International Nuclear Contamination Supervision Unit, . . . have been for years . . . and at the moment I'm based in North Wales, in a little town called Pencraig. This is where I'll be, next month.'

'How safe will you be? Things aren't going to be easy, you realise that?'

He warmed to her. 'Yes, I do realise that, mother. But I'll be safe. What about you, though, in California? You and Max?'

'Dear Max! I can't tell you how marvellous he's been . . . still is.'

Craig sensed a movement behind him and turned. Standing there, leaning against the frame of the open door and dressed casually in green T-shirt and grey jogging trousers that sported a green motif which Craig recognised as the AmSport logo, was a pimply young man, twenty two, perhaps twenty three years of age. He had flame-coloured hair and a small but prominent birthmark above his right eye. He obviously had no intention of retreating, of giving Craig the privacy that he required.

'Listen, mother, I'll have to go. Can I call you again?'

'So soon?' She was genuinely disappointed. 'We've hardly talked.'

'I'll call you tonight . . . maybe tomorrow. Will that be alright with you?' Without waiting for a reply, he switched the phone off and saw her distressed face give way to a blank screen.

'I take it that you've had permission?' The accent was unmistakably American. He continued to lean against the door frame.

'Permission?' Craig had got to his feet with the intention of leaving the office.

'To use the phone. Calling California no less!'

Craig looked at him sharply, unsure of who he was dealing with. 'No, not yet. But don't worry! I intend to clear it with the company.'

'Oh! I'm not worried, man.' The stranger had an arrogant sneer. 'But

I'll sure be checking that you've settled for the call.' Before Craig could react, he'd turned and walked out of the office.

* * *

The following evening, Craig kept his word to his mother and his promise to Alistair by phoning both of them, but not without checking with Rees Morgan beforehand. 'Is it okay if I use the phone in your office again this evening, Rees? I've paid for yesterday's call, and I'll naturally settle for this one as well.'

What he had done yesterday was to leave a fifty euro note, together with a scribbled note of explanation, under a paperweight for Rees' secretary to see.

'Settle? What do you mean, settle?'

Craig had phoned him before leaving Hafod for Storage Site 5 and Rees had answered on his handset at home. Neither could see the other.

'I called my mother in California from your office yesterday afternoon but I had to cut it short. Hope you don't mind, but there was no one around to give me permission to use the phone. I left money for the call on your secretary's desk.'

'Left money?' Rees sounded genuinely puzzled and then offended. 'You left money for a phone call?' Again he paused. 'Listen Craig!' He now sounded curt. 'You use my phone anytime you wish . . . no need to ask anybody's permission . . . but don't you insult me again by offering to pay for your calls. I'm too much in your debt for that. Pay? What the hell made you think you had to, anyway?'

Craig laughed nervously, not knowing rightly how to respond. 'Fear of being reported, I suppose.' But Rees' continued silence implied that he had to explain. 'It's just that someone said that there'd be a check.'

'A check? On what?'

'On the call, and that I'd paid for it.'

'Someone? Who the hell is *someone?*' The old man now sounded genuinely angry, but not with Craig.

'I don't know, Rees. He was a complete stranger to me.' The conversation was becoming an embarrassment to him. 'Look! Whoever he was, he didn't mean anything by it, I'm sure. Probably just doing his job.'

'His job? What bloody job? What did he look like?'

'Why not forget about it, Rees? No harm done.'

But the old man wasn't listening. 'Young? Red hair? American?'

139

'Yes, but . . . '

'Right! Now you listen to me! From now on you use that office phone whenever you like and for as long as you like, and if that *young upstart* bothers you again, you just kick him in the balls. Have you got that? . . . And afterwards, just get hold of him by the seat of his pants and throw him out of the office. But that won't be necessary either. I'll make bloody sure of that.'

Yes, Rees was genuinely annoyed. The old man hardly ever swore; in fact, had a theory against it. 'Never trust a man who swears too much, because it's a sure sign of a shallow intelligence and an inadequate vocabulary.'

The conversation ended without Craig being told who the young upstart really was.

His conversation with his mother, that evening, was long and intimate and uninterrupted and it left him in a conflicting mood of inner contentment and regret. The reconciliation had been necessary for both of them . . . for the three of them, Alistair included . . . but it should have happened before now. It should have happened years ago, he told himself. The blame for that rested nowhere but on his own shoulders and that was the regret that now marred his contentment.

He'd never meet his mother again, not in the flesh. That was one fact he had to face, had to accept, but he now vowed to take every possible advantage of Rees' offer during the short time that was left to them. Whether they survived the aftermath of August the twenty sixth or not, one thing was certain – there'd be no further means of contact between them after that, because communication systems the world over would be down. In many respects, they'd be returning to the Dark Ages. An Ice Age even!

What euphoria he'd just felt soon disappeared. His heart was again heavy.

Chapter 10

July dragged to its close, as did the early weeks of August. For many, time crawled, so resigned were they to some form of unpleasant fate, and yet they instinctively clung to the belief that they, at least, would be spared, that they would survive. Craig O'Darcy was no exception. He jealously guarded what provisions he had, never leaving Hafod for more than a couple of hours at a time and always, before doing so, locking all the window shutters from the inside. He'd also acquired from Rees two toughened panels, made by Pencraig Roofing, that could be fitted against the door frames of the cottage. These he could bolt on to whichever side of his doors that he wished, inside at night whilst he was asleep, outside during the day whilst he was out. Dog, on its extended leash, was little more than an alarm system; hardly a deterrent against the hardened criminals who now roamed the streets.

But by and large, Craig felt relatively safe. Hafod was so remote, so off the beaten track that not many people even knew of its existence, leave alone that it was occupied.

The latter half of July saw a sharp increase in the crime rate. Throughout the country, many previously law-abiding citizens were becoming desperate as they saw their meagre provisions diminishing from day to day, with weeks still to go before the real predicament. Television reports painted a gloomy picture, showing gangs of youths roaming otherwise empty city streets. Armed squads of army personnel, faces hidden behind surgical masks, were seen removing emaciated bodies from houses and taking them away for multiple cremations, leaving gaunt but tearless relatives on doorsteps to watch them go. Suicide statistics had reached an all time high.

In Pencraig, things were little better. The initial results achieved by the Vigilantes were reversed almost overnight, following a vicious attack on one of the teams. A gang had lain in wait one evening and had beaten two of them senseless before they could call for help and support. Cliff, one of Phil's team, had received serious brain damage from which he'd later died, whilst his partner, Carey, had suffered multiple injuries that included badly fractured arms and legs, broken ribs and a collapsed lung. The two had also been stripped of their anonymity and their identities disclosed to the rest of the criminal fraternity. It hadn't taken long after that for the connection with Pencraig RC to be made and for the whole squad to come under strong suspicion of involvement, Craig included. Anonymous threats of retaliation and revenge were received by each and every one of them, and the Vigilantes, fearing for themselves and their families, eventually decided to disband, leaving Rees Morgan a very disappointed man.

During that time, Simon Carvel had become rather a sad case. The July allocation from Central Depot for which he'd looked forward, had failed to arrive and, as the days passed, he'd become increasingly agitated and had even considered leaving for Buckinghamshire without it. News finally came through that the truck had been hijacked somewhere along the way, leaving all government employees in the Pencraig – Portharian area to suffer the same concerns as had plagued ordinary citizens for many months. But Simon Carvel had been devastated by a far worse calamity. Two days prior to his intended date of leaving he'd gone down to Portharian to check on his stored provisions, only to discover a splintered door frame and an empty garage. Whoever had been responsible had drilled out all the locks and then ripped the door off its hinges using a crowbar or a similarly heavy lever. Simon had returned to Pencraig that day a broken man. Not only did he no longer have any food but all his fuel had also gone. Without help from somewhere, there was no way he could now drive down to Buckinghamshire, to the *'great place'* that he'd talked so much about. And even if he could, what point was there in moving to a house that was bereft of all basic requirements?

By the second week in August, Craig could see that Simon was becoming desperate. Once or twice he noticed him in rather dubious company and he gradually became convinced that his one-time colleague was now well and truly part of the town's criminal establishment. This particularly worried him, because Simon not only knew that he, Craig, had stored provisions but he also had a fair idea of where to come looking for them.

Work at Storage Site 5 had been completed by the first week in August, leaving the forces of law and order – the police and the army, most of them territorials – as the only remaining government employees in the area. But, with hope diminishing of any further rations arriving from Central Depot, a growing unrest had become apparent even amongst them, making Craig realise just how well-founded Rees Morgan's earlier fears had been.

On the twelfth of August, his C-phone rang. At the time, he was pouring diesel into the generator that supplied Hafod with its limited supply of electricity.

'Yes? Craig O'Darcy here.' His watch showed 12.25.

'Mr O'Darcy, can you give us instructions on how to reach you? We're currently parked on top of a mountain pass on the A470, a couple of miles, as far as I can determine, outside the town of Pencraig. As you can imagine, we want to draw as little attention as possible when we get down there.'

He was immediately suspicious. 'Who is that?'

The caller became equally wary. 'You are expecting provisions, are you not?'

'Provisions?' For a second he thought that Central Depot had honoured its commitment to replace the stolen supplies. Then he remembered Alistair's promise. 'Ah! Of course! Listen! Stay where you are and I'll come to meet you. There'll be no need for you to enter the town at all, but you're not likely to find this place without me to guide you. I'll be there in less than ten minutes.'

'I'll need proof of identity.'

When he reached the top of the Dunant Pass he got the shock of his life. Not only was there a large truck parked in the lay-by there, with driver and co-driver aboard, but also an armed escort of motorcyclists on both flanks. He counted eight – four of them standing guard, guns raised – and whistled softly. Big Brother did indeed carry a hell of a lot of clout.

The lead rider dismounted and came to meet him, raising his visor before saluting and introducing himself. 'Corporal James Higgins, sir!' After a precursory glance at the government employee tag that Craig offered for inspection, he indicated, with a slight turn of head, the truck behind him 'This is your sealed delivery.' His instructions were then brief and pragmatic. 'What we intend, Mr O'Darcy, is to leave the truck with you, so that you can unload at will. That way, we can return immediately without drawing undue attention to our mission. You appreciate its covert nature, of course, and the need for urgency.'

'You're leaving the truck?' He sounded surprised. 'Until when?'.

The corporal smiled. 'You get to keep it, sir, for what it's worth. I doubt whether Central Depot will have further use for it.'

Craig smiled back at him. 'Generous, I must say. Just one thing, corporal. The only attention that we're likely to draw within the next few minutes is from some quarry workers as we drive up to where I live. I appreciate the strength of the escort that's been provided, but it's going to raise a few eyebrows I can assure you. May I suggest that only the truck and its driver follows me home. I can then deliver him back here for you. Since he's leaving his truck behind, then I presume he'll be riding pillion with one of your men on the way back?'

'I get your point, Mr O'Darcy, but my brief was to escort the truck to its destination. However, if you consider your option to be the lesser of two risks, well . . . ' He obviously preferred Craig's alternative and they settled on it. 'Here you are, sir!' He was holding two keys on his extended palm. 'Whatever you do, don't lose them, because they'll be your only means of getting into that container. And you're going to be needing both of them, for the two security locks.'

The journey, skirting the old Cefn Quarry workings and up towards Hafod, attracted little attention. There no longer being any work going on at Pencraig Roofing, the number of men who reported in every morning had dwindled to a mere handful, and *they* were only there for one another's company and for the free cup of tea or coffee that was on offer mid-morning and mid-day. A few curious glances were now directed towards the truck as it whined its way up towards the ridge and then out of sight, but those who did show interest had recognised Craig O'Darcy's bike going on ahead so they didn't become unduly inquisitive.

'Just park it there and lock it.' Craig was pointing to where the track ran through a little cutting, about fifty yards beyond the cottage. 'That way it won't be visible from down there.' He pointed in the direction of the town in the distance.

The driver obliged, returned with the ignition keys for Craig, and mounted the Norton pillion to be taken back to the Dunant Pass where he could rejoin his colleagues.

Less than half an hour later, Craig was staring in amazement at what Alistair had sent him. The truck, for a start, was part of a fleet especially constructed for Central Depot. Its container's walls were of solid steel, its rear doors, as hinted by the corporal, having computer-key-operated locks. Those keys were usually sent by separate delivery, as an added precaution against theft, but an exception had obviously been made in this instance, for which Craig O'Darcy was now grateful. It was common knowledge that some of these vehicles had been hijacked in the past but had later been found intact because the thieves had been unable to break into them, even with oxyacetylene torches. Provided that he put the engine out of commission so that the truck couldn't be driven away by anyone, then the container would be the ideal place, he now argued, for him to store all his provisions.

A quick and excited assessment showed him a wealth of stock – deep shelves stacked tight with tinned foods, powdered milk and soup, jars of jams and other conserves, pots of honey, sealed bags of rice, salt and various herbs, not to mention the piles of blankets and the rails of warm clothing. Back to back with the driver's cab was a large refrigerator unit full of meat, fish and freeze-dried vegetables. Close inspection told him that the electricity for this came from a patchwork of small solar panels set in the steel roof of the vehicle. All in all, Craig reckoned that Alistair had sent him the equivalent of a month's allocation for the entire government workforce in the area.

All he needed now was a way of camouflaging the truck's presence and he believed that he had a ready answer for that. He knew that Pencraig Roofing had some cladding panels left over from the Storage 5 contract and that Rees would be more than willing to let him have what he required. If he could only find a way of propping up the slate-grey panels at each end of the cutting then the spot wouldn't attract too much attention, at least not from any great distance, and the truck would remain hidden.

Without further ado, he opened the lorry's bonnet and debated how best to incapacitate the fuel cell engine, concluding that removing the injectors would be his best option. He'd have to borrow tools from Pencraig Roofing for the job, but it was best to wait until the day shift had gone home, which wouldn't be long now anyway, before approaching Rees. 'I'll have to explain this to him,' he thought. 'Even offer to share with him if there's anything here that he needs.'

*   *   *

The old man was genuinely pleased when told of Craig's good-fortune. He immediately supplied the tools and the panels, together with pick-up-truck transport to the site. He even accompanied him to inspect the job and to offer advice.

'I can't tell you how glad I am for you.' He was just getting over his shock after inspecting the truck's contents and there was now a mischievous twinkle in his eyes. 'This means that you'll be staying for certain, doesn't it?'

Although Craig had decided some time ago to remain in the area, he hadn't, up to now anyway, committed himself fully as far as Rees was concerned. Since his position as rugby coach was no longer a relevance, he couldn't help wondering why the old man should be so anxious for him to stay. It warmed him, though, to see how genuinely pleased he now was, at the sight of his friend's good fortune.

He smiled in return. 'Yes. I reckon I shall be staying, old friend, and you and Sinéad . . . and Ffion, of course . . . are welcome to share some of

145

this with me.' Why had he included the daughter, he asked himself.

Rees laid a grateful hand on his arm. 'No need for that, Craig. I've made adequate provision for my family. But I appreciate the offer just the same.'

For the next twenty to twenty five minutes they worked in comparative silence, Rees giving the occasional instruction and Craig providing the manual effort.

'Two should be enough.' The old man was watching the second injector being removed. 'There's no way that that engine will start now.'

'Do you reckon I should take the wheels off as well, in case somebody tries to tow it away?'

Rees thought about it. 'Quite a contract!' He was looking at the three sets of double wheels under the container, with another set under the cab section. 'But, yes. Better be safe than sorry. To do that, though, we'll need to go back down for hydraulic jacks, and a load of blocks to prop up the axles. There's a hell of a weight on it you know!'

It was getting on for half past six in the evening when the two of them finally stood back and surveyed the result of their efforts. The heavy vehicle now stood perched on eight towers of concrete blocks, no more than about two feet off the ground. Stripped of its shirt, Craig's upper body gleamed with sweat and his close-cropped hair clung wet to his scalp. The knuckles of both oily hands were bloodied from many a slip of the wheel brace and spanners.

Rees, for his part, although also exhausted, had a contented look about him. 'Tomorrow we'll work out a patent for hanging up those panels, to hide the truck as best we can. But now we'll go down for a hot bath and a tot of well-earned whisky or whatever, and then you can join Sinéad and myself for a meal.'

When Craig showed signs of protesting, the old man wagged a defiant finger at him. 'Don't argue! There's something I want to ask of you, anyway. A favour!'

'Okay, but I'm not coming empty-handed this time.' He smugly indicated towards the truck's contents. 'You can protest as much as you like, old man . . . '

*　　*　　*

Rees Morgan drove the pick-up, that they'd used to carry the materials up to Hafod, back to its parking space at Pencraig Roofing, leaving them with a half-mile walk to Plas Cefn. It was typical of the meticulous way that he ran his business affairs, Craig thought. If that was where the pick-up was supposed to be parked, then nowhere else would do. Anyway, the walk provided them with the opportunity that Rees needed, to talk, before reaching the house.

'Now what's this favour I can do for you?'

Rees hesitated. 'I want you to promise me something, Craig.' He again paused, as if unsure how to continue. 'If something happens to me, can you . . . will you . . . keep an eye on Sinéad . . . and Ffion?' His steely eyes were almost imploring. 'Do what you can to protect them I mean.'

Craig's laugh was brief and nervous. He played a hesitant finger along the uneven ridge of his nose and twisted the fingers of his other hand around the string-like handle of the plastic bag that he carried. 'And what's going to happen to you, for God's sake?'

'Nothing, I hope. But you can never tell, can you? Now, can I have your word?'

There was no ignoring the earnestness of the upturned face. The old man needed reassuring.

'No problem, Rees. I'll do whatever I can to help.' Again he laughed drily. 'But I doubt whether Ffion will need or welcome any help from me.'

Rees Morgan turned to look away and Craig was suddenly aware of how frail he'd become. The shoulders were narrower, the nape of his neck paler, thinner.

'What do you know about her, Craig?' The voice was sad and distant.

'What do you mean?'

'How much do you know about her?'

'That she's young and fit . . . very clever . . . Too bloody clever for me!' He laughed weakly. 'That she's a Maths teacher by day . . . gives evening classes in Welsh . . . That she's Welsh to the core . . . ' Zealot was the word he'd wanted to use but had thought better of it. ' . . . And that the name Craig O'Darcy isn't on her Christmas card list. Which is why . . . '

'You're mostly right. She is fit. She is clever. Reads a hell of a lot. Literature is probably her first love. Did you know that?'

Craig didn't, but Rees didn't wait for his response.

'She's got a photographic memory . . . or something very close to it. She scans pages rather than reads them, which means that she gets through a book in a fraction of the time that you and I would take. But you were wrong on one point. She's not Welsh to the core as you called it. In fact, she hasn't got a drop of Welsh blood in her.' Sensing Craig's surprise, he turned to look at him and saw the question forming in the young man's eyes. 'Don't misunderstand! I'm her father, all right. It's just that I've no Welsh blood in me either. Both my parents came from Liverpool. Evacuees during the second world war . . . '

'That's remarkable! And they didn't go back?'

'They couldn't. Nowhere to go to. Their homes had been blitzed, their families killed. Pencraig people cared for the two of them, raised them as their own. My father was officially adopted and his name changed from Collingswood to Morgan. In time, he became a quarryman . . . got to know my mother better – shared past, shared grief, that sort of thing – and they eventually got married.'

'So you're not . . . ?'

'Welsh? No, I suppose not. Theoretically at least! But my parents had a lot of respect for this place . . . for its people. As I do. As my daughter now does.'

'But Ffion? Where was *she* born?'

Rees smiled. 'Holland. That's where I met Sinéad. I was running a little arc-welding business in the shipyards of Rotterdam at the time.' For a second, his brow furrowed, as if with painful recollection, but it didn't last. 'Then, when Ffion was seven we moved to Marseilles. About four years there and then on to the States, to Baltimore and then Boston. I was into construction by then, and I struck lucky.'

'And then from New England back here to Wales?'

'You find that surprising!'

'I suppose I do. Standard of living . . . climate . . . All that.' He wanted to add, *You probably had the wealth to buy an idyllic home in Bermuda or Hawaii.*

Rees smiled a rather sad smile. 'I doubt whether you'd understand.' He paused, struggling to explain himself. 'It's just that this is where I belong. I've always felt that . . . Always known that this is where I'd return . . . where I'd be happiest. The people . . . the community . . . ' He laughed rather self-consciously. 'As I just said, I doubt whether you'd understand.'

'And Sinéad and Ffion?' Had Rees been selfish, Craig wondered.

'Sinéad understood.' The voice was uncompromising. 'Ffion, of course, welcomed the move.'

'Oh?'

'She was on her second year in Oxford at the time. Came up here regularly on hill-climbing weekends with some friends. Visited her grandparents' grave . . . '

Craig recalled and now understood Rees' earlier reference to his own *adoptive grandparents.*

' . . . She phoned me in Boston to say how sad the place looked. Told me about the unemployment, the boarded-up shops, the empty houses. She also mentioned the silent quarries. That saddened me more than anything, I think. Anyway, I made my own enquiries, found that Cefn Quarry was up for sale, bought it and . . . Well, you know the rest. Two years later, a maths teaching post was advertised in Pencraig and Ffion successfully applied for it.'

'With an Oxford degree?' Craig made no attempt to disguise his amazement.

Rees nodded. 'First class, no less!'

'And that would be . . . what? . . . seven years ago?'

'Nearer eight.'

'And then learnt the language?'

The old man smiled and shook his head. 'Sinéad and I have always had a policy, ever since Ffion was born. When its just the two of them, they speak nothing but Irish. Ffion and I, however, have always communicated in Welsh. When the three of us are together, though, then we use English.'

'Wasn't that confusing for her?'

'Why should it be?' The smile became somewhat patronising. 'You English have a problem with such things, haven't you? For you there can only be one language, one culture. You expect your language to be spoken the world over and over the years you've spent billions to make that possible. What is it about you that makes learning someone else's language, studying another nation's culture, such an anathema?'

Craig was taken aback by the unexpected criticism, until he saw the smile tugging at the corners of the old man's mouth. Then the wrinkles disappeared as the lips were pulled into a grin. 'If you can't answer me, lad, then what chance would you have in an argument with my daughter?' He laid a hand on Craig's arm and they continued towards the house. 'In Rotterdam, we lived close to a German couple who'd baby-sit Ffion for us. They had no English. And certainly no Irish or Welsh! Would it surprise you, therefore, if I said that my daughter was fairly fluent in German by the time we left Holland?' He again smiled, 'Mind you, her French isn't at all bad, either!'

Craig slowly digested the information. 'And that explains why I command so little respect from her?' There was a peevishness in his tone that he couldn't conceal.

'Ah! But that's not true. She does respect you. You can take that from me.'

Craig's shrug suggested that he needed more convincing. The old man obliged.

'I'm afraid that my daughter feels rather bitter towards life at the moment. Has done for the past three years. She has no interest in men, that's for sure . . . '

What was he saying, Craig wondered. Was he suggesting that she was a lesbian?

' . . . But, given time, that should change. The wound will heal.'

'I don't understand.'

'Ah! You've not heard? That explains it then!' Rees held his young friend back by the arm. 'A little over three years ago, my daughter was due to get married. Local lad. Gwyn Stevens. He was employed here at Pencraig Roofing, as a draughtsman.'

The old man paused, Craig waited.

'He was killed.'

'God! I'm sorry! . . . How did it happen?'

'Accident. He owned a superbike, not unlike the one that you ride, actually. We've got some treacherous roads around here, as you know only too well. Narrow and winding. Apparently he skidded on some wet leaves . . . straight under the wheels of an approaching truck . . . Ironically, a Pencraig Roofing truck!'

There was a sense of guilt in the way he uttered the last sentence, but Craig's thoughts were elsewhere. They'd returned to the evening when he'd given Lowri Daniels that lift home from chapel, and been seen by Ffion. He now recalled the contempt on her face as he'd driven off. Or had it been something other than that? Could it have been pain? Could it have been sorrow? Had he reminded her of her loss? Had he inadvertently opened up the wound that Rees had just now referred to?

They walked the rest of the way in silence.

* * *

The evening had one other surprise in store for Craig O'Darcy.

Sinéad had thanked him for the packs of frozen vegetables and tins of fruit that he'd brought her but it was Rees who'd shown the most appreciation, on seeing the two boxed bottles of Middletons Irish whiskey appearing out of the large plastic bag. 'You do realise, I hope, that this is just about the most expensive malt that you can buy in Ireland?' And when Craig had shrugged to show his ignorance, the old man had added, 'That brother of yours is really something, I'd say.'

150

The conversation during the meal was lively and interesting, far more relaxed than when Ffion had been present. The two men had just retired to the front lounge to enjoy a tot of the Middletons when they heard heavy footsteps running down the stairs and a young man suddenly appeared in the room with them.

'Oh! Sorry! I didn't know . . . ' He was obviously surprised at their presence and made to retreat just as quickly.

'Tristan! Come here!' Rees had jumped to his feet. 'I'd like you to meet our guest. I believe you owe him an apology.'

The flame-haired young man who had censured Craig about his phone call to California now fidgeted uncomfortably under the old man's gaze. The right eyebrow beneath the birthmark twitched nervously. For a moment he appeared to grow obstinate but then decided to comply.

'Yeah! I'm sorry, man. Didn't know who ya were, did I? Never seen ya before, had I? Thought maybe you were . . . '

Rees cut across him 'You took too much upon yourself. Just don't do it again.' And then as introduction, he added, 'Craig, this young man who was so rude to you recently is Tristan, my son. I hope that you can forgive him.'

As he instinctively extended an arm to shake the limp hand, Craig was aware of the startled look on his own face. In the two years that he'd known the family, he'd never heard a son being mentioned.

Suddenly the young man was gone and Rees had resumed his chair. 'Young people these days! You know what they're like.'

'I'm not that old myself, Dad!' He hoped the comment would dispel the tension and it did. Rees laughed and turned towards the wall-screen television, to bring it to life.

'You never told me.'

'That I had a son? Never had reason to, I suppose.'

'What does he do?'

'Do?' The old man's voice was suddenly filled with contempt. 'He's twenty two years of age . . . failed student . . . drop-out . . . shacked up, somewhere in New Jersey, with a divorced mother of three who's twice his age and whose children are almost as old as he is.' He allowed himself a rueful smile. 'He's back now though. Had nothing more to offer her, I suppose.' Then, by turning up the volume on the television, he indicated that Tristan was not his favourite subject of conversation.

The programme was called THE ULTIMATE BUZZ and the presenter claimed that what was about to be shown was 'historical video footage of man's fortitude in the face of disaster; visual proof of forbearance the world over in the dark days leading up to what is to be the worst disaster in the history of mankind.'

For the next forty minutes, the two of them sat in silence and disbelief as a catalogue of incredible world-wide preparations unfolded. The first featured a group of twelve seismologists preparing, at great personal risk, to record the unprecedented tremors that were expected to rip apart the San Andreas fault in California. 'Stupid buggers!' was Rees' only retort, whilst Craig silently prayed that his mother was well enough away from such dangers. More incredible was the team of vulcanologists camped on the rim of Vesuvius, waiting, so one of them claimed, 'to witness from a ringside seat' the true fury of *Il Gigante Che Dorme*, The Sleeping Giant. Then came the hot air balloonists gathered on the High Veld of South Africa. Their array of deflated multicoloured airships – fifty seven of them in all, according to the presenter – were shown from a circling aircraft as a montage of the world's most successful companies, each balloon proudly displaying the name of its sponsor. The brave airmen, their spokesperson maintained, were there to take full advantage of the incredible thermals that would come in the wake of Eros 2's explosive impact. Those thermals, he said, would take them twenty, perhaps twenty five miles, up into the Earth's stratosphere, at speeds never before experienced by hot air balloonists. 'You'll have breathing apparatus, I presume, but what about temperature? Won't you freeze to death up there?' The questioner seemed bemused. 'No way, man! We'll be bathing in those thermals. It'll be like the tropics up there.' *Loony* was the only word that came to Craig's mind.

'And this has to be the greatest buzz of them all.' The presenter seemed both amused and amazed as he gazed at his split studio screen. 'What we see here is Easter Island . . . ' The left half of the screen to which he was indicating showed a satellite view of the South Pacific island. ' . . . and over here on the right the island of Tristan da Cunha in the South Atlantic. Now let's take a closer view of what's happening on each of them.'

As he spoke, the satellite camera zoomed in to detail two wide and sandy beaches populated by literally hundreds of people either lying on the sand or surfing the waves. A terrestrial camera then took over, to focus on groups of wide-eyed youngsters, far-gone on pot.

'Sometime between four and five o'clock GMT on the morning of August twenty six, all these surfers – an estimated twelve hundred in all, from all corners of the globe! – will take to their boards for the greatest journey, the greatest thrill, of their lives, as they seek to ride the first of the giant tsunamis to sweep up through the Pacific and Atlantic Oceans. None of them will survive the trip – they fully realise that – but for them this will be the ultimate buzz – the UB as they call it. Amongst them are a number of well-known international surfing champions who will be hoping for a clear ride over hundreds of miles of open ocean at speeds never before experienced by sea-going craft, let alone by unprotected human bodies. On Easter Island, we're told that the dream of the majority is to stay afloat long enough to reach the Tropic of Capricorn, whilst the more optimistic talk of crossing the Equator. A handful of them believe they can reach the coasts of Mexico, California or even Alaska! On Tristan da Cunha, there's talk of reaching the coast of Western Africa, others think that by avoiding the Cape Verde Islands and the Azores, they can even get as far as Greenland, all in a matter of twenty four hours or less. Whether that is possible or not, whether anyone has that sort of stamina, that level of skill, remains to be seen, but it will be an incredible test of mental and physical strength and endurance. Journey's end for most will be quick and decisive; for others, if they get to approach land, the trip will become a true nightmare as the tsunami finally hits the shallows and crests to a terrifying height of hundreds of metres . . . '

'Can you believe these people?' Although addressing Craig, Rees couldn't drag his eyes away from the screen. 'What the hell do they hope to prove?'

The presenter seemed to hear the question. 'You, the viewers, will, no doubt, condemn their efforts as suicidal antics but this is our young people's way of thumbing their noses at Fate. As one young surfer put it – *We'll ride the whirlwind rather than stand meekly in its path.*'

Rees was still tut-tutting as the programme drew to its close with shots of the American and Chinese space stations orbiting Earth, both manned by experts in various fields of science, both craft well stocked with seeds and plants, ready to replenish a ravaged Earth, and each with its own arsenal of weapons of defence.

On switching off the telescreen, Rees turned, 'Remember your promise!' There was an intensity to his voice and to his stare.

Craig wanted to ask 'Why me? Why not ask your son?' But he reckoned he'd already been told why. 'I will.'

Chapter 11

Simon Carvel cursed loudly as he listened to his stomach growling. His face was pasty, tight skin on prominent cheekbones, sunken eyes in dark sockets. Days had passed since his last solid meal, four eggs stolen at considerable risk from a nearby hen coop. The owner of the hens, he knew, owned a gun and would not hesitate to use it against any thief. But the pangs of hunger often made light of such dangers.

A sudden shower sent him scurrying up the steps of his caravan, and as his gaunt face appeared in one of the windows, it took on the wild look of a hunted animal. Colourless lips could be seen mouthing 'Fuck'n weather! Fuck'n town!'

The rain fell heavier, as if to mock him; large drops drumming on the thin metal roof above his head and splattering on the paved area between the vans, its spray shrouded by the steam that was now rising out of the warm ground. The distant range of mountains no longer showed, enveloped now by grey mist and murky wetness. Behind him, on the other side of the van, an empty Mercedes truck served as an idle and mocking reminder of how different things could have been for him.

A skinny mongrel nosed its hungry way from pillar to post, zigzagging forlornly in search of improbable titbits. Nothing else, apart from the driving rain, moved. 'Fuck'n weather! Fuck'n town!' His stomach once more growled, like the rumble of distant thunder.

Gradually, the rain eased, the dark clouds parted and patches of blue sky again peered through.

A movement way to his left failed to draw his interest. Nor did the sudden purring of an engine bring a flicker to his eye. Had he but noticed, he would have seen a rider, in gleaming wet black leather, stop in front of one of the vans, yank his bike up on its stand and stride towards the door. His knock was answered through a partly opened window, enough for him to make his enquiry and for the suspicious resident, whoever it was, to point towards the static that was home to one Simon Carvel.

It took a few seconds for Simon to recognise Craig O'Darcy as he suddenly appeared in his line of vision, looking up at his window.

'Hi, Simon! Can I come in?'

With a certain reluctance, he moved to open the door.

'Simon! How are you?' Craig was removing his helmet as he spoke.

Carvel merely grunted, turned his back and returned to his former position at the window, leaving the open door as the only invitation to enter.

'I heard you had some bad luck.' He looked around with some distaste. Simon was living in considerable squalor. Items of dirty clothing, including T-shirts and underpants, were strewn here and there on the bench seat that ran along two of the walls; dirty crockery took up most of the table area and filled the sink; a glimpse through a partly open bedroom door suggested that things were no better there, whilst the stench that permeated from the bathroom made him wish that he'd left the caravan door open behind him. 'How are you managing?'

'How do you think I'm fuck'n managin?' No turn of head, no angry look, just a dispirited monotone response.

'You've still got the Mercedes truck, then?' He gestured towards the opposite window, at the lorry parked outside. 'Actually that's how I was able to find you.' He laughed briefly. 'It seems that the truck is better known than its owner around here.'

Carvel continued to gaze out dispassionately, making Craig O'Darcy wonder whether his former colleague had heard a word of what he'd said.

'How are you for food?'

It was Simon's turn to laugh. A long cold cackle. 'If you've come beggin' O'Darcy, then you can fuck'n well forget it.'

'Actually, I thought I could help. Tell me, what became of the house you were going to move to? Buckinghamshire wasn't it?'

'What became of it? What do you mean *What became of it*? It's still fuck'n there as far as I know.'

'The last time we talked, you were full of it. Couldn't leave this place soon enough, so you said. What happened?'

'Some fuck'n Welsh bastards skinned me. That's what happened! As if you didn't know! Took everythin. Food, clothes, fuel . . . Every fuck'n thing I had.'

'You know who they were, then?'

'Know? How the hell would I know them?'

'You said they were Welsh.'

'Had to be. Never trusted the bastards.'

Craig O'Darcy winced. He'd almost forgotten about Carvel's prejudices. 'I could get you fuel if you still want to go.'

Simon looked at Craig through lifeless eyes. 'Why? Why would you help me?'

'Why not? After all, we did spend some years working together.' Realising that the man was suspicious of him, Craig went back to his bike and to the two bags fitted on each side below the pillion, gulping in the fresh air as he did so. When he returned, he had the detached bags under his arms and, leaving an open door behind him this time, he pushed away a plate with the small bones of a cooked rabbit still on it and proceeded to empty the contents onto the table behind Simon, piling one thing on top of the other to make use of the little space that was available. Out came several packs of frozen sausages and bacon, tins of beans and spaghetti, powdered eggs and powdered milk, and finally a full bottle of whisky, but not the Middletons that Rees had enjoyed.

Simon Carvel's face became a child's face at Christmas, especially when the bottle of Scotch appeared. Eyes that were previously lack-lustre now shone, dilated pupils suddenly filled with life.

'Go steady on that, Simon.' Craig pointed to the bottle as its cap was being unscrewed. 'Empty stomach and all that!'

'Just a drop, to remind me of the taste.'

The *drop* that he poured into the greasy tumbler was a treble measure at least, Craig thought, as he watched him gulp it down. Worriedly, he wondered whether the litre bottle would last the night and he began cursing his own lack of foresight in bringing the whisky. In his present physical state and mood of desperation, Simon could quite easily be dead from alcoholic poisoning by morning.

'I'm grateful O'Darcy.' And his face showed it.

'Go steady on the drink, Simon. Get some food into you first.' He looked around. 'I take it that you have the facilities here to cook your own? Electricity and all that.' The rabbit remains were confirmation enough, he realised. 'There's not a lot there, so you'll need to ration it.'

Suddenly he felt anxious to leave.

'I know that you've never been too keen on this stuff . . . ' Carvel was indicating the bottle of Scotch ' . . . but how come you can manage the food?'

It was a question that Craig didn't want to answer. 'Hopefully things will get better once the panic is over. I can hold out until then.' The last thing he wanted was for Simon to suspect that he had an abundance of stores. 'I'll be seeing you.' Quickly, he returned to the bike and zipped the now-empty bags into place.

'Call again!' Simon was watching him from the open doorway, the raised bottle in his hand, as much as to suggest *and bring another one of these.*

Chapter 12

In the week that led up to the impact, feelings were running high the world over, with people reacting differently to their impending fate. News bulletins showed New York and Tokyo streets empty of traffic and pedestrians, apart from a few despairing looters, and down-and-outs resigned to whatever destiny they thought awaited them. Americans of various ethnic backgrounds were seen barricaded into roughly constructed log cabins in the Rockies and the High Sierras, their anxieties symbolised by the menacing gun barrels that panned the outside world through specially constructed windows and vents. One camera crew had trailed the surrounding redwood forest in a futile search for wildlife, finally concluding that every living creature – *'apart from the termites!'* – had been killed for food. Equally futile was the search for the Amish community of Pennsylvania. The carefully tilled lands of the Pennsylvania Dutch were shown stripped of all produce, their homes ransacked by inner-city gangs. Views of Salt Lake City showed a Mormon community under siege and the great Tabernacle deserted. In Quito and Rio fly-ridden corpses were shown rotting in the streets, with rats and mangy dogs feeding off them. Reporters the world over talked of murders and suicides and early deaths from famine and disease. There were even rumours of cannibalism in some areas but no one seemed too keen to follow that lead. Only in China was there any semblance of discipline. Whereas Shanghai and Hong Kong were deserted, and life in Beijing was anything but normal, out in the countryside work continued on the crops and in the paddy fields and tea plantations. Wheat and sweet potatoes were shown being harvested, fruit being gathered and stored. The overall impression was that, up to now, the threat of Eros 2 had made little or no difference to life in the communes.

In Pencraig the desperation continued.

'Do you realise that on average we've been burying ten to twelve people a week over the past month or two?' Rees Morgan was pacing the floor between his wife's chair and the window. 'What it must be like in the cities, God only knows. Our burial caverns are fast filling up and I'm not sure that we can do much more. Coffins were at a premium three months ago, now you can't buy one for all the tea in China. The material just isn't available.'

'What would they be doing with the bodies, then?' Her voice was a mixture of concern and dread.

'They're just being deposited as they are, on the shelves of Tomb

Chamber 3. The stench in there is something awful by now. Thank God those glass panels keep it airtight, I say.'

'Holy Mary, mother of God!

Removing corpses from homes and taking them to the burial caverns was the responsibility of special volunteer groups whose incentive for undertaking the morbid work was purely humanitarian, coupled with the practical necessity of controlling the spread of diseases.

'What of us, husband?' Sinéad had got to her feet to face him. Her usual self-control had deserted her. 'Are we to be deposited on a shelf, as food for rats?'

Rees placed a gentle arm around her shoulder. 'No danger of that, my dear. There's a corner of Chamber 1 that's already reserved for us as a family. Quilted coffins and all!' His smile suggested that he was making light of her fears. 'As for the rats, well we eliminated those a long time ago.' He saw no point in reminding her that plagues of the disgusting rodent were now openly roaming the streets of every town and city throughout the country and that Pencraig was no exception. It was an acknowledged fact that rats could sense death and that they swarmed around the homes of the seriously ill and the dying. There had even been reports, in instances of people dying alone, of the rats not even bothering to wait for the final breath to be drawn. But, since Sinéad no longer watched the news reports, Rees saw no reason to enlighten her.

'There be only three days left, Rees! And then . . . ! Oh Mary, mother of God, have mercy on us.' A shiver racked her body and she instinctively crossed herself and reached for her rosary. All of a sudden she looked ten years older. '*Is iomdha lá 'sa g-cill orainn.*'

Rees tried to laugh. He wanted to dispel her anxieties. '*Many a day shall we rest in the clay!* And how often have I heard you say that in the past?'

'Ah! But now it is so close, husband! So real! So threatening, is it not?'

'Listen, Sinéad! Haven't I promised to care for you? Haven't I said that all will be well?' He watched her dismal nod of head. 'Tomorrow Ffion will be moving back in with us and we'll all be together to face whatever happens. And if anything should happen to me . . . '

He felt her grip on his arm tighten.

' . . . if anything happens to me, then Craig O'Darcy has promised all the help you'll need.' He saw her frown. 'That young man's all right, Sinéad. I have a lot of regard for him. He won't take advantage.'

'He's *your* friend, not ours. You know what it's like between him and Ffion. If something happens to you, as you put it, what obligation will he feel?'

Rees looked her directly in the eye. 'I have only his word for it, Sinéad. Would you rather put your faith in Tristan?'

She quickly looked away, conceding the argument.

Chapter 13

By the evening of August the twenty fifth, tension had reached breaking point. Literally everyone who cared was glued to a television screen, for the final *Doomsday Discussion*, a special twenty-four-hour-plus presentation. Few doubted that this would be the very last thing that they were ever likely to see on television. There had been talk in London and Brussels of contingency plans in Europe to ensure communication links for the post-impact period but not many people gave thought to anything beyond the disaster itself.

Like so many others, Rees Morgan and family had their evening mapped out. They would have an early supper, at six, with Craig O'Darcy again as guest. Then they would tune in to Anita Beuwerk, and remain with her until the final countdown, not so much to listen to her cross-examining her guests as to watch on the split screen Hubble B's pictures of Eros 2 hurtling towards Earth. Their interest, like that of most other viewers, was masochistic. The asteroid, slowly tumbling and now visually getting closer, had a hypnotic effect on them all.

They would stay with the programme to the bitter end, when they were promised satellite pictures of the actual impact. And then, finally, they would all seek the vantage point at Hafod to witness what was being called a *false dawn* on the southern horizon.

Late afternoon, Craig had phoned his mother from Plas Cefn. It took longer than usual for the connection to be made and for a time he feared that the service had already been terminated, that the whole C-phone company workforce had taken french leave. But he persevered, knowing that the service was fully automated anyway, and his persistence was finally rewarded. The line wasn't good though. Only the odd word and phrase was discernible, but the picture, at least, was clear and he could fill in many of the gaps by reading his mother's tired lips. It was a little after eight in the Californian morning and she had just got up. He could tell that it had been a sleepless night for her, and a tearful one. Hearing his voice renewed the crying but they were now tears of joy, giving sparkle to old and weary eyes.

'. . . so glad . . . Craig . . . last chance . . . voice and to see you.'

'It's lovely to hear your voice as well, mother, and to see you looking so well.' The last bit was a forced lie. In fact, he was shocked to see the deterioration since he'd last spoken to her, three days earlier. 'I can't tell you how concerned I was about getting through to you. But you'll have to speak slowly. There's a lot of static interference on the line and I'm having trouble hearing you. How's Max?'

'He's fine.' The worry that suddenly clouded her face suggested otherwise. ' . . . spoke . . . 'tair yesterday . . . said . . . phone again . . . day.'

'You say Alistair phoned you yesterday? And that he's phoning you again today?'

She nodded. There had to be better reception at her end of the line, he thought.

'From where? South of France?'

Again she nodded, as if too tired to speak.

'When he does, can you please ask him to give *me* a call as well? He's been very good to me, mother, and I'd like to thank him for it. But I just can't get through to him. Hopefully he'll have better luck from his end.'

' . . . glad . . . friends now . . . in touch . . . one another . . . Promise?'

'Yes, I'm glad too that we were able to get in touch after so long, and you can be sure that we'll regularly contact one another after all this is over. He's asked me to join him and . . . and Sue in the south of France and I'll probably take up his offer when things have settled after this business tonight.' The white lies came out effortlessly. 'I'll have phoned you again before going, of course.'

'Yes . . . course.' But the sadness that now filled her wet eyes told him that he couldn't fool her.

They talked aimlessly until the line got too bad for both of them and then they muttered their final farewells. As her face faded from the screen, he saw the tears run freely over her worn cheeks and down to the point of her wrinkled chin. Then she was gone, and he too was crying.

That evening, when he joined the family for supper, he was surprised by Ffion's unexpected smile. The flicker of compassion that he saw in her eyes both pleased and puzzled him and left him wondering. He wasn't to know that she'd overheard much of his conversation with his mother that afternoon and that she'd even shed a few tears herself as she listened to his sobbing.

They ate a frugal meal, none of them showing much appetite. Tristan's reference to *'last supper'* didn't go down well with any of them and when the time came for them all to settle in front of the wall-screen afterwards, he'd disappeared.

'Probably gone for a walk,' Ffion suggested. 'Just as well!'

Sinéad, sensing criticism in her daughter's tone, felt a need to defend her younger child. 'He'll be more worried than he's letting on. Anyway, it's such a clear and warm night, the walk will surely do him no harm.'

Craig thought he heard a throaty 'Huh!' coming from Rees but he couldn't be sure.

Dead on seven o'clock Anita Beuwerk appeared on screen without any of the customary presentation. No special lighting, no atmospheric music . . . nothing other than a bare studio. Dressed in ordinary slacks and loose top and almost devoid of facial cosmetic, she glaringly lacked her usual composure. She looked worn, appeared older.

'Good afternoon, America. Good evening, Europe, and greetings to all our other viewers, wherever you are. The time is nineteen hundred hours GMT, exactly . . . ' She glanced at her wrist-watch as if for confirmation. ' . . . four hundred and thirty one minutes to impact. 'Welcome to *Doomsday Discussion*. Today's programme, naturally the last in the series, comes to you direct from the Glenn Research Center in Cleveland, Ohio. NASA's Eros 2 Command was re-located here two years ago, prior to the enforced evacuation of Houston, Texas, one of the many seaboard cities of the U.S. of A. that is expected to succumb to the impending tsunamis and rising ocean levels.

'I make no apology for our lack of presentation this afternoon . . . this evening.' She made the correction with the hint of a wry smile. 'We are, indeed, struggling to bring you this, our final programme, with what few staff are still available, which is why I would like to pay particular tribute, right at the start, to the dedication and professionalism of Moira Castle, our producer, Ken Boyd, our stand-in cameraman, Buck Zacharia our sound man, Mahmoud Asif our sole technician on site, and finally Joy Albinos and Dannii Prior who'll be manning the switchboard for your calls.' She shifted position in order to give the lone camera a different profile of her face. 'Understandably, most of our resident production crew have chosen to share these crucial hours at home with their families. However, I, Anita Beuwerk, am here to spend the next few hours in your company, provided, of course, that our satellite link holds out. During that time we shall hear the views and thoughts of a number of distinguished guests, amongst them Archbishop John Simpson, Primate of All England, and His Eminence Cardinal Stefano di Cambio from Rome, both of whom, on the stroke of 0200 GMT, will lead us in prayer, beseeching God to spare our world, our civilisation, from extinction. In the meantime, we invite you, our viewers, to phone in, to air your views and your anxieties with the rest of us, during these troubled times. Throughout the programme, we shall all be able to keep close watch, thanks to NASA's Hubble B Space Telescope, on the final hours of Eros 2's long journey as it approaches Earth. Then, when it enters Earth atmosphere we're hoping that its descent will be picked up by NASA's special satellite cameras which will transmit the final seconds before impact. Antarctica, we are told, has fairly thick cloud cover tonight, so we won't be able to witness the actual impact, but we can expect some pretty dramatic pictures of the blast just the same. Much will then depend on what effect the blast will have on our satellite transmission but we hope to stay in touch long enough to give you some idea of the terrifying aftermath in the southern hemisphere and the dreaded tsunamis building up in the southern Pacific and Atlantic Oceans . . . '

They listened in silence as she then made prearranged C-phone contact with representatives of various governments in their respective safe retreats, asking them about their countries' contingency plans for the short-term future. Most of them supported the view that firm policing would be necessary to bring back some semblance of law and order. Some outlined the steps taken by their respective governments to safeguard their countries' national treasures. Viewers heard that the Jewels of the English Crown had been removed from the Tower of London to a secure secret location where they would remain under heavy armed guard, as would the contents of the British Museum and the major Art Galleries, until such time as new permanent repositories could be erected for them. Similar precautions, it was said, had been taken with the ancient papyri and priceless artefacts of the Mediterranean cities. A representative of the White House staff claimed that the United States had completed the transfer of all priceless artefacts, two years previously, to special earthquake-proof galleries at carefully selected locations in the mid-west.

'It has been proposed that, as soon as it becomes physically and practically possible after today's developments, an international commission be set up to analyse the world situation and that that Commission's mandate will be to catalogue all existing food reserves with a view to pooling resources and arranging a fair distribution of supplies amongst the nations. Is such a plan at all viable . . . effectible? How do you respond to the proposal?'

All of them, apart from the U.S. congressman and the representative of the National People's Congress of China, expressed qualified support for the concept, after which an unseemly altercation developed with recriminations from both camps. Anita Beuwerk allowed the bickering to go on for several minutes, in the mistaken belief that it provided a welcome distraction for her anxious audience.

Throughout the talking, the split screen continued to register Eros 2's

163

progress, with the digital milometer in the lower left hand corner showing its distance from Earth decreasing in thousand mile units. For Craig O'Darcy, the whole scene had a magnetic, mesmeric quality. The awesome lunar-like detail now visible on the asteroid, its relentless tumbling approach, made the squabbling of the politicians seem so trivial, so puerile.

'We may as well indulge ourselves. What do you say?' Rees had reached for the bottle of Middletons and three tumblers and Craig sensed an uncharacteristic pessimism and resignation in his tone. In the meantime, Sinéad was fingering her rosary. 'What will *you* have, Ffion?' He knew that she never drank spirits. 'A glass of red wine perhaps?'

She waved away his offer and got up to look out through the window.

They sipped at their drinks in silence, trying not to look at the threat on the screen in front of them. But no matter how hard they tried, their eyes were continually drawn back to it.

'It's such a lovely evening.' Ffion was thinking aloud as she gazed up at the clear evening sky. 'You'd never think . . . ' She felt no need to finish the statement.

The others turned to look at her. Standing, as she was, in the bay window, with the security bars around the outside of it, Craig had the impression of a prisoner resigned to her fate. Rees got up to join her, laying a gentle hand on his wife's shoulder as he passed behind her chair. Sinéad's attempt to smile merely contorted her face. Craig felt the whiskey sting his dry throat.

Thousands of viewers were now either phoning in or e-mailing their comments, virtually throttling the NASA Center's sophisticated communications system. But the opinions being expressed, whether discerning or facile, did little to alleviate the tension for Craig and the others. One e-mailer from Seattle demanded to know why NASA's plans to deflect or destroy the asteroid had been such a dismal failure, another from Scotland wanted to know whether she, in the northern hemisphere, would hear or feel anything at the time of impact. The Center's spokesperson, attempting to reply, was clearly a minion who'd been sent to face the flack. His answer to the first question was garbled and defensive. He talked of the world's finest space scientists having had state-of-the-art technology at their disposal, with no expense spared; he praised courageous cosmonauts who had 'gone hunting' for Eros 2, their mission to position nuclear devices at its tail and so project the asteroid forward, to cross Earth orbit early; and in subdued tones, he referred to the unfortunate malfunction that had sent the European *Icarus* craft veering off course, to shoot aimlessly out into deep space, taking with it not only its nuclear payload but also Mankind's final hope of averting the holocaust. His answer to the question from Scotland was briefer but equally guarded. 'You could well feel a tremor but it's highly unlikely that you'll hear anything of the blast.'

The minutes crept by. Pictures from Mecca showed a few Islamic pilgrims circling the Kaaba, muttering prayers to Allah. In a half-empty Hindu temple in Delhi, priests were offering an ill-affordable goat as sacrifice to their gods. By contrast, Vatican Square was seen brimming with worshippers listening to words of assurance from Pope Paul VII. These scenes were followed by ones of deserted streets in Brisbane and Sydney, New Orleans, New York and Los Angeles, London . . . 'Eerie!' was Ffion's verdict, as she stood with her father, backs now to the window. 'Like something out of Hollywood. Post nuclear war sort of thing.'

The others knew what she meant. The scenes were bizarre and unnerving.

'Do you recall a programme last month, called 'Ultimate Buzz' I believe, that showed the surfers on Tristan da Cunha and Easter Island?' Anita Beuwerk looked drained. 'I have to report tragic developments in both places. It seems that food supplies on the islands ran out almost three weeks ago and that since then literally hundreds of the youngsters have died, either from famine or been killed in brawls. Those who are left are now doomed since their only means of transport from the islands will have to be their surfboards. Ironically, however, they'll be too weak to ride them. It seems that their final adventure – their UB as they so ambitiously referred to it – has turned sour for them all . . .'

'Holy Mary, mother of God! Does she have to be so insensitive?' Sinéad was clearly moved. 'There'll be mothers listening to her! Mothers who have been worried sick about those poor misguided souls.'

'And fathers!'

Disregarding Rees' interjection, she went on, 'Just think how they'll be feeling now, if they're watching this programme . . . as most of them probably are. Sweet Jesus forgive the woman!'

Craig found it difficult to share her level of concern.

The digital LED counters on screen showed 259 minutes and 177,000 miles / 283,000 kilometres before impact. Every crater, every wrinkle on Eros 2's carbonaceous surface had become scars on his mind.

* * *

Simon Carvel was watching the same thing, only on a much smaller screen and with somewhat different thoughts. He'd survive, he told himself. He'd make damn sure of that.

No question about it. Craig O'Darcy's recent visit had given him hope, had given him tenacity, had given him plans. Tomorrow morning, whilst the rest of the world was still reeling in shock, he . . . they . . . would go searching. And then, with luck, he'd be equipped to set off for his retreat in the Chilterns.

How many would he need with him? Two? Three? Two would be enough, he decided. The fewer to share with, the better. Dave would be one. Dave was a must. Dave had a gun! A twelve bore! But who else with him? Not Chris. He was too unpredictable. As was Vince. Tony would be his best bet. Tony, like Dave, could be ruthless. And strong! And he had a wife to fend for. Between them, Dave and Tony would do the dirty. All he'd have to do was lead them to the fountainhead. Granted, he'd never been to O'Darcy's place before, but he had a fair idea of how to get there. Anyway, Dave would know. Tomorrow, he told himself, Craig O'Darcy would have to yield all his saved-up PA rations, either that or die in a foolish attempt to guard them. These were hard times. No room for scruples.

The LED digitals at the bottom of his small screen read *Minutes To Impact: 223. Distance From Impact: 153,000 m / 244,000 k/m*

'Come on, you fucker!' he muttered. 'I'll get the better of you yet.'

* * *

'Tristan! Is that a Welsh name?'

Sinéad and Ffion had just left the room, with the former expressing concern about the whereabouts of her son.

'Yes.' And then, as an afterthought, he added, 'But in this case, no.'

Rees, pacing the floor of the room, sounded so adamant that he drew an enquiring glance from Craig, a look that the old man chose to disregard.

'Can I ask you a question, Rees?'

In response he received a steely stare, as if to suggest 'Depends!' Then he saw him nod his white head.

'When did you leave Pencraig?'

'When I was sixteen.'

'And you came back, when?'

'Getting on for eight years ago.'

166

'And you spent all those years away, where?'

Rees smiled. 'That's three.'

'Pardon?'

'You wanted to ask one, but that's already your third.'

Craig's face reflected his sudden embarrassment and he ran a nervous finger over the break in his nose. 'I'm sorry. I didn't mean . . . '

'Pulling your leg, that's all.' It was a strained laugh. He drained his glass and returned to his chair, keeping one eye on the wallscreen as he reminisced. 'When I left home I wasn't sure where I was headed. Liverpool seemed a natural choice, but I didn't get a job there, so I drifted through a few towns and cities in England. Slept rough . . . that sort of thing.' His eyes gradually became glazed with honest recollection. 'Did that for almost two years. Can you believe it? Two wasted years . . . !'

The self-recrimination was evident, the remorse genuine, in his far-off look.

' . . . When I think back on those wasted years, I feel nothing but shame . . . ' Then, he was out of his brief reverie, his eyes once more alert. ' . . . You only get one life, son, but young people don't seem to realise that, do they? At least I didn't. It's only as you get older that you start regretting the wasted years.' His forefinger began prodding the air in front of him, as he sought to drum his point home. 'When I see young people . . . and not so young people, for that matter . . . sitting on pavements, hanging around shop doorways, begging for euros, it really sobers me and I'm reminded *There, but for the grace of God, go I.* I could have been one of them! A dropout! My whole life could have been spent in squalor, with just a mangy dog for company. Imagine that!' There was a new intensity in his gaze. 'Imagine waking one morning and realising that it's your birthday . . . that you're forty, fifty, sixty, whatever, and that life has passed you by, that you've spent your years sitting on pavements, living on hand-outs from the state and on other people's charity, or lack of it. Just think! A whole life of not striving for anything. A lifetime without ambition; of kidding yourself that you want no part of the rat-race. And then, one day, it hits you square between the eyes that life has passed you by, and that there'll be no second chance. God! Can you imagine anything worse?'

Craig was surprised by the level of contrition.

Eros 2 continued to tumble, and Marilyn – NASA's *darling little bombshell module'* – once more crept into view but only as a silvery blur. The face of the asteroid was also less distinct. Hubble B's automatic focusing system was now struggling to cope with the asteroid's

hypervelocity.
Minutes To Impact: 150 Distance From Impact: 103,000 m / 164,000 k/m

* * *

Tristan returned just before midnight, looking pale and edgy, the tension obviously getting to him. He'd been walking, he said. 'Where?' Rees asked. 'As far as Pencraig Roofing and back.' 'Why there?' 'Why not there?'

Rees was suspicious, Tristan defensive, and Craig embarrassed by his own presence.

He'd noticed the bulge of a C-phone in the young man's hip pocket, and suspected a different motive for his absence. But, with his own apprehension nearing fever pitch, he was in no mood to add fuel to the old man's suspicions. Of late, he'd become very aware of Rees' uncharacteristic distrust of people. *'These are strenuous times, son. You can't trust anybody these days, not even your closest friends. Bear that in mind! And watch your back!'* The intensity with which he'd uttered those words, a couple of days back, had surprised Craig O'Darcy. *'Does that include me?'* had been his joking response. *'Of course not!'* Rees had snapped. *'Otherwise you wouldn't be welcome in my home. I put a lot of faith in my judgement of character, lad, and if I'm wrong about you, then I'll really be disappointed.'*

'I'm going up to my room. I'll watch it there.' Tristan clarified what he meant by nodding sulkily towards the wallscreen.

Craig watched him leave the room and again felt embarrassed by his own intrusion. The family needed to be alone together, he told himself. He could sense it in Sinéad's worry and irritability, in Tristan's petulance. He got up. 'I think I'll go up to Hafod, now.'

'What? Now?' Rees made no effort to hide his surprise. 'I thought the whole point of coming tonight . . . '

Craig appreciated the sentiment. He knew full well why he'd been invited here for supper. Rees hadn't thought it right for him to be alone in Hafod, not tonight of all nights. It was also a comfort for him to see Ffion's face reflecting her father's sentiments. Sinéad, however, merely looked towards the floor and remained silent.

'I'm grateful for your hospitality . . . ' The forced formality of his own words made him smile. 'but best I be there when it happens, I think . . . to keep an eye on my things, just in case.' He knew how weak the excuse sounded but as he spoke he felt his resolve being bolstered.

For a second Rees looked stubborn but then came the look of resignation. 'You're right, I suppose. But you will be able to watch?' He nodded towards the wallscreen. It was his way of referring to the smaller screen that he'd presented Craig with, a few days earlier.

'Yes. No problem. The picture's clear as a bell.' Which wasn't quite true, because Hafod's generated electricity could, at times, be fitful.

'Good.' But Rees didn't sound particularly convinced. 'You'll come down in the morning, though? There'll be things to discuss.' He'd forgotten about their intended visit to Hafod, to watch for the *false dawn*.

As he walked towards his bike and as he heard the front door close behind him, an emptiness, an unfathomable loneliness gripped Craig O'Darcy; a feeling of being naked under the night sky. The sudden screech, from a nearby pine, of a wood pigeon frightened by the roar of the Norton engine merely added to his melancholy.

Before leaving the house, he'd seen *Minutes To Impact: 124. Distance From Impact: 85,000 m / 136,000 k/m* and he'd synchronised his watch accordingly.

The journey around the disused quarry, although familiar to him, tonight took on a surreal quality. Moonlight danced on the pyramidal tips to right and left, skipping from one cold slab of slate debris to another as the bike's climb continually changed the angle of reflection. Deep purple shadows appeared cave-like in comparison, whilst ahead of him derelict buildings were silhouetted like demons' crowns against the night sky.

When he had to climb no higher, he brought the Norton to a halt, so that he could take in the scene. To his left, the level track to Hafod. Ahead of him, in the distance, Pencraig roofs were bathed in the harsh cold light of moon and stars. Gone was the familiar warm halo of glowing amber that street lighting used to radiate. Would he ever see it again, he wondered. 'Probably not,' he concluded sadly.

Below him to his right, mostly in shadow, Pencraig Roofing Ltd stood silent and still. Only a month ago, he reminded himself, the place was a hive of industry supporting a workforce of fifteen hundred local people. Tonight it was nothing.

A quick glance further right, over the interlocking spurs of slate tips, showed him the way he'd just come and he could just about detect in the distance the front bay windows of Plas Cefn peeping from behind the tall pines. It was a scene he didn't care to dwell on and he gave throttle to the bike.

He was glad of Dog's bark to welcome him home but it only

heightened his sense of isolation. 'Come on!' he said aloud, as he unclipped its leash. 'We'll have ourselves a treat. A whole tin of dog food for you and a mug of coffee with a dash of whisky in it for me. What do you say?' He removed the outside doorway panel, unbolted the door proper and they both entered.

Even the briefest of naps was out of the question and he found himself first of all thinking about his mother and then attempting to pray. 'Please God, look after her in the difficult times to come. Spare her and Max, spare Alistair and Sue, spare Rees and his family, spare Ffion . . . ' He stopped. That couldn't be the way to pray, he told himself. Surely, what he'd just done was to talk to himself, and he had to admit that it all sounded ridiculously selfish.

That was when his C-phone bleeped. Taking it to be Rees at the other end, he didn't particularly hurry to answer. 'Hi!' No need even to corroborate his name.

Since no face appeared on screen, he therefore presumed that the caller had no access to a camera. 'Is that you, Rees?'

'Craig?'

It wasn't Rees' voice. It wasn't his pronunciation either. And then it dawned on him. 'Alistair? Is it you?'

'Yes. I've had no end of trouble getting through to you. Tried all day yesterday, without any success. Same today. This was to be my final attempt. Thank God I was in luck. How are you bearing up?'

'I'm glad you called. I had no number to contact you. Where are you? South of France?'

'Yes. We finally made it. Been settled in for over three weeks now. Tell me, did you get the supplies that I sent you?'

'I did, and I can't tell you how grateful I am. There's enough there to bide me over for years I think.'

'Good. Pleased to have been of help, old boy. I gather that you spoke to mother earlier on. I'm glad. It upset her, I think, but in the nicest way possible. She won't die happy, of course, when her time comes, no more than the rest of us will, but at least she's . . . comfort . . . seeing . . . talking . . . two of us.'

The line had begun to crackle. 'Alistair! I'm afraid I'm losing you. I don't know how clearly you can hear me but I'd like to thank you again for the mega favour that you did me. Take care of yourself. Good luck, brother . . . ' He was surprised by the tears that brought a croak to his voice.

' . . . be thinking of . . .who knows, maybe . . . ' The line went dead.

Craig wiped his eyes with the back of his hand, looked at his watch and did some quick mental arithmetic. Minutes to impact – 97: Distance from impact: 67,000. The kilometres he couldn't be bothered with.

He turned on his T.V. wallscreen, for confirmation

* * *

Simon Carvel watched his silent screen. He'd turned down the sound when that Simpson clown in his ridiculous mitre had started grovelling before his god, seeking ' . . . forgiveness for Thy people, sinners all . . . '

'Primate of All England, my foot!' He'd laughed his scorn out loud. Now some *fuck'n Cardinal* in Rome was at it, but without available translation. Total gibberish, he told himself. Again he laughed. Laughing in the face of danger showed courage.

NASA's bottom screen detail had altered slightly. It now read *Seconds To Impact: 270. Distance To Impact: 3,100 m.* Both figures were seen rapidly falling, the miles by fleeting hundreds rather than thousands. Kilometres, presumably, were no longer worth bothering with. Eros 2 itself was just a blur.

* * *

In Plas Cefn, Rees Morgan and family held their breath. Up in Hafod, Craig O'Darcy did the same. Had any of them ventured out, they would surely have noticed the deathly silence that had gripped the outside world. Nature herself had stopped breathing.

Suddenly the screen format changed, bringing a gasp from all of them. Eros 2 vanished and a satellite picture now showed Antarctica as a segment of the Earth's curvature, presumably from a perspective that would detect the radiant and pick up the final seconds of the asteroid's journey. Much of the continent was under cloud but breaks here and there revealed some of the icy wastes, ghostly white in the moonlit dusk.

On *60 seconds* the digital counters disappeared, as did the insets of Anita Beuwerk and the Rome gathering, and the screen now showed nothing but sky, cloud and glimpses of spectral ice. Final countdown had begun. Rees felt Sinéad's nails biting into his wrist. On the other side, Ffion had drawn closer to her father and now held firmly on to his arm. Tristan's knuckles were white as he gripped the arms of his chair. Up at Hafod, Craig O'Darcy was too preoccupied with events to listen to Dog's low fearful whine or to notice its trembling.

171

Simon Carvel lay face down on his bed, with a pillow pressed tight over his ears.

*   *   *

At exactly thirty eight seconds counting, Eros 2 burst into Earth atmosphere like a huge rocket igniting, bringing gasps of wonder and fright from all who witnessed the scene. The satellite camera, having no chance of tracking it closely, remained on long exposure and watched its luminous tail quickly extending as it burnt its way at an awesome rate towards its polar target. As his fingers dug into the worn leather of his chair, as his knuckles whitened, Craig was aware that the briefest of commentaries was in progress, presumably from one of the NASA staff in Cleveland. He heard the words ' . . . now through the ionosphere and into the outer stratosphere . . . ' There was barely time for anything else to be said. Travelling at over eleven miles per second, Eros 2 – now white hot and a far far cry from the grey lump of cratered rock that Hubble B had been stalking for the past six years – took just another four seconds to plummet into an overcast Antarctic sky, dragging its burning residue behind it. Then the whole cloud cover was lit up from beneath, becoming transparent for the merest fraction of a second, before it was whirled away by a rising flash of intense heat and pure energy. And as the whole continent disappeared beneath out-swirling billows of fire, a breathtaking shower of burning rock hurtled skywards. Then the screen went blank. Transmission had been lost, but not before viewers had heard the NASA voice in Cleveland, Ohio, blurt out in whispered tones words that would remain with them for the rest of their lives – 'God help us all! The gates of Hell are now wide open.'

PART 2

'Death is not the worst evil,
but rather when we wish to die and cannot.'

(*Sophocles*)

Chapter 1

'God help us all! The gates of hell are now wide open.'

In one respect, the event was an anticlimax. At least, that's what the viewing turned out to be when, as the mushroom of flame and steam began to form, with burning ejecta bursting through it like spray from some colossal Roman candle, the picture suddenly disappeared, leaving nothing but a screen full of white static spit whose crackle, within Hafod's confined space, took on deafening proportions. Craig O'Darcy, mouth gaping, heart pounding, felt the exhilaration drain out of him, to be gradually replaced by a sense of cold frustration and bizarre disappointment. The greatest disaster in the history of mankind, he told himself, was taking place at this very moment in time but he was being denied the chance of seeing it unfold. For several minutes he remained transfixed, vainly urging the picture to return.

Finally, he became aware of Dog at his side, bristling all over and whining with fright. The noise added to his own tension, heightened his own alarm. Why should the animal be so frightened, he wondered. However intelligent Dog might be, it couldn't possibly comprehend the relevance of what it had just seen on a television screen. Or could it? The more he thought about it, the more convinced he became that the animal quaking at his side was sensing the greater disaster that was unfolding on the other side of the world.

Finally, he got out of his chair but then remained stock still, the soles of his feet feeling at the solid floor beneath him. Was the Earth shaking? Or could it be just his own fevered imagination? His own trembling, perhaps? It had to be the latter he told himself. Slowly he made his way towards the door and swung it open. Behind him, the screen continued to crackle loudly but the unearthly silence of the outside world caught his breath. 'It's after two in the morning,' he told himself. 'You can't expect to hear lambs bleating or birds singing.' Not that there were many lambs left in any case, or sheep for that matter, thanks to the poachers. But neither was there the rustle of breeze through grass or the faint sound of dislodged rubble on a distant tip, noises that were long familiar to him, that were an integral part of his life here at Hafod.

Apart from a few tufts of white cloud away to the west, the night sky was clear, with the moon nearing its full. Everything around him was ethereal. In the distance, the sea in the bay shimmered and he could even make out the white foam as the waves gently licked the beach at Caer Môr, so many miles away. Nearer to him, every rocky outcrop glistened, every blade of tough grass shone white as if covered with hoar frost. And then he thought he heard the earth growl, a barely detectable rumble, deep in its bowels. Instinctively, his eyes turned south, for signs of the *false dawn* that some had been predicting. But there were none. The rumbling was also imagined, he told himself. Had to be! Except that he could still hear it!

Standing there, in the doorway of his remote cottage, taking in the peaceful scene, he found it impossible to accept what was happening on the other side of the world. What he'd just witnessed minutes ago on his small TV wall-screen had been surreal. Something out of Hollywood, he told himself. Imagined! What else?

But then he felt a rubbing against his legs, heard the pitiful moan of his dog as it fearfully sought comfort, listened again to the crackle of the wall-screen in the room behind him, and he knew the reality. Suddenly the loneliness gripped him like a huge black hand and he was filled with a consuming gloom.

*   *   *

Down in Plas Cefn, Rees and family felt a similar frustration, as if they'd suddenly found themselves in a game of blind man's buff. After the months of anxiety and expectation they were now left to wonder how many of the predictions they'd been hearing over the last two years would be substantiated and to what extent the gates of hell had really been opened. The first tsunamis were expected to hit the coast of Britain in eighteen to twenty hours' time. It would take weeks, perhaps months, for any other repercussions to be felt.

'Are we going up to Hafod as planned?' It was Ffion's question, and it was in Welsh.

'We should, I think. Craig must be feeling really lonely up there.'

She looked askance at her father and was angered by the hint of a smile on his lips. 'That's not what I meant, and you know it. If there's anything to be seen in the sky, any sign of the *false dawn* that some people have been talking about, then I'd like to see it. We certainly can't see anything from down here.'

Rees turned to his wife who was mouthing silent prayers as her fingers passed from one rosary bead to another. 'What do *you* say Sinéad? Ffion wants to go up to Hafod to have a look.'

'In the name of Mary, mother of God, I'll not be leaving this house tonight, and nor should you, husband!'

At first, Rees was tempted to make light of her concern but then reconsidered. 'You're probably right . . . as usual,' he added. Then he turned towards his daughter. 'Best not to leave the house unattended, don't you think? You never know . . . ' He was implying that thieves might take advantage of their absence.

'Tristan will be here, won't he! After all, we'll only be gone half an hour at the most. Nobody's likely to come prowling, not tonight of all nights.'

Although her brother didn't understand what she was saying, he still picked up the testiness in her tone. It always riled him to hear the two of them prattling in Welsh. Damned bad manners in his opinion, especially since they were just as fluent in English. His father had never bothered to teach him the language, unlike his mother who had made an effort, at least, to instil some Irish into him, albeit in vain. Back in Boston, where he'd spent most of his juvenile years, Welsh and Irish had had no relevance whatsoever for him. Unlike Ffion, he'd never seen Pencraig, or Wales for that matter, until a few weeks ago, and Ireland was just as foreign to him. He'd stayed on in the States, first of all to continue if not complete his high school and college courses and then to give basketball coaching to junior grade kids. That work hadn't paid well but money was never a major problem; his mother had seen to that. Okay, so the heroin habit had become costly but that was a fairly recent thing, only becoming a problem after he'd arrived in Pencraig, where it was so difficult to lay hands on the stuff. Supplies to the town, spasmodic at best, had now ceased altogether due to the greater demand in the larger towns and cities. He had found a local source of methodone however and that was some consolation. The only problem there, though, was that no amount of cash could buy the damn thing. It had to be barter with foodstuffs and he was finding it increasingly difficult to lay hands on the provisions to bargain with. The situation was frustrating, to say the least. 'One thing's for sure,' he kept telling himself, 'this place won't be seeing me for much longer, no matter what Eros 2 makes of the world.' But his irritation was blinding him to his own naivety. *Where would he go? How would he get there? How would he survive once he got there?* were questions that he preferred to ignore.

'Are you coming or not?' Ffion was half way to the door.

'Yes, alright. Your curiosity will have to be satisfied I suppose.' Rees shrugged at his wife, as if to say 'I've got to humour her' and followed his daughter out, calling over his shoulder as he went, 'Keep the doors locked until we get back.'

*　　*　　*

Standing at the open door of his static caravan, Simon Carvel was laughing humourlessly. 'What a fiasco!' he shouted into the unearthly silence of a moonlit world. 'God! What a fuck'n fiasco!'

Most of the van doors on the estate were open, with their tenants gazing out apprehensively. They'd all watched the televised impact and now felt vulnerable and in awe. Most of them stood looking south as if expecting to see at any moment a maturing mushroom cloud rise above the mountains there. Simon Carvel's irreverent bawling found little or no accord with any of them, not even with the most obdurate.

He'd had plans for tonight but both Dave and Tony had cried off, saying that they needed to be with their wives during these crucial hours. And although he'd poured scorn on their worries, and despite his current public outburst of derision, he was secretly glad that no firm plans had been made because, with the suspense now ebbing out of him, he suddenly felt drained and tired, desiring nothing more than a soft bed to fall on. 'Craig O'Darcy's provisions will have to wait twenty four hours, that's all!' And as he slammed the van door shut, he muttered, 'The gates of hell will open for him alright!'

*　*　*

The Leech made light of the ruts in the path up to Hafod. When it reached the upper level, Rees switched off all lights and proceeded by moonlight. Ffion didn't question his action, which was just as well because her father couldn't have explained it anyway. He'd done so instinctively, almost subconsciously, as if he felt that the Leech's penetrating beams were alien to its new surroundings.

'It's so beautiful up here, dad. So peaceful. It's hard to believe what's just happened.' She was speaking in a hushed whisper. 'What's *still* happening,' she corrected herself.

Her father nodded quietly.

'There's no need to go any further, is there? If there's anything to be seen, then we'll see it from here.'

Rees shrugged. He knew what she was thinking. She was still recalling the mischievous comment that he had made earlier about Craig O'Darcy's loneliness. 'I'll have to take it as far as Hafod anyway. Nowhere else to turn round.' The length of old tramway ahead of them, as far as the blocked-off cutting where the provisions truck was concealed, was bathed in moonlight.

Craig, crouching outside his cottage door, fondling Dog's ears to give

177

it comfort, tensed when he heard the crunch of tyres over uneven ground and glimpsed the burnished grey vehicle, lamps dead, slowly creeping up on him in spectral fashion. His immediate reaction was to retreat and bolt the door behind him, but then he recognised the purr of the Leech's powerful engine. 'It's okay, Dog,' he muttered reassuringly as he felt the bristle and heard the deep growl that had more fear in it than menace. 'They're only friends.'

'Hi, Craig!' There was a hint of a smile on the old man's face as he got out of the car. 'Had to come, to keep Ffion here happy.'

His daughter snorted. 'Huh! Who wanted to come this far, anyway? Not me.'

Craig felt the sting of her words and his sense of loneliness returned, stronger than ever, turning his welcoming smile into a sad one. With the tip of his forefinger he nervily rubbed the break on his nose.

'She wanted to see the false dawn.' Rees, oblivious of his friend's discomfort, was gazing at the night sky to the south. 'Any sign of it?'

Craig turned towards Ffion, expecting to see her looking in the same direction as her father but she was, instead, looking directly at him. Her eyes were moist! But were they any moister than usual? What could he see in them? Was it remorse? Was it compassion? Could it be a mute apology? She looked away before he could decide.

'Just like every other fine night. What do *you* say, Craig?'

'Never expected anything else, actually. It's ridiculous to suggest that we might see the glow of the explosion from this side of the world. Who said that we would, anyway?'

Rees didn't know. Nor did Ffion, who now answered. 'It's been mentioned once or twice on the *Doomsday* series, that's all, and since I never heard anybody suggest otherwise then I naturally assumed that it might just be possible . . . But obviously not,' she concluded, indicating with an embarrassed gesture towards the southern skyline. 'I just wanted to satisfy my own curiosity, that's all.'

'Would you like something to drink? Tea? Coffee? Something stronger?'

Rees looked at his watch. 'At twenty past three in the morning, a cup of coffee would suit me fine.' And his daughter nodded agreement.

They stayed for close on half an hour, during which time the three of them discussed the likely scenario over the next weeks and months, recalling some of the predictions that they'd heard on the *Doomsday* series; expressing concern about some, scepticism with regard to others.

'The tsunamis are our first worry. From what we've heard, they'll start pounding our shores anything between eighteen to twenty hours from now.' Rees looked at his watch and then at his daughter. 'That'll be sometime between five and eight o'clock tomorrow evening . . . this evening rather!'

'Then we'll have to find a good vantage point to watch them arrive, especially if they're going to be as dramatic as they've been telling us.'

'You could come up here, of course. It's as good a spot as any.' Craig looked at each of them in turn. 'A lot of the bay is visible from here, and we'll be high enough to see and to appreciate everything that happens.'

'Appreciate? Did you say *appreciate*?' Her eyes narrowed as she fought back a smile.

He also smiled. 'You know what I mean.' And then, to stress the point and hopefully create an impression, he added *'Ti'n gwybod.'* He hoped that his memory was serving him well, as he recalled the drilling during those early Welsh classes. *Dwi'n gwybod* – I know; *Ti'n gwybod* – you know; *Mae o'n gwybod* – he knows; *Mae hi'n gwybod* – she knows . . . *'Ti'n gwybod,'* he repeated as he saw her smile widen.

'Da iawn*, Craig!' she said, in a way that a teacher might encourage a slow pupil. *'Da iawn!'*

He'd never seen this side of her character before and the experience was warmly gratifying.

Once or twice, he caught her looking around the room, studying her surroundings, and this embarrassed him. 'Very basic, I'm afraid,' he explained apologetically, pointing to the few articles of second-hand furniture in the room and to the worn leather armchair on which Rees was now sitting.

'I like it! Really!'

Her eyes told him that she meant it.

'I'm glad you did it up, dad.' She was referring to the cottage itself. Then she turned again towards Craig, 'And I'm glad that you took up our offer.'

'Our'? he thought. Had Rees discussed the matter with his daughter, all those months ago? Had she had some say in letting him live at Hafod? It would please him if she had.

---

* *Very good*

Chapter 2

By mid afternoon, a huge crowd of Pencraig townspeople had congregated on the slopes overlooking the town, from where they could look down the Arian Valley as far as Portharian in the distance. They also had a fair view of the northernmost part of the Bay of Branwen but the town of Caer Môr to the south-west was blocked out by a series of undulating hills. Close on five thousand had taken to the slopes, many of them children, implying that most families were represented here. But no one would have left an empty house behind, for obvious reasons. The constant chatter underlined the suspense and the tense atmosphere of expectancy.

The higher elevation was giving Craig O'Darcy a wider panorama. He could follow the coastline for miles beyond Caer Môr even, as it curved gently in a south-south-westerly direction, and had there not been a haze on the horizon due west he'd even have been able to make out the shadowy silhouette of Ireland's Wicklow Mountains. Despite his high vantage point however, he was oblivious to the gathering of townspeople below. They were hidden from him by the ridge of the slope that served as their grandstand.

Simon Carvel had no worries about leaving his caravan unattended. Apart from the odd blanket or two, he didn't think there was anything else there that was worth stealing. They weren't even worthy of his concern, he told himself, seeing that he had exciting short term plans to feather his nest and fill his larder. He'd become fed up with having to scrape the odd meal from stealing a rabbit or a chicken, a cabbage or a pocketful of potatoes from someone's back garden. He needed longer term security and he now knew where to find it, who to claim it from. And now, as he made his way towards Summerhill Crescent, where Dave lived, listening as he went to the excited chatter of the silly townspeople who had taken to the slopes, he felt a spring in his step and a new-found youthfulness in his heart.

Dave had to come first. Dave took priority over Tony, simply because Dave had a gun. With a double-barrel pointing up his nostrils, O'Darcy would be in no position to offer resistance. He'd be given the choice of either handing over his provisions or having his kneecap, or lower leg even, blown off.

'Is Dave in?'

'Who wants to know?' The woman in the upstairs window was eyeing him with suspicion. She'd refused to answer the door.

'Tell him Simon Carvel's here. We need to talk.'

'About what?' It was obvious that she didn't much care for the stranger or for his alien accent.

'Just tell him I'm here!' He felt like adding 'you cow!' but thought better of it.

Dave eventually appeared in the doorway and mumbled an apology about being in the toilet. He was a lanky forty five year old with thinning fair hair. His stoop, adopted at an early age at school where he'd been overly conscious of his height, was now further necessitated by the low doorway. He was dressed in baggy light-brown corduroys, supported by a pair of worn braces over a grubby and collar-less grey shirt. He was in the process of pulling on a jacket, threadbare at the elbows. The man, baptised Dafydd Elfed Evans, was known to most of the townspeople, but more as a familiar face than an acquaintance. He owned an old scrambler bike that, on open throttle, had a distinctive roar and, up until a few months ago when fuel became impossible to buy or steal, he could be seen daily, gun strapped across his back, heading for the miles of open moorland above the town. *Riding the range* was how he liked to think of it. Most people knew him to be an incorrigible poacher. He had otter boards stashed away at many of the local lakes, but the water bailiffs, wary of the gun that he always carried with him, had never tried too hard to catch him red-handed at his poaching. Rabbits and deer were never safe either, with him around, and there was little doubt that he'd even been helping himself of late to the odd lamb or two, as less-alert army look-outs had found to their cost. And when he wasn't out hunting, he'd take his .22 rifle down to the refuse tips below the town, where the rats gave him target practice.

'Are you ready then?'

'What? Now? What time is it?' He spoke in deep monotones and with a heavy Welsh accent.

Carvel, in shirtsleeves, glimpsed at his watch. 'Three twenty. We still need to call on Tony.'

'I thought we needed to meet first, like. You know, to discuss what to do. To plan, like.'

'I've already done the fuck'n plannin 'aven't I? All we need do now is go up there and take what we want.'

'But where are we going, like? Where's the stuff being kept . . . you know, the stuff you've been talking about? Who owns it, like?' He seemed hesitant. Reluctant even.

'You'll see. Now hurry up, and try to keep that damn gun out of sight.

You can't walk around with it strapped across your back like that.'

'Why not? Who'll notice?'

He had a point, Simon realised. There might be more people around today than had been seen for months, all heading for the slopes overlooking the town, but the familiar sight of Dafydd to some, Dave the Poacher to others, with gun strapped across his back, wouldn't unduly interest or worry any of them. Incorrigible poacher that he was, he'd never been known to steal from any of them, nor to threaten anyone.

As they made their way towards the new estate where Tony lived, Simon Carvel, struggling to keep up with the long-legged poacher, again cursed his luck at not having diesel for his lorry. What use was an otherwise reliable Mercedes truck, parked next to his static van, if he couldn't move the fuck'n thing? He knew that they'd definitely need transport of some kind to cart away all of O'Darcy's supplies. It was a problem that he'd slept many nights on, without finding a satisfactory answer. His one remaining hope was that Craig O'Darcy would have his own personal supply of fuel. If so, then the plan would be to overcome O'Darcy, tie him up, then take enough diesel down to the truck and return in that for the goods. And if O'Darcy proved awkward, then Dave would just have to deal with him permanently. These were hard times, after all. There were lives at risk, not least his own, and he couldn't afford not to be ruthless. That was why Dave and his gun were a must. But Tony would be needed as well, as back-up. If things turned physical – O'Darcy was no weakling was he? – then Tony was the one to have around. He had the strength of an ox and could take O'Darcy on any day of the week.

'What? Now?'

Bloody same reaction from this one, he thought, irritably.

'I expected some warning. Where are we going? Exactly where is this ready supply of food being kept?' Tony pulled his bungalow door shut behind him

'You'll see.'

Although Dave and Tony had responded in like fashion, any similarity between them ended there. Whereas Dave was rangy and awkward, Tony was squat and well co-ordinated, with dark lively eyes that indicated a higher degree of intelligence.

'Where the hell are you taking us?'

They had just slunk past Plas Cefn and were now on the rough track leading up towards Hafod. Dave knew of the cottage's existence, Tony didn't. Neither of them knew who lived there.

'You'll see.'

For the past twenty minutes little had been said between them, with the lanky Dave, once he'd been pointed in the right direction, setting a brisker pace than the other two could keep up with.

'Has your record stuck or what?' Tony was obviously irritated by Carvel's evasiveness.

'You'll see!'

'How the hell do you know where to go, then?'

'Ah! I have my contacts.' And with a flourish of superiority Simon reached into his pocket, produced a mini-phone and tapped it gently against the side of his nose, implying that Tony was being too inquisitive. 'Trust me!' he added.

Half way up they heard the noise of a car engine behind them and instinctively jumped for the nearest possible cover. Then, from their individual hiding places they peered at the Leech climbing past and watched it until it had disappeared over the brow of the hill above them.

'That was Rees Morgan's LR!' There was an element of concern in Tony's voice. 'I don't want him to see me here.'

'Why the hell not? What's so fuck'n special about him, anyway?'

'There's no way I'm doing anything whilst he's around.'

'Why the hell not?'

'Because I've got a lot of respect for the man. If he's involved then you can count me out.'

Carvel sensed the resoluteness and decided to play his cards differently. 'Okay. So we stick around until this Rees Morgan bloke goes back. But let's find a better hidin' place than this.' And he indicated the ruined buildings above them.

*   *   *

Craig was busily cleaning the Norton, which he'd parked outside the cottage door, when Rees arrived. He'd caught a few hours fitful sleep up to mid-day and had done nothing since but twiddle his thumbs and look for ways of filling in the time. The first of the tsunamis wasn't expected until five o'clock at the earliest and he'd become bored by the waiting and by his own idleness. In retrospect, the decision to clean the bike was a ridiculous one, ridiculous and pointless but, under the circumstances, it served a purpose. Up to now, Dog had lain curled on the warm slate, its sleep a fitful one judging by the constant twitching of its ears and tail. Rees' arrival brought it to its feet.

'Good morning.' The old man had the window down as he brought the Leech to a halt but he made no move to get out of the vehicle. 'Did you catch some sleep?'

Craig took the few steps needed to join his friend by the vehicle. 'Yes, I had a few hours. How about you?'

The rueful smile implied that Rees hadn't slept at all. 'When you get to my age then you don't need it as much.'

'How about . . . the rest of the family?'

'Oh! They slept all right.'

Craig looked at his watch. Rees was early, he thought. 'Are you coming in?'

'No. I've just brought you this.' He produced a bowl of jelly trifle off the seat beside him. 'Sinéad thought you'd like some.'

'That's very kind of her.' But he doubted whether the kindness had been Sinéad's idea at all. Rees' more likely. Ffion's even! 'Quite a treat! I haven't had trifle for . . . well, for donkey's years,' he finished lamely.

'Anyway, enjoy it. We'll all be joining you in . . . ' It was Rees' turn to look at his watch. ' . . . a little under an hour. We'll get here by five. Nothing will happen before then, not if the experts are to be believed anyway. And if there's time, you can clean my car.' He smiled as he turned his eyes towards the shining Norton.

Craig also smiled, somewhat self-consciously. 'It passes the time. Something to do.'

The old man nodded knowingly. 'See you later,' he called, as he turned the Leech in the small space available.

*   *   *

As they listened to the extra-long-base wheel convertible Leech LR returning down the hill, one word came to Simon Carvel's mind – *Diesel!* 'Why the hell didn't I think of him earlier,' he thought aloud, and fingered the mini-phone in his pocket.

'Who? Think of who?'

'Never mind.' He got to his feet and gingerly picked his way through the rubble that had once been the roof of the building. A thick wooden lintel above the doorway, now supporting nothing but air, looked as if it might collapse at any minute, making Simon wary as he passed beneath it. 'Better get goin'. Wind's pickin' up. Looks like the fuck'n weather's goin' to change.'

A stiff wind had picked up but it was a warm one. Above the distant horizon, a bank of dark cloud meant that a cold front with heavy rain was moving in from the south-west.

'Come on! No time to lose!'

The three were now looking along the level stretch of track leading towards Hafod, a twenty foot high escarpment running parallel to it on their left, mountain pasture falling to their right, with the rooftops of Pencraig beyond and the Bay of Branwen in the distance.

'From the information I've had, that's the place we're looking for.'

About two hundred metres away, the stone gable of the cottage blended well with its background but the gleaming bike parked in front was drawing attention to itself.

'Doesn't look much, like!' Dave had hardly spoken since they'd left the town. 'Last time I came this way the place was empty. No windows, holes in roof . . . '

'Well you haven't been this way for quite a while then, have you boyo?' Carvel's impatience was showing and his tenseness was all too obvious.

Tony had dropped slightly behind, his face suddenly a mixture of doubt and concern. 'Tell me, Carvel. Who's house is that? Because if it's who I think it is, then . . . '

'Then what?'

'Then you can count me out.'

'What?' He'd raised his voice more than he intended. 'What the hell do you mean, count you out?'

Tony looked resolute. 'If that's Rocky's place then I'm going back now.'

'Rocky?' Carvel cackled humourlessly but with some relief. 'Who the fuck'n hell is *Rocky* when he's at home?'

'I call him *Rocky*. Some call him *Coach*. Is that *his* house? Is that where Craig O'Darcy lives?' Eighteen months ago, everyone at the rugby club had come to hear about the cottage that Rees Morgan had provided for the new team coach but Tony, for one, had never wondered where that cottage might be. He was quickly making the connection now, though, having just seen Rees Morgan come and go.

'What if it is? What fuck'n difference does it make?'

'It makes all the difference mate. Count me out.' And with that he turned on his heels and left a bewildered Dave and a seething Simon Carvel to watch him go.

*   *   *

185

If it hadn't been for the sounds of agitated conversation, Craig might not have noticed them until they'd got much closer. As it was, he was witness to whatever argument was taking place and he saw the departure of one of the trio, the one who looked very much like Tony the Neck, Pencraig RC's one-time hooker and town Vigilante.

He now watched as the other two debated amongst themselves. The poacher fellow – Dave something or other – was easily recognisable, toting that gun across his back, and there was something vaguely familiar about the other one as well, the one in shirtsleeves, but he was too far to make out. Their mere presence aroused his suspicion. His cottage was far from any beaten track. In the year and a half that he'd lived here, Craig couldn't recall more than half a dozen walkers, at most, taking this route past his cottage. His hand instinctively felt for Dog's head as it rubbed against his knee.

He watched them draw nearer and was on the point of retreating indoors and locking himself inside when he recognised his ex-colleague. Simon Carvel had lost a lot of weight, he realised, and he had the drawn features and empty eyes of someone who was either seriously undernourished or addicted to drugs. In Simon's case, it was probably both.

The chance to withdraw indoors was gone.

'O'Darcy, my old friend!' The greeting was louder than it needed to be and its tone of familiarity both insincere and exaggerated. 'Long time no see!' The two were now within twenty yards of him.

'Simon!' He was watching them closely, feeling distrustful and ill at ease in the presence of the gun. 'What brings you up here?'

'Goin' huntin', with Dave 'ere. Accordin' to him there's plenty of food to be had round this way.'

Craig caught the warning glint of amusement in Carvel's eyes, at the same time noticing that whilst *he* had come to a halt, his partner had continued walking past the cottage gate but had now stopped and turned to face him from the other direction.

His heart was racing. He felt threatened. A low growl from Dog, tugging at its leash, further heightened the tension.

'Thought you might be willin' to help an old friend, O'Darcy.'

He took time to answer. He was more interested in what the Poacher was doing. 'Maybe. What do you want?'

'Some food would be nice. Whisky too, perhaps. What do you say?'

Over his shoulder, Dave was eyeing the strangely blocked-off cutting in the distance. The area was familiar to him; he'd never seen those panels before.

Carvel noticed Craig's concern. 'Worried about Dave, are you? No need to be.' And then he, too, noticed the panels. 'What goin' on over there, then? You wouldn't be hidin' anythin' from us, would you O'Darcy?'

His hunter's instinct must have warned the poacher that Craig was going to do a runner. With one deft swing of the arm, he whisked the strap over his head and in two seconds had the gun pointing straight at its target. He must have thought the action enough in itself because he didn't bother to voice any warning. He looked nervous though, and in a way unsure of himself, a fact that added to Craig's fear.

Simon Carvel laughed humourlessly. 'Dave here's so impulsive, you know. He'd just as soon shoot you as look at you.' Which was actually very far from the truth, because up to now the Poacher had never seriously threatened any man or woman, certainly not with a gun. In fact, the look on his face now suggested that he was more than startled by the role that he was expected to play.

Craig allowed his shoulders to sag, giving the impression of a beaten man. 'Okay then Simon. You've got me over a barrel. I suppose I've just about got enough to share with you both. Some meat and a few other things, and maybe there is one bottle of whisky left.' He was making a point of not looking in the direction of the panelled-off cutting. 'You'd both better come in and I'll see what I can spare.'

Carvel again cackled. 'What you can spare, you say? Sorry, old boy, but you'll have to do a damn sight better than that. What's the old adage at times like this?' He made a phoney show of remembering. 'Ah, yes! Of course! *What's yours is mine; what's mine's my own.* But before we get to that, why don't you tell us what you've got hidden over there.' He was nodding towards the cutting and the hidden truck. 'Dave 'ere seems quite intrigued by it.'

'Safety precautions . . . so I'm told, anyway.' He tried to assume a tone of disinterest. 'Some old quarry workings . . . dangerous apparently.' He was surprised at how easily the lie slipped out.

The Poacher, however, was having none of it. His head was shaking sagely from side to side and Craig realised that he was too well-acquainted with the area to be so easily fooled.

'Ah! It seems that my friend doesn't agree with you, O'Darcy. I wonder why?' And with that he began walking towards the cutting, leaving Dave to keep watch.

With increasing anxiety, Craig watched him go. He knew that the panels had only been intended to hide the truck from afar. They'd been

187

hastily erected and anyone who got close enough would have no trouble in looking past them at what was hidden behind. He saw Carvel pause and, even from that distance, heard his drawn-out whistle. Then, by squeezing between panel and rock he disappeared from view, leaving The Poacher suddenly looking unsure of himself, as if he'd been left to deal with the situation alone.

'If you kill me you'll be in a hell of a lot of trouble, you realise that?'

The barrel of the gun dropped about ten degrees. 'Won't kill you. Just shoot your leg off, if . . . ' He left the threat unfinished. His ungainly height, his stoop, his deadpan face, his hungry look reminded Craig of a cartoon vulture character in a Disney film, only this cartoon wasn't drawing any laughter. He was obviously nervous, and keen for Carvel to return.

'Whatever you do, you're going to be in trouble . . . unless you leave now, of course, in which case I'll forget about the whole thing.'

The Poacher attempted a sneer. He was calling Craig's bluff.

'I've got a lot of friends in this town and, if anything happens to me, then they'll come looking.'

'Who'll know, anyway?'

Although he couldn't be one hundred per cent certain of whom he'd seen with them earlier, or what their argument had been about, Craig nevertheless decided to gamble. 'Tony the Neck for one. He's a good friend of mine, as you've probably gathered by now. And if anything happens to me, he'll tell Rees Morgan, in which case you'll have the whole Pencraig rugby squad looking for you . . . The Vigilantes!'

By now, the Disney Vulture was looking distinctly ill at ease. The part he was having to play was obviously out of character for him. Any other species of animal looking up the barrels of his gun would be dead meat for certain, but shooting at another human being was something else entirely. *Which is why he's keeping his finger well away from the trigger,* Craig reasoned. *And in any case, the gun is hardly loaded. Nobody of his experience would surely be carrying a loaded gun across his back. I could take him on.*

But calling the Poacher's bluff – if bluff it was – wasn't a risk worth taking.

Dave was a loner, not used to dealing with situations where people were involved, which was why he now found it difficult to cope. By shifting uncomfortably from one foot to another, he was enhancing his impression of a Disney Vulture.

'I'm expecting some friends up here any minute now. Rees Morgan for one!' Craig could see the man's growing uncertainty and discomfort.

'You bastard, O'Darcy! You fuck'n bastard!'

As Simon Carvel reappeared, screaming, from behind the partition, his face contorted by rage, Craig felt his heart sink. The Poacher, on the other hand, looked distinctly relieved. Carvel, finger pointing accusingly, was striding angrily back towards them, his indignant shouting being picked up by an ever-strengthening wind, which had the odd drop of rain in it. The dark sky was getting closer.

'No wonder that final posting allocation never arrived. It was you who stole the fuck'n thing!'

Craig looked at him with scorn. He was less afraid of Carvel than of The Poacher. 'Don't be so stupid, Simon! How the hell do you think I could manage that?'

'How should *I* know? What I do know, though, is that the fuck'n government food truck is now parked behind that panelling. You hijacked it, you hid it, you stole my final PA you bastard! If it hadn't been for you I'd now be fuck'n hundreds of miles away from here, well away from this God-forsaken country.'

'I didn't steal your posting allowance . . . yours or anybody else's. That truck . . . that empty truck . . . was sent to me by my brother.' Worth the try, he thought, but Carvel wasn't likely to swallow the half-lie.

'Ha! And why would your brother, whoever he may be, send you a fuck'n empty truck? Tell me that, O'Darcy!' He was now standing directly in front of Craig, his angry spittle being carried away by the wind.

'To live in! He didn't know I had this cottage, so he thought I might need somewhere warm and dry to live.' The lie was effortless but hardly convincing.

'Then let's check this *empty* truck of yours.' Stressing the adjective underlined his cynicism. 'Where's the key?'

'I don't have it.'

'Don't fuck with me, O'Darcy! Give me the bloody key!'

The situation was now serious, Craig realised. If he was forced to give Simon Carvel the key, then he'd be waving goodbye to his stock and to his future. With the poacher's gun to back him, all Carvel would then have to do would be to sit tight and help himself at will to whatever food or clothing he wanted, knowing full well that no one could break into the truck in the meantime. Risks would have to be taken, Craig realised, if he was to turn this situation around. But they'd have to be calculated risks. Would The Poacher, for instance, shoot to kill? Would he shoot at all? At a human being? Craig suspected that he might not; that he'd be reluctant to pull the trigger. But could he gamble his life on just intuition? Was the gun loaded, even? Again he suspected not but again he had to way up the risk that it might be.

'Come on, O'Darcy! I'm waiting! Gimme the fuck'n key! I want what belongs to me.'

'Whatever's inside that truck, Carvel, doesn't belong to you. It wasn't me who stole your allocation.'

'I'm counting to three, then Dave's goin' to blast your leg off. No key, no leg! As simple as that. One . . . two . . . '

Craig took a crumb of comfort from the fact that The Poacher was now looking distinctly nervous and unsure of himself.

'Alright! I'll get you the key.' He'd calculated the risk and now made to turn. Dog's growling and tugging at its leash was his only hope.

'Hold on! Where is it? Tell me where you're goin'.'

He paused and looked Carvel coldly in the eye. 'You want the key?'

'I don't trust you, O'Darcy. Tell me where it is and I'll get it myself.'

'Fair enough. It's sewn into the dog's collar. Help yourself!'

The Essex man stared at the bared teeth of the animal and the bristle on its back. 'Very fuck'n funny! Now get it and give it to me.'

Craig had noticed that Dog was more preoccupied with The Poacher, standing some five metres away, than with the man who was doing all the shouting. It was smart enough to realise where the real threat was coming from. Large drops of rain, the start of a heavy shower, were now falling..

'Come on! I'm gettin wet! If you want to keep both fuck'n legs . . . '

Slowly, Craig bent over the dog, using some of his body to conceal what his hands were really doing. Two yards away, the Norton waited on its stand, keys in the ignition.

That was when the sky really opened up. The dark curtain of rain that had been creeping in from the south west had finally arrived and was now closing tightly around them, making their world suddenly dismal and dark and very wet. Huge raindrops pounded the roof of the cottage, danced along the length of a now lacklustre Norton and turned every surface stone into miniature fountains of spray and steam. Carvel cowered as he felt his thin shirt become quickly saturated. The Poacher stooped even lower and struggled to pull together the lapels of his coat, to keep the rain from running under his collar. The movement sent the gun barrels pointing skywards at the very time that Craig released Dog from its collar. 'Get him, Dog!' he quietly urged and the animal duly obliged, throwing itself straight at the man who reeked of the blood of wild creatures.

Craig didn't wait to see what ensued. In a leap he was astride the bike, feeling the cold slippery saddle wetting his buttocks. Feverishly he groped for the key. The engine fired, roared angrily and, with Carvel screaming wildly and The Poacher busily fending himself against Dog's unexpected attack, he gave the bike throttle. The stand sprang back into place as the rear tyre chewed the wet ground and then he was off, fighting to control the bike as it half-skidded its way past Carvel and out onto the uneven track. Head well down over the handlebars, to present as small a target as possible, he splashed and bounced through the gathering puddles as he struggled to put distance between himself and The Poacher's gun.

An eternity of seconds went by before he heard the first of the barrels being discharged. He expected to hear the whistle of pellets and the stinging pain as some of them found their mark but when they didn't come, and when a safe distance had opened up, he began to feel concern for his dog. Then came a second blast. If The Poacher had harmed Dog . . . ! But now wasn't the time to think up ways of avenging himself.

When he reached Plas Cefn, he found Rees, Sinéad, Ffion and Tristan sheltering under the front porch, dismally studying the wet grey sky. They showed surprise when the Norton skidded to a halt on the tarmac, next to the Leech LR, and when a drenched and distressed-looking Craig O'Darcy hurried towards them.

'Craig! Anything the matter?' Rees Morgan showed concern. Instinctively he looked at his watch. Ten minutes to five. 'We were about to come up to Hafod, only the rain delayed us. Has anything happened?'

Craig composed himself before answering. They couldn't have heard the gunshots because of the noise of the rain, he realised. He quickly recounted what had just taken place and how concerned he was about his dog. Before he'd even finished, Rees was stepping out into the rain. 'Come on! The two of us are going up there, now.'

'They've got the gun!'

The old man waved away Craig's concern. 'I know him. I know Dafydd. He won't use it. Not on me. Nor on you either.'

'In which case, I'm coming as well.' And as she spoke, Ffion, head bowed by the weather, was running after them towards the Leech.

Craig followed and then heard Sinéad and Tristan coming up behind.

*   *   *

Simon Carvel knew that they had very little time to take what they wanted out of the cottage. O'Darcy wouldn't be long before coming back with help, which meant that they'd have to hide the stuff somewhere safe and not too far away, and return for it later. The more he thought about what had just happened, the more he wondered what might be stored in the government truck in the cutting, what might have been his, then the more frustrated he became. He blamed Dave for the failure.

'Couldn't you have taken out the bike, or somethin? Blown off the fuck'n wheel or . . . or . . . ?'

The Disney Vulture scowled at the criticism, his stoop becoming even more pronounced as he did so. 'I had no chance did I, like. That mutt came at me like a bloody whippet. Bit my arm the bloody thing did!' He first of all pointed to the tear in his coat sleeve and then pushed it up to show the blood and the teeth marks.

Carvel muttered unintelligibly and turned towards the cottage, throwing another wistful glance as he did so towards the hidden truck in the distance. 'Come on! Let's see what O'Darcy's left us with.'

After a quick inspection of the chest freezer and of the pile of boxes with the saved-up rations, Carvel was delighted to discover three full bottles of scotch. 'Right! Let's hurry, before he comes back with help. There's no way we can carry everythin down today. We'll have to hide most of it. Any ideas where?'

The Poacher gave the problem some laboured thought before nodding sagely and pointing south in the direction of the cutting and beyond. 'Old hut near slate tip.'

'How far?'

Again came the ponderous mental calculation before deciding. 'Quarter mile, probably. Not much more, like.'

'Right! So let's go. Start with the boxes! . . . Bugger this rain!'

The boxes would take at least three trips to remove, and Carvel doubted whether they had enough time before O'Darcy returned with reinforcements. He also doubted his own strength. Weeks of starvation had sapped his energy and left him frail and without muscle.

He was approaching the cutting on his second delivery, his hair and clothes dripping wet and his numbed arms raised to keep the heavy box on his head balanced, when he heard the protesting whine of the Leech climbing the hill somewhere behind him. Dave, somewhere ahead, had already lapped him and was on his third run. The noise sent Carvel scurrying breathlessly to get beyond the cutting and out of sight.

* * *

By the time they reached Hafod, twenty minutes or more had elapsed since Craig had made his getaway. There was no sign of either Simon Carvel or The Poacher but there was no Dog either to welcome them. Craig found its mangled body where it had fallen, one shoulder blown away by the close-range cartridge and the continuing flow of blood profusely staining the wet ground.

Craig felt Rees' hand grip his arm. The others were still in the car, sheltering from the rain that was now abating. The hand then began to pull gently in the direction of the cottage and Craig allowed himself to be led indoors. Ffion soon joined them.

'Did they get much?' The old man was pacing the stone floor in obvious anger. 'They didn't stay long, did they?'

Craig threw a disinterested look around the room. The boxes of provisions, that had been piled in the corner of the room, were gone and vaguely he wondered how two men could have carted so much stuff away in such a short time, but he was too gutted about the loss of his dog to dwell on the question. He walked over to the freezer unit. That was still full.

'They must have been quick!' Rees strode quickly through the door and out onto the rough track outside, to peer down through the wet gloom. But there was no movement anywhere on the acres of rough pasture between him and Pencraig in the distance. 'They'll pay for this!' he growled as he returned indoors, aware that Sinéad and Tristan, from inside the Leech, were watching him go.

'I wouldn't worry about it Rees. There's plenty of food left.' If there was any paying back to be done, he thought, then it would be Craig O'Darcy's revenge and no one else's.

'To be sure, it's stopped raining at last.' Sinéad was joining them, as was Tristan. They both looked around them, surprised no doubt by the spartan conditions of Craig O'Darcy's everyday life.

'In which case I'll go and bury my dog.' He stopped when he realised that he had no tools to dig with.

'We'll take him into the old workings for now,' Rees suggested sympathetically. 'I'll find a proper box later, to give him a decent burial . . . '

Craig, still rather dazed, saw Tristan's smirk.

' . . . Have you a blanket or something in which to carry him?'

For answer, Craig rolled up the rug that he had in front of the fireplace and without a word, for fear of his voice cracking, he went outside. Rees followed him, leaving Ffion to gaze sadly after them and Tristan to sneer.

Between them, they wrapped Dog's bleeding body in the rug and carried it into the cavern where Craig had his firewood and drums of diesel stored. There they found a dry shelf of rock and laid the bundle to rest there.

'He gave me the chance to escape, Rees, and I now feel as if I betrayed him. I had no right to turn him loose on them.'

'Nonsense. A faithful dog will gladly do that for its master. Just think! It might be you lying out there in a pool of blood. Anyway, just bear in mind what's going on in other parts of the world.' He hoped the comment would put things into better perspective for his young friend.

They returned to the cottage to find Ffion and Tristan arguing but the quarrelling ended abruptly as they entered. It was obvious that Tristan had said something objectionable, probably about the fuss being made of a dead dog.

'Right then! Now shouldn't we be doing what we came up here for? Shouldn't we be looking out for that great big wave that they've been promising us? I've brought a couple of pairs of binoculars. They're in the Leech. I'll get them.' And with a glare at his son, Rees went outside, leaving the others to follow. Craig chose to lag behind for a few minutes, to compose himself.

Chapter 3

It was after seven o'clock and the crowds overlooking the town of Pencraig had dwindled to a mere thousand or less. Most had got tired of waiting for the arrival of the spectacular tsunamis that had been predicted and had gone home, surprisingly disgruntled by the non-event. Now a rumour was circulating that it had all been a massive hoax by the Americans, even the impact itself.

Up at Hafod, they were taking turns at keeping watch but by now, they too were becoming increasingly discouraged. Not that they, more than anyone else, wanted the great devastation to happen, but the months . . . years . . . of hype had reached a climax of fearful anticipation that needed to be appeased.

Since the cottage could offer little in the way of refreshments, Sinéad and Tristan had returned to Plas Cefn for supplies of tea, coffee and biscuits. It was only after they'd gone that Craig ruefully remembered the truck and its almost limitless provisions. Now they were all, with the exception of Ffion who was outside on watch, dispiritedly sipping at their tea or coffee and occasionally thinking up small talk that would have been better left unsaid.

'Seven twenty!' It was Rees' turn to look at the clock. 'What say we give it another ten minutes? If nothing has happened by then, then I suggest we all go down to Plas Cefn for supper. It's getting murkier and the wind's picking up again, by the sound of it.'

'In which case I'll go and take over from my sister until then.'

Craig involuntarily winced as Tristan's broad American accent cut through the room's oppressive atmosphere just as the sudden burst of a police siren might disturb a funeral service at a roadside cemetery. As he watched him leave, flame-coloured hair bobbing with every step, he was struck – not for the first time – by the incongruity within this family that had befriended him. Sinéad – Irish to the hilt; strikingly attractive even in her mid-fifties; clever but always feigning otherwise: Rees – years older (seventeen or eighteen, Craig guessed) than his wife; Welsh to the core but without a drop of Welsh blood in him; exuding a healthy self-composure; possessing considerable entrepreneurial skills and clarity of thought and vision; a figure who personified success and who commanded respect almost to the point of envy: Ffion – highly intelligent (a Maths degree, first class, from Oxford testified to that, as did her command of five languages); surly and morose though, often to the point of rudeness . . . but perhaps a little better of late; fervidly Welsh and up until recently on a personal crusade to save a dying tongue that wasn't even hers, by right; suffered personal tragedy three years ago: lacking feminine pride (judging by her unfashionable dress and frequently unkempt hair) but nonetheless attractive, in a way different to her mother: Tristan – new kid on the block; unmistakably American in speech and dress; moody, disgruntled and showing signs of increasing frustration and probable drug addiction; not likeable and not wishing to be, Craig thought.

He shook his head and smiled ruefully to himself. The family was an enigma; he'd just have to accept the fact.

'Dad! Mam!' Ffion's shout sounded like a breathy gasp that seemed to fill the outside world. *'Brysiwch!*' Come on! Quick!'

Craig was first out, Sinéad last. Tristan was already there, alongside his sister, staring in utter disbelief towards the south-west and its distant horizon. Except that the horizon, as they had known it, was no longer there.

'Do you see it?' She was in awe.

The overcast sky had brought an early dusk. It was no longer raining but a strong wind had blown up, plaintively whistling over the ridge behind them. The faint smell of sulphur tingled their nostrils.

For a second or two, Craig couldn't make out what he was seeing in the distance. His immediate impression was that a snow-capped range of mountains had dramatically risen out of the sea, forming a solid barrier right across the Bay of Branwen and stretching away towards the Irish coast. But the fancy didn't last. What he was seeing, as his eyes focussed, was a frightening wall of water sweeping up the bay.

'Holy Mary, mother of God!' Sinéad clutched at her son's arm.

The others remained in stunned silence, family pressing together in their fear while Craig stood slightly behind, looking over Ffion's head, and feeling strangely isolated and alone.

As it rapidly swallowed the miles of open sea, the giant wave seemed to be ever-growing in height, remorselessly devouring the coastline into a cauldron of boiling foam, the likes and magnitude of which none of them had ever before witnessed.

'I can't hear anything.' Tristan was thinking aloud, his voice a frightened whisper. The crashing waves, he thought, should be audible despite the crying of the wind in his ears.

It took an eternity of seconds for his sister to provide the answer, in equally hushed tones. 'It's travelling maybe faster than sound!'

Almost before they could realise, Caer Môr in the distant dusk had

---

* *Hurry!*

been completely enveloped, town and castle swallowed by the swirl of crashing surf that fringed the ever-towering wall of water. Then the full rage and roar of the sea assailed their ears.

A faint wail of distant horror told them that the watching crowds above Pencraig had also heard, had also seen.

'My God!' In his long life, never had Rees Morgan witnessed such a display of Nature's anger. From the safety of a helicopter, he'd once watched Etna erupting, and before that he'd been lucky enough to survive a South Carolina hurricane that had taken a motel roof from over his head, but what he was seeing now was even more awesome.

Despite the fact that they were miles away from it, they all gasped as the tsunami drew level with them, cresting at well over two hundred and fifty metres, Craig reckoned, and curling forward to pounce and to ravage. For the merest fraction of a second, they were looking along the whole length of it, along its foaming ridge as it stretched into the gathering dusk, and Craig, despite his awe, recalled the would-be surfers of Tristan da Cunha and Easter Island and realised the total absurdity and naivety of their intentions.

The finger-like peninsula, sweeping westwards towards and beyond Aberheli, stood directly in the path of the wave and they all held their breath in fearful anticipation. Then, as they watched, the sea between wave and shore suddenly disappeared, sucked in and devoured to give the monster even greater height. Its roar was deafening, its appetite insatiable.

And then it struck.

Portharian, a ghost town these past few weeks, disappeared under the thrashing mass of turbulence, swept away like dust under a giant broom. Mile upon mile of land, as far as their eyes could see, disappeared beneath the raging white surf, and Aberheli too was gone.

'The gates of hell . . . '

Craig couldn't be sure whether it was Sinéad's or Ffion's whisper but the words were well-timed he thought. Hell had, indeed, broken loose. What they were now witnessing was a global accident unprecedented, unparalleled in man's history. No human being had ever before seen devastation of this magnitude and lived.

And now an offshoot of the wave was thundering up the Arian Valley towards them, a huge demented torrent stripping the slopes clean of their vegetation. Centuries old oaks, survivors of storms and forest fires, were being ripped effortlessly out of the ground and used as bullets and battering rams on all before them. Rocks, weighing several tons, were being hurled forward like mere lumps of polystyrene. It was a game that only gods – or devils! – had the power to play.

A heavy warm drizzle began to fall, only it wasn't drizzle at all but spray being carried over the miles by the wind. Relentlessly, the churning tide swept up the valley in a scene reminiscent of something that Craig O'Darcy had seen as a child in a Hollywood disaster movie, when the great Hoover dam, seven hundred feet high and almost twice as long, had been blown to smithereens by a terrorist nuclear device. Ogling in wonder in his cinema seat, he had watched the liberated waters of the Colorado River cascading through the Black Canyon to wreak dramatic havoc on an unsuspecting Las Vegas city, where U.S. senators and the president's doomed son were gambling at the tables. 'But that was Hollywood!' he reminded himself. 'This is real!' A scene being acted on the screen of life, with himself and Rees and Ffion and the rest of mankind as mere bit-players in the action.

Time stood still as they watched, in stunned silence, the whole valley being ravaged by waters that were now laden brown with churned-up earth and littered with flotsam of torn branches, tree trunks and an indescribable array of household debris. The violent ebb and flow in the wake of the initial assault was sending a succession of waves to pound the slopes, causing further landslips here and there to compound the disaster. The little group, clutching at one another in their fear, felt as though they were peering into a boiling cauldron that was barely large enough to hold its bubbling stew.

'Thank God!' A nail-biting eternity had elapsed and Rees was realising that the flood had finally peaked. 'Another two hundred feet higher and it would have taken Pencraig as well.'

The peninsula in the distance, at one time virtually submerged under the foaming, seething waves, was now reappearing in part, as dots of little dark islands that were once the summits of its highest hills.

'And would the worst now be over?' Sinéad, voice subdued, was searching her husband's face for an answer.

'For a time, maybe. Nobody can tell for . . . '

'No, Dad! No!' Ffion was staring into the gathering gloom, her agitated voice being swept off her lips by the strong wind. 'There's another one coming!'

The second tsunami was smaller than the first and broke up earlier as it hit the backwash of the first. Even so, it was enough to send another tide of surging foam over the low-lying peninsula and to cause further violent activity in what had once been the Arian Valley.

They witnessed three in all that evening, each getting progressively smaller. Then, when it became too dark to see, they turned for home, dispirited and in shock. It was within a few minutes of a quarter past nine.

'Join us, Craig! You can sleep in Plas Cefn tonight . . . '

'Plenty of room,' Ffion urged.

But Craig sensed Tristan's quick glance at his mother.

'That's very kind of you but I think I'd better stay here.'

'It's not a time to be alone.'

'I'm more than grateful for the offer, Rees, but if those two decide to come back . . . ' He felt no need to elaborate.

'I doubt whether Dafydd will bother you again.'

'Dafydd?' And then it dawned on him. 'Oh! You mean Dave? The Poacher!'

'I don't think you'll be seeing him around again.'

Craig got the impression that Rees had something in mind; an intention, perhaps, to warn The Poacher off.

'I'm more worried about Carvel, actually. Anyway, I intend to sort that problem out myself . . . tomorrow.'

'Do you think that's wise?' It was Ffion's voice but since he couldn't see her face in the dark, he was unable to decide whether the question had been prompted by concern or derision.

'Wise or not, I intend to sort it out.' His voice was cold and calculating. He still remembered the mutilated body of his dog.

*   *   *

Simon watched the first and second tsunamis from the roof of his caravan, whilst at the same time struggling to stay upright in an almost gale-force wind. Although he'd only been able to carry a handful of O'Darcy's stuff down with him, he was still wary of thieves, which was why he wasn't going to leave the van unattended. There was also the distinct possibility, of course, that O'Darcy himself might come looking. From his rooftop vantage point he could keep an eye out for both of them, O'Darcy and thieves alike and, if danger threatened, he'd have enough time to climb down and lock himself safely in.

He and Dave had had to return home by a circuitous route, to avoid being spotted from above by O'Darcy and the others, and they'd had to leave the bulk of the stolen provisions where they'd hidden them, in the ruined hut near the slate tip. The plan was to go back for them at the first

199

possible opportunity but the trouble was, he needed Dave to guide him there. And that was the reason for his irritability now. He didn't trust The Poacher, any more than he trusted anyone else. 'What's to stop the bugger helpin himself to the stuff?' he kept asking himself. 'He could be up there, even now, loading the food . . . my fuck'n food! . . . into sacks.'

The lingering suspicion agitated him, made him edgy and more bad-tempered than usual. Short of going back up the mountain in the gathering gloom, there was absolutely nothing he could do. And even if he did try, he doubted whether he could ever find the exact spot where the stuff had been hidden.

His concerns were soon forgotten when he saw the first of the tsunamis. Because of the rising ground to left and right of the caravan park, he could only look due west, towards the Bay of Branwen in the distance, and the estuary of the River Arian with the peninsula beyond. It was a tunnelled view. Caer Môr and the southern bay were hidden from him. As was the Arian Valley itself, thanks to some other vans and buildings that were restricting his view.

The chilling wail from the slopes above the town, barely audible against the wind, and the sudden crashing sound of water way to his left, were his first warnings of the tsunami's arrival. Fighting to keep his feet in the strong wind and feeling the warm drizzle whipping his face and probing his thinning scalp, he craned his neck and peered into the murky distance. He could smell the brine and the seaweed. Despite his growing apprehension, he'd always doubted whether there'd be much to see. All along, he'd been derisive of the 'exaggerated' predictions of so-called experts. But now the tension had finally got to him. Even Simon Carvel was now renouncing his cynicism.

The wail might have warned him but it certainly didn't prepare him for what was to come. In the split second that it took, he glimpsed the wave, and then saw Portharian and most of the visible peninsula beyond disappearing under a crashing wall of water and white foam. He could only gape in utter bewilderment at the suddenness and at the scale of what was happening. A whole town, a whole peninsula way into the gloom, engulfed by the one wave . . . a devouring monster of a wave that was now turning the distant scene into something ironically resembling the snowy wastes of Antarctica.

'Fuck'n 'ell!' was all he could mutter.

Simon Carvel fell to his knees on the caravan roof, stunned and horrified by the sight. Somewhere behind him the faint wailing and groaning continued. He couldn't see, as others could, the destruction now being wrought on the picturesque Arian Valley.

He remained mesmerised for many minutes, oblivious of his drenched clothes and barely moving except to combat the fierce wind. Eventually, he got back to his faltering feet and was on the point of climbing down off the roof when the thrashing sound of the second wave reached him and a new turbulence filled the distant bay. He watched as the slowly emerging coastline once more disappeared under a new deluge that was pounding and pummelling its way inland, its fizzing and seething clearly audible over the miles that stood between them.

For the time being, the cache of stolen food and the fear of Craig O'Darcy's revenge were forgotten.

Chapter 4

It was a night of fitful sleep for Craig O'Darcy, full of little nightmares. Simon Carvel and The Poacher featured in every one of them, as did the bleeding body of his dog. The last and most vivid had him on a surfboard, riding the crest of a great wave that was forever growing under him until he could touch the clouds. Far beneath him, small and insignificant, Carvel and the Disney Vulture scurried like two Lilliputians, weighed down by cardboard boxes laden with food. But there was no sign of Dog and he was distraught. And then the wave was collapsing and he was falling, falling into the frothing waters of the Arian Valley. And as he plunged and sank, and kept on sinking, the water that was drowning him turned red and he couldn't understand why. And then, Dog's bleeding body drifted towards him and he suddenly knew what had coloured the waters. He was swimming in Dog's blood!

He woke sweating and rolled off the bed. Five to six! The cottage door was wide open, just as he'd left it, and the stone floor inside was still wet from the rain and the salty spray of the night before. It wasn't raining now, though, and the wind had died down.

He knew why he'd left the door open. He'd half hoped that Carvel and his gun-happy friend might return to threaten him again, in which case he had every intention of calling their bluff this time and beating the two of them senseless. And if they weren't bluffing? Well, how much did he have to live for, anyway?

Shirtless, he went outside to see the extent of the destruction. There'd probably been more tsunamis during the night, he imagined, each one smaller than its predecessor.

The morning was dank and grey and he felt the warm humidity caressing his skin. For six o'clock in the morning, it was unnaturally warm, he thought, even for midsummer. The sky was overcast but didn't threaten rain. He took the few steps necessary from his front door to reach the track and looked down on a sea of white mist stretching almost as far as the horizon. Even Pencraig had been swallowed by it. It was like looking down from an aeroplane on a bed of unbroken cloud.

'Inversion of temperature,' he muttered, trying to recall the cause of this climatological phenomenon. Was it warm air being held down by colder air? Or the other way around? The latter, he decided, as his thought process became clearer. Cold air trapped under a belt of warmer stuff, keeping the mist to a set level. But nothing that a bit of sun or daytime warmth couldn't disperse. He'd have to wait until then to see what devastation there had been and whether the tide of destruction had receded.

He turned to go indoors again. On the path, where he had dropped it yesterday, lay Dog's tether, twenty feet of it curled and discarded, and wet with yesterday's rain. One end was still tied to its rusty peg near the cottage door, the other, with its collar clip, lay lifeless. Craig now picked it up and fingered it nostalgically until it became just a blur through his tears. First duty today would be to get a pick and shovel so he could dig Dog's grave. Second duty would be to find Dog's killers.

*   *   *

The mist lingered until mid-morning, by which time the day's rising temperature had dispersed most of it. In the meantime, Craig O'Darcy had honoured his first duty and was now taking in the distant scene as it gradually unfolded. Agitated voices on the breeze faintly told him that Pencraig people had returned to the slopes above the town to satisfy their own curiosity.

The sight was worse, more disturbing, than he'd even feared. Ten miles away, where Portharian had once flourished, there was nothing but a restless sea. The hill that the little harbour town had nestled up against, was now an island; a bare marker to where the port had once stood. Running west and south from that point, the coastline had changed beyond recognition, inundated in part, rocky and bare in others where soil and vegetation had been so violently eroded. But what really dismayed him was the state of the once-picturesque Arian Valley. Apart from the very upper ridges of the valley sides, not a tree nor a square metre of greenery was to be seen. The whole valley was a dismal brown with outcroppings of bare rock where none had been visible before, all rising out of the muddy waters of the valley floor. No dark green pastures there, as in the past. No lazy, meandering river. Nothing but a restless lake of mud licking at the valley sides, and looking like a nicotined finger pointing eastwards out of the Bay of Branwen.

The scene resembled a huge, drowned quarry and as he took in the reality of what had happened, of what had changed, Craig O'Darcy's sense of disappointment was replaced by a deep melancholy. The feeling of loneliness returned, like a black mist over his mind. He liked his solitude, yes, but this was something else. What he was looking at now was complete desolation. What he felt was utter despondency and forlornness. Why, oh why had Nature so ravaged herself?

*   *   *

Rees Morgan didn't expect his C-phone to be working so he wasn't really disappointed when proved right.

Craig had been down early to borrow a pick and shovel from the Pencraig Roofing site and Rees had left him to it, knowing that he wouldn't want company whilst burying his dog. He'd go up to Hafod later, he thought, to view the devastation, when the mist had cleared. Right now he had his own work to do.

Having failed at the third attempt to use his C-phone, he climbed behind the wheel of the Leech LR and made for town. Before setting off, he'd had to wipe a matting of leaves and twigs and blades of grass off his windscreen, reminders of the destruction and the strong winds of the night before.

His mission was clear to him. To warn off the two men who had raided Craig O'Darcy's cottage and shot his dog. Dafydd Evans, The Poacher, he could deal with, he felt sure of that, but the Englishman was an unknown quantity. He hadn't taken to him from the very start; had marked him down even then as a potential troublemaker. But the fact that his judgement had been one hundred per cent correct was no consolation to him now, though.

His first priority was to find somebody to accompany him as back up. He'd done his thinking during the night and he'd made his choice. Tony the Neck, Pencraig RC's one-time hooker, would be ideal for the job in hand. And the fact that he knew where he lived made things easier. Eight minutes later, and engulfed by the thick cold mist, he was knocking on the door of Tony's dormer bungalow.

From an upstairs window, Tony the Neck gasped as he recognised the Leech parked outside. Quickly he soft-footed downstairs in time to catch his wife before she could answer the door.

'I'm not in!' he hissed. 'Gone out! Say anything but *don't* tell him I'm here.' And with that he retreated to the top of the stairs to listen.

'How are you, Dianne? Tony in?'

She couldn't have shown more surprise had the king of England himself been standing there.

'Oh! Mr Morgan, sir! I didn't expect . . . ' The *'sir'* was spontaneous and tinged with genuine respect.

She was plump and pretty, and Rees liked her. She had an open, honest face. He smiled. 'Is he here?' he again asked.

'Tony? Um! . . . No . . . uuuh! . . . He went out . . . um! . . . earlier.'

The *'Uuuhs!'* and the *'Ums!'* spelt nervousness and a lie and he wondered why.

204

'Any idea when he'll be back?'

'Um! . . . Afraid not. He didn't say.'

'Oh! Pity. Tell him I called.'

Perched heavily on tiptoes at the top of the stairs, Tony the Neck listened to his own heart pounding and wondered guiltily how Rees Morgan had come to know that he'd been with Carvel and The Poacher the day before. Dianne heard his sigh of relief as she clicked the door shut.

'What was that about Tone?' And when he didn't answer, 'What did Mr Morgan want?'

When he told her, she too looked worried.

* * *

Craig O'Darcy had his jaw firmly set as he mounted the Norton and kicked life into its engine. He knew what he had to do but didn't know where to start, whether with Carvel or else The Poacher. If the latter, then how would he counter the gun? That was his biggest worry. Last night, he'd been so incensed by the callous way that his dog had been killed, that he'd planned all forms of revenge on the two of them. Now, however, in the cold light of day, things looked different and he was having to reconsider his intentions. One thing was for sure, though! The shit would have to be well and truly scared out of Simon Carvel. He'd seen the truck, knew what it contained! And he'd be thinking of ways of getting his hands on it. Craig knew him well enough to realise that he'd come looking again.

Yes, Carvel had to be settled, but not only that. What they'd stolen would also have to be retrieved! Not because he, O'Darcy, was short of provisions himself, but because neither Carvel nor The Poacher should be allowed to profit from what they'd done.

'Yes, I'll get my stuff back from the bastards!' But his resentment suddenly disappeared under a wave of conscience. 'And I'll give it to somebody else who needs it.' The decision made him feel better.

He'd just passed Plas Cefn and entered the main road when he noticed a solitary figure appearing out of a lingering pocket of mist and walking up the hill towards him. When he got close enough to recognise him, curiosity and suspicion made him brake and pull up.

'Tony! What brings you up here?'

Tony the Neck coloured as he detected the note of distrust in the question. 'Hi, Rocky! Fact is . . . ' But he didn't know how to express the *fact*.

'Up here yesterday as well, weren't you?'

'Oh! You saw me then!'

'Yes, I saw you. Their guide, were you, Tony?'

The Neck, looking distinctly uncomfortable, now started to protest with some righteous indignation. 'That's not true! I didn't know where you lived. Not a clue! Honest!'

'But you know now.'

'Yea! Dawned on me when I saw Rees Morgan coming and going. When I realised it was your place, I wasn't going to have anything to do with them, so I left them to it. And that's the truth!'

'You left them to it! And they stole my food and shot my dog. Thanks, Tony! I owe you.'

The sarcasm didn't go undetected and The Neck's colour deepened, his face adopting a hangdog expression. 'Hell! I'm sorry, Rocky. Honest! It's just that I thought that if I walked away, then they'd do the same.'

'But it didn't happen.'

'No.'

'What now?'

'What do you mean?'

'Why are you here now?'

'Oh! I see what you mean. Fact is, I was on my way up to apologise to you and to Rees Morgan.'

'Rees? Why Rees?'

'Well, he knows doesn't he? You told him.'

'And how would you know that, Tony?' Craig was certain that he hadn't mentioned Tony's name to Rees Morgan, or to anybody else for that matter.

The team's hooker again fidgeted and shifted his weight from one foot to another. 'He called at my house earlier . . . um! . . . That's what my wife said, anyway. I was . . . um! . . . out at the time. Anyway, I was thinking I could help in some way. Make up for what I did, like.'

'What you didn't do, you mean.'

'Yea, I suppose so. So where are you going now, then?'

'What's it to you, Tony?'

'You're right. None of my business. It's just that I thought that if you were hoping to get your stuff back then I could give you a hand.'

'No, I'll deal with it. How did you get mixed up in it, anyway?'

'Dave . . . You know! The Poacher! . . . introduced me to Carvel. Said he was a friend of yours . . . You know how it is. Common acquaintance . . . that sort of thing. I just didn't think that . . . '

Craig suddenly felt sorry for The Neck whose remorse was undoubtedly genuine. 'It's all water under the bridge now, anyway, so forget it.' And with a curt but friendly backhand tap on Tony's upper arm, he gave throttle to the bike and left him there to wonder whether he should still go looking for Rees Morgan or not.

* * *

It proved a frustrating morning for Rees. When he called at The Poacher's house and asked to talk to Dafydd, he was told that he'd left the house at least an hour before and that she, Janet, had no idea when to expect him back. 'Always out, he is. Never know where he goes to or when to expect him back. Done nothing wrong, I hope, Mr Morgan?'

Rees had to restrain a smile. To his knowledge, Dafydd Elfed Evans – Dave The Poacher – had never done much right! 'Just ask him to come up and see me, Mrs Evans. He knows where I live. He also knows that there are things we have to discuss, sooner or later.'

Reluctantly, he turned for home. It wasn't often that he failed to accomplish what he'd set out to do but, for now, dealing with The Poacher would just have to wait. Without back-up, he didn't think it wise to confront the other one.

* * *

At ten thirty in the morning, Simon Carvel was already into the whisky that he'd brought down with him from Craig O'Darcy's place. He relished the sting of it in his throat. It invigorated him; fuelled his incentive. Okay, so maybe it aggravated his peptic ulcers, but what the hell . . . ! Life wasn't meant to be a doddle. He lifted his glass in a mock toast – 'Cheers, O'Darcy! Here's to more of the same' – and then laughed without humour.

The reference to *more of the same* brought the other two bottles to mind, the ones he'd had to leave behind with the rest of the food, up in the South Quarry ruins. There'd be a lot of stuff going to waste there unless he . . . they . . . collected it soon. Trouble was, only The Poacher knew the exact spot to go looking for it. He, Simon, didn't. So what was to stop the thieving bugger from helping himself at will?

The thought brought on another fit of restlessness and he decided to go looking.

* * *

Through the thinning mist and the curtainless window of the static van, Craig O'Darcy watched him get to his feet and make for the door. It struck him how haggard and scrawny his ex-colleague now looked and it made him wonder what he could have been living on these past few weeks. Stolen, whatever it was, he concluded wryly, frowning as he did so, aware that his level of compassion wasn't at an all-time high.

He'd left his bike far enough away so that Carvel wouldn't be alerted by the purr of its engine. He now quickly closed the gap between himself and the caravan door so that when it was unlocked and swung open, and Simon appeared on the top step, Craig was there to confront his ex-colleague.

'Fuck'n 'ell! Where did you come fr . . . ?' He'd jumped back in fear but Craig had him by his scraggy neck even before he could finish his question. Slowly he began to throttle him between forefinger and thumb and watched dispassionately as the pale frightened cheeks turned pink, then red and finally a shiny purple. It was only when the eyes started to roll that he finally let go, pushing Carvel's bony frame away from him and onto the table which immediately collapsed with a loud crack, sending its load of dirty crockery crashing to the floor, with Simon tumbling after it. Craig saw him look at his hand and at the sudden flow of blood where he'd been cut by a broken plate.

'Get up, you bastard!'

But the Essex man had no wish to get to his feet only to be knocked down again. 'Go . . . steady . . . O'Darcy!' he croaked, struggling to breathe.

'Steady? You steal my food, you kill my dog, and you want me to go steady?' The anger was genuine but he was also putting on an act for full effect. A half step forward sent the frightened man scurrying backwards on his back side, clattering through more broken crockery as he did so. 'Where's my stuff, Simon? You tell me now or I'll crack your skull like I would a boiled egg. I mean it!' A raised fist accompanied the threat and Carvel crossed his bloodied arms over his face to protect himself against blows that didn't arrive.

'I don't . . . know, . . . do I? You'll have . . . have to . . . ask Dave.'

'Don't piss around with me, Carvel! I know where that came from.' He pointed towards the bottle of scotch that had been his, twenty four hours earlier. 'And those!' He indicated the empty tins of beans and fruit cocktail that adorned the top of an already filthy butane gas stove.

'That's all I . . . I brought down with me . . . Honest!' His voice was still hoarse as a result of Craig's savage grip but his breathing was now less laboured. Then, on impulse, he decided to confess to the whole truth, as it suited him. 'Plus three or four more tins in the cupboard . . . I couldn't carry more than that, O'Darcy, . . . and that's God's fuck'n truth.'

'None of your blasphemy, you lying sod! So where's the rest of it?'

'You'll have to ask The Poacher. Honest!' His face was slowly returning to a more normal colour but it was still flushed. On each side of a rather conspicuous Adam's apple, the imprints of Craig O'Darcy's forefinger and thumb stood out like painful weals. 'It's still up there, somewhere . . . Some old quarry building, that's all I know, but don't expect me to take you there. I couldn't.'

It was pretty obvious that he was telling the truth. Craig, nevertheless, raised a threatening finger to warn him again. 'I'm finished with you, Simon. I helped you. Gave you food. Even some of this!' He got hold of the three-quarter-full bottle of scotch and slipped it into the deepest pocket of his leather jacket. 'I'd even have given you more, if you'd only asked for it. But now . . . ' He was speaking through clenched teeth. ' . . . now you can go to hell!'

Stopping at the door, he turned. 'If I ever see you or your friend near my place again, I'll know why you're there. So be warned! If I have to, I'll settle the two of you, once and for all.' He hoped that his show of pent-up anger would convince Carvel that this was no empty threat. A white lie wouldn't go amiss either, he thought. 'Just remember this! Your poacher friend isn't the only one with a gun, and don't think that I'm likely to forget what happened to my dog.' With that, he turned, rattled the steps with heavy feet and strode purposefully into the thinning mist, in the direction of his parked Norton Jaguar.

When he eventually found where the Disney Vulture lived, he got the same sort of message that Rees had had a little earlier. Dave had left home over an hour and a half ago and she didn't know when to expect him back. 'What's he done, like? Why do you want him?'

'Just tell him that the man who lives up in Hafod has been looking for him. He'll know who it is. And tell him that he'll be seeing me again, only he won't know where, or when.'

He knew she was watching him go and that her unanswered questions remained etched on her face.

* * *

Later that day, Rees came up looking for him.

'Good news! I know where your stuff is hidden . . . at least, most of it.

So let's go and get it!'

He didn't bother to ask where the old man had got his information. He merely assumed that The Poacher had admitted to what he'd done and that Rees had dealt with him accordingly.

Seven or eight minutes later, they were standing, heads bowed, in a hut that had walls of slate slabs and a low roof that had partially collapsed.

'One box missing!'

'Yes. He admitted as much. I let him keep that much, if that's okay with you.'

'You let him keep it?' Craig sounded incredulous.

'Well, I thought that that would be the tactical thing to do, seeing that you're not likely to go short.' He was, of course, referring to Alistair's truckload of generosity. 'That way he won't be bothering you again. You can take that from me.'

He wanted to tell Rees that he'd sooner *have* the Disney Vulture come looking again. Simon might be the treacherous instigator but it had been The Poacher, after all, who had pulled the trigger on Dog. He'd already settled with Carvel, now the other one had to have something coming as well.

'You want to carry these back now?' Rees laid a hand on the pile of three boxes.

'Don't know.' Nor did he care much. 'I thought I'd give them away.'

The old man didn't show any undue surprise. 'To anyone in particular?'

'Not really. Anybody who needs it, I guess.' And then a thought struck him. 'Tony the Neck will get some of it.'

He didn't bother to explain why nor did Rees ask.

Chapter 5

Summer drew to its close but the weather stayed warm throughout September and the best part of October, during which time a number of smaller tsunamis pounded the coast. National and international communications had virtually broken down, due mainly to the failure of the energy services. There were plenty of power stations still capable of generating electricity but so many pylons had been brought down and underground cables affected by the giant waves and by rising sea levels that the National Grid was no longer operational. Nor was there a ready supply of gas to any of the regions.

Craig had gone up with Rees in the Humming Bird to survey the extent of the devastation and the scene had sobered the two of them. Not only did they find all the estuaries inundated but coastal areas in general had been badly decimated, stripped clean of their vegetation and soil cover and now had salt water lapping over them. Craig estimated that sea level had risen by perhaps three or four feet and that it was still rising. He was reminded of the German oceanographer's prediction on the *Doomsday Discussion* programme – 'anything between seventy and eighty metres', that's what Von Pappen had said – and although Alistair, his brother, had protested vehemently on that same programme, and had used words like 'alarmist' and 'ridiculous' and 'nonsense' to discredit the professor, he had nevertheless admitted later, albeit privately, that the prediction wouldn't be too far off the mark. In which case, Craig quickly calculated, as he now looked down on an unfamiliar North Wales coastline skimming by, the current level hadn't yet reached anywhere near von Pappen's minimum! The predicted long months of precipitation – rain, hail, snow – were yet to come, whilst the Arctic ice-cap, already sitting in a bath of relatively warm water, was slowly but surely melting.

In the course of their conversation the evening before, Craig had repeated what Alistair had told him about Wales becoming virtually an island in the wake of all the tidal activity, at which Rees had become quite agitated and had declared an interest in surveying the border with England, which was why they were now following the North Wales coastline in the direction of the Dee estuary and staring numbly at ghost towns that had canals for streets.

'Escaped the big waves, though.' Rees was shouting to be heard above the whine of the rotor blades, as they circled what had once been the funfair town of the north. 'Llandudno, Colwyn Bay and now Rhyl! But at least, they're all intact . . . as far as I can see, anyway.' Apart from upturned cars and smashed store windows, the only visible destruction was to the large funfair, sitting almost on the promenade at the western end of the town. There, the Big Wheel tilted precariously at an angle of fifteen to twenty degrees off the perpendicular, whilst the ribbed frame of the roller coaster was nothing more than a jumble of metal sitting in shallow brine.

'They haven't had any big waves here, have they?.'

'More sheltered than our coastline,' Craig offered as explanation. 'High tide now, though!' He was surveying the wide strip of coastal lowland that now looked more like paddy fields in the wet season. 'It'll probably retreat as the tide goes out.'

But Rees was shaking his head in disagreement. 'I doubt it!' he again shouted. 'A lot of this land is no higher than sea level,' 'There's been trouble here in the past with high tides. The sea defences have had to be rebuilt here more than once, over the years, otherwise the sea would have claimed this lot ages ago.' With a wave of his hand he indicated the thousands of houses and bungalows that now lay half submerged in trapped sea water. 'Things won't ever be the same again, though, will they.'

It was more statement than question, and Rees was right, Craig thought. Things weren't going to improve, of that they could be certain.

As they approached the Dee estuary, Rees gave the Humming Bird more height and Liverpool's dockside edifices came into view in the distance, clustering around the familiar landmark of the Liver Building. A deserted, water-logged Wirral Peninsula was an indication of its uncertain future, proof that the rising waters would be claiming all of it before long.

'Can you take the controls?' They were turning inland and the old man wanted the respite to look around.

Craig duly obliged and pointed the Humming Bird's nose towards the ancient city of Chester, now seemingly afloat on a huge flood plain that extended for miles and miles into the heart of England.

'He was right, wasn't he?'

'Who?'

'Your brother. Didn't he tell you that the Cheshire Plain would go? . . . '

Craig nodded but remained silent.

' . . . And this is just the start! We'll be seeing much higher levels than these.'

In twenty minutes, the ancient border town of Shrewsbury came into view, much of it standing in what could only be described as the flood plain of the River Severn.

'How far do you want to go, Rees?'

'The whole hog. As far as Gloucester if need be. I want to see just how well-informed that brother of yours really was.'

The further south they got, the greater the devastation that they witnessed. The normally fertile lands of the shires of Worcester and Gloucester were nothing more than a hideous sea of mud, as far as the eye could see. It wasn't only the orchards and the hedgerows, the clumps of deciduous woodlands and the fields of wheat, that had been swept away, but farm buildings, villages, whole towns even, had virtually disappeared overnight, just as they'd seen happening to Caer Môr and Portharian.

Neither of them was inclined to talk. The scale of the destruction had them in awe. It was Craig who finally broke the silence, speaking as if to himself. 'Alistair wasn't far wrong, was he?' And then louder, 'It must have been terrible here.'

The old man nodded sadly. The stump base of a tower and the expanse of mud-filled ruins in the distance convinced him that the city of Worcester and its majestic cathedral had also fallen victim to the power of the sea. 'Take me home, son.' He looked drawn, defeated.

Later, as they flew a diagonal course over the Cambrian Massif, they felt relief at seeing a semblance of life as it had been. Little white farmhouses squatted in pockets of upland greenery, sheltered by tall autumnal oaks or majestic copper beeches, their very remoteness a safeguard against forays by desperately hungry town-dwellers. Craig noticed that the farmsteads that they flew over had specially erected pens, housing a selection of livestock – pigs, poultry and rabbits in the main, but also limited numbers of sheep and even the occasional cow and calf. 'If anyone's going to survive the bleak years ahead then it'll be these farmers,' he thought.

Invariably, the sound of the Humming Bird brought people running out into the open, villagers to wave and to shout excitedly in the belief that long-awaited salvation had reached them, farmers to stare distrustfully.

They got home in less than half the time of their outward journey. Rees was tired.

Two days later the cold winds arrived.

Chapter 6

Craig O'Darcy had completed his round of nightly press-ups and other exercises to strengthen midriff and neck muscles and had then gone to bed wearing only his underpants. As usual, he'd discarded the solitary sheet because the night was unseasonably hot, reminiscent of the sweaty nights that he and Sally had spent in Rio, three years ago. It had been their last holiday together.

The memories disturbed him, not so much the passionate and frequent love-making to the rhythm of the steel drums of the Mardi Gras outside their window as the little tell-tale signs that their four-year-long relationship was coming to an end. Sally's *post-sex irritability*, as he'd referred to it at the time, had led to a lot of bickering between them, and it was only after they'd returned home, him to Sellafield B, her to Nottingham, that he'd begun to realise why. She'd become involved with someone else, shortly before they'd flown out to Rio; of that, he had now become convinced. He was equally convinced that their sessions of passion in Rio had had nothing at all to do with love, at least not as far as Sally was concerned.

For two hours or more, he tossed and turned on his bed, unable to settle comfortably in any position for long. His body was too warm, too sweaty; his mind too full of Sally, too full of bitterness and exasperation.

He must have dozed off eventually, but it couldn't have been for long because it was still dark when he woke up. Not that that, in itself, meant anything, because with the window shuttered and the panel bolted onto its door frame, Hafod could be dark even at mid-day. What had woken him was the cold . . . that and the dream that had become a nightmare. One minute he was cuddling up to the warm, naked body of a faceless woman who could have been Sally, could have been Ffion, – could have been Sinéad even! – the next he was hugging Dog's stiff body and staring into its cold empty eyes. It was the shivering that had woken him.

Through the open door between bedroom and kitchen-cum-living-room, he could hear the wind filling the chimney stack with a cold, doleful resonance that drowned even the hum of the generator outside. With trembling fingers he groped for the bedside lamp. Ten to seven! Since the discarded sheet offered little comfort, he had no option but to get dressed. The slate floor felt like ice beneath his bare feet.

'Bloody hell!' he shivered, as he pulled-on the paper-thin T-shirt and the green shorts that he'd been wearing the day before. 'What the hell's going on?' Then, on tiptoes, he padded towards the narrow wardrobe that held all his clothes. Fleecy shirt, jeans and thick woollen socks – unimaginable wear just a few hours ago – were now barely adequate against the freezing cold. He rummaged for his winter-training tracksuit and pulled it on over his clothes. Off the top of the wardrobe he dragged the Himalayan-style sleeping bag that he'd last used during the Hornets' pre-season training in Lapland over two years ago. 'I'll need this tonight, for sure,' he muttered, and spread it over the bed.

When he took the panel off the door frame and opened the door itself, the wind slashed at his cheeks and ears, causing him to recoil indoors and to slam the door shut again. A faint smell of sulphur filled his nostrils. Again he looked at his watch; again with a lack of understanding. Just after seven! Late October! Dawn should have broken, he told himself, but it hadn't. Nothing but pitch darkness outside. His watch had to be wrong. But it wasn't! The little digital clock on the windowsill confirmed as much.

*   *   *

Simon Carvel lay huddled in his narrow bed shivering, teeth chattering. Unlike O'Darcy, he'd gone to bed early – What else was there to do? A dark caravan offered no options. He was down to his last four candles and beginning to realise the need for rationing. 'I should have rationed the fuck'n rabbit too,' he'd mumbled, belatedly, before dropping off to sleep, but the stolen little herbivore had been too tasty and his rapacious intestines had had to be appeased. His stomach hadn't been so satisfied for weeks and bodily contentment had, for once, overcome the mental resentment and irritability that was eating at his very soul.

He'd slept soundly whilst a disturbed O'Darcy had been reliving, albeit bitterly, his last erotic involvement with Sally. But then the early morning cold had arrived unannounced and had penetrated the thin walls of the static van much quicker than it had probed the thicker stone walls at Hafod. Unlike O'Darcy, Carvel had no way of knowing what time it was. Not that he cared much. Time was no longer of any consequence to him. In his dreams he'd been tackling a huge bowlful of spiders that kept scurrying off the spoon before he could get them into his mouth. He knew that he had to eat them all, or die. And yet, although they were avoiding him, he could still feel them dancing around in the emptiness of his stomach. Each side of him, The Poacher and Craig O'Darcy had been tucking into platefuls of hot dinners, with a selection of mouth-watering desserts to follow. *Bastards!* he thought. Then he'd woken up. The dream had been so real! 'Fuck'n bastards!' he muttered.

As he clutched at his sides to keep warm, he felt his bony fingers fitting neatly between his ribs. All the clothing that he owned was now piled on him and over him in an effort to counter the freezing wind that was rocking his home and his bed.

He was again hungry and his irritability had returned. He blamed Craig O'Darcy for all the misfortune that had beset him. Somehow or other, that bastard had been able to hijack the very last government delivery and was now sitting pretty; being spared the nightly hassle of creeping into people's back gardens to steal eggs or the odd chicken or rabbit, or whatever little else was still available.

'If it wasn't for you, O'Darcy, I'd be settled in my own house now, with my family for company. And I'd have been gone before those bastards in Portharian stole my supplies from me.' Knowing that his parents had safely moved to the house in Buckinghamshire was no consolation to him. Knowing that his sister and her wimp of a husband had joined them there and were now living in the luxury that should have been his, really galled him. 'You'll pay for what you've done, mate! You'll fuck'n pay!' But uttered through chattering teeth, the threat didn't sound too convincing. If I could only get my hands on some more methodones, he thought, then I'd have something to bargain with, with that Yank.

He hadn't seen Dave since that day they'd gone up to O'Darcy's cottage. He'd called at The Poacher's house many times since, only to be told by his wife that her husband wasn't in. And then, despite O'Darcy's threats, desperation had driven him in search of the ruined hut where he and Dave had hidden the stolen boxes of food. When he eventually found it, however, the boxes were no longer there. At first, he'd blamed The Poacher but by now he was convinced that O'Darcy had claimed back what had been taken from him and that he'd avenged himself on The Poacher for shooting his dog. He might even have done away permanently with him and left his body to rot in one of those bleak mountain hollows. O'Darcy, he thought, could by now be a cold-blooded murderer who'd never have to face justice. The thought incensed Carvel enough to make him forget his discomfort, at least for a brief while.

* * *

'Get up! Help me build a fire.' Rees stood over Tristan as he lay rolled up in a king-sized double duvet, with little more than a mop of ginger hair showing.

216

A muffled grumble was the only reply.

'Come on! Stir your stumps!' Thinking that his son would follow him, Rees made for the downstairs lounge and Plas Cefn's only open grate. As he descended the stairs, he cursed the fact that they no longer had any central heating in the house because all mains electricity and gas supplies, throughout the country, had been disrupted. 'My fault!' he muttered. Five years ago he'd been tempted to install nuclear cell heating, then new on the market, but had been put off by rumours of teething troubles in the system. Then, a little over two years later, when the threat of Eros 2 was made public and when he began to foresee how things might turn out and how crucial the new system might prove to be, he was too late. The offer was no longer available. All the country's plutonium had been earmarked for safe storage and no amount of political or public pressure could get the European government to change its mind.

Wrapped in a wind-proof anorak and with torch in hand, he made his way out through the back door and aimed for the long outbuilding at the far end of the parking area. In the early days of the quarry, this was where the manager's offices had stood and it was here that the quarrymen used to queue at four thirty every Friday afternoon to claim their hard-earned wages. Like so much else on the site, Rees had had the building renovated when he moved to Plas Cefn.

He unlocked the door and the double-halogen beam of his torch picked out the back-up generator. Once he'd got it going, he turned towards a pile of newspapers and magazines that filled the corner of the same room. As soon as he'd heard about Eros 2, Rees had had the foresight to save every bit of paper that he could lay his hands on, until such time when no more was available. He now took down a bundle and made for a second room that was stacked from floor to ceiling with pine logs. After minutes of waiting in vain for Tristan to join him, he returned indoors with half a dozen logs piled precariously between the flat bed of newspapers and his raised chin. He had to return for firewood.

It took time for the logs to kindle properly. In the meantime he'd boiled the kettle on the small propane gas stove, that he'd brought from Pencraig Roofing's canteen, and was now taking two cups of black coffee upstairs, one for Sinéad, the other for Ffion. Tristan, who was still curled up in his duvet, could get up and make his own.

His watch showed eight forty but it had to be wrong, he thought, because it was still dark outside.

It would take another hour at least for the room to warm properly.

The rest of the house was an iceberg since the electric blowers, feeding off the generator, hadn't had time to do their work yet.

*   *   *

By mid-day, most people were beginning to realise what was happening; why the darkness, why the cold.

'It'll be what those meteorologists have been predicting all along.' Sinéad had moved away from the fire and was now peering out through the window into the cold gloom. She could see no cloud movement in a leaden sky. 'Mary, mother of God, protect us! Something up there is blotting out our sun.' Her face, her voice, were full of concern and fear.

'It'll clear.' But Rees' reassurance failed to raise any hopes.

A little sunlight and warmth did penetrate the murk during late afternoon but it lasted no more than an hour and a half before the heavy clouds had again closed ranks. During that time, Craig O'Darcy came down from Hafod to check on his friends. It was ironic, he thought, as he made his way down on the Norton, that he, living where he did and previously with the most basic of lifestyles, should now have a source of energy when most other people no longer had one.

When he arrived at Plas Cefn, he found Sinéad in relatively high spirits, convinced that the worst was over, that the threat had passed. Rees and Ffion, however, were more subdued; Tristan surly and morose. The smell of a meal cooking pervaded from the kitchen. The house was pleasantly warm.

'You've got the generator going then?' The question was rhetorical. 'It must be really cold down in Pencraig.'

It was Rees who answered. 'Yes. I can't get them out of my mind.' He was thinking of the houses that had little means of heating. 'The older people in particular . . . those that are left.' He laid a hand on Craig's shoulder. 'You've a fair idea how many have been dying during these past few months. God only knows what suffering there'll be there now.'

In Pencraig as everywhere else, the mortality rate during the past year had been high, many dying from weakness and hunger, others from illnesses due to lack of medication, and others as a result of vicious attacks from men . . . and women . . . who'd become desperate for food. A system of communication had been established many months ago whereby neighbours kept a watchful eye on one another and reported any fatalities to any one of a dozen members of the burial squad. Everyone realised the importance of having dead bodies removed as quickly as possible. Things were bad enough as they were without the threat from swarms of rats or other wild animals spreading typhoid, cholera, rabies, bubonic plague or other deadly diseases. Many houses no longer had running water and therefore little or no sanitation. Attempts had been made to ration a dwindling water supply but people were in no mood to reason. It was every man for himself and, for many, the law of the jungle now prevailed.

The burial squad worked to a rota, in teams of three, and had a purposely adapted van at their disposal. They were also supplied with surgical masks for protection against disease. For their trouble they were given basic provisions from the reserves that Rees Morgan had held back for contingencies such as this and which were being stored under lock and key in the great metal containers on site at Pencraig Roofing. But even those reserves were now becoming rapidly depleted.

All that the burial teams could do was respond to reports of fatalities and remove the bodies to the chamber vaults in the quarry where they were then piled, coffinless, onto the shelves there. And since the air-conditioning system no longer functioned underground, even the corridors now reeked of rotting flesh. The burial squad's task was a repulsive one but, in such times of hunger, it had its rewards.

'There must have been a lot of volcanic activity somewhere or other.' Craig was referring to the dust-laden sky and there was concern in his voice. He was thinking about California, about the San Andreas Fault and the likely scenario there. He was thinking of his mother and Max in a cold log cabin up in the snow-capped mountains of the Yosemite. Could they still be alive, he wondered. He didn't hold out much hope.

Without a word, Tristan got up and left the room, leaving Craig convinced that it was his own arrival that had prompted the sullen departure.

Rees remained thoughtful and it was his daughter who responded to Craig's observation. 'You think that's volcanic dust?' She had joined her mother at the window and both were now staring at a sky that wasn't quite as dark or as threatening as it had been earlier. 'You're probably right. It's blocking out the sun.'

'You can actually smell the sulphur when you're out there.'

'And did I not say the very same thing?'

'Yes, mother, you did.'

'You'll stay for a meal with us?'

Craig turned to look at Rees, who'd made the offer, but he also glimpsed the quick look of reproach on Sinéad's face. 'No thanks. I've just eaten, actually,' he lied. 'I only popped down to make sure that all of you were okay. Is there anything I can do while I'm here?' He nodded towards the grate. 'Help you carry in some logs, perhaps?'

'Tristan can do that.' The old man sounded brusque. 'It's about time he did something.' The reproachful tone seemed intended for Sinéad but she didn't respond.

'In which case, I'll be going.' As he made his way towards the door, Craig half turned towards Ffion. '*Hoo-il va-oor!**' he ventured.

She half smiled. '*Hwyl fawr!**' she responded, by way of correcting his pronunciation.

Sinéad remained at the window.

The journey back up to Hafod was cold for him in more ways than one.

---

* '*All the best!*'

Chapter 7

That night, Craig O'Darcy slept more soundly than he'd done for several weeks, thanks mainly to the comfort and the warmth of his sleeping bag and to the fact that he'd lost so much rest the night before. His dream was both pleasant and frustrating. He was sitting at Rees' table and the meal before him was sumptuous. But the food was too far from him and, no matter how hard he stretched for it, it still remained just beyond his reach. None of the others was having a problem, though. They were all devouring the feast at an amazing rate, all except Rees who was too busy drumming the table with his fist. And then he realised why he couldn't get at the food. Sinéad and Tristan were pulling the tablecloth towards them, and with it the food. That's why Rees was drumming the table! He was protesting at his wife's unfair tactics.

Craig was suddenly awake without knowing what had woken him. The darkness that engulfed him was icy and he knew that the sky had filled up again; that those leaden clouds had returned. And then the fervent knocking began again and he felt that he was being dragged back into his dream. But this wasn't a knocking muffled by tablecloth! This was harsh and forceful and echoing. 'Good God! Someone's at the door!'

After fumbling for the bedside lamp, he unzipped his warm sleeping bag and hurriedly dressed. By the time he'd got his shirt on, he was at the front door and struggling to open the bolts that held the security panel in place.

'Who's there?' Suspicions had begun to form, making him wary of unbolting the door proper. 'Who is it?'

'Me! . . . Ffion! . . . Please come! . . . Please, . . . Craig!' There was no doubting the panic in her breathless voice.

He had the door open in seconds and she half tumbled into his arms. She was wearing an Eskimo-style parka with a fur-lined hood.

'Thought I'd . . . never . . . get . . . here. Please come.' Her words came out in puffs of vapour.

After slamming the door against the biting cold wind, he supported her towards the centre of the room. 'Calm down. Tell me what's happened.'

She took two or three heavy breaths. 'Someone tried to break in . . . to steal food. Guns! . . . They had guns! . . . Lot of shooting.'

'Good God! Is anyone hurt? Your father?'

'He's been shot . . . And my mother . . . I don't know how bad. Please come, Craig! . . . Dad wants you.'

'Good grief! Any idea who they were?' He was already reaching for his own lined parka and fleecy over-trousers.

'No . . . Didn't see their faces. They started shooting at all the windows.'

Seconds later they were on their way down to Plas Cefn, with Ffion sobbing on the pillion behind him. In one gloved hand she grasped the butt of an old billiards cue that Craig had been keeping as a possible means of protection but which now seemed ridiculously inadequate. Her other arm desperately clung around Craig's waist as the Norton bumped its way over the uneven track. The halogen torch, that had led her up to Hafod, was now stuffed inside Craig's jacket.

'Are they gone?' They were half way down before he'd thought of asking the question.

'Yes. Think so.'

'Who the hell opened the door for them?' He again had to shout.

'No one. They . . . they didn't get in. Bars on windows . . . to stop them.'

'So how was Rees shot?'

'Dad wouldn't . . . open the door for them . . . so they . . . they pushed the gun barrel through a window and . . . and fired at him.' She was still sobbing.

'And Sinéad? Your mother?'

'She was standing at . . . at her bedroom window, I think . . . There's blood. Dad told me to . . . to get you.'

'Where's your brother?'

'Don't know. I . . . I ran to get you.'

For the first time since he'd known her, Craig sensed her frailty. But he also realised that it had taken a lot of courage for her to venture out, not knowing whether the attackers were still around or not, and to find her way by torchlight up to Hafod.

When they reached Plas Cefn, the door was firmly locked, although peppered with shot where the attackers had tried in vain to blast their way in. The steel-mesh-reinforced uPVC, although showing scars, had otherwise been unyielding. Ffion knocked and shouted through one of the broken windows while Craig stayed alert for any attack from behind. Tristan, face pale and frightened, eventually opened for them. He was shivering from cold and terror.

Rees was sitting at the top of the stairs, holding a bleeding thigh, his face a mask of mental rather than physical pain. A trail of blood showed how he'd got to where he was.

'Sinéad!' he shouted at them. 'Help her!'

His wife was lying where she'd fallen, in the bay of her bedroom window, a pool of blood, dull black around the edges, still growing beside her. In stark contrast, shards of shattered glass glistened like diamonds all over the floor and the bed.

Craig immediately realised that her wound was larger and different to Rees'; uglier; flesh more mangled. Different gun, he thought. Rees had been shot with a .22 perhaps, Sinéad maybe with a twelve bore. Closer inspection showed him that she'd been shot in the side, between hip and right breast. In ordinary times she could have been taken to hospital and the wound might not have been considered life-threatening, but he hardly needed reminding that these were not ordinary times. The local hospital had shut its doors months ago, after nursing staff had been scared off by gangs of youths on the rampage for drugs. No surgeon lived locally and he knew that of the panel of four GPs who used to serve the area, at least two had died recently. He also knew that the others, if they were still in the land of the living, were hardly likely to respond to a call out. He had no idea where to find them, anyway.

Sinéad began moaning loudly. Feeling was gradually returning to her numbed flesh. Then an uncontrollable trembling took over as her body temperature dropped. The loss of blood was taking its toll.

'Blankets! Quick!' With most of the windows broken, there was nothing that could be done about the ice-cold draught that was sweeping through the whole house.

It was Ffion who responded. She dragged the double duvet off the bed, shook free the shards and then helped him cover her mother's trembling body. A crippled Rees Morgan, propped up by the frame of the bed, his face blanched with worry and cold, could only stand and stare. Tristan, was even paler. Fear had drained an already gaunt face of all its colour and, standing in the bedroom doorway, wrapped in a thick cream-coloured blanket, he now appeared ghostlike.

'Is there a heater that we can use to warm the room?' Even as he asked it, he knew how futile the question was. But Ffion nevertheless went looking. In the meantime, he kept tucking the duvet around Sinéad's body in a vain attempt to control the shivering. He'd packed a white sheet tight against the wound to try and staunch the flow of blood.

Whilst playing for the Hornets, Craig had been on a number of compulsory First Aid courses. He'd also seen a variety of injuries on the field of play – lacerations, dislocations, fractures, neck injuries, concussions . . . – and had helped to deal with some of them whilst waiting for paramedics to arrive. But Sinéad's condition was way beyond anything that he could cope with and he knew that the others were realising the fact. Worse was knowing that there was no one else, either, that they could turn to.

He got up and joined Rees. Ffion returned, eyes wide and wild, her arms piled high with bed clothing from other rooms. 'For God's sake, come in and close the door behind you!' she irritably ordered her brother as she pushed past him in the open doorway. 'It's impossible to keep her warm in this draught. Better still, why the hell don't you go and look for something to patch up that window?' Without waiting for him to respond, she returned to the hopeless task of keeping her mother warm.

'Not good is it, son?' The old man had aged a lot since the night before.

'It's the loss of blood, I'm afraid. She badly needs a transfusion.'

Rees' stare intensified and a mild excitement gripped him, the excitement of a drowning man clutching at straws. 'It's possible to do that here, isn't it? You can do that, can't you? She can have my blood.'

Craig regarded him sadly. His old friend had probably seen some emergency surgery being performed on TV. 'I might, Rees, if I had the equipment. But there are other considerations . . . other difficulties. For a start, are your blood types compatible . . . ?'

He saw him shake his head, frustrated by his own ignorance, turning the blame onto himself.

'Anyway, Rees, I don't have the necessary sterilised equipment . . . ' He laid a comforting hand on the old man's shoulder. ' . . . and apart from that, she's still bleeding heavily, so any transfusion would be a waste of time, I'm afraid. Let's wait until the bleeding stops, then we'll see what can be done.' He could sense the despair all around him. The room was full of it. 'Now can I look at *your* leg, to see how bad that is?'

When Rees didn't protest, Craig looked up at Tristan who, oblivious of his sister's earlier command, still stood in the open doorway, scared and shivering. 'Get me some scissors and bandages.' And when he saw the lack of comprehension, he added firmly, 'Now! And close that bloody door behind you!'

It took longer than expected for Tristan to return. When he did, he held but a pair of scissors. 'Couldn't find . . . bandages.' He gave the impression that the word was new to him.

Craig impatiently snatched the scissors out of his hand and started to cut the inside thigh of Rees' trouser leg. Underneath was another pair and under that a pair of long thermal underpants, soaked with blood.

Eventually, he was able to study the wound.

'Ah! That's good! Just a flesh wound.'

The bullet had passed right through what little flesh there was on the thin leg, but closer inspection told him that it had also ripped through a muscle. That was what was restricting the old man's movements and giving him so much pain.

Craig tore at one of the sheets that Ffion had brought and used the strips as bandage to stem the slow flow of blood. 'That should do it.' But none of the others took any notice. Their eyes were on Sinéad. Their ears were full of her suffering.

* * *

It was twenty past eight in the morning when Sinéad died. Apart from Ffion's sobbing, the only other sounds were the doleful whistling of the wind in the pines outside and the muffled hum of the generator somewhere at the back of the house. With great care, they'd been able to lift Sinéad onto the bed without inflicting too much extra pain on her, and it was only as the mattress depressed under her weight that she let out a loud groan. Just over two hours later she drew her last breath.

It took several minutes for the family to face up to their loss. Rees spoke first, his voice empty, it's tone robotic. 'You'll help me bury her, Craig.' It wasn't a question.

'You can leave everything to me, Rees.' Even as he uttered the words, Craig was realising the significance of his promise. He was committing himself to the unenviable task of depositing Sinéad's dead body in one of the underground chambers that he'd visited with Rees some months ago. And he'd undertaken to do so alone!

'Thank you. I have her coffin ready. I've kept it safe. Nobody else knows where it is. Nobody except me . . . ' His eyes, like his voice, were vague. Neither of his children had the will to interrupt him. 'I'll show you!' He made to move but with a groan sank weakly back into his chair.

'Leave it for now, dad.' Ffion's eyes were welling up again. 'I'll make us something hot to drink.'

'Why don't we all go downstairs? There's nothing else we can do here.' Craig tried not to sound callous but he felt that he had to escape the funereal atmosphere of the bedroom where Sinéad's body now lay, covered with a single white sheet. He also felt the need to exercise, to help his own circulation. So, since no one objected, he picked Rees up in his arms, like a mother might pick a baby out of its cot, and the two of them led the way down to the lounge where the well-stocked log fire of the night before still glowed beneath a coating of flaky white ash. The room was not warm, though, not with both windows – front and side – shattered.

'Have you any idea who they were, Rees?' He prodded at the embers before gently placing a couple of logs on them. By now, the old man had been put to recline on the sofa and since he didn't see him shaking his head, Craig went on to ask 'Was Carvel one of them? What about The Poacher? Was he there?' This time he did turn in time to see Rees give another shake of the head.

'I didn't see any faces. Didn't recognise any voices.'

'I did, though!' It was Ffion who stepped forward. 'Simon Carvel was there. I realise that now. I'd know his voice and ugly laugh anywhere.'

'He laughed? Why would he laugh?'

'I don't know, do I? . . . But maybe Tristan does.' She turned to look at her brother, who blushed at the cheeks whilst at the same time becoming pinched and even whiter around the nostrils. Craig also looked at him, questioningly.

'Me? For God's sake! How the hell should I know?'

'Didn't you hear him? . . . ' Ffion's annoyance was kindled by her brother's pretence. 'What was it he called out? Something about you owing him. Owing him what, little brother?'

'How the hell should I know?' he repeated. 'I don't even know the guy you're talkin' about.'

She glared at him for a second or two. 'You know!' she muttered accusingly. But with that she turned away.

The lights flickered, went out for a second or two and then came on again.

'I'd better check the generator.' Rees seemed oblivious to the exchange that had just taken place. 'Better make sure there's enough fuel to keep it going.' But he made only a half-hearted effort to rise.

'I'll do it.' Craig blew warm breath into his cupped hands, looked for the halogen torch and then made for the back door.

He was in the act of pulling the door shut behind him when he heard the raised voice. It was Rees' and he was talking to his son.

'If I find that you were in any way responsible for your mother's death, you little shit, then you'd better look out.'

Tristan could be heard protesting but he wasn't very coherent to Craig partly because of his American drawl. Then there was nothing but silence. Craig closed the door with greater care than he would otherwise have done. He didn't want them to know that he'd overheard. As he got to work refuelling the generator, however, he became increasingly convinced that the family had a skeleton in its cupboard.

* * *

Back at 5 Stryd y Bryn, Simon Carvel had to face the wrath of three youths.

'You guaranteed us fucking food!' The eldest and tallest was shouting intimidatingly and waving a .22 Magnum Plus gun barrel under Carvel's nose. He'd delayed the confrontation until they'd reached the shelter of Carvel's new home.

'Yeah!' in unison from the other two, both looking drawn and frail, with eyes deep-set in dark sockets; lips and nostrils as blue as their hands. Their shivering was audible, as was Carvel's, because despite having layers of clothing on, the bitter cold was getting to them all.

Carvel himself was in no mood to back down. The gun didn't frighten him, no more than the wild narcotic look on their threatening faces. He was past fearing, and he, too, was angry. He, too, had been denied. He, too, was desperate. 'Don't you fuck'n blame me, you trigger-happy bastard!' The target of his rage was the one whose numb fingers could barely hang on to the twelve bore. 'If you hadn't shot that woman, he'd have opened the door for us.'

'Who? Your Yankee fucking friend? So why didn't he anyway?'

Carvel answered scorn with scorn. 'What? After Billy the Kid 'ere had shot his mother? Grow up, for God's sake!'

The three looked uncertainly and somewhat sheepishly at one another, thus allowing Simon Carvel to continue.

'I'm tellin you somethin that you should fuck'n know for yourselves, anyway! That Rees Morgan has a whole stock of food stacked away somewhere in that quarry. How else does he pay the burial squads every week for gettin rid of the bodies?'

'I wasn't the first to shoot.' The lad with the twelve bore had adopted a sulky look but none of the others was listening.

'To hell with the food! You said that he had plenty of crack as well.' The tone of voice suggested that the third of the trio was desperate for reassurance.

'Yea, yea! Plenty of that too.'

The sickly-looking lad, by far the weakest both mentally and physically of the three, was, however, unable to discern the lie. And he wasn't to know that, as part of the same deal, Rees Morgan's son had received similar promises from Carvel. The Yank would supply the food, Carvel the methodones. That was the deal! Only there were no methodones, no drugs, for him either.

'But the fuck'n plan's dead in the water now, thanks to you bloody amateurs.'

Simon Carvel had moved from his caravan into 5 Stryd y Bryn the previous evening when the elderly couple who'd occupied the house, were found dead during the first of the cold snaps. There were many such houses now available in the town as the population continued to fall. The secret, however, was to move in as the bodies were being carried out. That way, all the furniture and wood fixtures could be safeguarded against neighbours desperate for firewood. One had to foresee the burial squad's next most likely candidate and be on hand to claim the property when the opportunity arose. Carvel had had his eye on 5 Stryd y Bryn for weeks before its inhabitants finally succumbed to the hardship and the cold.

'If the food's there . . . if the crack's there . . . then we'll fucking get it, somehow or other.' The youth with the rifle brandished his weapon with a new-found determination but heard no encouragement from either of his friends. Nor did Carvel say much. He knew that Rees Morgan and family wouldn't be able to stay long in their big house, not with all its smashed windows letting in the freezing draughts. He had only to wait, but in the meantime he needed to feed himself and to keep warm. For that he would need one of the guns that was currently being brandished before him. Weren't they his by right, anyway? Hadn't it been his knowledge, his know-how, his plan, that had given them the weapons in the first place? He'd known about these three tearaways, who lived on the caravan site, for some time, had even feared being attacked by them, but then he'd decided to use them to his own advantage and, as bait, had promised them drugs.

His original target had been Craig O'Darcy. That way he saw himself killing two birds with one stone – on the one hand, claiming what was rightfully his and, on the other, avenging himself for the way O'Darcy had treated him. But the fact that his ex-colleague's cottage was so remote was a problem in itself, especially now in the bitterly cold weather. Rees Morgan's place was more accessible and probably offered easier pickings. And anyway, he already had a contact inside the house. But they'd still need guns! That was what had made him think of The Poacher. Not that he was going to take Dave Evans into his confidence again, – there was no chance of that – but he had to find a way of getting his hands on the man's guns.

A plan had come to him, eventually, and he'd taken the other three with him to Summerhill Crescent, where The Poacher lived. Once there, they'd furtively stretched trip wire across the front door of the house and two of them had then pelted the windows with rocks before pretending to run away while the other two remained hidden close by. The Poacher had predictably come rushing out of his house, gun in hand, and had been sent sprawling by the trip wire, giving the two who were hiding nearby the chance to get the better of him and to claim his gun. They'd then claimed the second gun from the house. After that, Carvel had given Dave Evans and his wife no further thought. They'd be frozen to death by now anyway!

He had to claim back one of the guns now, though, he realised. He couldn't risk the wrath of three distraught addicts when they eventually found out that they'd been tricked and that the crack they'd been promised didn't exist . . . never had existed. The best approach, he thought, was to take the bull by the horns.

He approached the one holding the twelve bore. 'If you'd just fuck'n waited! The plan was to get them to open the door by threatening to shoot out all their windows. But no, you had to get trigger-fuck'n-happy . . . ' He could see the other mouthing his protest, but he was almost there. ' . . . Once you'd shot at that window, killed that woman, there was no way they were goin' to open for us . . . ' He snatched the gun out of the purple-cold hands, in a show of further anger. ' . . . Was there? Not after you'd scared the shit out of them.'

The lad continued to mumble sulkily, half complaining that he was being unfairly accused and half conceding that his accuser had a point. The fact that he no longer had the gun didn't seem to bother him; at least he could now push his freezing hands deep into his coat pockets.

Carvel now turned on the others. 'Get back here tomorrow. We'll try again then.'

The three left. They'd been dismissed.

Chapter 8

Craig O'Darcy got help from an unexpected quarter to bury Sinéad Morgan. News of her murder had reached town and those who heard, although long-accustomed to untimely death, were nevertheless horrified. There was no couple more highly thought of, more respected amongst Pencraig people than Rees Morgan and his wife and a crime against them was a crime against the town itself.

The news travelled quickly, despite the fact that people were being confined to their homes by the cold weather, by the dark days and by their fear. Many of those who heard were so shocked by the news that they had to let their neighbours know, no matter what else threatened. That Sinéad Morgan, of all people, should have been murdered in her own home, was shocking in itself. That the defences at Plas Cefn, the barred windows and doors, had been breached, was frightening. It confirmed what they already knew, already feared, that no home was now safe, that everyone's food supplies, however plentiful, however meagre, were under threat.

By the time the story had been told second and third hand, the facts had been compounded, so that what Tony the Neck heard was that every member of Rees Morgan's family had been slaughtered and their bodies left lying in the dirt of Cefn Quarry.

'What?' Dianne, his wife, couldn't believe what she'd just heard him say. 'Now? You're going up there *now*? Seven o'clock at night? In the dark? In the cold? To do what, for God's sake?'

'To give them a decent burial. Anyway, it'd be almost as dark if it was mid-day.' Tony's voice lacked conviction. He didn't fancy going, any more than his wife wanted him to go, but his decision had been instinctive and his resolve now needed to be strong.

'The burial squad will do it. It's their job, Tony.'

He laughed cynically. 'When did the burial squad last go out? Tell me that!'

'*I* don't know, do I, Tone? You're one of them! *You* tell *me*!' The recrimination in her voice reflected her panic.

'My team hasn't been called out for five days, Dianne. Nor has any of the others, as far as I know, what with the cold and the fact that the van has frozen solid and is no longer serviceable.'

Since she already knew the fate of the van, she couldn't argue the point. Instead, she stood in silence and watched him pulling a thick jumper over the one that he already had on. Then he went for his fleecy-lined anorak and a pair of gloves, and finally the black balaclava.

'So what can *you* do, all on your own?'

'Don't know yet, do I? But I'll feel better after I've tried. Where's the torch?'

Twenty five minutes later he was standing breathless outside Plas Cefn, gazing up at the broken windows within their cages of steel bars. *Eerie*, he thought. *Looks more like an empty prison than a home.* All the more eerie because two of the rooms were still lit. Lights in a house of death seemed incongruous and he felt loath to go any nearer. And then he noticed the bike. Rocky's Norton Jaguar! No sign of Rocky himself, though. Had he been here when it happened? Had he, too, been killed? Fearfully, Tony the Neck approached the front door, his heart leaping each time he felt clusters of frozen chippings crunching beneath his feet. He told himself that he was trembling because of the cold, not because of fear.

'What the hell do you want?'

He'd reached the door and the sharp voice, so close to him, really sent his blood coursing. It had come from the dark window to his right.

'Rocky? Is that you?'

'What do you want, Tony?'

There was no escaping the tone of suspicion but the face remained hidden in darkness.

'Is it you, Rocky?' When no answer came, he continued, 'Heard, I did, about what happened here. Thought I could do something.'

'Like what?'

'Give them a decent burial, I thought. Nothing wrong with that, is there?' He suddenly felt irritated at having to justify an act of compassion. 'Why the hell are you hiding, anyway?'

Gradually, Craig O'Darcy's face appeared out of the shadows and pressed up against the bars. '*Them?* Who were you going to bury, Tony?' The suspicion was still there.

'Mr and Mrs Morgan and the others.'

'Others?'

'Ffion and her brother. Someone said they'd all been murdered. Is it true? Tell me it's not!'

'I think you'd better come in.' And with that, Craig went to unlock the door.

*   *   *

After being directed by Rees, the two of them took the Leech to collect Sinéad's coffin from a small locked room at Pencraig Roofing. It was made of shining white uPVC with deep purple padding inside. There were four others exactly like it in the stack, each one bearing a name. Rees' was there, as was Ffion's, as was Tristan's, as was . . . Craig stared in sudden shock as the beam of his torch picked out the name of CRAIG O'DARCY.

'Weird!' Tony was at his shoulder. 'Didn't you know?'

'No. No idea.'

'Must think a lot of you, though. Must think of you as one of the family, I'd say.'

His words put things in better perspective and Craig felt the shock receding.

Although they could easily have carried Sinéad's coffin manually between them back to the house, neither of them fancied the walk by torchlight. It would have been spectral to say the least – a gleaming white coffin borne by two dark-clothed bearers, one tall and muscular, the other squat and robust. *Burke and Hare stuff!* Craig thought ruefully. *I'd do it though, if there was any chance of Simon Carvel being around to see it. The sight would really scare the shit out of him, and I'd like that.*

They then used the Leech to take Sinéad to her final resting place. Despite the air-tight glass doors on each of the prepared caverns, the stench of death filled their nostrils as soon as they opened the double steel doors into the underground corridor and sent them both rushing for the cubby holes where the face masks were kept.

'Bloody hell!' Craig's muffled voice echoed away into the eerie distance. 'I thought those glass doors were supposed to be air tight?'

Tony shouted back, 'They are! But those chambers are now full. For the past month or so we've been having to lay bodies in the other chambers . . . in the unprepared ones. No doors at all on those! That's where the stench is coming from.'

A sudden squeak out of the darkness ahead told Craig that the rats were at work. He felt his flesh creep and he shivered in disgust. 'For God's sake, let's get this over with.'

The shelf reserved for Rees' family was just inside the entrance to the No. 1 Vault Chamber. Even by torchlight, it took them no more than five minutes to deposit Sinéad's coffin and to lock the glass doors behind them. Then they were out again in the open air, their faces being whipped by the cold wind.

'Thank God! I don't want to go in there again in a hurry.' He felt no shame in admitting his revulsion, in showing his fear. 'It can only get worse. And God only knows what it's like in the town if the burial squad's no longer taking the dead away, what with the rats and everything.'

Tony the Neck climbed into the passenger seat next to him. 'At least the cold weather is freezing the bodies and keeping them from rotting. Wind-chill in winter makes it much colder above ground than it is in there. You probably know that.'

'Yes. Rees mentioned it more than once.' He wanted to ask '*But what's going to happen when the weather improves?*' but refrained. The idea didn't bear thinking about.

When they arrived back at Plas Cefn, Ffion and Tristan, at their father's insistence, had amassed a liberal supply of foodstuffs and clothing for Tony, as an acknowledgement of the family's gratitude, and although he protested loudly at what he called their 'excessive generosity', it was a very happy Tony the Neck whom Craig O'Darcy delivered home in the Leech, minutes later, to be welcomed by a wide-eyed but equally happy Dianne.

Before making his way back to Hafod, Craig and Tristan collected two rolls of thick plastic sheeting from one of the Pencraig Roofing sheds and then Craig bullied the brother and sister into helping him pin it over as many of the windows as they could. *Keep them busy and take their minds off their grief*, he thought. Temporarily at least! Rees, on the other hand, remained motionless on the couch, face blood-drained, chin on chest, eyes staring. He was slowly coming to terms with his loss.

'I can't tell you how sorry I am, Rees.' He'd left Ffion and her brother to cover the remaining window upstairs. 'Such a shame . . . Such a needless loss.' He was finding it difficult to express his sympathy.

Suddenly Rees caught him in a wild stare, his eyes blank yet penetrating.

'Tristan isn't my son, you know.'

'I don't understand.' Craig's surprised look confirmed as much.

'Sinéad was unfaithful to me. Tristan is not my son.'

'Let's not talk about things like that now, old friend.'

But Rees had a need to purge his soul, to face his grief. Blurting out the truth would be his catharsis.

'When we were in Rotterdam . . . she met someone . . . one of her own . . . '

Craig didn't ask him to explain. He presumed that Sinéad had had an affair with an Irishman.

' . . . Ffion was six at the time . . . We didn't stay long in Holland after that.'

'Look! Why torture yourself, old friend? It all happened a long time ago.'

But Rees now seemed to be talking to himself, his voice distant, his face expressionless. ' . . . Things were never the same after that. He was younger than me. Sinéad was younger than me . . . '

Craig was well aware of the age difference between Rees and his wife.

' . . . She couldn't forget him . . . '

'Sinéad adored you, Rees. You know that.'

But he wasn't listening. His mind was in another place, another time.

' . . . When we were in bed . . . When we made love . . . *he* was always there. *Him* not me! Always kept her eyes shut, she did . . . Never wanted the light on. She wanted to see *him*, not me!

The old man fell silent. Then, as footsteps were heard on the stairs, he hissed the word 'Slut!' with unexpected venom, just as if he were adding a final punctuation mark to the whole episode. But then he was crying uncontrollably and muttering to himself, 'I'm going to miss her, Craig. God! How I'm going to miss her!'

The next minute, Ffion entered the room to find her father sobbing. Tearfully, but without really understanding what she was seeing, she crossed the floor towards him and laid a consoling arm over his shoulder. In contrast, her half-brother remained standing in the doorway, his ashen features made more conspicuous by the abundance of flame-red hair that framed them.

A little later, a confused Craig O'Darcy left the three to console one another as best they could.

* * *

Half past nine the next morning, he heard distant gunshots from the direction of Plas Cefn. By the time he'd pushed the Norton out of the cottage, where he now garaged it out of the extreme cold, the shooting had stopped. Minutes later he arrived at the house to find the plastic sheeting that he'd taken so much trouble to pin up, riddled with buckshot. There was no sign of the gunmen, nor was there any reply to his loud knocking. Carvel and friends had gone, but so had Rees Morgan and family. Craig feared the worst.

Chapter 9

For two whole days he searched for Rees and Ffion, starting with the outhouses at Plas Cefn before moving on to Pencraig Roofing, knocking desperately on each of the locked doors on site, including those of the metal containers that housed the contingency supplies. To no avail, however. Then he walked amongst the slate tips of the old quarry, hoping against hope to come across a building that his friends might have sheltered in. But no luck there either. His only remaining hope was that they'd found an empty house somewhere in town and that they'd settled safely in there, without Carvel knowing. The fact that the 6 x 6 LR had also gone didn't add all that much to his optimism; it could have been Carvel who had taken the Leech.

That night the wind picked up again and it was a very cold and dejected Craig O'Darcy who climbed into his Himalayan-style sleeping bag. Before sleep eventually overcame him, he'd taken two solemn decisions. One was to settle with Simon Carvel once and for all, and at the earliest possible opportunity. The second was more significant. He would suspend his disbelief; he would imagine there was a God; he would pray to Him for the safe deliverance of his friends. 'Dear God . . . ' Did that sound as if he was writing a letter? Was he blaspheming? 'Help me, O God, to find my friends. Care for them, wherever they are. Keep them safe. Keep everybody safe, please, please God . . . ' He sounded bloody pathetic, he thought. *Keep everybody safe!* What was he asking? The impossible? But God was supposed to be . . . What was the word? . . . Omnipotent. God could do anything He wished. Wasn't the world His oyster? He could play around with people's lives just as He pleased. So why *couldn't* He keep everybody safe?

'How the hell can I pray to someone . . . something . . . that I don't believe even exists?'

He was making his frustration known to the cold night air. How ridiculous it was to believe that there was a totally incomprehensible deity up there pulling the strings, controlling people's lives as if they were spineless little puppets.

'To hell with it!'

But despite himself, he again returned to Ffion's reasoned argument. What if he, Craig O'Darcy, was no different to the bed louse that she had referred to, blindly and stubbornly convinced that the Earth mattress on which he spent his days . . . months . . . years . . . constituted the full extent of all worthwhile creation? What if his Sun was but a lit bulb in one small room? What if there were other dimensions of intelligence, of Time and of Space that he, Craig O'Darcy, couldn't even begin to understand? And what if those other dimensions were inhabited by other powers, other presences that were far far superior to anything that he could comprehend?

'Dear God, help me to understand . . . help me to accept . . . Help me . . . Help us all.'

*   *   *

The next fortnight became the most melancholy period in Craig O'Darcy's relatively short life. During the first few days, he made his way down to Plas Cefn in the hope that the family had returned, only to return dejected each time. What with the perpetual gloom and the constant cold, he soon lost count of time because by now the only difference between day and night was that the days were not quite as dark nor quite as cold. Most of his hours were spent either huddled in front of a roaring log fire that seemed to be sending all its warmth up the chimney, or curled on the narrow bed that he'd dragged through from an even colder bedroom. More than ever he had reason to bless the warm sleeping bag that the Hornets had supplied him with, a few years ago, for their *Pre-season Toughening Adventure Course* in Lapland, and with a wry smile he recalled how loudly he and the rest of the squad had moaned about the 'ridiculously extreme conditions' that they were having to endure for the sake of their sport. The Land of the Midnight Sun had never thrown anything as cold or as dark as this at them, though!

The thermometer that used to hang on the outside wall of the Pencraig Roofing offices now stood on the window ledge outside Hafod. He studied each day's drop in temperature, from a few degrees Celsius above zero at the start of the Dark Period to a shivering fifteen, then thirty and now a life-threatening eighty six degrees of frost. Out of the wind, and with the help of the fire and a warm air blower running off the generator, he managed to keep the cottage just above freezing.

Craig had carried every bit of clothing, that Alistair had sent him, from the truck and into the cottage, as well as a supply of various foodstuffs that should last him the best part of three months, he reckoned. He'd also carried in a huge pile of logs and peat bricks from his stack in the old quarry cavern. Now, with so much packed into the two small rooms that he called home, his movements were being severely restricted. But as things were, free movement was the least of his worries.

236

When his third visit to Plas Cefn, hoping to find his friends returned there, proved futile, he continued on down to the town to seek out Simon Carvel. More than ever, he wanted to wreak revenge on the man.

The layers of clothing that he had on over his rubber wet-suit, the ski mask that covered his face beneath the helmet, the sheepskin gloves on his hands were all but scant protection against the freezing wind as he kept the bike down to a crawl. Eventually, when he reached town, he found the streets to be deserted and he was dismayed, though not surprised, to find so many empty houses with their floorboards, and their doors and windows if of wood, ripped away to be burnt – certain proof that the tenants had died of hunger or cold before their homes were stripped bare by desperate neighbours. Quarry Terrace, with its two rows of fifteen houses facing one another, was a painful illustration of the true extent of the tragedy. The street had but one remaining inhabitant, and the solitary candle, flickering dimly behind drawn curtains, brought home to Craig O'Darcy the depth of his own loneliness and dejection. All the other houses were empty shells, with the wind howling in and out of their gaping black doorways and broken windows.

When he reached the Pencraig Caravan Site he found all the static vans not only empty but totally vandalised, with not a scrap of combustible material left in any of them. The place looked like a breaker's yard, with devastation everywhere. *God!* he thought. *What it must have been like here! Desperate people reduced to wild animals in their attempt to stay alive.* Carvel was nowhere to be seen. Nor anyone else, for that matter!

He didn't loiter but returned directly to Hafod and spent the rest of the day in a deep melancholy, now convinced that Rees and Ffion could no longer be alive.

* * *

Craig O'Darcy wasn't the only one baying for Carvel's blood. Had he tarried in Pencraig some twenty minutes longer that day, he might have seen a strange looking creature exiting a house in Summerhill Crescent and making his way furtively from street to street. The gait was that of a man but the form resembled a very large sheep walking on its hind legs. Dafydd Elfed Evans, alias Dave the Poacher, had prepared for the cold in his own way. Every sheep that he'd rustled or killed during the past twelve months had been painstakingly skinned and the pelts amateurishly cured and sewn together, now giving him excellent if smelly protection against the cutting wind.

Back at the house, with its front windows inadequately boarded against the weather, Janet his wife was a corpse, and had been for the past eighteen hours. It had taken that long for Dave to come to terms with his loss, during which time he'd brooded long on revenge, on how best to seek retribution on the man who'd broken his windows, cruelly tricked him and stolen his guns. He already knew that Carvel had moved out of his caravan home and that he now occupied a house in Stryd y Bryn*. But which house? That was the question. Although only four of those twelve houses seemed to be still occupied, he had no easy way of picking the right one. He couldn't very well knock and expect wary and frightened people to answer the door, especially to somebody dressed as he was. And he certainly didn't want to unwittingly knock on the right door and find himself looking down the barrel of one of his own guns. All he could do, therefore, was to observe the street. A face in the window was all he needed, provided it was the right face.

* * *

For Craig O'Darcy, sleep that night proved fitful. He'd spent most of the previous day in bed, because that was where he was least cold. Even the flames of the log fire had lost their cheer. Sometime during the night he heard the rumble and felt the tremor of a distant earthquake. There had been many like it during the past two months but he had no way of knowing how high any of them featured on the Richter Scale or where their epicentres were. He had no way either of knowing how much more devastation was being caused by the resulting tsunamis. The waves were no longer audible to him and the perpetual darkness made it impossible for him to see as far as the distant bay. What he suspected, though, was that the ocean itself had begun to freeze and that the ice was keeping some sort of check on the waves.

When sleep did come, it was nightmarish. There he was, on Pencraig's High Street, struggling to free himself from under a pile of nude frozen corpses. But cold dead hands groped for him . . . for his ankles, his wrists, his throat and he was being pulled down again into an icy darkness. And the corpses had faces that he knew! Ice-blue faces grinning horribly, fiendishly, at him. Carvel was there, silently mouthing obscenities! The Disney Vulture was there, with Dog's bleeding body! Sinéad was there, her mouth distorted by a macabre grin, her tongue blood-red and snakelike. And suddenly, Rees and Ffion were there too, but they were shunning him, had their backs to him. No matter how fervently he

---

* *Bryn Street*

pleaded, or how loudly he called, they were ignoring him as if he were a total stranger. And so he wriggled and wrestled to extricate himself, but the harder he struggled the deeper he sank in the sea of ice-cold flesh. He was like a man in quicksand precipitating his own fate by striving too hard to save himself. But he had to try. What were those lines that his English teacher was forever quoting? *'Do not go gentle into that good night . . . Rage, rage against the dying of the light.'*

Suddenly he was awake and cold because his unwitting restiveness had let the freezing night air into his sleeping bag. He could feel it creeping under the layer of clothing that he had on, and running like melting ice along his spine. Shivering, he wrapped himself tighter in its material, vainly trying to regain the warmth that he had lost. A dull glow in the grate told him that the fire needed stoking but the prospect of climbing out of his relative comfort wasn't at all appealing. *I'm in a no win situation,* he thought. *Do I get up now and half freeze to death or do I let the fire go out and freeze later?* He smiled ruefully into the darkness. The latter wasn't an option, was it? Anyway, there was something else that intrigued him, worried him; a strangeness that he couldn't quickly fathom. He wanted to reach out for the bedside lamp to find out what was wrong but he lingered and lingered, loath to lose more of his warmth into the enveloping darkness.

What *was* it about the room that disturbed him? Was it the stillness . . . the silence? But why tonight more than any other night? Finally, he reached out for the bedside lamp and threw the switch. Nothing! Again he tried, again without success. *Damn it!* he thought. *The bulb's gone! Either that or the trip switch. More likely the trip, though!* The generator had occasionally surged of late, thus tripping the supply into the cottage.

And then it struck him. The generator! He couldn't hear its soft, constant hum.

'The bloody generator's packed in!'

If he thought that he had an option before, he didn't now. With a groan, he climbed out of the bag and groped with his stockinged toes for the sheepskin slippers that he knew to be there. Then he groped with his hands for the halogen torch next to the bedside lamp and suddenly the room was full of moving shadows, thrown by the stack of logs, by the towers of food boxes, by the twenty five litre containers of half-frozen spring water . . . Near the door, the chrome on the Norton Jaguar winked at him.

Awkwardly, he pulled a thick sweater over the one that he already had on and then pushed his legs into an extra large pair of moleskin trousers, the bottoms of which he tucked into an extra pair of knee-high woollen stockings. The snow boots came last.

Roughly, he scratched at his ten day beard and adjusted the woolly cap that he'd grown so used to during these last days . . . and nights. A few seconds later he had a candle lit and was pushing a couple of tinder-dry logs into the glowing embers and topping them with bricks of peat for good measure. He'd soon have flames, if not too much warmth, he told himself.

The wind had dropped, its familiar moan no longer filling the chimney. That, at least, had to be good news.

Once he had his anorak with hood on, and the ski mask to protect his face, he unlocked the cottage door and directed a halogen beam into the early morning gloom. The unexpected movement outside sent his heart pounding into his throat, until he realised that what he was seeing was a heavy fall of snow out of a dark and menacing sky. Borne on the wind during the night, it had drifted against his front door and now formed a chest high wall, the colour of concrete, between him and the outside world. It was like standing at a window and looking out on another planet, one that had only two colours, black and grey; the sky an ugly black, the snow a dirty grey. The flakes, larger than any that he had been accustomed to in the past, didn't float down on the wind but fell at the pace of rain.

It didn't take Craig O'Darcy long to realise why that was, or why they were the colour they were. The snowflakes were larger, heavier, simply because they were laden with volcanic dust from the atmosphere and he was left to wonder what colour the earth would eventually be, if or when the skies cleared and the weather decided to improve.

His surprise lasted but a few seconds. The longer he stood there, the colder his house was getting. So, without another thought, he waded into the grey drift and yanked the door shut behind him. The smell of sulphur still hung heavy in the air.

Beyond the drift, the snow cover was only about eight inches deep, so his movements towards the back of the cottage weren't too seriously restricted. Following the beam of his torch and with his head bowed away from the wind, he trudged around the side of the house towards the now-idle generator.

Any hopes that he might have had of restarting it plummeted when he saw that the drifting snow had backed up against the scarp face at the rear of the house and that it had completely covered the hut that housed the generator. Under normal winter conditions, it would have taken him fifteen minutes at the most to clear such a drift, but these weren't normal conditions; this wasn't ordinary snow. He needed no reminding of that! Five minutes of shovelling in this temperature would be the death of me, he thought ruefully.

With that he retraced his steps towards the relative warmth of the cottage, seriously wondering now what was to become of him. The prospect of death didn't particularly frighten him. 'What is there to live for, anyway?' he mumbled as he struggled to close the door against the crumbled drift.

Chapter 10

The Poacher, again a wolf dressed in sheep's clothing, made the same journey from 4 Summerhill Crescent down towards Stryd y Bryn in the heart of town, only now he had to contend with the additional hazard of newly fallen snow, whilst at the same time carrying an old oil drum across his shoulders. What made the drum heavier than usual was the bagful of stones it contained.

He was long used to skulking through the town at all hours of the night on his poaching forays, but this new greyness had turned familiar streets into an alien world, even for him.

Cold and exhausted, he finally found the street that he was looking for, the street where Simon Carvel lived. During his visit yesterday, he'd begun to suspect that of the four houses remaining intact here, only two could possibly have anyone alive in them now. Only in those had he seen flickering fires casting shadows onto drawn curtains; the other two had been dark and lifeless and the drifting snow hadn't even begun to melt on their cold window panes. But if their tenants were now dead, their half-alive neighbours couldn't have realised the fact, he thought, or they would surely have braved the elements to do some looting.

Simon Carvel could already be dead. Dave had considered that possibility before setting out from home that morning, but his gut feeling – a hunter's intuition some might call it – was that Carvel's fate and his own were inextricably linked. There was a score to be settled and there was no way that the Englishman could have departed this Earth without first of all paying for what he'd done to Janet. If Carvel was going to die – And he was going to die! And soon! – then he had to know who was responsible for his death; he had to know the reason for his dying. Justice would be done and would be seen to be done, by the avenger and the guilty alike. Didn't the Bible condone such vengeance? 'An eye for an eye and a tooth for a tooth'. Exacting retribution might not accomplish anything in the long run, he told himself, but it would be morbidly satisfying.

By the time he reached Stryd y Bryn, the falling snow had clung to his sheep's clothing and he himself had become as grey as his surroundings. He now approached the two houses whose flickering firelight still boasted some inner warmth. They were only three doors apart and he took up a position in the middle of the road, directly between them, from where he could detect any movement of their curtains. He then reached for one of the lumps of stone that he'd brought with him and proceeded to drum the empty tin can as loudly as his painfully frozen fingers would let him.

The noise didn't echo long and hard as he'd expected it to, but was being strangely muted by the surrounding snow.

* * *

Simon Carvel hadn't been out of bed for almost a week, only to urinate or defecate in a stinking corner of the room, or periodically to stoke up his fire with peat bricks. He'd hardly eaten anything in all that time, only a few dried biscuits and some barely warm baked beans. Not that he didn't have the food; in fact, his shelves were better stocked now than they'd been for months, *'thanks to the foreign git'* who used to keep the petrol station on the corner, diagonally opposite to where he now lived, and who by now, was probably just another lump of dead meat.

Since moving into Stryd y Bryn, Carvel had had his eye on the boarded-up service station, simply because there used to be a shop attached to it, selling all manner of goods, including crisps and biscuits, sweets and fizzy drinks, not to mention fleecy sports wear and a limited stock of camping appliances. The shop and garage buildings had been ransacked by looters months ago and they now looked distinctly unpromising. But before the looting, Murati, the Welsh-Albanian owner, and his wife and two children had disappeared but had since returned, judging by the dim light that could occasionally be glimpsed in a room at the rear of the building.

Carvel had noticed the light during one of his nightly forays and had gradually put two and two together. If the family had returned, he argued, then they must have had something worthwhile to return to. Provided, of course, that they'd gone away in the first place!

The more he'd thought about it, the more he'd become convinced that Murati hadn't left the premises at all during the looting but had found a safe place to hide until all would-be looters had lost interest in him and in his shop. And he, Simon Carvel, had a fair idea where that hiding place would have been. Hadn't he been a regular customer for petrol at the station, during his early days in Pencraig? And hadn't he gone searching for Murati, one evening, just on closing time, to explain to him that his bills would be settled monthly by Sellafield B's finance department? And hadn't he then found the proprietor, that day, coming up some steps from a cellar under the concrete floor of a back room? *'I check level of petrol and diesel in tanks.'* That had been Murati's flustered explanation at the time, when in fact he wasn't obliged to explain anything, especially to a relative stranger. It was only after moving into 5 Stryd y Bryn and seeing the chink of light in the garage's back room that Simon Carvel had started putting two and two together and had realised where Tómas Murati and family had been hiding all those weeks ago. More importantly, he'd realised where they'd also been hiding their provisions. Okay, so maybe Murati had never sold groceries, as such, but that didn't mean that he hadn't had access to wholesale food depots in the days before strict rationing. He would have been a bloody fool not to have taken full advantage of that fact and Murati, as Simon Carvel knew only too well, was no fool. In fact, *'the foreign git'* as he invariably referred to him, had been one of the shrewdest businessmen in town.

And so, last week, Carvel had gone foraging, cradling a loaded twelve-bore shotgun in his arms. The first cartridge had blown away the lock on the back door of the service station and the threat from a second had sent the terror-stricken Welsh-Albanian scrambling to put his own body in the direct line of fire. 'No shoot! Please no shoot!' he'd cried. 'Please no hurt family.'

How readily the *foreign git* had then emptied his cellar, Simon now recalled with a certain satisfaction. Not only that, but he'd even agreed to carry the food and the fuel over the road to 5 Stryd y Bryn, pleading continuously as he did so for his family to be spared.

Looking back at it all now, Carvel felt that he'd been too magnanimous by far in allowing the bastard to keep a token supply of the food. 'Bloody waste!' he'd thought afterwards. 'They'll all have died of cold by now anyway.' Still, it was good for his conscience to know that he'd shown some Christian charity.

Slowly, he crept out from under the pile of bedclothes and tottered towards the corner to urinate, shivering violently as he loosened some layers of clothing. Recently, he'd been having a lot of trouble passing water, a complaint he attributed to a worsening prostrate condition brought about by the cold. And now, as he dribbled, he watched the steam rising from his warm urine.

Before returning under the bedclothes, he decided to eat something and wash it down with a cup of luke-warm coffee. An iron grill had been roughly constructed over the peat fire and on it sat a saucepan, half full of water flecked with soot. It had been there for days but the water never boiled. I could open a tin of beans, he thought, and leave it in the water to thaw. But that would take time and in this cold, time was something he didn't have. So he settled for a handful of plain biscuits and a mugful of tepid, unsweetened black coffee, and turned towards the relative warmth of his bed.

That was when he heard the noise. At first he couldn't make out what it was or where it was coming from, but it certainly frightened him, cutting as it did across the prevailing silence, just as the sudden crack of a lion tamer's whip might make a tense circus audience jump.

It had come from the street outside . . . ! Was *still* coming, he realised! The banging was getting louder . . . angrier . . . frighteningly intimidating. Slowly and with heart racing, he approached the window and parted the curtains enough to peep out. The drumming immediately ceased, as if a schoolboy had been caught doing mischief by his headmaster. He peered into the darkness but all he could see was a grey world under a black ceiling. No movement. Nothing. It reminded him of a nightmare world where all colour had given way to cold grey and pitch black. He brought the curtains together again and turned towards the room once more.

* * *

Dave the Poacher had seen the curtains part but hadn't been able to determine whether the face had been that of a man or a woman. The inhabitant of the other house, however, had been less cautious, giving The Poacher more than a glimpse of his frightened, bespectacled face beneath a woolly cap, as it was pushed forward against the window pane. It was a face that bore no resemblance whatsoever to the face that he had been hoping to see. One down, one to go!

He now dragged his tin drum directly in front of the fifth house in the street and began again his eerie tattoo, right under its ground floor window.

As the seconds crawled by, what strength he had began to ebb and his hands and feet grew steadily colder. Even his resolve was waning. And then, as he was about to turn away and leave the steel can lying in the snow, a movement caught his eye. A shadow was cutting across the flickering light of the room. Then the curtains were thrown open and a wild, frightened face appeared menacingly against the glass. For what seemed an age, the two of them stared into one another's eyes, with neither showing signs of recognition, The Poacher alienated by his bizarre dress, Simon Carvel by his hollow eyes in dark sockets and by his long hair and wispy beard.

It was The Poacher who showed the first signs of recognition and then

245

the look of realisation and subsequent fright appeared on Carvel's face as well. The next minute he was gone and the curtains had again been closed. The Poacher didn't hesitate. He knew Carvel's next move and he knew full well what he himself wanted to do.

Stepping back, he pulled the first stone out of its bag and hurled it through the window in front of him, to hear the sound of breaking glass being quickly muffled by the heavy atmosphere. A second stone, aimed at one of the two upstairs windows, fell disappointingly short of its mark and he seriously wondered whether he had the breath or the strength to try again. But the memory of Janet dying of cold because of Carvel's greed gave him the additional impetus that he needed and his second attempt brought more shards of glass plunging into the snow at his feet.

It was then that all hell broke loose. A gun barrel – ironically his own – was fired at random, and with a thunderous roar, through the shattered pane of the downstairs window. With the instinct of the hunted rather than the hunter, Dave threw himself face down into the snow and remained perfectly still, fearing the sound of a second discharge and the searing pain of hot pellets tearing at his flesh. But his fears didn't materialise, because Carvel couldn't see him through the gloom. His fleece had snow clinging to it and he now blended in with the thick carpet of grey all around him.

When the second cartridge was eventually fired, it was again at random and the shot was followed by a weak scream of anger and despair as Carvel realised who had paid him the visit, and why.

Half-frozen and with fingers and toes badly frost-bitten, Dafydd Elfed Evans, alias The Poacher, turned for home, where his wife's corpse awaited him. Janet had been avenged and that was all that mattered. Come tomorrow morning, he vowed, he would return to 5 Stryd y Bryn and claim whatever Carvel had left that was worth taking. And whilst down there, he would check on whether the other two houses, those that were still intact in the street, were occupied or not. If not, then he would claim one of them for himself.

* * *

Simon Carvel groped desperately back towards his bed, barely aware of the discarded biscuits crunching under his stockinged feet. A sudden stabbing pain in his left heel told him that he'd trodden on the mug that he'd earlier dropped and broken. He could feel the warm blood flowing. But it didn't matter. Nothing mattered any more.

As he pulled the worthless pile of blankets over and around his hunched up body he felt strangely at peace with himself. Whether he was still shivering or not, didn't matter. Whether or not The Poacher returned to wreak more revenge didn't matter either. Nothing mattered except his dream. The chair was rocking gently beneath him on the veranda of his little palace in Buckinghamshire, the warm sun tingling on his upturned face; the wooded slopes of the Chilterns affectionately encompassing him and the scent of freshly cut hay filling his nostrils. Next to him, sat his father. He couldn't see the old man but he could tell he was there by the sweet aroma of his pipe tobacco. Behind him, the happy tinkle of cutlery and crockery echoed all around the kitchen, telling him that the old lady his mother was busy preparing lunch. A leg of lamb was roasting in the hot oven; he could smell it, could hear it sizzling away. An array of saucepans were simmering on the hobs – sweet-tasting carrots . . . garden peas still in their pods . . . corn the colour of the sun . . . new potatoes – Jerseys, no less! – and gravy. Only his mother could make such gravy, and soon she would be calling them to table. There was no sign of his sister or her wimp of a husband, and that was good.

A smile creased his tired face as he pulled his knees up to his chin and into a foetal squat. This was contentment, he thought. He could sleep now.

PART 3

'Long is the way
And hard, that out of hell leads up to light.'
(John Milton: 'Paradise Lost')

Chapter 1

As the cold days and the dark empty weeks crept by, Craig O'Darcy kept more and more to his bed. The silent generator meant that his only remaining source of light and warmth, apart from the tired glow from the grate, was the thick church candle that had now taken the place of his bedside lamp. Although he tried to conserve as much of it as he could, lighting it only when he needed to get out of bed to stoke the fire, to nibble at some food or to answer the call of nature, yet it was already down to a third of its original height, its wick having burnt itself into a little crater that encased the flame and caused it to splutter in its own pool of molten wax. As far as the fire was concerned, he'd worked out that four logs, stacked into the grate in a particular fashion and then topped with two bricks of peat, would last six hours before needing to be replenished.

And so he lived in a twilight world, in a drowsy state of half-awareness, sometimes going two or three days without food. He would sleep for hours at a time, irrespective of whether it was day or night; a state of stupor in which his heartbeats became lazy and long. His whole body had drifted into voluntary hibernation, which was a blessing in one sense, in that it relieved him of his melancholy and suicidal despair.

Once, he checked the time and date on his watch – *04.10: Sunday: December 23: 2026* – and remembered thinking cynically 'Christmas the day after tomorrow. I wonder how many presents I'll get?' When he next bothered to look it was the twenty ninth of January, 2027. Not that it mattered. Not that anything mattered anymore. This was how things were now, and this was how things would stay. Warmth and light and comfort were things of the past. Friends and family were gone. It was a world without life, without growth. Mother Nature herself had died.

Not once, during those long months, did he allow the fire to die out. However soundly he slept, some instinct would always waken him when the fire got low. Or maybe it wasn't instinct at all! Perhaps it was just the cold. So when, one day, he awoke to total darkness he felt inexplicably disorientated. Was he curled up on his left side rather than his right, and therefore looking away from the grate rather than towards it? Was he staring into the blackness that was the wall between him and the next room? The feeling scared him, because he *wasn't* lying on his left side at all. He *was* looking towards the open fireplace! And yet it was dark, without an ember glowing. He'd slept too soundly! He'd slept too long! Why would he have done that?

The questions bewildered him. And yet, it had been a wonderfully dreamless sleep and he felt so rested; ebullient even!

It took him a full minute to realise the truth but when he did, he fairly jumped out of bed. His eyes had dilated sufficiently and he could now tell where the window was, its shutter mounted in a barely perceptible frame of pale light. More thrilling was the warm air that filled the cottage. He wasn't as cold! He wasn't shivering! That was why he'd slept so well. That was why he felt this sudden surge of energy and excitement. He groped for the torch and searched for his snow-boots.

Unbolting the security panel over the door frame proved difficult because he was all thumbs. Finally, however, he got it done. He swung open the door to be confronted by a grey wall of snowdrift, the upper half of which immediately collapsed inwards over his lower body and onto the stone floor of the room. Instinctively, he shaded his eyes against the sudden glare of painful sunlight. Then he was wading almost chest high through the drift, at the same time filling his lungs with a mixture of healthy air, wonderment and considerable relief. When he eventually reached the track in front of the cottage, he found that the undrifted snow was no more than two feet deep, its surface frozen like that of a crisp *meringue.*

The sight was as nothing he'd ever seen before. In the glare of a mid-morning May sun that was shining through wispy cloud cover, the greyness had suddenly become a silver carpet, whilst distant rock faces glinted with the thaw. The whole scene was surreal. It was like looking down on a breathtakingly beautiful but lifeless planet, one that only Hollywood's imaginative minds could have conjured up. 'Haven't I had that impression before,' he asked himself, 'but under different circumstances?'

The roofs of Pencraig were indiscernible and it was difficult to imagine that under all that glitter in the distance, the Arian Valley was just a scar of muddy brown. Today, at least, its name – Silver Valley – suited it. The Bay of Branwen was no longer visible either, no longer there! All he could see was a flat expanse of silver, melting into an indistinct horizon. The sea had frozen and been covered by the grey snow.

He stood there motionless for at least ten minutes, unconsciously thanking God, over and over again, for his deliverance. Then he turned towards the cottage and once more held his breath. Apart from the black hole of an open doorway and the panes of glass that were slowly releasing their grip on the drifted snow that had clung to them these past months, the rest of the house was just a mound of silvery grey, as was the cutting way to his right, where he'd stowed his food truck. 'It's certainly hidden now!' he thought, with the ghost of a smile.

The only blot on an otherwise perfect scene was the blackness of the southern sky. It told him that other places were still in the dark, still in the cold. It also told him that the conditions that he now revelled in could only be temporary and that, given time, the Arctic winter would return, perhaps with greater vengeance. But that was a prospect he didn't want to dwell on, now.

He soon had the fire re-lit and a lump of frozen spring water melting in a saucepan on it. A cup of sweet coffee would make his day, he decided, as would a hearty breakfast of whatever was available. The thermometer on the window sill showed seven degrees above freezing. Outside, it had to be warmer even than that.

It was only when his stomach was full and his exhilaration had ebbed that his melancholy returned. 'So you're alive! So you think that you're living in a magical world! You bloody fool! What happens now? Where do you go from here?'

Sullenly, he ran the fingers of both hands like a comb through his shoulder length hair and furiously scratched deep into his wiry beard. 'I'll go down to Plas Cefn,' he decided out loud. 'Who knows . . . ?' But the hope of finding his friends having returned there, of finding them alive, quickly ebbed.

Plodding through the dust-laden snow proved more tiring than he'd imagined. Up to a point, its frozen surface would hold the weight of each step but then his foot would break the crust and he'd be up to his knees again in clinging snow.

When he eventually reached the top of the track that snaked down towards Plas Cefn, he paused to take stock of what should have been familiar surroundings. Below him to his left, the site of Pencraig Roofing in deep shadow was just a sobering battleship-grey. Straight ahead, half a mile or so away, he could make out the sunlit mounds that used to be the walls bordering the A470 as it climbed towards the Dunant Pass. Nearer to him and slightly right, the splendid pines that once had sheltered Rees Morgan's home now stood awry, having succumbed to the winds and to the weight of snow. Craig wondered yet again why he'd felt so elated a few minutes ago.

That was when he caught a movement, out of the bottom corner of his eye, between the interlocking spurs of slate mounds below him. It was but fleeting and he couldn't be sure. Whatever it was – *if* it was! – had now disappeared. Instinctively, his heart had started to race. Had he seen anything? If he had, then whoever it was . . . whatever it was . . . was making it's way up the track towards him. He stepped back into the shadow of a ruined quarry hut and waited, knowing that whoever . . . whatever . . . was coming would be effectively blinded by the glare if he . . . it . . . looked up in his direction.

Seconds turned to minutes and he became convinced that his eyes had deceived him, but still he kept them glued on the bend of track that emerged from behind the mound. And suddenly there he was! A lonely figure, head down, trudging so slowly through the snow that he barely seemed to be moving. Every step was an effort and he paused often for breath.

'He has either walked far or else he didn't have the strength to start off with,' Craig thought. 'If I don't go down to meet him then I could be waiting here for another hour or more.' It never crossed his mind that the stranger could be a threat.

The nearer he got to his unannounced visitor, the more certain he became that it was a man. Short – five foot six perhaps? – and hunched. No way of telling his age. Hardly surprising that he had a thick beard. What man wouldn't have by now? From the waist down, his clothes had to be soaking wet but he seemed unaware of the cold. An extra coat was slung over one shoulder and his puffing could be heard from afar.

It was that puffing that kept him from hearing Craig's approach. The two were within twenty yards of one another when the one coming up stopped for breath and lifted his eyes to see how far he yet had to go. The silhouette of Craig O'Darcy – six foot four and with long unkempt hair and beard – blocking the track above him must have given him a turn but, instead of showing fright, the shorter man straightened and stiffened, preparing to defend himself.

Craig was the first to speak. 'Who the hell are you? What do you want?'

The eyes glinted, then gradually softened. 'Rocky? . . . Is that you?' His recent efforts and the sudden shock had left him breathless. 'Is it really you?'

'Bloody hell! Tony the Neck! You're alive!'

The thick beard opened up in a broad smile. 'Alive? I should hope so . . . Am I glad to see you.'

The next minute they were tied in a clinch.

'How have you been coping? . . . Your wife? Is Dianne alright?'

'Yes, we're both well, thanks to you and Rees Morgan . . . '

Craig assumed that he was referring to the generous supplies of food and clothing that he'd been given.

'. . . It hasn't been easy, though . . . not for anybody, I guess.'

'So where were you going now?'

'To look for you. To look for anyone who might still be alive.' A pained expression crossed his face. 'There's no sign of anybody at Plas Cefn.'

'I've no idea where they went to, Tony. One minute they were there, the next they were gone. I can only fear the worst, I'm afraid. You know, of course, that Sinéad died? And that Rees was shot?'

'Yes. I helped you take her down to the burial chamber if you remember.'

'Of course.' He laughed long and with new-found humour. 'The cold weather must have frozen my brain!'

Tony also laughed, without really knowing why. 'And how was Rees Morgan when you last saw him?'

'Not good. Wherever they went to that day – him and Ffion and . . . ' He couldn't recall Tristan's name. ' . . . and the American . . . ' He wasn't going to call him Rees' son, not after what Rees himself had told him on the day of the shooting. ' . . . I don't think he had an earthly of surviving those cold months. In fact, there can't be much hope for any of them.'

The two stood silent for some time, reflecting on their loss.

'So what are your plans now, Tony?'

'If the weather stays like this . . . if it continues to get warmer . . . then I . . . we . . . have a problem.'

'*We?* What do you mean?'

'No, I didn't mean you and me! I was thinking more of Dianne and myself.'

'You need food.'

'Well, yes, the situation is getting to be a problem, but that's not all. You see, Rocky, as the weather gets warmer the town's going to be a very unhealthy place to be living in . . . what with all those unburied bodies thawing out.'

'Yea, I see what you mean.'

'I was really hoping to find somewhere else to live. Somewhere far enough away from the problem.'

Craig laughed briefly and this time without humour. 'You'd be welcome up at Hafod, but I'm afraid there's not enough room there even to swing a mouse, leave alone a cat.'

'I know that. Plas Cefn was where I had in mind.' Suddenly, he seemed embarrassed at having made the suggestion. 'I mean, if the place is going to be empty . . . But if any of the family intend coming back there, well that's another matter.'

Craig remained silent. He could see Tony's point, could sympathise with him and Dianne, but the thought of anyone other than Rees living at Plas Cefn was difficult for him to stomach.

Tony sensed his reluctance. 'Of course, if you object, Rocky . . . '

'Hell, no! You and Dianne are going to have to move, and Plas Cefn is the obvious place for you. It's just . . . ' He couldn't put the thought into words.

'Yea. I know what you mean, mate. Anyway, let's wait and see if the worst of the weather is over, first of all, then perhaps . . . *What* . . . ?'

Because of their difference in height, they'd automatically swapped positions on the slope, with Tony now looking down towards the snow-hidden complex that used to be Pencraig Roofing. His eyes had narrowed; his expression one of frozen excitement.

Craig quickly turned to look in the same direction as him, down over some of the smaller mounds of quarry rubble. In the distance, close on half a mile away, a lone figure could be seen trudging slowly towards the snow-covered offices of Pencraig Roofing. Even as they watched, they saw him stumble, slowly regain his feet and then stumble again.

'Who the hell can he be?' Tony had his hand shading his eyes against the glare. 'Where the hell did he come from, do you think?'

Whoever it was, Craig thought, he couldn't have come up from town. Not on that route, anyway. The only possible explanation therefore was that he'd been sheltering these past months in one of the Pencraig Roofing buildings and was making his way back there now. But who could it be? Suddenly, Craig O'Darcy felt a surge of excitement and hope.

Instinctively, the two of them started waving their arms in the air and yelling to draw the stranger's attention, their excited voices stirring the eerie silence. It took a second or two for the sound to travel, then they saw the figure stop, could almost see his panic as he turned this way and that, frantically trying to decide where the shouting was coming from and whether it presented a threat or not.

'Come on! Let's go down there!' Craig's first few steps were too eager. He'd forgotten how heavy the snow really was to plough through and he now found himself tripping head first into it.

'Try stepping in my footprints.' Tony was pointing towards the trail he had left. 'It'll be easier,' he added, stating the obvious.

With gathering impatience, they followed the track down, soon losing sight of the solitary figure. They had no option but to take the circuitous route that the track offered them and they were soon hemmed in by the mounds of buried slate waste. Once out of the pale sun and into the shadows, they began to shiver with cold and Tony hurriedly struggled into his coat again.

Eventually, and after what seemed an age, they reached level ground and knew that they were standing on what should be a tarmac surface. To their right, three hundred metres away, stood Plas Cefn, cold and lifeless; way to their left, the grey stillness of Pencraig Roofing.

'He's gone!' Tony's voice was heavy with disappointment. The stranger had disappeared.

'Can't have gone far. We're bound to find him. Come on!'

'Can you be sure?' Despite his physique, Tony the Neck was now tired and the five hundred metre trudge through deep virgin snow, to where the stranger had been standing, appealed little to him. The long cold months, the enforced rationing, the morning's exertions . . . they were all now taking their toll. 'It could be wasted effort.'

'No. We'll find him, all right. We only have to follow his trail.'

And so, cold and wet from the knees down, and getting colder and wetter by the minute, they ploughed their way slowly through the snow until they eventually reached what they were looking for.

Craig pointed to the trail. It led towards the back of one of the buildings. Suddenly, he called out, 'Whoever you are, it's safe for you to come out. My name's Craig O'Darcy and I've got Tony . . . Tony the Neck . . . with me.'

His shout was met with a squeal of excitement and relief, and a figure appeared from hiding. 'Craig? Is it really you?' She was crying. 'It can't be! Can it?'

'My God! Ffion?' Who else, except her father, ever gave his name that pronunciation? 'You're alive! Thank God! Thank God for that!' His relief was euphoric as he pushed his way towards her. She came to meet him and then she was clinging to him and crying uncontrollably. The strain, the tensions of the past six months were now being released.

He let her cry, while Tony looked on. Eventually she sniffled and stopped, seemingly embarrassed by what she regarded as a show of weakness. 'I'm sorry. It's just that . . . '

'No need to explain. You've been through a lot.' He removed her fur cap and her hair fell in long tresses onto her shoulders. He smiled. 'You've changed.'

'Yes, I know. But a lot more has happened than just my hair having grown.'

Craig felt as if he'd been reprimanded for being insensitive. 'Yes, I realise that. I'm sorry. I should have asked about your father . . . your brother. I've thought a lot about Rees . . . about you all . . . during these past months. Is your father all right?' Even as he spoke, he knew it wasn't the question to ask, because the tears were welling up in her eyes.

'Dad only lived about three weeks after Mam. His leg turned gangrenous and he suffered a lot. But there was nothing I could do, except give him some pills to try and deaden the pain.'

She looked and sounded so pitiable that he once more pulled her towards him.

'But couldn't you have let me know where you were? I might have been able to help.' He was thinking of his First Aid training but he refrained from adding, 'I might have been able to save him.'

'We tried. Dad sent Tristan to look for you but he came back and said that you were dead . . . that you'd frozen to death.'

'Why would he say that?'

'I don't know, unless it was an excuse not to go all the way up to Hafod, what with the weather being so cold.'

'The little bugger!' Craig felt genuinely aggrieved. 'And where is Tristan now?'

'I think *he's* probably dead as well. Dad sent him away. Told him that he didn't want him near him. I tried to reason with Dad but he'd have none of it. I couldn't understand it. I just don't know how he could do such a thing. Dad, of all people!'

As he listened, Craig became convinced that she knew nothing of what Rees had talked to him about and that she still believed her father to be Tristan's father as well. She knew nothing of her mother's infidelity all those years ago. Rees had kept it from her.

'But why did he? Send Tristan away, I mean.'

'Because he found out that Tristan was partly to blame for Mam's death, that's why. When Dad confronted him, Tristan admitted that he'd been having dealings with Simon Carvel. It seems that he'd known for some time where Dad was hiding the keys to the Contingency Food Supplies here at Pencraig Roofing. My brother had been secretly supplying Carvel with rations . . . over a number of weeks, apparently.'

'But why would he do that?'

She shrugged to suggest that the answer was obvious. 'Carvel gave him drugs in return. I'd suspected as much myself, actually.'

'So your father . . . what? . . . banished him?'

'Yes, that's exactly what he did, I suppose.'

Craig had always known that Rees could be ruthless in business but he'd never suspected him of being callous. 'But where did he banish him to?'

'He gave him Plas Cefn and everything that was in it, plus a good supply of extra food.'

'Where have *you* been staying, then? I mean, since . . . You know!'

It was Tony's question and Ffion turned now towards him.

'Since the shooting you mean? Come on! I'll show you."

She led them away from the site of Pencraig Roofing and Craig recalled that this was the way Rees had taken him in the Leech, that day they'd gone underground to see the old quarry workings. But instead of then bearing right, towards the incline that led down to what Rees had called the C-floor entrance, Ffion bore left and upwards, up another snow-covered incline that already bore a set of her tracks.

Although it was only about thirty metres in length, climbing it proved arduous. Eventually, however, they reached the top and stood there panting.

'Where are you taking us?'

She looked at Craig. 'You've been underground haven't you? Dad took you once, didn't he?'

'Yes, but not this way.'

'He took you in along the C-floor?'

'That's right. Way down there, somewhere.' He pointed vaguely downwards.

'We're now up on the A.'

Tony was nodding. He was better acquainted than Craig with the old quarry workings.

'Did Dad ever mention his contingency plans to you, in case things went wrong?'

'He mentioned them, but he never told me what they were.'

'Then you'd better come and see.' She turned towards a set of steel doors in the rock face, similar to the ones that Craig had seen leading into the C-floor. 'Cefn Quarry had only four adits,' she explained, 'to the A, B, C and F floors. The F was the one being used for the burial chambers, as you probably know! What Dad did was to block off the top floor – the A – from the other levels. Maybe he showed you?'

'No, he took me *down* from the C, not up.'

'Anyway. This is what he prepared.' She swung open one of the double doors, pulled a torch from her coat pocket, and they followed her inside.

The first thing to greet them was the grey wheel-convertible Leech Land Rover.

'Dad made me drain all water out of it,' she explained, 'in case it froze. Who knows? One day it might become useful again.'

Craig nodded. He'd taken the same precaution with his Norton.

Skirting the Leech, they made their way, single file, further into the mountain. Craig heard Tony, behind him, shudder with the cold.

'The roof gets lower from now on, so watch you don't bang your heads.' Her voice echoed eerily, as if she were speaking in a vacuum.

Eventually, they came to a huge rock chamber opening out on their left. Within it, the halogen beam picked out a flat-roofed structure, roughly twelve metres square, similar in shape and colour to the concrete bunkers that Craig had seen in old films about the Second World War. He immediately recognised the cladding panels as the type used in the galleries at Storage Site 5.

'This isn't where you've been living these past six months, is it?' Tony sounded incredulous. 'Good grief! It was cold enough above ground . . .'

She half turned towards him. '*Now* it's colder, yes. That's because it's so much warmer outside. But when the weather, and especially the wind, was really cold out there, it wasn't too bad in here, you know. But this isn't where I've been sleeping though.'

The torch-light led them further along the icy cold passage and Craig found himself marvelling at her courage in spending so many months alone in this God-forsaken environment. If ever there was a hell-hole to be alone in, then this was it, he thought. Eventually they were faced with a brick wall where the passage had been blocked off but before that, a second chamber opened out on their left.

This was larger than the first, as was the building inside it. This structure, like the other, had been constructed of Pencraig Roofing panels and Ffion now approached the door, to enter. Out of the shadows behind the building came the familiar hum of a generator.

'This is where I've been living,' she explained. 'You'll find that it's got double-cavity walls insulated with thermostyrene. Dad was very . . . very thorough, as you . . . know.' She again began choking on her grief.

Before reaching the door, she swept the beam of her torch towards two capsule-shaped tanks lying up against the outside wall and then at the piping leading out of them and in through the wall. 'Propane!' she explained.

Tony whistled softly. 'So that's what he wanted them for! I sold him these, months ago. Eighteen hundred litres each . . . that's what they hold.'

The security lock was voice-activated and, as Ffion addressed it, they heard the door click open. Once inside, they were surprised at how warm the room was, and when she threw a switch to light it up, they soon saw why. Behind the door stood two large heaters with a cooking stove in between, all connected to the propane tanks that they'd just seen. Only one of the heaters was currently glowing.

'I've been trying to economise as much as possible,' she said. Dad always warned that it could be a very long winter . . . five . . . ten years even!'

It struck Craig that she was constantly referring to her father.

'Mind you, I never would have been able to last out that long. Six months was awful, five years would be a nightmare.'

Opposite them, near the far wall, two mattresses had been made up as single beds, each having a thickly quilted sleeping bag spread over it. One mattress was sullied by a dark stain that Craig took to be dried blood. Rees' blood! She'd left it lying there, all this time! A small lamp and a knee-high pile of books separated the two beds. Three other mattresses were propped up on their sides with some folded-up chairs. Craig counted four of those. A fifth chair stood open in a semi-reclining position, near the working heater. Along the left-hand wall, ceiling-high shelves supported an array of canned food. A table held the remains of a recent meal, with a stool in front of it. Four other stools had been tidily pushed beneath the table and showed little sign of use. Adjacent to the door and to their left as they entered, more shelves, these stacked with folded blankets and a variety of warm clothing. Another closed door took up part of the right-hand wall, as did a row of large clear-alkathene containers, six in all. Of those, one was still full, another part full and the remaining four empty. Craig presumed that they contained or had contained drinking water.

His mind was full of questions. Rees had had contingency plans for his whole family, but why the fifth bed? . . . the fifth chair? . . . the fifth stool? He thought he knew the answer to that one. Hadn't there also been a fifth coffin, with his own name on it? The fifth bed, the fifth chair, the fifth stool had been intended for him. Rees, bless him, had included Craig O'Darcy in his contingency plans!

'Where does that lead to?' He nodded towards the closed door.

'Just the toilet.' She crossed the floor and swung the door open. It opened inwards to reveal another door that opened in the other direction. Beyond the second door, they glimpsed a little box-extension to the room they were in. 'There are chemical toilets in here but it's ventilated, so it's much colder, which is why I have to keep these doors shut.'

'Your father had thought of everything, hadn't he?' Tony had stood silent until now. Craig suspected a hint of bitterness in his tone but then he noticed the wry smile. 'I supplied him with most of this stuff, you know – the heaters, the shelving, the toilets, the insulation . . . – but he never told me what they were for. Best bit of business that I ever did, actually. He paid me in kind for them.'

'What do you mean?'

It was Craig's question but Tony's answer was directed at Ffion. 'Your father gave me a choice – cash or food.' He grinned. 'I don't need to tell you what I took. How else could Dianne and myself have lasted this long?'

'Yes, I had wondered about that.' Craig turned back to Ffion. 'What about the other building? The one in the other chamber?'

'Food mainly, a tank of clean water, some tools, a lot of books . . . '

'Books?' Tony sounded disbelieving.

'Yes. Mostly my own but some of them have come from the local library, the ones that I was able to salvage before people took them away to burn.'

'Oh!' Tony sounded critical of one, at least, of her priorities.

There was one question that Craig found difficult to ask. What had she done with her father's corpse? His eye kept returning to the blood stain.

'You're thinking of Dad!'

He smiled sadly at her but said nothing. Did she have a sixth sense, he wondered.

'Yes. I was wondering what . . . where you . . . ?'

'What I did with his body.'

'Well, yes.'

'He's out there . . . ' A pained expression returned to her face. ' . . . in the snow.'

They stared at her.

'What else could I do?' And she started to sob. 'He was dead! I couldn't keep him in here, could I? As much as I would have liked to.' Once again she was crying and once again Craig had to console her. It took time for her to continue. 'I . . . I got his . . . his coffin and . . . and put him . . . put him in it. Then I took him out . . . into the cold . . . Then the snow came.'

Good God! Craig thought. She'd nursed her father for three weeks and watched him die a painful death. She'd then gone out into the freezing cold to get the coffin and had dragged it all the way back here. But how had she known where to go looking for it? Rees must have told her! He'd have known that he was dying, and he would have told her. My God! The anguish must have been unbearable for both of them. Even in his death throes, Rees would have worried about leaving his daughter alone, to fend for herself in a cold and friendless world. And then, after he'd died and after she'd got him into his coffin, she'd had to drag him all the way out again into the open, squeezing her way past the Leech. How on earth had she coped? Not only with the physical effort but with the trauma of it all?

'But the snow's started thawing now, so we'll have to take him down there.' As she indicated to the burial chambers way beneath them, a wild look came to her eyes. 'You'll help, won't you? You'll help me take him to join Mam?'

Her cheeks were wet and Craig had some more consoling to do.

'Leave that to us. There's no rush. The snow won't clear for a while yet. We'll have to wait.' The idea of Tony and himself having to carry a laden coffin through all that heavy snow, when in fact they could barely walk in it, didn't bear thinking about. The other option appealed even less. There was no way they could or would attempt the underground route that Rees had taken him on, all those months ago. The catacombs were definitely not an option! Anyway, the need wasn't desperate. Rees' body would remain refrigerated under the snowdrift for some time yet.

'I think I'd better be going.' Tony, uncomfortable with the whole situation, was shuffling his feet. 'Dianne will be getting worried.'

'But *you'll* stay, Craig!' She didn't try to disguise her panic. She needed the reassurance.

'Yes, of course!' No question of that! 'But why don't Tony and Dianne join us here? The place may not be big, but it's warm and there's enough food for everybody.' He had his mind on the truck, the contents of which he'd barely touched as yet.

They watched Tony's face for his reaction. It was obvious that the idea appealed to him but he was having to wrestle with the difficulty of accepting. In the end, he shook his head sadly. 'I only wish we could. Believe me, I appreciate the offer, but I'm afraid that Dianne would never make it up here, not through that snow . . . And there's no way I could carry her!' They all smiled. Dianne was corpulent to say the least.

They accompanied him out into the open but before he left them,

Craig made him another offer. 'If the thaw continues, then you and Dianne are welcome to move to Hafod to live.'

'But if the thaw continues, you're not going to be staying underground, are you? You'll be needing somewhere yourselves. Will you move into Plas Cefn, then?'

'Most probably. Come to think of it, what's to stop all four of us living there? It's big enough. There are difficult times ahead and we'll have to depend a lot on one another, won't we?'

Tony nodded. 'Let's wait a day or two to see what the weather does. If it keeps improving, then Dianne and I will have no option but to move. Either that or risk disease. I'll see you then.'

*   *   *

It was getting on for three o'clock in the afternoon as they watched Tony the Neck's squat figure receding in the distance, shouldering the heavy pack of supplies that Ffion had given him. He had just passed Plas Cefn and was nearing the main road when Craig decided to return to Hafod to collect some of his things.

'Why? There's all you need here!' There was a hint of desperation in her tone.

'Everything except clothes to fit me, Ffion. I need to change.'

He was looking forward to ridding himself of the foul-smelling clothes that he'd lived and slept in over the past few months. The relative warmth of the underground room meant that he could now start thinking of washing himself.

'But you promise to come back? You promise that?'

He smiled sympathetically at her. This wasn't the Ffion that he'd known. Gone was the composure, the self-assurance, the old aloofness. Six months of trauma had left their mark. 'I'll be back in . . . ' He looked at his watch. ' . . . an hour and a half at the most.'

'I'll come with you!' It was a spur of the moment decision, brought on by a sudden attack of panic.

'Come if you like, but it's going to be very tiring, I can promise you. You know what it's like, trudging through this heavy snow . . . getting wet . . . getting cold. No, it's better that you stay here.'

'I'm coming!' She linked her arm in his, as if stubbornly attaching herself to an anchor.

His *'hour and a half'* proved too optimistic because at half past four they were still up at Hafod, although at last preparing to leave. The journey had almost got the better of them, especially Ffion, and time had been spent getting the fire going properly to get some feeling back into their hands and especially their wet feet.

And so, after he'd locked the cottage door and bolted the security panel onto its outside frame, they set off on their arduous downward journey. Because of the thaw, the feet marks in the snow now held ice-cold puddles and their soaking feet were all but frozen again. The wind had also picked up, a cruel reminder that they should have come better prepared. Often they paused for breath and once, briefly, for Ffion to stare dejectedly at her parents' empty home in the near distance. Much of the plastic sheeting, badly torn by the wind or shredded by Carvel's buckshot, dangled out between the bars of its shattered windows and Craig imagined the wind-driven snow now carpeting the lounge and the bedrooms. It was a picture of despair. Tomorrow, if the weather permits, he thought, I'll go over there and check what's happened to Tristan.' In their earlier conversation with Tony, they'd talked about moving back there to live but Tristan's name hadn't been mentioned. It was as if they'd all assumed that the young American was already dead. What if he was still alive, though?

They were dead-beat and half frozen by the time they reached their underground home and it took a long time for them to regain lost warmth. Frost-bitten fingers and toes became tortured as their circulation improved, and Ffion cried with pain. Later, some hot soup gave them cheer.

That evening, Ffion needed a lot more comforting and by the time they were ready for bed there was little doubt that they'd be sharing the same sleeping bag. Before that, though, Craig enjoyed his first proper wash for months

'Take me, Craig,' was all she said as he slipped in next to her, 'and don't be too gentle with me.'

Her eagerness, the pressure of her firm body, aroused him and he took her at her word. The old haunting recollection of her at the Club pool returned, to add to the flame and to turn the next few minutes into nothing other than pure animal lust. Within seconds she was making her rapture known, whilst his delight became a long muffled groan. Twice more, before morning, they groped for one another. The third time was gentler, more prolonged, and Craig heard himself muttering over and over again his love for her. She, in return, clung to him desperately, as if afraid that she might sleep and then wake to find him gone.

Chapter 2

They slept late that morning. Eventually they got up, washed in warm water and whilst Ffion was preparing breakfast, Craig went to see if the thaw was continuing.

The sky had hardly changed since yesterday but what had melted then had frozen again overnight, so that the snow had an even crisper feel to it now and crunched sharply underfoot.

After breakfast, the two of them dressed warmly and went out for some fresh air. A slow thaw had again begun and Craig reckoned the air temperature to be perhaps a little warmer than yesterday's. As they trudged, he felt Ffion gripping his arm and pressing herself against him in her new-found contentment.

'That's where Dad is.'

She briefly pointed towards a large drift near the adit entrance. The bluntness of her tone surprised him. She might just as well have been pointing to a book on a shelf or a star in the sky. But then he realised that she'd been living with her grief, with her loss, for the best part of six months, whereas he'd only just come to know about Rees' death.

'Oh!' What could he say? 'But don't worry. Tony and I will take care of things when the time comes.'

'I bet you've had many girlfriends in your time.' As she tugged at his arm, she was smiling at her own sudden change of subject.

'Not many,' he mumbled. Until last night, Sally had been a painful memory that gnawed at his intestines.

'And slept with them all.'

'Not really.' He felt strangely embarrassed by her questioning.

'You didn't show any lack of experience last night, anyway. Did you?' The suggestive grin and the quick squeeze of the arm told him that she was teasing him. It was a side to her character that was new to him and he was excited by it.

'Neither did you, madam!' he retorted, playfully referring to the fact that she hadn't been a virgin.

At which, a cloud of pain passed over her face and she turned away.

He realised his blunder. He'd forgotten about the fiancé whom she'd lost in a motorcycle accident almost four years ago. 'I'm sorry!' he muttered. 'I didn't mean to . . . '

Her sadness soon passed and she was again smiling broadly at him and pushing her body up close. 'Promise you'll make love to me again tonight?'

He laughed, out of relief more than anything else. 'I promise.'

'Just like last night?'

'You bet!'

'And just as often?'

'You call that often? I didn't even reach second gear last night.'

They laughed. They tussled. They kissed.

'I'm looking forward to it, especially now that you're so sweet-smelling.'

He jokingly got her by the throat as if to strangle her and they again laughed.

'So tell me honestly! Have you ever been in love before? I need to know.'

It was his turn to look away. 'I thought I was . . . once.'

'What was her name?'

Her curiosity surprised him. 'Why do you want to know?'

'Just in case you start calling out for her in your sleep, or use her name when you're making love to me, that's why.'

She was again teasing but he also sensed a dogged resolve to get what she wanted to know. He, in turn, decided to make light of it all.

'Her name was Sally, she lived in Nottingham, she was bloody awful in bed . . . and she gave me the boot.'

'I don't believe the bed bit. Anyway, why would she do that?' She wasn't smiling any more. 'Give you the boot, I mean?'

'Found somebody else, I suppose.'

'Did she fool around?'

'Probably. I wasn't really in a position to know. I was at Sellafield, she was down in Nottingham.'

'Was she a flirt . . . like Lowri Daniels, for instance?' Her smile was rather crooked now, her tone somewhat resentful.

He hadn't really thought of Sally as a flirt, not until now, but Ffion's question made him consider. He'd always felt so proud to be in Sally's company; seeing men's heads turning appreciatively to gaze after her. Sally had revelled in that sort of attention and he'd noticed the provocative way that she achieved it. A swirl of the hips, a flashing thigh, tight sweaters . . . And the eyes! God! How she could use her eyes to get them drooling! Those eyes gave every man she talked to reason to think that she fancied him, that he could get her into bed. How naïve had he really been, he now wondered. But yes, in retrospect, Sally had definitely been a flirt.

'Well? Was she?'

'Was she what?'

'Don't play games with me, Craig O'Darcy! Was your Sally a flirt?'

'Yes. I suppose she was.'

'Then you're well rid of her. You're better off with me.'

She smiled. He smiled. They kissed.

'Poor Sally! Her loss! I bet she regrets it by now.'

'I bet so too! Just look at the hunk that she's lost.' He straightened to his full height but she ignored his banter.

'As Mam used to say . . . ' And, in a voice and accent that were very reminiscent of her mother's, she recited, in Irish to begin with and then in English, '*It'll be the flirt herself that gets left on the shelf.*'

They laughed.

'Can you help me, please?'

The unexpected voice made them both jump with fright. They'd been so engrossed with one another that they hadn't noticed him standing there, in the shelter of one of the workshops. What frightened them even more was his outlandish appearance.

'Who the hell are you?' Craig took a threatening step forward, to place himself between Ffion and the stranger.

'Would you have food?' The voice sounded weak. 'Please. I don't know where else to turn.'

Craig took another step towards him, gradually getting over his initial shock at seeing such a strangely-dressed visitor. With only a wild pair of eyes and an unkempt beard visible from within a shapeless suit of fleece, he had no way of knowing whether the man was an acquaintance or not.

'We might. Do we know you?'

The answer didn't come directly. 'Yes. I think you do, but . . . '

'But what? Who are you?'

'You might be holding a grudge against me. My name's Dafydd Evans . . . Dave Evans.'

Craig shook his head, then glanced at Ffion, to see if she could help.

'The Poacher!' she whispered. 'Dave the Poacher!'

Craig felt the blood coursing through his veins. The Poacher! The Disney Vulture who'd killed his dog! 'You've got a bloody cheek! Coming here . . . asking for help, after what you did.'

'But I gave all the food back,' he garbled, 'All except what Mr Morgan let me keep. That's God's truth!'

'I'm not talking about the food. I'm talking about what you did to my dog, you bastard!'

All of a sudden, the Poacher was protesting vehemently. 'It wasn't me that killed your dog! And that's God's honest truth.'

'Don't take God's name in vain, you murdering bastard.' He felt Ffion's hand gripping his arm in an effort to restrain the verbal attack, but he'd have none of it. '*You* were the one with the gun. Remember?'

'I may not be a religious man, Mr O'Darcy, but I would never ever take the Lord's name in vain. When you rode away on your bike that day, your dog attacked us . . . bit me, like. But I could have dealt with him, because I have a way with animals, you see. But the other Englishman . . . the one who said that he was your friend and who said that you had a lot of food that belonged to him . . . well, he took the gun from me and he shot your dog from close range. I was going to leave him for doing that – I only kill for food, you understand – but he now had the gun and he threatened me with it. That's God's honest truth that is.'

'But you obviously didn't take much persuading.'

'That's true. My wife and me, we needed the food you see. But it wasn't me who killed your dog. I like dogs. I have a way with dogs.'

He was so convincing, and sounded so pathetic, that Craig had to believe him.

'Let's give him food.' Ffion was at his shoulder, whispering. 'He's genuine. I think I can vouch for that. He's never harmed anyone. Not to my knowledge anyway.'

'Only one!' The Poacher had overheard what she'd said.

'What do you mean, Dafydd?' It was her turn to step forward. 'Who have you harmed?'

'The other Englishman. The one you call Carvel.'

'What about him? Where is he?'

'He's dead. I saw to that, like.'

Craig and Ffion both stiffened. 'You mean you killed him?'

'I suppose I did, but only because he did the same to Janet.' Slowly he went on to describe how Carvel had tricked him out of his house by breaking all his windows and how Janet, his wife, had subsequently frozen to death.

'Sound familiar?' Craig had turned towards Ffion. She nodded.

'And how did you deal with Mr Carvel?'

'Did the same to him, didn't I? Broke his windows, like. Made *his* house cold.'

'An eye for an eye.'

Although the words weren't meant as criticism, The Poacher took them as such. 'I don't usually . . . What do you say? . . . *dal dig* . . . ' He looked towards Ffion for translation.

'Bear a grudge,' she offered.

'That's right. I don't usually bear grudges and I don't believe in that thing about eye for eye and tooth for tooth . . . at least I don't think I do, like, . . . but he made Janet suffer didn't he? And, in a way, he killed her. I couldn't let him get away with that, could I?'

'He had it coming,' Craig muttered. Then louder, 'And now he's dead? You're sure of that?'

'I'm sure. I've been living off his food until four days ago, but now I've got nothing left, see.'

'So you came here. Why?'

'Where else could I go, Mr O'Darcy? There's no more food or anything in town. I don't think there's anybody else left alive there even, apart from me, like. But I thought maybe . . . You know! . . . maybe there was food up here. People used to talk about how Mr Morgan kept a secret supply, . . . so I was hoping.'

He must have seen some slight reaction on the two faces in front of him because he became even more earnest.

'I wouldn't want it for nothing, like. I'd work for it. Do whatever you want.'

Craig and Ffion turned to face one another and to discuss in hushed tones.

'He could have a point, you know, Craig. There can't be many people left alive here apart from the three of us and Tony and Dianne. We could do with his help, especially now that the weather's getting better.'

But Craig was more wary. 'I don't know. Can we trust him?'

'I think we can . . . and I think we should. If there are others still alive, and there might be I suppose, what if they come up here to threaten us? Dave could be very useful to us. Him and Tony.'

Slowly he nodded, then turned towards The Poacher. 'Okay! We'll give you some food . . . what little we can afford . . . but you must promise not to let on to anyone else.'

'May God bless you!' And he genuinely meant it. 'But don't worry about anyone else getting to know about your kindness. As I said, like, there can't be many, if anyone, still alive in Pencraig.'

'Stay there then, Dave, and we'll go and see what we can afford to give you.'

Fifteen minutes later the two of them returned, each carrying a large bag crammed with tinned food. Craig also had a quilted anorak thrown over his arm.

'I've opened one can for you. You're obviously famished.' She passed him the tin of cold beans and they watched in silence as he devoured the contents.

'Can you manage these bags? They're pretty heavy.' He looked frail and exhausted.

For answer, he grabbed at the handles, as if afraid they'd change their minds. He was overwhelmed by their kindness, his deep-set eyes glistening with gratitude. Before he left, he again blessed them and promised to return the next day to help Craig patch up the windows at Plas Cefn. They watched him struggle doggedly into the distance and wondered how long it would take him to make the long journey home under the weight of his newly-gained provisions

*   *   *

Dave was as good as his word, as was Tony. They were both up at the house by eleven o'clock the following morning, having first of all waited for the night's hard frost to relent. Dave was once more recognisable, having discarded his sheep's clothing in preference to the anorak that he'd been given. Needless to say, he and Tony had been pleasantly surprised to find one another still alive.

Craig and Ffion were already at Plas Cefn, waiting for them. They'd found Tristan in the front lounge, huddled in front of a cold fireplace, and ironically with a considerable supply of food beside him. He'd been dead for months and the sub-zero conditions had effectively refrigerated his body.

Ffion cried briefly and then pleaded with Craig and the others to get his coffin. They obliged, but Craig then insisted that she leave them alone so that they could lay her brother out. He knew full well that there was but one way to get the curled-up body into the coffin – rigid joints would have to be straightened, bones would have to be broken.

It proved neither easy nor pleasant. As the first knee broke under Craig's weight and as the leg straightened, Tony made an excuse to keep Ffion company. Dave, however, stayed to see the job through. It was a much harder task than either of them had imagined. The amount of physical effort required surprised them both, not least to straighten the spine. And as the vertebras cracked, both of them were overcome by nausea. Finally, however, Tristan was laid to rest in the coffin that already bore his name.

Ffion wanted her brother to be taken to lie side by side with her father in the snow near the adit entrance until such time as they could both be removed to the chamber vault, but Craig would have none of the irony. Instead, he convinced her that it would be wasted effort on their part, that Tristan should be buried in a convenient drift near the house, from where he could more easily be taken down to the burial chamber, once the snow had sufficiently cleared off the road.

By late afternoon, all the windows had again been covered with thick plastic sheeting, which was just as well, because as Tony and Dave prepared to leave, both of them delighted at being allowed to share Tristan's untouched supplies, the wind had picked up to a near gale.

The extra generosity proved providential for both of them because by morning, the heavy black clouds had returned with a vengeance, to fill the sky and to block out the sun's light and warmth once again.

Chapter 3

'Why do you do that?'

He looked up across the board.

'Why do I do what?'

'Run your finger along the break of your nose like that?'

'Oh! Didn't realise. Does it bother you?'

'Not really. It's just that I've noticed you do it every time you're worried . . . and you're worried now.' She was smiling because she was once again getting the better of him, this time at Super Scrabble. The word 'zigzaggy', confirmed by the Oxford Dictionary, had just given her more points than his entire total so far. Her smile, though, was far too smug for his liking.

One thing they'd agreed on, when they'd realised that the cold weather was back to stay, was to live their lives as normally as was practically possible. That meant keeping regular mealtimes and retiring at roughly the same hour every night, since neither of them wished to return to a semi-comatose state of hibernation. It also meant filling in their time profitably and Ffion had drawn up a list of suggestions on how best to do that. Reading was to be one pastime, playing games another. They also agreed that he should take language lessons. Monday and Tuesday mornings would begin with forty five minutes of Welsh; French on Wednesdays and Thursdays; German on Fridays and Saturdays. And to improve his vocabulary in each, they adapted the game of Scrabble to suit their needs. Sundays, however, were English Super Scrabble days. Most afternoons were for exercise and for reading.

'Good grief! You've got a whole library here!'

She'd led him into the cabin in the other cavern. It had shelves stacked high with all sorts of tinned and dried food as well as two huge crate-cupboards full of books.

'Both crates have been specially lined,' she explained as she'd opened the larger of the two. 'They're damp-proof. The smaller one only has duplicates.'

'Duplicates?' He'd laughed at the idea, had questioned her priorities. 'Books? And duplicates? Bloody hell, Ffion! Surely there were more important things to think of?'

But she'd challenged him. 'What if every book ever published had been destroyed? Have you thought of that? The tragedy that would have been! And I naturally wanted duplicates of the more important ones, just in case.'

'Naturally.'

She'd sensed his cynicism. 'Aren't there any books that you would have wanted to salvage?'

'Can't think of any. I've never been much into reading, I'm afraid. Except for a few old comics, I can't think of anything worth saving, leave alone keeping duplicates of.'

'Craig O'Darcy, you're a philistine! That's what you are!'

But she'd known that he was joking and he'd smiled.

'So tell me what literary classics you've safeguarded for posterity. All Welsh, I bet.'

'Stop being so facetiousness! *The Bible*, naturally, came top of my list! English and Welsh versions . . . *The Complete Works of Shakespeare* of course . . . Chaucer, Milton . . . a full set of Dickens . . . History books, including English and Welsh editions of John Davies' *History of Wales* . . . anthologies containing the works of all the major poets as well as volumes of Welsh poetry dating back to the epic stuff of the sixth century . . . collections of Celtic legends, not least the Welsh *Mabinogion* . . . Tolstoy, Dostoyevski, Chekov . . . Moliere, Maupassant . . . Homer, naturally . . . Aristophanes, Sophocles . . . Plato and Aristotle . . . Books on Geometry, Calculus, Astronomy . . . Dictionaries, medical and otherwise, 'The Paramedic's A – Z' . . . Do I need to go on?'

'Bloody hell! All of it heavy-going, I'd say, except for the one on astronomy perhaps. Haven't you any spicy novels that I could cut my teeth on?'

At the time, he wouldn't have believed it, but a few days later they were reading 'Macbeth' together. And although the archaic syntax gave him problems, and multisyllabic phrases like *'The multitudinous seas incarnadine'* caused him to stutter and to swear, he gradually came to relish some of the character parts. And as the days passed, they took turns at rendering their favourite soliloquies out loud, even attempting to act some choice scenes together. Needless to say, Ffion's Lady Macbeth far outshone anything that Craig could offer. 'As You Like It' then gave them light relief and by the time they were back to the tragic stuff, he was more than ready for the challenge of Lear and Othello. He made a particular meal of the scene where he had Desdemona by the throat on her bed, threatening to choke the life out of her unless she surrendered to his demands. As he readily admitted afterwards, Shakespeare could be great fun.

Another unexpected surprise for him had been their brief sessions of biblical readings. He'd baulked at the idea to begin with, readily admitting that he'd never even *held* a Bible in his hands before then, but when Ffion made him read the Sermon on the Mount he became somewhat captivated by the melodic repetition of the 'Blesséd are verses' as he came to refer to them . . . Blesséd are the poor . . . Blesséd are the meek . . . Blesséd are the merciful . . . Blesséd are the pure in heart . . . Blesséd are the peacemakers. . . Blesséd are they . . . He liked the sound of the words as they rolled off his tongue. And he'd added one of his own – 'Blesséd are they who are still alive.' He'd then listened to her rendition of them in Welsh and had had to admit that they sounded just as melodic.

'Let's go for some poetry! I think you'd enjoy it.'

The suggestion had come one afternoon and he'd willingly lain back with his eyes shut and listened to her reading.

When she finally closed the anthology, she'd paused before asking, 'Well, which one did you like most?'

He'd taken time to consider. 'That Hopkins fellow I think. Gerald something-or-other.'

'Why?'

'Must I say why? I just enjoyed the sound of it, that's all.'

She'd smiled and left it at that. Later, she'd read him a verse or two from Fitzgerald's Omar Khayyám before handing him the volume. From then on the 'Rubáiyát' became his favourite reading and he often recited verses out loud, memorising some of the quatrains as he went along. With time, however, the monotony of the metre and Omar's underlying pessimism got to them both.

And so the days became weeks and the weeks months. Every so often they took pains to trim one another's hair, and Ffion paid special attention to Craig's beard, trying to give it some style. At first, he'd taken it upon himself to check on the state of the weather every couple of days but it became so desperately cold in the tunnel every time he opened the outside doors that he soon decided that a fortnightly check would be frequent enough. In fact, it was a good job that the doors swung inwards, otherwise the thick blanket of frozen snow would have prevented them opening at all. It was also fortunate that the adit entrance was sheltered from the prevailing wind or it would be buried in drifts by now.

Occasionally, they talked of Tony and Dianne and of Dave the Poacher, and wondered pessimistically about their chances of survival. The outside temperature, they knew, could be anything between forty and ninety degrees below. 'Tony should have accepted our offer' was an often-used phrase to end those conversations, especially when they felt embarrassed by their own relative warmth and comfort. Craig was the more conscience-stricken of the two, because he knew how desperately cold things could really be on the surface. He also realised how privileged he and Ffion really were. There could be no more than a few thousand people in the whole world who'd have had the opportunity to prepare as thoroughly as Rees had done, and most of those would have been high-ranking politicians like Alistair, key scientists, doctors and surgeons, top engineers and architects, botanists . . . Various governments, he felt sure, would have planned for the post-impact years by safeguarding that sort of expertise. It had also been rumoured at the time that huge purpose-built buildings had been erected in various countries to house not only different species of creatures, ranging from wood lice and butterflies and bees to giraffes and buffaloes and elephants – a sort of multi-location Noah's Ark – but also state-of-the-art genetic laboratories.

As time passed, their games and their sessions of group reading had become less frequent and the language lessons and the acting had ceased altogether. They'd reached a stage where they couldn't escape each other's irritability. Craig blamed it on Ffion, maintaining that their rows always started with her. She'd become withdrawn and ill-tempered of late and it was starting to show again now.

He backed away from the Scrabble board, tired of the game, annoyed by her smugness, by her competence. 'What say we have a party today?'

'To celebrate what, for God's sake?' There it was! Her peevishness!

'To celebrate May the sixteenth! To celebrate the fact that we've been locked in here for a year to the day.'

'Stupid!' Abandoning the game, she went to lie on her bed and buried her head in a book, but Craig knew that she wasn't reading. She was too fidgety by far and, as the minutes passed, he noticed that no pages were being turned. He also realised that they were heading straight for another row.

He regarded her, long and hard. 'Of course! That's what I am! Stupid! What else? Always stupid!'

For answer, she turned her back to him, still pretending to read, and this annoyed him more.

'Educational snob, that's what you are, Ffion. Just because you've been to Oxford . . . '

Her shoulders were shaking and he assumed that she was laughing at him.

' . . . Damn you! I should have stayed at Hafod.'

When she turned, he realised that she hadn't been laughing at all. Her eyes and her cheeks were wet and he suddenly felt rather foolish and ashamed.

'Maybe you should,' she sobbed.

'I'm sorry. I thought . . . thought that . . . ' he began lamely and left his explanation unsaid. 'What is it? What's the matter?'

She sat up. The tears now flowing.

'For God's sake, Ffion! What is it?'

'I think I'm . . . ,' and then in a hushed voice, 'pregnant.'

The possibility had often crossed his mind during their early months of love-making, and he had worried over the implications but, as time went by, he'd come to think that, for whatever reason, she just wasn't able to conceive. Which was why he now felt so stunned by what he'd heard.

'Are you sure?'

Slowly she nodded her head.

'How long have you known?'

'Two months.'

'Why didn't you say anything?'

'I had to be sure.'

'But now you are?'

'I think so.'

'So that means . . . ' He used his fingers for counting. ' . . . December?'

She again nodded.

Eventually he overcame his shock, sat beside her on the matress and placed an arm across her shoulders. 'You'll be all right. There's plenty of time. Things will have improved by then, you'll see.'

But his voice lacked conviction and she sensed it.

Chapter 4

'Have you thought how we're going to stay alive once these supplies run out?'

They were standing in the storeroom, taking stock of the depleted shelves. Ffion, heavily pregnant, and wearing layers of warm clothing, was looking around for somewhere to sit and Craig pointed her to an empty shelf that she could lean on. He'd noticed how agitated she'd become of late, due mainly, he thought, to her increasing concern about the fate of their child once it was born. Which was probably why she'd insisted on accompanying him now, to take stock of their situation. He'd pleaded with her to stay in the warmth of their living quarters but she'd stubbornly refused.

'Let's not worry about that, now. The supplies in the truck up at Hafod have barely been touched, and some of your father's Contingency Reserves are still left at the site. We can last out for months again, if need be.'

'And after that . . . ? Or when the propane tank is empty and we no longer have any heating? What then?'

Craig watched her run an anxious hand over her distended belly. How was he to dispel her mood of pessimism?

'After that, we just take things as they come, that's all. Let's not meet sorrow half way.'

Two days later, on December the third, she gave birth to a healthy-looking baby girl and Craig, with the help of 'The Paramedic's A – Z', helped her through a prolonged and difficult delivery. Afterwards, Ffion's instinctive regret was not knowing how much the baby weighed, whilst Craig, in sheer relief, jokingly wondered what Santa Claus might bring.

'So what do we call her?'

They'd discussed names before now, but they'd all been boys' names. Neither of them had seriously considered the possibility of anything but a son.

'Whatever it is, it'll have to be . . . '

'Welsh! . . . Yes, I know!' He smiled contentedly at the two of them, watching the child sucking at its mother's breast. The birth was their first joyous experience in months and he was determined not to spoil it in any way. 'What do you suggest?'

'Branwen.'

'Branwen?' He looked surprised. 'That's the name of a sea!' He was thinking of the nearby Bay of Branwen.

Realising what he meant, she laughed out loud. 'Craig O'Darcy! How silly can you be?' She motioned him to come nearer to be kissed. 'The bay got its name from a girl in the first place! Branwen is a girl's name.'

'Oh?' He pretended to look sheepish and hurt. 'So tell me about it.'

'If you'd read the Mabinogion, as I've suggested to you many a time, then you'd know! Pass it to me!' She pointed towards a finely bound Gregynog Press volume of Welsh legends and when he passed it to her, she one-handedly thumbed the pages until she finally came to a title page – 'Yr Ail Gainc: Branwen Ferch Llyr'.*

He expected her to start reading but instead, she looked up and began summarising from memory.

'Llyr was king of Britain – same name, by the way, as the one that gave Shakespeare his *Lear*! When he died, his son Brân Fendigaid – a giant of a man – took to the throne. Branwen was his sister and she had been given as wife to Matholwch, king of Ireland . . . '

Craig smiled, sat back, and listened to her telling the tale. She had a way with words and, as they rolled over her tongue, he began to see her as an itinerant storyteller in some dim Celtic past.

' . . . But Branwen was cruelly treated by her husband. She was kept prisoner in her room in the palace and Matholwch ordered that no ship was to cross the sea to Britain, lest Brân should come to hear about his sister's suffering . . . '

Craig watched and listened, amused by the fact that the story was being told not so much for his benefit as for that of the suckling child.

' . . . And she befriended a bird – a starling – that came to her window, and the more she talked to it, the more it seemed to understand what was being said. And so a plan began to form in her mind. She took pains to describe her brother, the giant king, to the little bird and then, when she was convinced that it understood, she beseeched it to act as her messenger, as her postman. She wrote a note, describing her misery, and tied it under the starling's wing before sending the little bird on its long journey over the miles of open sea . . . '

He listened as she went on to tell how war broke out between Britain and Ireland and how Branwen was rescued and how her brother, the king, was killed.

'And so the bay was named after her?'

'Yes. The whole Irish army was destroyed. Not a man in any of the five kingdoms of Ireland was left alive. And only seven of the Britons

---

* 'The Second Branch: Branwen, Daughter of Llyr'

survived, with Branwen herself making eight. But she was so heartbroken at having been the cause of all that devastation and killing that she, too, soon gave up the ghost and died.'

Craig smiled. 'Sad tale! Let's hope that *our* little Branwen finds more luck in life.'

The baby was sleeping contentedly at its mother's breast.

Chapter 5

During their twenty-two-month incarceration underground, they experienced several earth tremors, but nothing really frightening or life-threatening. Either the Richter value of the quakes was small or their epicentres were many miles distant. In early March, however, they were woken, not so much by the violent shaking of everything around them as by the deep and angry rumbling rising out of the bowels of the Earth; a thunder being magnified by all those empty caverns in the mountain below them, as if all the bass stops of a mighty organ had been pulled open on a discordant note. It went on and on for what seemed an age and Craig instinctively pulled Ffion into his arms whilst she, in turn, clasped her child to her breast. They listened, terrified, to muffled thuds and crashes, as if bombs were falling on a far-off target. Then, suddenly, a close-by eruption of noise made them jump, causing little Branwen to start howling. Ffion, herself, was too tense, too terrified, to cry.

The tremor lasted for ten seconds or more and was followed by a series of lesser aftershocks. To the frightened parents, however, the experience seemed to last a lifetime. Eventually, everywhere became quiet again.

'That was the worst yet! It's a good job we're safe down here.' Craig had felt anything but safe and he hardly expected his sham optimism to fool her.

It didn't. 'There have been roof falls in some of the other chambers and a big fall in the one next door, I'd say. We'll have to go and see.'

'I'll go.'

'But not until we're sure it's safe, you won't!' The fear was still in her eyes. 'Give it half an hour, just in case there's some more loose stuff to come down.' She seemed to know what she was talking about. 'You heard those falls in other chambers below us. I only hope the roof of this one is safe.' She looked up to indicate her concern. 'Dad said that this had the safest roof of all, so we should be all right . . . hopefully.'

When he eventually got to the next chamber, the sight unnerved him. After cautiously inspecting its high ceiling with the beam of his torch and finding no imminent danger there, he ventured inside, only to discover that a huge block of slate, at least two to three tons in weight, had been shaken loose from above and had crashed onto one corner of their storeroom, causing the rest of the structure to lean precariously to one side. A quick inspection told him that some of their food had been lost, but that the main casualty was their reserve of warm clothing. Wryly, he imagined how relieved Ffion would be that her books were unscathed. The water constantly dripping from the roof posed some kind of threat to them, though . . .

That's when he stopped to take stock of what he was seeing, what he was thinking. He remembered how Rees had once told him that one of the greatest problems of underground quarrying had been the surface water that continually seeped through into the caverns. In those days, according to Rees, pumps had had to be in constant use to keep the working areas from flooding, and today, if the old man was to be believed, all levels from the G-Floor down were well and truly flooded, and possibly frozen too, by now.

When he first become aware of the dripping water, Craig's instinctive reasoning was that the roof-fall had, in some way or other, made it easier for surface water to drain through. It was only gradually that he realised that there shouldn't be any running water at all, not unless . . . !

He rushed back to tell Ffion and waited impatiently for her to voice-activate the door so that he could be let in.

''Get your coat! Come on!'

'What is it? What's wrong?' She was misinterpreting his excitement for panic.

'I think it's thawing!' And then louder and even more animated, 'I think the warm weather's back with us!'

When they pulled open the outer doors, the blinding sunlight hurt their eyes and Ffion instinctively shaded her baby's face against it. The air was so warm, it was unreal.

The snow was waist high and frozen hard to a depth of a foot or more. But it was melting, because its surface now was nothing but thick slush that indicated that the thaw had been in progress for some time. Craig now gathered some of it in his hand and watched it quickly melt and run through his warm fingers. He grinned widely at Ffion; she grinned back and leaned forward against him.

'Thank God!' she muttered.

'Yes,' he readily agreed. 'Thank God!'

Later, he climbed out and walked around in the fresh air, feeling elated. He was convinced that he could smell the Spring. The sky was overcast with no blue to be seen but it was ordinary cloud cover. Gone was the blanket of sub-micron dust that had blocked out the sun's light and warmth.

He'd have liked to climb higher up the slope to be able to study the southern sky but every step he took ended with him slithering back further than where he'd first started. He took great comfort from the fact that the sky to the west – what he could see of it – showed no threat and this gave him heart. After all, that was where the weather, like the prevailing wind, usually came from.

Below him, the buildings of Pencraig Roofing were just mounds of silver grey. Plas Cefn, in the distance, was more conspicuous because of the blue plastic sheeting of its upstairs windows; ground floor level, with its front door and three bays, was hidden by huge drifts. Only two of the big pines were still standing and even they were leaning precariously, supported only by the gable end of the house.

He returned to take charge of Branwen, so that Ffion, too, could fill her lungs with the warm, healthy air.

*   *   *

It surprised them how quickly the snow cleared. They'd expected it to take weeks if not months, but within four days the dark grey of the slate rubble had started to show. By the end of the month, patches of yellows and browns were beginning to show on distant hills and the sound of running water constantly filled the air, as more and more streams were formed by the quickly melting snow. It was a sound that gladdened their hearts and gave them hope.

By mid-April, apart from the stubborn drifts and the pockets of snow that never saw any sun, only slush remained, and Craig could no longer escape his obligation to dig two coffins out of their temporary graves, to take them down to the Vault Chambers. His conscience, if nothing else, told him that Rees – and Tristan too, probably – deserved a better resting place than they'd had up to now. He knew that he had to act before the coffins became exposed to the sun when the bodies within them would begin to thaw and to decompose. But how to take them down to the vault chambers was another matter! It all depended on whether he could get the Leech to start or not.

Some of the melted snow at the adit entrance had flowed into the mouth of the tunnel so that the 6 x 6 LR now stood in trapped water at least a foot deep. If left where it was, the rubber of its tyres would soon perish. It also meant that Craig and Ffion got their feet wet every time they used the adit entrance. So, they began to plan not only the removal of Rees' and Tristan's coffins but also moving themselves to Plas Cefn to live. The latter was an easy enough decision to make; the fear of another quake saw to that. But first they had to sort out the Leech.

281

'I just can't get it to start.' Craig had just returned for lunch, baffled and irritable. 'I've been at it all morning. The battery's fully charged and the radiator's been filled – I've seen to those – and I've checked everything else there is to check. I may not know much about these fuel-cell machines but, according to the dials on the dashboard, the tanks are three quarters full, the heat exchangers are A1, the fuel cells are okay, as is the humidifier . . . So what's wrong I just don't bloody well know.'

At the time, Ffion was in the process of feeding Branwen. As she listened, her look of sympathy gradually gave way to a ghost of a smile.

'You find it funny?' But *he* wasn't smiling.

'You know that it runs on hydrogen?'

'Of course I do. I've just told you that the tanks are three quarters full. And before you start giving me lessons, let me tell you that I'm familiar with the process of electrolysis. I know, for instance, that if hydrogen combines with oxygen and water then you can have electricity. Am I right? And the Leech has an electric motor! Right again . . . ?'

Her smile broadened. His churlishness seemed to amuse rather than aggravate her.'And you know, of course, that the hydrogen is pumped into the tanks at very high pressure . . . ?'

'So?'

'And, as a nuclear physicist, you'll surely know that hydrogen is highly inflammable . . . '

'Stop playing with me Ffion. I've never claimed to be a nuclear physicist. What the hell are you trying to tell me?'

His comments went unheeded. ' . . . In which case, you'll know about the safety device.'

She suddenly saw him biting his lip.

'What safety device?'

'The one that automatically cuts off the supply if the car has been stationary for a long period.'

'Bloody hell! Why didn't you tell me sooner? So how do I switch it on again?'

This time her smile was sympathetic. 'I'm sorry, love. It hadn't occurred to me until now or I'd have told you. All you need do is switch on the ignition and then do nothing for a full thirty seconds. The computer board will check for any faults or any leaked pockets of gas and if there are none then you'll see a green light come on. It should start after that.'

*   *   *

282

That afternoon, he dug Rees' coffin out of the snow and single-handedly managed to load it into the back of the Leech. He then drove over to Plas Cefn to search the snowdrift where they'd interred Tristan's coffin.

'Need a hand?'

He almost jumped out of his skin. He'd been too engrossed in his work to hear anyone approaching. He turned to see three pale but beaming faces looking at him – Tony! . . . His wife, Dianne! . . . The Poacher! – and his mouth fell open in disbelief.

'Good God! You're not alive, are you?'

Tony laughed out loud; the other two continued to smile. 'I think we are! Either that or we're three of the most tangible ghosts you're ever likely to meet.'

The next minute Craig was embracing each of them in turn, aware, as he did so, of their thin frames.

'How did you manage? Where did you get the food? How did you survive the cold?' He was looking from one to the other. 'And where the hell have you been till now? Why didn't you come up sooner?'

'If you'd only shut up for a minute, I'd tell you.' Tony feigned a playful punch at Craig's solar plexus. He, too, felt euphoric, despite his feebleness.

'Better still, why don't you first of all help me with this other coffin, then, when we get back from the burial chamber, you can tell Ffion and myself . . . and Branwen of course! . . . all about it.'

'Branwen?' The three looked confused. 'Who the hell is Branwen?'

But Craig merely smiled and said 'You'll see! Now, will you help me? Dianne can join Ffion while we're at it.'

Once they'd laid Rees and Tristan to rest alongside Sinéad, Craig turned to Dave, 'Shall we go for your wife as well?'

But The Poacher, after a second or two to consider, shook his head. 'What for? There's no coffin is there, like? Janet would want to be left where she is, I think.'

The other two nodded. The choice for him wasn't a difficult one to make.

Half an hour later, the five of them were sitting around the table, sipping hot cups of instant soup. Dianne had had her own little surprise, one that Craig got to know about from an excited Ffion as soon as he arrived back. 'Craig! What do you think? Dianne is expecting! Don't you think that's wonderful?'

Craig readily agreed. Yes, it was very wonderful, under the circumstances.

As Ffion later told him, Tony and Dianne had been wanting to start a family for years but without success. There had been one early miscarriage, apparently, and doctors had told Dianne at the time that she needed to lose a considerable amount of weight before she could hope to conceive and successfully carry for the full term. It was ironic, therefore, that this pregnancy had been made possible by the enforced diet of the past three years.

'But how the hell did you survive? The temperature . . . ? Food . . . ?' If anything, Craig marvelled more at The Poacher's survival than that of Tony and Dianne even.

Tony smiled into his soup before answering. 'The day that we left you – How long ago was it? Two years, must be! – I persuaded Dave here to come and live with us in the bungalow.' Briefly, he pointed towards the walls that surrounded them. 'Do you remember me telling you that it was me who supplied the thermostyrene insulation for these wall cavities . . . ?' He waited until he saw Craig nod. ' . . . I'd just had a cancelled order at the time. Arnolds, the housing contractors had intended to build six new bungalows in Portharian and had ordered the cavity insulation for them. But then the news broke about the asteroid and that put everything on hold.' He smiled and laid a loving hand on his wife's arm. 'Best thing that could have happened to us, actually, because when the time came, I was able to use a lot of the stuff to double-line the inside walls and roof of my own bungalow. Made a hell of a difference during that long winter, I can tell you . . . !'

Craig noticed The Poacher nodding agreement.

' . . . And then more snow came and the drifts more or less covered the house, which was great, because they also helped to keep out the freezing winds. And like yourselves, I'd made sure that I had a good supply of propane. Of course, we've had to ration our warmth just like our food but I doubt if we could have lasted more than another month or two. '

'But food? You couldn't possibly have had enough to last you all these months?'

'We've got a confession to make, actually. A couple of days after we last saw you, and when we realised that the cold weather was back to stay, Dave and I decided to come up to Plas Cefn to help ourselves to what was there.'

Ffion smiled at him. 'Yes, the kitchen was well-stocked of course . . . in addition to what . . . what Dad gave . . . my brother.' She successfully fought back the painful memory. 'But how did you get in?'

'The day we put your brother in his coffin it was. I'd noticed the stock of food then, when I wandered into the kitchen. Anyway, Dave and I came up here and used a power-grinder to cut through a couple of the steel bars on the bay window. I hope you don't mind? We had to make the journey two days running, to carry all the food down. The wind was bloody cold, I can tell you! Wasn't it Dave? Actually we didn't think we were going to make it back the second time.'

'But where have you been these past few weeks, since the snow's cleared?'

The three of them laughed and it was Tony who again explained. 'Didn't I just tell you that we've been snowed under? Our bungalow's pretty exposed to the weather, as you know, and the drifts literally buried the whole house. We had no idea that the weather had improved until this morning. That's when we heard snow sliding off the roof and the next thing we saw was sunlight coming in through the dormer windows. You can imagine how we felt!'

'So what happens now?' It was Ffion's question.

Dianne looked at Tony, Tony at Dave.

'That's why we're here. We were hoping that we could come to some sort of arrangement.' He looked at Craig. 'You once suggested that Dianne and I could live with you at Plas Cefn, at least until it was safe to return to Pencraig . . . when there's less danger of disease. We could help you with whatever repairs have to be done.'

Tony didn't notice Dave's unease; Craig did. 'No problem. And that includes you of course, Dave.'

For answer, The Poacher began to mumble his thanks but the gist of what he was saying was that it would be better for all concerned if he lived alone.

'Well if you prefer, you're welcome to use the bungalow Dave. You know that. But is it worth the risk, staying in town? I mean . . . ' He wanted to mention the risk of disease from decomposing bodies but realised that he couldn't, at least not without appearing insensitive.

By way of interruption, Craig got to his feet. 'I think,' he said, 'that I can suggest an arrangement that might suit our friend better.'

Chapter 6

'Branwen! Tyrd o fan'na, rwan! Ti a Dylan!•

The four year old, startled by her mother's harsh command, stopped dead in her tracks and looked sheepishly towards her younger, smaller companion.

'If you tread on those lettuces, I'm going to become very angry.'

Dianne joined Ffion in the open doorway. 'They're getting to be quite a handful, aren't they?'

Ffion's scowl gave way to a wry smile. 'The garden isn't exactly flourishing, is it? We can't afford to have them spoiling what little we have.'

Together, the two women returned indoors, happy that the youngsters had now left the vegetable patch for the relative safety of their usual play area.

'Do you know what surprises me about them? They're so young and yet they can distinguish between the two languages. Dylan will patter away in English to Tony and me and then straightaway answer you or Dave in Welsh. And Branwen's just the same with you and Craig. I find that astonishing. Don't you . . . ?'

Ffion paused in her stride but said nothing, allowing Dianne to continue.

' . . . You've even got Branwen learning to *read*, haven't you? In both languages!'

Ffion shrugged. 'I do what I can.'

'It's important to you, isn't it? That they learn Welsh.' They'd reached the kitchen and Dianne watched her friend quietly but firmly nod her head. 'Do you mind if I ask you why?'

'Same reason that I'm anxious for her to learn English. Same reason, in a few years' time, why I'll be hoping to pass on to her what little French and German I myself have . . . '

'But why? I mean, what's the thinking behind it? As long as we understand one another, as long as we can communicate . . . '

Ffion reached for a cloth and began wiping the kitchen top, thus taking a few seconds to consider her answer. 'Language is to do with more than just communicating, don't you think? Or maybe I should say that it's to do with more than one kind of communicating. You see, Dianne . . . when Branwen is older, I want her to be able to appreciate what's on those bookshelves in the other room. I want her to be able to

---

• *Branwen! Get away from there, this minute! You and Dylan!'*

286

read Shakespeare and Milton. To let *them* communicate with her if you like! I want her to share the imagination of . . . ' She waved a hand to suggest that her daughter would be spoilt for choice. ' . . . Raoul Dahl, Mark Twain . . . Chekov even, when she's old enough! And James Joyce, of course! Mam would have wanted that! . . . And in time, I want her to have the chance, if she ever wants it, to *listen* to the thoughts of Aristotle and Plato, and Darwin and Newton . . . ' She paused, and Dianne could see in her eyes an obsessive determination. 'But I also want her to know about her own people. I want her to appreciate Welsh history and Welsh literature and to take pride in her heritage. And I especially want her to be able to turn to the New Testament when she feels the need to . . . , which will be quite often I imagine.' She stopped and smiled, somewhat embarrassed, realising that she'd got carried away. 'Tell you what, Dianne! Why don't we prepare a little picnic and take it up to the men? The kids will enjoy the walk.'

Up at Hafod, Tony and Dave were helping Craig to put the last of the wheels back on the truck. It had been a relief to find that the rubber of the tyres hadn't perished too badly. They'd spent all morning pumping air into them, with the use of an ordinary foot pump. That, in itself, had been a long and tedious task but they'd finally managed it and now Tony had climbed up into the cab and had switched on the ignition.

'Nothing! I can't understand it. There's plenty of hydrogen in the tanks, the battery's been fully charged and we've filled the radiator. According to the dials, the heat exchangers are okay, and so is the dehumidifier. So why the hell won't it start? Give me a diesel engine any day, I say! These bloody fuel-cell engines are just a load of trouble. Fact is, we should have tried starting the damn thing before wasting time and effort on the tyres.'

Craig smiled to himself. 'A little word of advice, Tony! Switch off the ignition, then switch it on again and leave it for a full half minute without doing anything. If a green light appears on the dash, then there should be no problem.'

'Well bugger me!' The truck was purring contentedly and Tony was smiling broadly. 'Good for you, Rocky!'

Craig assumed the air of a professional mechanic and smiled knowingly back at his friend. It had been Tony's idea to get the truck on the road again, after he'd come across a large supply tank of hydrogen, complete with pressure hose and nozzle, on site at Pencraig Roofing. But it had taken them another twelve months or more to finally get round to the task, simply because there had been other, more pressing jobs to do.

As far as Craig was concerned, Tony had been a revelation. Not only had he been the driving force who knew exactly how to utilise the individual talents of each and every one of them, but his own plumbing and other skills had also proved invaluable. With the wide range of tools available to him at the Pencraig Roofing workshop, he had first of all re-established a fresh water supply for Plas Cefn and had made the solar roofing again operational so that now they had hot water and central heating as well, if they wanted it. He'd also provided Dave at Hafod with a supply of cold water, piped directly from the spring outside. And, having done all that, he'd then got to work on erecting windmills to supply the Plas and the cottage with generated electricity, so that they no longer had to depend entirely on the generators that had served Craig and Ffion so well during the cold years. And it had also been at his instigation that the three of them, suitably equipped with face masks, had gone down to Pencraig to collect as many panels of double glazing as they could lay their hands on – many of them out of Tony's own bungalow. He'd then adapted those, as best he could, to replace the ones that Simon Carvel and his young tearaways had broken at Plas Cefn, the night that Sinéad and Rees were shot.

Dave had also proved his worth. As their rations had diminished, The Poacher had quickly realised where his responsibilities lay, so, once the thaw was complete, he'd equipped himself with Rees Morgan's fishing tackle and had begun his rounds of the area's many lakes, targeting those that he knew to be the deepest. The shallower ones, he realised, would have been frozen solid and their fish stocks wiped out, but the deeper lakes offered more hope. His success, however, was limited, until he decided to take the Leech down to the coast. There, on one memorable day, he'd hit upon a shoal of mackerel and had returned to Plas Cefn with his usually impassive features creased by a broad smile of success. For the next three days they'd feasted without ration and felt better than they'd done since their world had changed.

Leaving Tony to rev up the engine, Craig turned to join Dave who was now gazing quietly towards the distant bay, where white patches, here and there, showed that the sea hadn't yet thawed out completely. The ravaged coastline, the absence of Caer Môr's windows glinting in distant sunlight, the brown scar that had once been the picturesque Arian Valley were all painful reminders of the Earth's recent trauma. But there was growth as well! Trees on distant slopes, too remote to have been chopped down for firewood, were now in leaf. There were bushes that had sprung up, and there was colour where the occasional broom and hawthorn flowered. All in all, things were improving quicker than any of them had ever imagined. As yet, the sea hadn't claimed as much land as had been predicted but its level could be seen to be rising as the thaw continued. The distant promontory was noticeably diminished and waves now lapped where once the River Arian had lazily meandered.

'Can you hear it?' Dave was holding an excited finger in the air, his eyes eagerly searching an overcast sky.

'What? Hear what?'

'Sh! Listen!'

Craig listened. It was a song he recognised. 'Skylark?'

The Poacher's smile was uncharacteristically broad and he nodded. Then he was pointing. 'There! Can you see it?'

But Craig didn't have The Poacher's keen eyesight.

It was the first bird that they'd heard in over seven years and they signalled Tony to switch off the truck's engine and to listen. That was when they heard a different sound, coming at them from the south, a whirring from afar.

'Are my ears playing tricks or what?' Tony had joined them, the high pitch of his voice betraying his excitement. 'That can't be a chopper, can it?'

For what seemed an eternity, they kept their eyes peeled on the distant ridge of mountains.

'There!' Dave was pointing towards the darkest of the clouds.

It took a second or two for the others to spot it coming, then they were all three waving furiously to attract the pilot's attention. At first it seemed that he was going to pass them by, but then he saw them, circled, waved and finally found a place to bring it down about a hundred metres away on the track, with its rotors spinning perilously close to the scarp face.

They were then surprised to see two men, wearing white overalls and surgical masks beneath protective headgear, climb out of the aircraft, both carrying security screening scopes similar to the ones that Craig had seen used at Sellafield B and at Storage Site 5. One of them was also carrying a white box. Behind them, two bearded soldiers appeared in battle-dress, their guns at the ready.

No word was said while the three of them were frisked with the scopes, then one of the soldiers drew nearer, to within twenty yards of them. He wanted to be heard over the noise of the rotors.

'What are your names?'

They shouted back and saw him make a note of each answer in turn. He then wanted to know how many of them had survived and how they'd been able to do so. Although objecting to his authoritative manner, Craig nevertheless complied but made his explanation as curt as possible.

'Apart from one farmer and his wife, up in the wilds of the Cambrian Massif, you're the only other survivors that we've come across up to now.' The words belonged to one of the two in overalls.

'Good God!'

Craig wasn't as surprised as he sounded, though. Nor were the others for that matter.

'And who are you, then?' he asked. 'Where have you come from?'

The loud whine of the chopper and the flapping of its rotors, meant that he, too, had to shout.

'We're checking survivors for contamination. But you've probably guessed that already, haven't you?' A grin appeared behind the mask.

'What sort of contamination? Radioactivity?'

'Amongst other things . . . Bubonic plague, typhoid, dysentery . . . exposure to solar ultraviolet flux . . . you name it! We need to know. Tell me, have you come into contact with any rotting corpses?'

'No.'

'Drinking water? Where do you get it from?'

Dave extended an arm in the direction of the escarpment behind the cottage. 'There's good water coming out of the rock over there. You'll find nothing better, like.'

'Artesian well?'

'S'pose so!'

'I'd still boil it if I were you. Better to play safe.' He cast a quick look around. 'You're lucky, you know, to be living on these upper slopes. The acid should drain quickly from your soil and, as time passes, you should find things improving around here; vegetables and stuff like that will start to flourish.' His conversational tone suddenly gave way to a more practical one. 'Now then, we'll have to take some swabs and blood samples, if you don't mind. Can we use the cottage?'

'You still haven't answered my question.'

'What question was that, sir?' They'd arrived indoors and he'd placed his white box on the table. He now unclasped the lid and took out a number of swabs, individually packed in resealable plastic sachets.

'Who are you? Where are you from? By what authority are you here?'

'Not one but three! Questions I mean!' He was still smiling as if intent on establishing their full co-operation. 'The two of us are medical scientists. They . . . ' He indicated towards the two soldiers outside. ' . . . belong to the Security Force. We're all here by the authority of the

Senate.'

'What senate?'

The grin gave way to a look of faint surprise, but he didn't pause in his work. 'What Senate? Why the Welsh one, of course! We'll need to take saliva and nasal swabs off each of you and, if you don't mind, we'd also like you to give urine and blood samples. How do you manage for food, by the way? How did you manage over the cold years?'

Although he looked at each of them in turn as he asked his questions, it was on Craig that his eyes finally settled.

'As I've already told your mate, just now . . . ' He indicated towards the soldier who'd now posted himself just outside the door. ' . . . we prepared for it. And now we're growing some of our own food. We'd taken the precaution of storing plenty of packets of seeds and beans and such, for planting.' He saw no point in explaining how indebted they were to Rees' foresight and Alistair's generosity. 'Now maybe you'll tell us how all of *you* survived. And have you any idea what it's like in other places? . . . England? . . . Europe?'

'Europe? No idea, I'm afraid, except that the Channel . . . the English Channel I mean! . . . escaped the full brunt of the tsunamis, being as it were in the shadow of Spain and France, but the waves were still big enough to sweep over thousands of square miles of the French coastline; Belgium too, most probably. And as for Holland, well . . . !' He didn't bother to finish, his tone implying that they could use their own imagination.

'And England?'

Craig saw him shrug and heard him make a clicking noise with his tongue. 'Bad, I'd say. Possibly worse than here in Wales. Some, like yourselves, were better prepared than others, having had access to fuel and food and proper shelter but otherwise . . . ' He again shrugged. The unfinished sentence suggested a lack of hope.

'London's gone?'

''Fraid so! The English Cabinet now meets in Sheffield. Can you believe it? And like us, here in Wales, they've been trying to re-establish some form of communication network. But it'll take years, most likely.' He sealed the last of the swabs in its little plastic sachet and labelled it accordingly, then passed each of them a bottle for an urine sample. 'You'd be surprised at how much devastation there's been.' And he nodded through the open door towards the brown scar of the Arian Valley as an example of what he meant.

'And you? Where are *you* based?'

291

'On the Beacons . . . the Brecon Beacons. We're in a specially constructed lab there. They . . . ' He jerked his head back to indicate the armed security. ' . . . are camped about twelve miles away, in Brecon itself.'

'So all of you were catered for?'

'We were cared for under the government's contingency plans, yes.' His voice held no hint of embarrassment that he'd been singled out for preferential treatment.

'How many of you?'

'Hard to tell, really. There are eighteen of us scientists, plus our partners and children, plus staff . . . cooks, cleaners et cetera. Sixty in all perhaps.'

'And them? The so-called Security Force?'

'About two hundred, so they tell us. All well armed! Then there are the Senate members and their families and the civil servants and their families. Three to four hundred of them probably. They're based at Brecon as well. Then there are the Service Engineers, the so-called artisans – builders, electricians, plumbers, carpenters et cetera – also based in Brecon, plus a team of architects, of course. It's anybody's guess how many of those there are. And finally there are the Wild Life Conservation Centres, three of them in all in Wales; one on the Beacons, not far from us, another near Llandrindod Wells and the third somewhere up here in Snowdonia. *Their* staff number well over a hundred. Which reminds me!' He and his colleague had now finished packing their equipment. 'We're supposed to keep an eye out for any wild life. They started releasing birds, some of them game birds, and insects over six months ago and they've recently released hares and rabbits and red squirrels into the wild. Have you seen any?'

'Funny you should ask! We've just heard our first skylark, but that's about all we've seen.'

'They'll come! And after we've reported back and told them you're here, I think you can expect delivery of a few sheep and cattle for rearing. Have you any farming experience?'

He looked from one to the other and saw them shaking their heads.

'But we'll manage, like.' The Poacher gave one of his rare smiles. 'How about fish? Not many trout left in these lakes, now. Pheasant? Grouse?'

'I'll pass on your request.'

Tony: 'Potatoes is what we don't have . . . for planting, I mean.'

'Yes, okay!' As he made a further note, distant voices made him raise his eyes and he strode towards the open doorway, closely followed by the other four. 'Are those your families?'

Ffion, Dianne and the children had just come into view and now stopped at the sight of the helicopter and the white-overalled strangers. Then, as they drew nearer they were suddenly frightened by the sight of the soldiers, whom they hadn't noticed until now. At Tony's beckoning, however, they drew nearer and when they eventually arrived, they too were asked to give swabs and blood and urine samples.

'Probably pointless,' remarked the more talkative of the two scientists, indicating, as he retreated towards the chopper, the box containing the samples. 'You all look too healthy to be harbouring any diseases.'

A few minutes later, the helicopter was but a dot in the southern sky. The little band of survivors turned towards one another, smiling with new-found hope.

Chapter 7

Six weeks went by before the next visit, this time by two helicopters flying in tandem. As soon as he spotted them coming in low over the southern skyline, Dave jumped into the truck and drove down to Plas Cefn to collect the others. Now the little group stood waiting as the throb of the rotor blades became deafening. 'Troop carriers!' Craig muttered, recognising their twin rotor format.

The scientist had been as good as his word. Each chopper had a cow slung beneath it in a specially constructed straightjacket.

They watched in silence as the cattle were gingerly lowered until their feet touched solid ground, no more than thirty metres from where they stood. Craig felt the downdraft from the rotors first of all flattening his hair and then swirling it in all directions. Signals from above instructed them to release the two frightened animals, which then stood around, turning this way and that, looking completely dazed and shaken.

Eventually both aircraft landed, somewhere beyond the ridge above them, and this time the rotors were silenced.

'They're for breeding only.' The instruction came from one of the accompanying soldiers – an officer judging by his demeanour – who now appeared, alone, on the ridge, thirty feet or so above them. He stood there, feet apart, hands clasped behind his back, a figure of authority pasted against a grey sky. There was no sign of overalled scientists this time. 'And we'll be coming back to check!' he again shouted.

The voice sounded menacing and Tony, for one, took exception to it. 'In which case, you'd better send us a bull as well, mate. You know! . . . Birds, bees and all that.' But his smile had very little humour in it.

The soldier attempted a withering look. 'They've already been artificially inseminated. I naturally assumed that you would have reasoned that out for yourselves.'

Whilst he was talking, other soldiers appeared on the ridge, carrying sacks and cages. They now stood perplexed, looking for a way down, and Craig pointed them towards a crevice, further on.

One by one they arrived, each carrying his burden which he then placed on the ground in front of him, before standing to attention. Eventually, eighteen of them in all stood there, staring straight ahead, as if paralysed, until their officer finally commanded them to be 'At ease!'

Although they were all bearded, Craig couldn't but notice how well turned out they were. All hair and facial hair had been trimmed to similar styles and their sage-green uniforms looked brand new, as did their gleaming boots. Each and every one of them looked supremely fit and Craig concluded that they'd been hand-picked for survival but that they'd had nothing much to do during the cold years except work on mental and physical disciplines. He, himself, felt ragged and soft in comparison. Self-consciously, he combed his own unkempt hair and beard with the splayed fingers of both hands. But the sight of them also unnerved him in a way that he found difficult to define. 'They're here with the best of intentions,' he told himself, but the proverbial warning about Greeks bearing gifts continued to plague him.

'We've brought you the potatoes that you requested for planting, plus a variety of shrubs, seeds and bulbs.' The officer then pointed towards the cages. 'And we've also got hares and rabbits . . . male and female, naturally!' The words were aimed sarcastically at Tony. ' . . . plus a variety of game birds. But we're not *giving* you these! In a few minutes, they'll be set free into the wild around here, where hopefully they'll increase their numbers fairly quickly. Only then will you be allowed to start hunting them. I hope that's clear? In the meantime, we've also brought you poultry.'

'*Be ydyn nhw, Mam?*' [*]

Little Branwen and Dylan had got over their initial shock at seeing the two helicopters and the swarm of strangers descending on them and were now staring in awe at the strange black creatures that had appeared so suddenly out of the sky to munch noisily on the coarse grass at the track side.

Ffion laughed at her daughter's fear. '*Dim ond gwarthag, mechan i! Wnawn nhw ddim byd iti.*' [**]

The officer raised an inquisitive eyebrow but said nothing. Then, on his order, the caged animals and birds were released.

As he watched the rabbits and the hares scurrying in different directions and the game birds flapping furiously to gain height, Dave was seen to smile contentedly. His world was gradually coming back to him.

'We'll be back next week with a delivery of sheep.'

'What about a sheepdog?'

The soldier looked at Tony, suspecting sarcasm, but realised that the question had to be genuine. 'Yes, I see your point. I'll see what can be done.'

---

[*] '*What are they, Mam?*'
[**] '*Only cows, my darling! They won't harm you.*'

'No. Don't bother!'

All eyes turned enquiringly towards Dave.

'A sheepdog would be useful, like,' explained The Poacher, 'but we won't be able to feed it, will we?'

Tony smiled ruefully and slowly nodded his head. 'Fair enough!' he acknowledged. 'I hadn't thought of that.'

'Maybe in years to come,' offered the soldier.

The helicopter pilots had appeared on the scarp edge above them and were now signalling that they should be turning for home, on which the officer bawled a command that sent the squad of soldiers jogging in single file towards the crevice that would lead them back to higher ground and to the troop carriers beyond. The officer himself, last to leave, cast a solemn, even critical, look at Ffion and the two children but said nothing.

They watched him go; saw him disappear into the crevice; saw him reappear at the top and watched him as he again drew nearer to them along the ridge. Eventually he reached his original position and took up the same pose as when he'd first arrived. 'We'll be in touch,' he called. 'Soon!' he added, somewhat intimidatingly. Then he was gone and the whine of the rotors again filled the air.

*   *   *

The next few weeks saw a lot of hard work for all of them. The sheep duly arrived – a dozen in all – with the promise of insemination for each of them once they'd had time to acclimatise. A litter of five piglets had also been dispatched. Dave, living where he did, automatically assumed responsibility for all the animals as they grazed the slopes below Hafod, whilst it was Ffion's role to oversee work on the gardens which were being extended almost daily over the slopes behind Plas Cefn. Every day, weather and other duties permitting, the men tilled more and more land for planting and the prospect of a reasonable harvest and of a more varied diet brought a spirit of contentment that none of them had ever again expected to experience. Tony even talked of making wine, come the autumn, whilst Craig, for his part, had found a new use for the huge trays that were once used in the production of Pencraig Roofing tiles. He'd filled them with soil and then converted them into mushroom beds. The others had joked about his efforts but the mushroom harvest, when it came, surprised them all, Craig included. But although the shed on site suited the purpose, Ffion still maintained that the darkness and the cool temperature of one of their underground caverns would offer better conditions for mushroom growing. Dianne's domain was the kitchen but she was also put in charge of the poultry. Dave spent what time he could afford, fishing.

Day by day, the world around them continued to improve. Apart from a couple of diminishing floes way out, the sea now seemed clear of ice and it was heartening to see little patches of green appearing here and there on the otherwise barren slopes of the Arian Valley. Sea level, however, was visibly rising, with more and more coastal lowland disappearing beneath the waves, a fact that made Ffion, one evening, recount an old Welsh legend about the drowning of an ancient kingdom beneath the waves of the Bay of Branwen. The distant peninsula had become appreciably shorter and narrower, with its western tip now but a cluster of tiny islands.

'Have you any other stories, like the one you told us the other evening?'

The question was Dianne's.

Other than Dave, and the children who were already in bed, they were all sitting on the veranda outside Plas Cefn, gazing at a colourful sunset. They didn't get to see too many clear skies; today, however, had been an exception.

'You know! The one about the drunkard who forgot to close the floodgates and who let the tide drown that chap's kingdom . . . ' She couldn't recall the names but the story had gripped her imagination. ' . . . The one about the bells still being heard on a quiet night, even though they're under the sea. '

Ffion smiled. 'Yes, there are a few more I could tell you, I suppose. Irish as well as Welsh, if you like.'

Their leisure hours had to be filled somehow or other.

'Go on then!' Dianne sank lower into her chair, looking as contented and as relaxed as a sunbathing holidaymaker.

'On one condition.'

'And what would that be?'

'That we come to an agreement like Chaucer's pilgrims did.'

The other three looked at her, then at one another, perplexed, until she felt obliged to explain.

'In his *Canterbury Tales*, Chaucer has a number of pilgrims coming together at The Tabard Inn in Cheapside, all intending to journey to Canterbury. Since their journey's going to be a long one, one of them – well actually, I think it's their host, the innkeeper – suggests that they take turns at telling stories on the way, stories that will entertain their fellow pilgrims and take their minds off the rigours of the journey. And that's what they do. Each of them has a tale to tell. So . . . ' She smiled mischievously. ' . . . in the absence of TV and radio, I propose that *we* do likewise. I'm quite prepared to do *my* bit, as long as each of you does the same.'

Dianne laughed to hide her discomfort. 'Oh, come on, Ffion! What does a thicky like me know that could be of any interest to the rest of you?'

'Or me?' Tony chipped in.

For answer, Ffion used the thumb of a raised hand to point behind her, towards the room where all the books were shelved. 'I'm no Sheharazade myself! If *I'm* to keep *my* end of the bargain then I'll have to do some more reading. Research if you like! So what's to stop the rest of *you* doing the same? And while we're at it, I propose that we have sessions with the children as well. What do you say?'

She looked at each of them in turn and waited patiently for each head to nod, albeit reluctantly.

*   *   *

Late July had seen them spending a lot of their time on the slopes of Moel Lwyd, collecting bilberries which they'd then put into the freezer, for future use. And when September came, they also found blackberries in plenty. Then, one day, Dave surprised them all by returning from one of his far-off wanderings on the Norton with a bag of sweet chestnuts. 'Plenty more where those came from!' he reported, and true to his word he returned there the following day to gather an even bigger store. The abundance of wild fruit available to them that autumn surprised them all. It was as if Mother Nature had licked her wounds and was proving how well she'd recovered.

In contrast, however, the last week in September proved to be a nightmare. Violent electrical storms broke out, bringing with them thick cloud-cover and falling temperatures that were reminiscent of the dark, cold days. Snow fell steadily for three whole days and their grey world returned.

Gloom descended on the whole group, tempers became frayed, conversations turned hostile.

'We've no option – have we?' Craig and Ffion had retired early, just as Tony and Dianne had done. 'We'll have to go back underground.' Her belligerent tone of voice, like the look on her face, underlined her aversion to the idea.

'We'll have to take the others with us this time. You realise that?'

'Of course I do!' she snapped. 'There are five mattresses already down there, so we'll only need to take another two . . . '

Craig found himself wondering who'd have to sleep on Rees' blood-stained deathbed.

' . . . If this weather keeps up then we'll all be dead within a few months anyway. Our supplies won't carry us through another long winter.'

She fell silent and lay there beside him, looking up at a dark ceiling. But he could still see her lips moving, despite the darkness. Her concern was Branwen; he knew that. Branwen and little Dylan too, most probably. She was now silently praying for their safe deliverance. He'd noticed how much more devout she'd become of late. There wasn't a day that passed that she didn't mutter prayers of thanks to her God for having protected them over the long cold years, and now she was at it again, pleading for more safekeeping.

'Her God!' Craig smiled ruefully at his own choice of words. Didn't he himself believe? Believe in what? A god who was prepared to destroy the world that He himself had reputedly created? A god who could watch, without feeling, from on high as little children suffered and died? A god with endless powers to do good but choosing to do nothing but harm? The thoughts disturbed him, confused him, because he could also recall Ffion's persuasive argument that evening, so many years ago, when he'd first sat to supper with them. Her bed bug analogy had left an indelible impression on his mind and he'd felt a need, ever since, to be convinced that a caring and a forgiving God did indeed exist and that an afterlife was on offer. In such insecure times, he didn't want to be sceptical, didn't want to be agnostic. He desperately wanted to believe that the day would eventually come when he would meet up again with all his loved ones in another life and in a better world. But Mother Nature's tantrums were once more making it difficult for him. As he dwelled on the thought, Rees' calm voice of reason came back to haunt him: '*We don't feel the need to tap into that great universal energy until something happens to bring us to our knees.*' Wasn't he back on his knees right now? Weren't they all?

Thankfully however, the heavy clouds proved to be but fleeting dangers. Within days, the skies had again cleared to make way for mild autumn days that Tony jokingly described as 'Riviera weather!'

Although the cold snap did no lasting damage, since all their garden produce was safely in store, one heavy downpour, some days later, did wash away a section of Ffion's garden, taking with it rows of blackcurrant and gooseberry bushes. But, in her mood of gratitude, she smiled at her loss and philosophically talked of lessons being learnt and of a need for more effective drainage.

Storms and bad weather apart, up to the onset of winter proper, Branwen and Dylan enjoyed a freedom to play and to roam, almost at will.

* * *

'So I decided to wait until your birthday before giving you the good news.'

While she waited for his reaction, she continued to smile at him, before adding mischievously, 'I take it that it *is* good news for you?'

It was almost eight o'clock in the morning and they were lying in bed, facing one another. Craig, after the initial shock, broke into a grin and eventually asked the all-important question, 'And when is it due?'

'Late June, I reckon. We'll see! And guess what!'

'What?'

'Who else, do you think, has been a bad boy and is also being given a bit of a shock this morning?'

The grin on his face reappeared. 'No! You're joking! Not Dianne as well?'

She nodded, more with her eyes than her head.

'Well! Well! And when is *she* due?'

'Two or three weeks ahead of me, she thinks.'

Craig pretended a stern look. 'And the two of you plotted together, did you?'

She laughed. 'Not to conceive, you idiot! Only for you both to be told the good news at the same time.'

* * *

Breakfast that morning turned out to be a bit of a celebration, with the children relishing the festive mood and being more boisterous than usual. They were still at table when Dave reported for work.

'The future's getting brighter every day, like,' was all he had to say when they told him. Then he was making for the door, where he turned to say, 'I was thinking of taking the Leech down to the coast. Thought maybe I'd try for some fish, like.'

The others nodded and smiled somewhat sadly as they watched him leave. Dave had to be lonely, they thought. And yet, he seemed content.

'That limp of his is getting worse.'

Craig nodded to Tony's comment. 'Yes. So's his cough. He's struggling. But then so are we all.'

'Yea. But we've got a lot to be thankful for as well. Don't you think? In fact, we're lucky to be here at . . . '

He stopped. Dave's lanky frame was again filling the doorway and he looked agitated.

'There's a helicopter coming. Should we go up there to meet it, like?'

He obviously intended going. What he was asking was whether the rest of them wanted to go with him. It would be their first contact with the outside world for almost five months.

It was a dismal enough morning, with the highest peaks enveloped in clouds and a freshening wind carrying the hint of light rain. Judging by the wet ground and the sound of rushing water in a nearby stream, it had already rained heavily during the night.

Before taking the wheel of the Leech, Craig cast a quick look around him and felt the euphoria of the breakfast table ebbing away. Ahead of him, the bleakness of dripping slate tips under a grey sky; behind, the gardens in their now sad and ravaged state.

Ffion, sitting directly behind the driver's seat, immediately sensed his changed mood as he took his place at the wheel. Leaning forward, she whispered in his ear words that had become familiar to him from past readings, 'If Winter comes, can Spring be far behind?' But they held no comfort for him.

As they rose out of the shelter of the quarry and into view of the distant bay, Craig had to take a tighter grip on the steering as the full wrath of the wind caught the Leech broadside, giving it an unexpected shaking. They could hear the gale howling angrily amongst the rocks and the derelict buildings.

Tony, sitting next to Craig in the passenger seat, lifted an excited finger to point. Directly ahead of them, a bright red helicopter was performing what looked like an air dance, swaying to and fro to the changing rhythm of the wind.

'It's a Humming Bird!' muttered Ffion. 'Just like Dad's!'

Rees' helicopter still stood idle on its helipad at Plas Cefn. Tony had often tried to persuade Craig to give the rotors a whirl, just to see whether the chopper was still airworthy but, urged by Ffion, Craig had been adamant in his refusal. 'No need for it, at least not for now!' That's what he'd said. 'We have enough contact with the outside world as it is. If we go looking for more, then we might live to regret it.' Tony had argued otherwise and, for a while, the matter had threatened to become a serious bone of contention between them. Finally, however, they'd agreed to disagree and the inactive Humming Bird was now no longer discussed.

'He's having trouble landing in this wind. What do they want, I wonder?'

The pilot had again circled and was bringing his craft in for another attempt, which this time proved successful.

'Coming to check on us, most likely,' Ffion offered, and the others sensed her disquiet.

They didn't bother seeking the shelter of Dave's cottage but sat instead in the Leech, waiting for their visitors, whoever they were, to appear. The throbbing of the rotor blades from beyond the ridge was being whipped away on the wind and coming back again.

'Here they come!'

Craig was first to spot them as they emerged out of the crevice in the distance.

'Soldiers again!' Ffion's unease was again apparent.

They watched as the four uniformed men, all armed, adopted a two by two formation once they reached level ground. A fifth person, in a dark overcoat with its collar turned up, took up position between them. Then, on command, all five began marching crisply towards the Leech.

'That's a woman!' Tony's surprise was genuine.

One by one they climbed out to meet her, leaving the children in the relative safety and warmth of the Leech. An onlooker would have been struck by the disparity of the scene, where an orderly and patently efficient squad of professionals was being confronted by a huddle of dishevelled individuals in working clothes.

'Good day!'

As she stepped forward, her armed guard unclipped their pistol holsters and then stood to attention. The threat was there.

'My name is Manon Burton, Deputy Minister, Department of Advancement.' She spoke with the voice of new-found authority. 'I'm here to check on a few facts and to fill in some census forms with you.'

'Oh! You're here as a clerk, are you?'

Craig nudged Ffion, for her to watch her step.

The stranger gave her a withering look, then with her right hand she slid a black leather case-folder from beneath her other arm. 'Can we go inside, please?' The question, as she nodded in the direction of the cottage, was aimed at Craig, and he obediently led the way.

She was tall – maybe five foot ten – and erect, with close-cropped well-groomed dark hair. Mid-thirties, Ffion reckoned, and maybe too young for the job.

Once inside the house, the official unbuttoned her black overcoat to reveal a black trouser suit that had its jacket studded up to her throat. With scope, she produced a black pen and began to pull some official-looking paperwork from her case.

'Black's in fashion this year!' Dianne whispered jokingly into Ffion's ear, taking care not to be heard by the guard who stood right behind her in the open doorway.

'It was in fashion about a hundred years ago as well' came the return whisper.

Dianne's brow creased enquiringly but her eyes continued to smile. 'What do you mean?'

'Hitler's Gestapo! That's what *they* wore!'

Manon Burton, Deputy Minister of the Welsh Senate's Department of Advancement, raised stern eyes as Dianne unsuccessfully tried to stifle a laugh.

'I have to point out to you that this census is obligatory, by decree of the Welsh Senate. Given the depleted state of our country's population, you must surely appreciate its importance. A similar census will be held every three years to begin with, and then, eventually, every five years. Now can we please get on with it?'

Painstakingly, she recorded details about every one of them, – FULL NAME, AGE, WHERE BORN? MARITAL STATUS, No. of CHILDREN and so on. There was also a special section FOR POSTERITY to record how each of them had survived the disaster brought about by Eros 2 – how they'd fought the cold; how they'd managed for food; what other difficulties they'd had to face and to overcome; had special relationships been formed?; had they experienced criminal behaviour, or even resorted to it themselves in their struggle to survive?; details of friends and relatives who had died . . . The questions seemed never-ending. In all, it took the best part of an hour and a half to complete the details on all five of them. Then she quizzed them about the success rate of the Senate's wild life policy and seemed particularly pleased to hear from Dave a list of all the birds and small animals that he'd come across during the past few weeks.

'No birds of prey or foxes, though,' the Poacher added, 'but there's good reason for that, I s'pose?'

'They'll be let loose in time, but only after other species have been given the chance to establish themselves properly.'

'I thought as much, like.'

She now turned. 'By the way! We've been having enquiries at headquarters about you, Mr O'Darcy.' She'd begun returning the completed paperwork into her case-folder.

'Enquiries? Sounds ominous!'

His brief laugh didn't fool any of them though, least of all Ffion, who now took a couple of steps forward.

'Who's been enquiring about him? And why?'

'Person by the name of Alistair Dalton. A relative, I believe?' She was still looking at Craig, ignoring Ffion.

'Alistair? My God! He's still alive, then?'

'He's alive, yes, and living in France . . . The upper Rhone Valley if my memory serves me correct.'

She had no need to consult her notebook. Deputy Minister Manon Burton was efficient if nothing else.

'But how did he contact you? I thought . . . ?'

'Satellite communication was re-established four months ago. We are now in contact with no fewer than nineteen different centres throughout the northern hemisphere – three in China, seven in Europe – including two in Russia – and the rest in North America.' As she spoke, her self-importance became even more evident.

'But how was that managed?'

'We had the equipment stored, of course, ready for use, as did those other centres. All we had to do was to wait for NASA to ascertain that Earth atmosphere was eighty five per cent free of submicron dust. Europe couldn't risk re-activating its own communications satellites before then, lest they be permanently damaged. NASA contacted the rest of the world with that information four months ago. Unfortunately, though, most of the satellites have failed to function. In fact, there are only five that are still operational. Three of those belong to NASA, one is Chinese and the other, thankfully, European.'

'It's still great news, though! . . . '

Tony's jubilation, however, wasn't shared by all of them. A look resembling a scowl had darkened Ffion's face, a look that only Dianne noticed.

' . . . What's been happening in the rest of the world, then? Have you any idea how many people are still alive world-wide? What about the southern hemisphere?'

The official shook her head slowly to Tony's questions. 'We have no way of knowing how many people are still alive. A conservative estimate puts it at no higher than fifteen million, but that's as much of a wild guess as anything. Sea levels, of course, are still rising which means that coastlines are retreating the world over. And as for the southern hemisphere, well, nothing less than total devastation, I'm afraid. The blast itself rendered the hemisphere helpless and many areas were then ravaged, if not by firestorms or huge tsunamis, then by violent earth tremors and eruptions and pyroclastic flows. As far as can be determined, Australia and New Zealand have, to all intents and. purposes, ceased to exist and God only knows what life, human or otherwise, still exists in Africa or on the continent of South America. The equatorial belt . . . most of the tropics . . . are still under thick volcanic cloud; still in the grip of a nuclear winter.'

'How would you know that? About Australia and New Zealand I mean.'

'Again by courtesy of NASA. Bear in mind that the manned American and Chinese space stations are still in orbit and that communication with them was also re-established some months ago. They had a pretty torrid time up there, we gather, but were fortunate to avoid any major damage from ejecta following the impact. You'd be surprised at how their on-board cameras can pinpoint what's happening here on Earth. In fact, they could easily produce detailed photographs of our meeting here, now.'

'Strange bedfellows!'

'Pardon?'

But Ffion didn't bother to pursue her own sarcasm, much to the annoyance of the official. At which point Craig hurried to dispel any tension.

'What about the U.S.? California?'

The Deputy Minister took time before again shaking a despondent head. 'According to NASA, the San Andreas Fault in California was the centre of huge earthquake and volcanic activity that lasted for almost three years. Still is, of course, but to a lesser degree now. From what they say, not a single fly in the whole region could have survived.' She detected Craig's dismay and saw Ffion reach out for his arm. 'I'm sorry! You had relatives there? I hadn't realised.' Her words, however, lacked any genuine compassion.

He tried to put on a brave face, telling himself that he'd known all along that his mother and Max couldn't have survived. 'Can you get a message to my brother in the south of France then, just to let him know that I'm okay?'

'Out of the question! Not allowed, I'm afraid, . . . personal messages, I mean. Not in the current climate, anyway. Maybe in three, six months time . . . who knows? By the way, I'm leaving you this information leaflet.' She placed a thin pamphlet on the table in front of her. 'Just the one copy though, I'm afraid. You'll have to share.' Her brief smile suggested an insincere apology. 'Frugality is of the essence in these troubled times, don't you think?'

Having buttoned up her coat, she made for the door and they all followed, to watch her being flanked once again by her four uniformed guards. But before a signal to march could be given, she raised an authoritative hand. 'I almost forgot!'

From the way that she singled out Ffion with her eyes, what she was about to say wasn't an afterthought at all.

' . . . Two other edicts by your Senate, the first of which is particularly relevant to your group, judging from a report passed on to me some months ago . . . '

Ffion scowled, the others merely looked baffled. *What report?* was the question not being asked.

' . . . To ensure future harmony throughout our country, no languages other than English will be tolerated . . . '

Ffion's hoot of incredulity made the Deputy Minister pause momentarily but she then continued as though uninterrupted.

' . . . And secondly, bearing in mind the rifts and the divisions that religion has created in the past, in all parts of the world, your Senate has now decreed that Wales shall have no centres of worship and that all forms of religious gatherings will be outlawed. Long live the Senate!'

The last statement sounded so ludicrous in its context that they all, apart from Dave, burst out laughing, a fact that brought a dark scowl to the Deputy Minister's face.

'You may laugh, but let me warn you! Anyone found guilty of insurrection in any shape or form will be ostracised and will receive no further funding or help from central government. You will, in effect, become social lepers and, when the time comes, no one will be allowed to trade produce with you.' Then came her parting shot, 'I say heed the warning, or suffer the consequences.' And with that she was gone.

Chapter 8

'We can't just disregard what she said.'

An emergency meeting of the group had been called at Plas Cefn for eight thirty, after the children had been put to bed, and now the five of them sat facing one another across the table. It was almost nine o'clock and the Deputy Minister's visit was still under discussion.

In the grate, a slow-burning peat fire gave off more smoke than warmth and its soot had settled in a fine dust over the floor and the furniture, causing the five of them to cough fitfully, Dave more often than anyone.

'We just have to consider what's on offer here.' Tony was now drumming the open pamphlet with the palm of his right hand. 'We can't jeopardise what's in here for the sake of . . . the sake of . . . '

Although avoiding Ffion's eyes, he still found it difficult to voice his criticism.

'For the sake of what, Tony? Somebody else's language? Somebody else's culture? Somebody else's credo? Go on! Say what's on your mind.'

'Okay, Ffion! So I will!' Tony, too, was warming to his task. 'They may be your language, your culture, your credo, as you call them, but I thought they were also the language and the culture and the credo of the people who thought up these rules.' Again he drummed at the pamphlet. 'They're certainly not of my making, nor Dianne's I'm sure.' There was, perhaps, just a hint of sarcasm in his tone. Now he picked up the leaflet and began picking out points with his index finger. 'According to this, there can only be three thousand seven hundred and forty six people left alive in the whole of Wales. It says that the Senate is now in the process of drawing out long-term plans to improve the infrastructure of the country and that includes building brand new homes for every single family. They claim that the houses will be so well insulated that extreme cold won't be a problem in future . . . ' He continued to peruse. ' . . . It also says, and I quote, . . . that every community, however small, will receive food aid on a regular basis, until such time as each one of them becomes self-sufficient. To achieve that goal, farming expertise and some machinery will be made available to ensure a thriving agricultural industry . . . There's even mention of a factory, that's been established in Brecon, to supply the regions with free clothing.'

He paused to watch Ffion push back her chair and walk over to the window. There, with her back towards them, she stayed, gazing out nostalgically in the direction of the silent, lifeless site that had once been

Pencraig Roofing, the frizz of her shoulder-length hair catching the sunlight like a halo.

Craig also watched her, wondering how she would respond to Tony's argument, and as he watched, as he waited, he recalled her aloofness of old. Those early classes when Simon Carvel had had his come-uppance! Those discussions when he, himself, had been so roundly put in his place. They were recollections that belonged to another life, to another world. Rees' world. Sally's world. He tried to remembered faces – Rees, his mother, Sally, friends . . . – but they were all blurred, already faded into a dim past. Craig felt an emptiness within him that was numbing. Times . . . people . . . places even . . . that would never return, only in memories.

'Well? What do we do?' Tony had tired of waiting for Ffion to respond. 'I say we have no option but to accept these terms.'

She turned. 'Wrong, Tony! We have an option. We could challenge them.'

'What? Challenge the terms? And risk losing what's on offer? No way! I'm not prepared to do that. In my opinion, the terms aren't unreasonable.'

'Of course they're not . . . for you!' She'd raised her voice and Craig, recognising the signs, feared the outcome. 'You and Dianne are in an all-to-win situation aren't you? It's not your language . . . your culture . . . that are under threat . . . '

'Maybe not, but you can't live on culture, can you? You can't eat it . . . drink it!'

She ignored his interruption. ' . . . and as far as religion is concerned . . . '

But he again cut across her. 'Okay! So Dianne and I are non-believers . . . '

She returned to the table. 'As I said, you're both in an all-to-win and nothing-to lose situation.'

'And you? You stand to benefit a lot as well, you and Craig and little Branwen. You've got to consider her, you know.'

Craig saw it coming. Tony had sounded reproachful and had touched a raw nerve. Ffion was bound to react. Her eyes were flashing.

'How dare you! How dare you even suggest that Branwen is not my priority. Do you think I want her to grow up to be a pagan? Do you think that I'd compromise on a decision like that?'

Craig saw Tony flush and his mouth fall open. Ffion had caught him unawares. By association, she had labelled him a pagan and it was an accusation that stung. Godless he might be, but never pagan. Pagan was an ugly word, synonymous in Tony's book with heathen and infidel. The word referred specifically to uncivilised tribes who lived in jungles and who drank blood, ate human flesh. 'It's all well and good to be self-righteous,' he parried,' but have you asked Craig what he thinks? What he wants?' He wanted to point out that the decrees of the Senate would be of no consequence to Craig either.

'Ask him yourself!'

And so Craig suddenly found four sets of eyes turning towards him for an answer. He had to pause to think. But he paused too long for Ffion's liking and she saw his hesitation as a lack of support and a betrayal.

'I managed well enough on my own . . . for months . . . ' Despite trying to sound resolute, she failed to hide the crack in her voice. ' . . . and, if need be, I'll manage again; me and Branwen and . . . and . . . ' She was close to tears as she instinctively laid a hand on her pregnant belly. 'I wouldn't give in to them before and I won't now.'

Craig just as instinctively reached out for her but his eyes remained on Tony. 'I'm with Ffion, No question.'

Dianne now broke in. 'Dave? What about you? Where do you stand?'

The Poacher looked nonplussed. He hadn't expected them to seek his opinion. 'I . . . I don't know, really,' he stammered. 'I've never been one for going to church or anything like that, like . . . '

'There we are then!' Tony sounded triumphant, as if he'd got the majority vote.

' . . . but that doesn't mean that I don't believe in God, does it?'

No one said anything and Dave felt obliged to continue.

' . . . You can't spend as much time with animals and with Nature as I have, without feeling that there is something . . . '

Tony let his frustration show. 'Something up there, you mean?' and he pointed derisively upwards, as if pouring scorn on the Poacher's intellect.

Listening to him, Craig recalled with some embarrassment his own sarcasm in this very room and on this very subject, years ago.

But Dave ignored the derision. 'Yes. Up there if you like . . . but all around us as well. I've tried telling myself that there can't be a God, just like you're doing now, like, but . . . ' He shrugged his shoulders as if to imply that he'd failed to convince himself. 'Anyway, as for the language thing, well, I've lived here all my life, haven't I? It's what I've spoken since I was a boy, like. I can't suddenly start thinking in English.' He paused. 'But you probably don't understand what I mean now, do you?' He looked around, and Dianne looked away. 'Anyway, I'm not going to stop now, am I, even if it's just talking to myself or to the animals up there . . . ' With a roll of his eyes, he indicated Hafod. ' . . . just because some strangers drop out of the sky and tell me to do so.'

* * *

'A pity that it had to happen.'

Craig now stood at the front door, listening to the Norton's sad hum as it faded into the distance. Tony and Dianne had retired moodily to their bedroom, having declared they'd be leaving Plas Cefn as soon as they'd found another suitable place to live in. 'There are plenty of abandoned farmhouses all over Wales,' Tony had said, 'and maybe it would be a good idea for us to move to another area to live.'

'Can't blame them, can you?' Ffion's tone was conciliatory. 'It's not their battle, after all.'

He looked at her. 'I'm glad you feel that way. I'd like to think that we can all part as friends.'

'Me too. But tell me, Craig. Should I have compromised?'

He gave it thought before slowly shaking his head. 'There was no compromise for you, was there? Surrender was your only other option.'

'Should I have surrendered then?'

He looked at her, smiled and ran the palm of his hand down her cheek. 'No. If you had, you wouldn't be the girl I fell in love with . . . and you certainly wouldn't be Rees Morgan's daughter.'

His words made her eyes glisten. 'Thank you,' she whispered.

'I could compromise, if you like?'

'What do you mean?' She was immediately suspicious.

'I could agree to work with him on the Humming Bird. Make it airworthy. Tony might appreciate that.'

'To what end, though?'

'Well, when the time comes, if no one in Wales is allowed to trade with us, then we could try further afield.'

Ffion considered and then smiled. 'Yes. Tomorrow morning, make him the offer. It would be nice if they stayed.' As she looked away, Craig sensed a new contentment in her. 'I'm going to name him after my father, you know.' She indicated towards the child she was carrying. 'I hope you don't mind?'

He smiled and took her under his arm. 'Oh? So it is going to be a boy this time then, is it?'

'Of course!'

'Rees O'Darcy! Hm! Sounds okay!'

'Correction! Rhys!'

He pushed her gently to arm's length and looked bemused.

'Rees is the anglicised form that my dad assumed whilst he was abroad. Shame on him, don't you think?' She was laughing though. 'I'll have you know that Rhys is a proud Welsh name that goes back to the time of the Welsh princes.'

He laughed. 'Wow! Rhys O'Darcy it'll be, then!'

'Correction! Rhys ap Craig.'

His raised eyebrows suggested that he thought she was joking.

'I'm serious. Rhys son of Craig. Ap! Just like your Irish O' or Mac. Surely you don't expect me to call him Rhys O'Craig or Rhys MacCraig do you?'

They laughed together.

'Okay! Rhys ap Craig it'll be.'

'Assuming that I'll marry you, that is!'

'What?'

Her grin was mischievous. 'Otherwise he'll be Rhys Morgan, won't he? And you and I will still be living in sin.'

'Good heavens! We can't have that, can we?' He took her hand and jokingly adopted a ministerial stance and intonation. 'Do you, Ffion Morgan, take me, Craig O'Darcy, to be your loving husband, to do all my bidding and to tend on me, hand and foot, at all times?'

'I do. I'm already doing all that, anyway, you male chauvinist.'

They laughed and she pecked him on the lips.

'And how does it feel to be Mrs O'Darcy?'

'Hm! I like it.'

'See those stars.' He was pointing south, towards an expanse of cloudless night sky. 'That's the constellation of Orion, otherwise known as The Hunter.'

'Dafydd's mate!'

'Uh?' He looked confused and then the penny dropped. 'Ah! I see what you mean. Hunter . . . Poacher!'

'I didn't know you were into astronomy. You know your stars?'

'Not really. Wish I knew more, actually. Now that we're having some clear skies again, I'll have to read that book we've got in there.' He indicated the room that they now knew as The Library.

'Look at the illustrations, you mean! You're no great reader, are you?' She pinched him playfully, throwing back at him words that he himself had used years ago.

'Those three, closest together, are what are known as Orion's Belt . . . '

Suddenly, he realised that he'd had this conversation before, with her father. ' . . . And you see that one, the bright star on the heel of Orion? That's Sirius, the Dog Star.'

'Oh!'

'Aren't you going to ask why?' He remembered that Rees had.

'Because every hunter needs a dog, presumably.'

'Oh!'

He sounded disappointed and she laughed.

'Actually, my dad taught me that, years ago . . . '

'Oh!'

'Yes, after you told him.' And she laughed again, louder this time.

Upstairs, Tony and Dianne already felt miserable. Ffion's carefree laugh added to their gloom.

'She's happy, now that she knows we're leaving.'

'I don't think so, Tone. She's more genuine than that. I'll miss her, you know . . . miss them.'

'Yea, I know, love. We've achieved a lot here . . . worked well together.'

'And Dylan! He'll miss Branwen, you know.'

'Yea, I know.'

'They'll miss playing together. And he'll miss Ffion as well. In a year or two he'll be old enough to start reading. She'd help him. You should hear how well Branwen reads, even now . . . Words in English and Welsh mind you! . . . and she's not yet five. She's even got us reading! Books that we wouldn't have dreamed of looking at before . . . Shakespeare even! Just think!'

He could hear the tears as well as the laughter in his wife's voice. 'Are you trying to tell me something, Dianne?'

'I'm not sure.'

'You think we should stay?'

'That's what I feel, yes. We've lived in Wales for years, Tone. We've been happy here . . . even liked listening to them talking in a language that we can't understand . . . ' She laughed briefly, her eyes bright with tears. 'And now our own son is doing it! But if we go away he'll forget it all, won't he?' She laid a sad hand on her lower belly. 'And our next won't even have the chance.'

'You think she's right in what she's doing.' It was more of a statement than a question.

'Who are we to say? I certainly can't see her doing any wrong. Can you, Tone?'

He put an arm around her. 'Tell you what, love. We'll discuss things with them again in the morning. Would you like that?'

Her tears said it all.

Downstairs, and oblivious to the conversation that was going on above them, Craig had pulled Ffion towards him until her face now rested against his chest. Squeezing her hard, he muttered into her hair, 'There's no need to worry, you know. Things will work out just fine, you'll see . . . in spite of everything and everybody. We've come too far to give in now, haven't we?'

'Far?' Her smile was rueful. 'Only as far as the gates of Hell and back!'

He freed a hand just long enough to push the door shut behind them, then, still clutching at one another, they made for the stairs.